Limited Signed Edition

If you collect limited editions of books, check out the special "COFFIN" edition of *EVOLVE: Vampire Stories of the New Undead*.

Protected in a magnetically sealed miniature pine coffin; packaged in an open ended black bag; identified by a unique wax seal; and certified as an original; is a hardcover copy of *EVOLVE: Vampire Stories of the New Undead*.

Each of these "COFFIN" editions is identified by unique number: on the lid, the box and the book. Each book is signed by all of the authors, the cover artist, the editor and the publisher.

Only 50 copies of this limited edition are available. You must order your copy directly from the publisher. Limited to one copy per customer. We expect the COFFIN edition to sell out quickly. Act fast to avoid disappointment.

Limited "COFFIN" edition — $250.00 US (Shipping included).

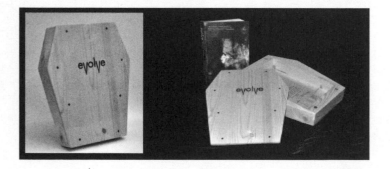

Order directly from the publisher
by email: publisher@hadespublications.com

Praise For
EVOLVE TWO: *Vampire Stories of the Future Undead*

"Nancy Kilpatrick is, quite simply, one of the finest anthologists of our time. *Evolve Two* contains beautifully written, edgy stories as mesmerizing as the archetype they celebrate—that predator par excellence, the vampire. From an homage to *Twelve Angry Men* to a trip to Mars; a heartbreaking deal made between two friends, and the promise of a year-long night—*Evolve Two* takes us far beyond Nosferatu's origins, and blasts us along the vampire's evolutionary trajectory. *Evolve Three*, please?"
—Nancy Holder
New York Times Bestselling Co-author of *Crusade*

"In her introduction, Nancy Kilpatrick tells us there will be no stereotypes in *Evolve Two*, and she's as good as her word. The characters in these very original vampire tales range from hip urban huntresses to vicious cage fighters to lonely astronauts, the settings from isolated farms to futuristic underground courtrooms to post-holocaust deserts. *Evolve Two* is speculative fiction at its full-blooded best."
—Lisa Morton
Stoker Award-winning Author of *The Castle of Los Angeles*

"Vampire tales to quench everyone's thirst—a killer anthology! Nancy Kilpatrick shows us the future of all things vampiric: angst, dreams, medicine, criminal trials, apocalyptic cravings, and of course, blood."
—Lois Gresh,
New York Times Best-Selling Author of *Blood and Ice* and *Eldritch Evolutions*

"*Evolve Two: Vampire Stories of the Future Undead* is a full-spectrum vampire anthology, with stories catering to all forms of the vampire legend. There's something here to please all undead aficionados (or perhaps that should be 'aficionados of the undead'...I can't speak to the vital signs of all the book's readers)."
—Kevin J. Anderson
Editor of the *BLOOD LITE* anthology series

Praise For
EVOLVE: *Vampire Stories of the New Undead*

"Penned by writers who wrangle words with beauty and blood splatters. Recommended."
—Chris Alexander
Fangoria

"A worthy anthology for vampire lovers."
—Laura Godfrey
Quill & Quire

"The stories in the book are as diverse as the regions of Canada that they were culled from. Many are fresh."
—Monica S. Kuebler
Rue Morgue Magazine

"...*Evolve* offers much to enjoy and delight, especially for readers sick of the usual tropes. If there were a hip vampire dialect, you could say it really sucks—and that's a good thing!"
Winnipeg Free Press

"Nancy Kilpatrick is to be commended for assembling a truly original compilation of vampire fiction for the 21st century."
SciFiGuy

"It's collections like *Evolve* that are absolutely vital to the continued growth and health of genre standbys like vampires. *Evolve* continually thinks outside the coffin."
Dark Scribe Magazine

"...a macabre buffet of the future undead. This collection is capable of entertaining a current obsession, beginning a new one, or resurrecting an old, albeit modified one. ...be sure to get your hands on this book."
—Chuck Gould
Horror Bound Magazine

"Overall this is a collection that should not be ignored. Each story stands on it's own as a solid piece of fiction, but together you begin to see the nature of the modern Vampire myth."
—*A Novel Approach*

Praise For
EVOLVE: Vampire Stories of the New Undead

"The premise behind *Evolve* is a simple one: just as humans have undergone a social evolution from the time a caveperson picked up that thigh bone and smashed his/her neighbor over the head, so vampires have evolved from the somewhat crude lurkers of the 18th and 19th century. One of the results of such evolution is that the evolved ones bear only a slight resemblance to the original. Evolve is an excellent example of this, demonstrating changes that would have made these vampires unrecognizable to Ur-vampire Dracula."
—Michael Mirolla
Rover, Montreal Arts Uncovered

"I had thought that vampires were a dead horse, that we had done everything possible with them, imagined them in every conceivable way, and every 'new' vampire story was simply a re-telling of the older ones. I am pleased to say that this anthology has proved me wrong. The authors in Evolve have done the unthinkable—they have given life to vampires."
—Lyndsey Holder
Innsmouth Free Press

"The vampires in the anthology are not the sparkly kind, in case you are wondering, but instead pay a much closer homage to Dracula with a few modern twists. The stories feel both familiar and, at the same time, new."
—Michell Plested
Get Published

"Overall this is a collection that should not be ignored. Each story stands on it's own as a solid piece of fiction, but together you begin to see the nature of the modern Vampire myth."
—*A Novel Approach*

Vampire Stories
of The Future Undead

Edited by Nancy Kilpatrick

EDGE SCIENCE FICTION AND FANTASY PUBLISHING
AN IMPRINT OF HADES PUBLICATIONS, INC.

CALGARY

EDGE

Edge Science Fiction and Fantasy Publishing
An Imprint of Hades Publications Inc.
P.O. Box 1714, Calgary, Alberta, T2P 2L7, Canada

Edited by Nancy Kilpatrick
Interior design by Janice Blaine
Cover Illustration by John Kaiine
Evolve logo by Ryanne Hamilton
ISBN: 978-1-894063-62-3

EDGE Science Fiction and Fantasy Publishing and Hades Publications, Inc. acknowledges the ongoing support of the Canada Council for the Arts and the Alberta Foundation for the Arts for our publishing programme.

Library and Archives Canada Cataloguing in Publication

Evolve two : vampire stories of the future undead
/ edited by Nancy Kilpatrick.

ISBN 978-1-894063-62-3

1. Vampires--Fiction. 2. Horror tales, Canadian (English). 3. Fantasy fiction, Canadian (English). 4. Short stories, Canadian (English).
    I. Kilpatrick, Nancy

PS8323.H67E963 2011   C813'.0873808375   C2011-901623-0

FIRST EDITION
(E-20110407)
Printed in Canada
www.edgewebsite.com

Table of Contents

Acknowledgments

The editor would like to acknowledge the invaluable emotional support of her friends who have, as always, gotten her through tough times, including several recent losses. She appreciates the numerical help supplied by William Greene Raley, her math major Mensa friend, who may or may not be a vampire! The brilliant artwork of John Kaiine gracing the cover perfectly reflects the contents—thank you John! To the staff at EDGE for all the hard work they put into creating and promoting beautiful books they can be proud to have had a hand in producing. And a special, grateful nod to Brian Hades, publisher of EDGE Science Fiction and Fantasy, for, once again, being open to a different sort of anthology, for getting behind it in so many ways, and for giving this vampirophile yet another chance to explore one of her many dreams.

Nancy Kilpatrick
Montreal 2011

INTRODUCTION
By Nancy Kilpatrick

"Why vampires?"
I'm asked that question a lot. I'm asked because I'm a writer and an editor and vampires have managed to infiltrate a fair chunk of my work. And I'm asked because I've been a collector of vampireobilia for thirty years and know quite a bit about the undead. Everywhere I am, when the nosferatu takes center stage, either in book, film, visual art or music form, I'm asked, especially at Halloween!

Once that 'Why?' question evaporates like a mist, it's quickly followed by further why questions, for example: why are these creatures of the night rearing their fanged heads so often these days? And: why would anyone find a vampire attractive—what in the world is there to be attracted to?

Please bear with me. I'm going to wax a tad esoteric for a moment about the first 'why', the proliferation of the nosferatu, then (hopefully gracefully) ease gently into the second 'why', their attraction.

Psychologist Carl Jung coined the term 'archetype'. It's one of those hundred dollar words that sounds educated and sophisticated so, once the media got hold of it, the word was bandied about quite a bit over the last couple of decades. Consequently, the original meaning has been seriously diluted, if not polluted.

Today, when many people use the word 'archetype', what they really mean is 'stereotype'. Most of us know that stereotypes are boring. Not to mention unfair. Nobody wants to be seen as a stereotype. It's ridiculous to lump together people or situations and say they're all the same, with no variations.

A stereotype is *not* an archetype. In fact, a stereotype is a *dead* archetype, one with the life sucked out (sounds like a vampire's victim!). An archetype is the original, a vibrant energy that is a pulsing template on which whatever comes after is formed. It's the spirit of the original. All that follows and emulates the original incorporates that spirit and is like it but also unique.

So, what does that mean when it comes to vampires? Picture this, if you can: If we took all the vampires that have ever existed in legend, mythology, literature, film, television, music and art and piled these thousands upon thousands of undead beings atop one another—(yeah, that's quite an image!)—what we would find is the one thing they all have in common. Each is different but there's a common thread in all of them and that thread is the archetypal vampire. What is the vampire archetype? Simply put: Vampires are predators; we are their prey.

And yes, even the sparklies like Edward Cullen can turn into a predator at any moment; it's in his nature, the nature of the vampire. No matter how polished and presentable the undead, our fear of their dangerous side is always percolating, as it should be, and the fear is also part of the allure.

According to Jung, archetypal energies kind of float around in our personal and collective unconscious, not doing much, just hanging out. Every archetype, including the Vampire archetype, has both a positive and a negative side and these powerful energies are eternal, shared by all humanity, although different cultures may ascribe different cultural traits to an archetype. We know that humans down through history have been aware of the vampire. The earliest writing, the Sumerian *Epic of Gilgamesh,* which dates to 2500 BC, is the first record of the death-bringer.

At least since then, the vampire has been lurking. Legends and folklore from many parts of the world talk about the vampire. We read about them in early English and French literature, we viewed them in German, British and American films from the silent cinema days, joined more recently by movies from Mexico, France, the Philippines, Russia, from all over the world. In one capacity or another vampires have appeared on our television screens through the 1950s, 1960s, 1970s and onward. There is no shortage of art and music, board games, breakfast cereals, dolls, jewelry, and on and on. Everywhere we look in the present and the past we see the vampire.

Jung discovered that these floating archetypal energies only surface in our awareness when something triggers them. When many people become aware of an archetype, it says that collectively we are bringing this energy out into the open for a reason. Something is up.

We all know that the vampire has become a big deal over the last few decades. We mortals are finding immortals *very* interesting indeed. We need something from them and, at the same time, we fear them. It's a paradox.

The current surge in their popularity started in the mid-1970s when several important books were published that shaped the vampire for modern readers and influenced film and television, art and music: *Interview with the Vampire* (Anne Rice); *Hotel Transylvania* (Chelsea Quinn Yarbro); *The Dracula Tape* (Fred Saberhagen); *Salem's Lot* (Stephen King). With the exception of King's novel/TV miniseries, these books presented the vampire in a new and evolving light. The vampire was more human, lived among us (although back in those works from the 1970s, that bit of info was known to only a select few fictional characters); and the vampire did not necessarily *always* have an evil intent.

That perception of the undead has grown and expanded. Today, nearly forty years after those ground-breaking novels, we have undead that not only live among us, but are a known entity, part of society. Some are bad asses, of course, but not all. And generally, they've grown more human and less feral.

What we as a species need from the vampire might be tied in with how we have allowed—even encouraged—the undead to evolve. The biggest question is: why did we want to humanize the vampire? Why take what is essentially 'other' and try to understand and then accept this non-human, supernatural force that is so threatening. Surely this goes against the traditional Homo sapiens distrust of 'other', the desire to defend ourselves and our loved ones from the unknown which is potentially threatening. And maybe that's the key to understanding why we want this creature which has always been loathsome to integrate into our world. It's almost as if there's a silent revolution on the go. What had previously been intolerable is now welcomed. We see that with a lot of groups; over the last decades, categories of people that were 'out' are now 'in', participating in society, winning their rights, which says that overall our species is more accepting. Despite the wars of today and the fear of those who are not like us and may even harm us, there seems to be almost a quiet but steady drive underway to accept what could not in the past be accepted. Our global village now includes vampires.

The vampire traits that we're all familiar with give a clue to why we find the undead an attractive lot and why we need them to evolve along with us. Vampires:

1. live forever, or at least more than one lifetime, but certainly long enough to gather some smarts so they can avoid the dumb mistakes we mere mortals seem hell-bent on making;

2. are youthfully gorgeous—despite not being able to see themselves in mirrors—and stay attractive *sans* Botox, or I should say they have *become* attractive in the last several decades—first we had to get rid of those old-school smelly, resuscitated corpses;

3. have no problem finding 'dates', to employ a euphemism. Their sexual charisma is legendary. What high school senior wouldn't love to take a vampire to the prom;

4. don't have to work. In fact, they are often wealthy, having managed some savvy investments over the centuries;

5. are physically powerful and mentally mesmerizing, and they refuse to play by normal human rules and regulations—unless they want to, of course. They're good manipulators, and this power in its myriad forms comes in handy when they fall outside the boundaries of behavior expected by mortals which, it seems, they do frequently.

Naturally, there are a few drawbacks to their existence, but the spin on those has changed too. Vampires:

6. traditionally sleep in a coffin and sometimes that casket must contain soil from their native land. More often today, though, they retire on satin sheets in darkened chambers that reek of opulence and/or edginess;

7. can be fried crispy by sunlight and are weakest in the daytime. But lots of humans are night people so a moonlit lifestyle isn't all that strange, especially for the young and palely attractive (see 2 and 3);

8. are allergic to garlic—but many people hate garlic—and wolfs bane (a plant in the buttercup family); most of us wouldn't know wolfs bane if we brushed against it and developed a rash;

9. will die if they are stabbed through the heart with a stake preferably widdled from hawthorn—but most of us would succumb to a stake through the heart made out of any material;

10. drink human blood to survive. Not all vampires drink blood—human or other—but it seems the majority do imbibe. For mortal vegetarians turned undead, this would be a hellish way to acquire nutrients. But, since most mortals will chomp on a medium-rare sirloin when they can get their canines into one, the liquid diet of the vampire might not be as repulsive as first envisioned.

As it turns out, most vampires don't kill their victims. It has become common for a vampire to take just a little blood and leave the human intact with a Band-aid to the neck. This makes them a tad more appealing to us.

And, more importantly, most vampires don't 'turn' those they bite. If they did turn their food source into ones such as themselves, well, check the stats on that: a vampire turns one tonight. Tomorrow night those two vampires turn two. The third night the four vampires turn four. In thirty-five days there will be 13,786,200,000 vampires (yes, that's thirteen *billion!*) wandering the planet, which is about 6,800,000,000 more than the total population of earth. (Total of Earth's population estimated as it increases daily.)

Even given contingencies like: the inability to move during daylight hours; the difficulty of long-distance travel which includes time zone changes and daylight savings time; a rebellious human population that fights back; turnings that don't 'take'; and vampires who, for one reason or another, murder each other—even with these variables factored in, it's pretty clear that in short order we mortals would be history. But, vampires are not stupid; they're not zombies (see 1). They would not intentionally kill off their food supply and starve themselves to death.

One of the biggest pluses and perhaps the one largely responsible for the popularity of vampires of late is their erotic appeal. Vampires are charismatic, rock-star sexy, oozing glamour and seductiveness, so much so that there's a lineup of volunteers ready and willing to open a vein, just for the titillation of it all.

This has not always been the case (see 2). But even the ugly ones from the past had a certain *je ne sais quoi*. People *did* let them into their homes, and yes, in the old days, courtesy being what it once was, the vampire had to be invited in. But why would anyone invite into their home a stinky, dirt and maggot-covered, pale-as-death being with fangs that they *knew* had died recently and was buried at the local cemetery because in their small town or village, they'd witnessed this departure and/or interment with their own eyes! *Plus* they were also aware that it was their *relative* who had died. Traditional lore has the vampire going after family first. Then extended family. Then friends. And family and friends of friends. They were a pretty incestuous lot.

Despite the terror of the person opening the door, and against all odds, vampires *were* invited in. The reason was simple: the undead mesmerized their potential victims. Like a hypnotist on stage commanding: *Bark like a dog!* The vampires of old demanded: *Let me in!* And people did.

Nowadays, earth is getting crowded. Plenty of us live in cities or large towns where the vampire could be our neighbor, or a classmate, or a co-worker, or the overnight gas station clerk, for all we know, or don't know. We're wary and not inclined to let strangers into our homes. We've changed, but so have the undead. They seem to have gotten over their self-imposed ritual of having to be invited, perhaps at the same pace as humanity's abandonment of traditional etiquette. Vampires have also overcome their aversion to crosses, holy water, bibles, and other religious paraphernalia. Could this have faded as church attendance declined sharply?

Along the path of their evolution, a good many of what we deem traditional vampire traits altered, or even vanished altogether. The vampire identified in myths and legends and the ones that first appeared in literature, these are not the same vampires we see today. In the past, they were never part of our world. They lived apart from us, cold and undead, soulless, dwelling between realms, skulking amidst the shadows, spawns of Satan, frightening us, extending their existence by ending ours.

They were departed family members coming back for kin. They were aristocrats, using the advantages of wealth and elitism to prey upon both their peers and the lower classes. They were persons born with a caul over the face, or the seventh son of a seventh son. They were religious heretics. Vampires in the past ran from the cross and drank blood until they were bloated and their victims drained. In some parts of the world they sucked souls, or energy, or the life force itself. Vampires were shapeshifters, able to become bats, wolves and rats. In some cultures they appeared more ghost-like or were invisible. They controlled the elements and the lesser creatures of nature, as well as humans. They were the ultimate supernatural force that only under a spell would a mortal perceive as intelligent, erotic and worth encountering a second time. The vampire was to be avoided at all costs if for no other reason than that you would very likely end up dead or undead yourself. That's why graves were opened, bodies exhumed, hearts staked, mouths filled with garlic bulbs and heads lopped off corpses which were then re-buried at a crossroads face down with a crucifix atop the casket.

But, all that's the past. Vampires have evolved. Considerably. Out with the old, in with the new. And almost everything we believed we knew about the nosferatu has undergone a shift.

Today's vampiric predators come in all flavors, from ethereal to sexy, dominant to submissive, tormented to torturer, and they can be the killer or the victim. They are everywhere at all times of day. They buy houses, register for night courses, own RVs and take vacations. And, they've learned restraint. They intermingle with us and interbreed. They drink blood substitute (although they probably prefer the organic stuff!).

Everything about the vampire has changed but one thing: they are still predators, we are still their prey.

A year ago I edited the anthology *Evolve: Vampire Stories of the New Undead,* composed of tales of the vampire we see today and would be seeing in the immediate future. It was a project I'd wanted to pursue for a long time. I'd hoped to extract this extraordinary creature from the past—which is how he/she has been commonly viewed—and show the new vampire, where the princes and princesses of darkness are at now and how that differs from where they were then.

Even before that innovative tome was in the hands of readers, I realized that I'd caught a glimpse into the further future and became excited by the idea of showing readers what I saw. The vampire. Beyond the year 2012.

I challenged writers to find the vampire we'd be seeing in 2025, 2075, 2175 and the year 3000. We know that the vampire now lives with us and has integrated into society—that's been the most recent common theme in vampire fiction, film and art, so that wouldn't reverse. But how would, how *could* these enthralling creatures of the night evolve further without blunting their edge? Will our world be so accepting that we allow the undead to live next door, to occupy the cubicle behind ours at work, to date our daughters without worrying about it? Would future vampires be so civilized that we trust them to rein in whatever violent instincts they possess and not have us over for dinner in the strictest sense of the words?

What about catastrophes, natural and other types, and things like pandemics—we're seeing signs of such events now. When the going gets tough, maybe the vampire will get going in a way that doesn't suit us.

As the future unfolds, we will change, and the undead must as well. I was eager to find out how our two species will relate to and interact with one another because in the days ahead, at least regarding vampires, we mortals will be dancing with death on a daily basis. We might come to like and even appreciate them, but that doesn't mean we will ever feel entirely safe. And can the vampire ever fully trust us, or see us as more than potential nourishment? All is possible, but what is probable? The future will undoubtedly be challenging.

Evolve Two: Vampire Stories of the Future Undead shows how two species—us and them—may or may not co-exist in the decades to come. These stories investigate whether or not we can mutually inhabit the same planet and even on future worlds, despite the fact that vampires can rip out our throats. Vampire may or may not be working to control their urges. We mortals may or may not be struggling to keep from staking them first chance we get. Perhaps we will come to some mutually satisfying way of dwelling together. Perhaps.

Have a read. See what *you* think about the future undead. The range of stories in *Evolve Two* will twist and turn you in a lot of directions but, once you come out the other end of this book, you will likely agree with me about one thing: we definitely have not seen the last of the Undead!

Nancy Kilpatrick
Montreal 2011

PRE-APOCALYPSE

The List

By Kelley Armstrong

Everyone laughed when I walked into Miller's bar. Never a good way to start an evening out.

Randy waved for me to ignore them and join him at his table. He had my beer waiting. There would be a list of supplies he needed me to steal, too, but that wouldn't come out until later. Don't ask me where he learned such good manners. Certainly not from his older brother, Rudy, who was snickering and whispering behind the bar.

"Ignore them, Zoe," Randy said, twisting the top from my bottle.

"What's going on?"

"You don't want to know."

Whatever it was, it was bringing a much needed air of liveliness to the place. Miller's might not be the worst dive in Toronto, but don't tell Rudy that or he might decide he can skip the monthly cleaning.

It isn't even a bar, really, just a dark cave of a room off an alley, with a Miller's Beer sign in the window. The sign used to flash, until Rudy realized it was attracting patrons and unplugged it.

It's not a private club, but it is racially segregated. Sorcerers, half-demons, witches, necromancers, they're all welcome. As for vampires, only one is allowed. I'd feel a lot more special about that if I wasn't the only vampire in town.

"How's the clinic going?" I asked.

Randy made a face, which meant 'the usual'. Chronically underfunded and in danger of closing, which is why I stole medical supplies for him.

"I had an interesting case today," he began. "This guy—"

"Hey, Zoe!" Rudy called. "Come here. Got something to show you."

"Don't do it," Randy murmured.

I walked over to the bar, reached across and snagged a beer bottle from the ice.

"Uh-uh," Rudy said. "You haven't paid for your first one yet."

"And I don't plan to pay for this one either. So what's up?"

The guy on the stool beside me leaned over. I resisted the urge to lean back. One advantage to not breathing? You don't need to smell anything you don't want to. As for the guy's name, it was either Dennis or Mo. I'd known them both for years. Still can't tell them apart. Both on the far side of sixty. Both missing half their teeth. Both half-demons. Or so they claimed. Never saw them demonstrate any powers other than the ability to sleep on rickety barstools.

For simplicity's sake, I usually call them both Dennis. Neither complains. Most times, they're past the stage of remembering their names anyway.

"You are not a real vampire," Dennis said.

I sighed. "This again? Fine. In the morning, I'll go drain the blood of a few virgins."

"Real vampires don't go out in the morning."

"Hey, I agreed to the slaughter of innocents. Don't push it. And don't ask me to pretend I can't see my reflection in a mirror, either, or I'll never look good enough to get those virgins back to my place."

"Can you sparkle?" someone across the room called. "I hear that's what real vampires do these days."

"Oh, I can sparkle. Just not for you."

A round of laughter. I headed back to our table.

"We got confirmation, you know," Rudy called after me.

I turned. "Confirmation of what?"

"That you're not a real vampire." He picked up a folded newspaper from the bar. "You aren't on the list."

I returned and took the paper. Two papers, actually. The first was the *Toronto Sun*, our daily tabloid. The other was an underground rag.

I read the *Sun* headline: "24 Vampires Call Toronto Home, researcher claims."

"Cool," I said. "Add me and we can field our own baseball team."

I skimmed the article. The researcher was an anthropologist who specialized in vampire lore, its origins and its connection to modern life. He'd compiled a list of people suffering from porphyria and deemed them 'real vampires'. The underground paper had reportedly found and printed his list of the twenty-four living in Toronto.

"It's a known medical condition," I said. "You need to drink blood and you have an aversion to sunlight, which means, when it comes to real vamps, it's only half right."

"Or maybe you're half wrong," Dennis said.

"No, Zoe's all sorts of wrong," Rudy said. "Which is why she isn't on the list. Meaning she's not a real vampire. Meaning I win a whole lotta bets."

I flipped him the finger and took the *Sun* back to our table.

"Hey, look. The guy's giving a lecture tomorrow at U of T," I said as I finished reading the article.

"Don't even think of going, Zoe," Randy said.

"Why would I do that? To mock the guy when he doesn't recognize a real vampire? That would be very immature."

I ripped out the article and pocketed it. Randy sighed.

I took Brittany the Vampire Slayer to the lecture. At seventeen, she's waffling about post-secondary education, so I'm trying to convince her that university isn't as boring as she thinks. And that vampire hunting really isn't a viable career goal. There are only about a dozen of us in North America. In five years, she'd have slaughtered the lot, and then what?

"I am not a vampire hunter," she grumbled as she trudged along beside me. "And why can't we take the subway?"

"Because walking is good exercise. A vampire hunter must be in excellent physical—"

"I'm not—"

"But you were. Remember how we met? You running at me with your garden stake, yelling, 'Die, bloodsucker'."

She reddened. "That was last year, okay? I don't know why you have to keep bringing it up."

"Because it was so adorable. And Brittany the Vampire Slayer rolls off the tongue much better than Brittany the Former-Vampire-Slayer-Who-Now-Just-Wants-to-Hunt-Bad-Guys-in-General."

"Not 'in general'. Not 'bad guys' either. That sounds so lame. I'm going to join the interracial council and hunt supernaturals who misuse their powers."

"See, now that's what I mean about redefining goals. That's very specific and feasible. However, working for the council is a volunteer position. You need to plan for a long-term, satisfying, *paying* career."

"I could work with you. Become a thief."

"The income stream is too erratic. But if you'd find that sort of work satisfying, we could look at something in the financial sector. For starters, though, you're going to attend public lectures with me, get a feel for a university education."

"And for each lecture, I get a shopping trip."

"That was the deal."

When I met Brittany, she had little appreciation for the finer things in life, like fashion. In a year, I've weaned her out of her track pants, sneakers and hoodies. I'm very proud of that. Of course, I'm also proud of the advances she's made in stalking and fighting under my direction, but I believe that just because a girl can kick ass doesn't mean she shouldn't look good doing it.

The lecture was very educational. I say that with scarcely a drop of sarcasm. I'm always fascinated by vampire lore. It's like when I was a young girl in Imperial Japan and my grandfather would recount our family's storied past as *samurais* and *shoguns*. While we knew less than half of it was true, it was enthralling nonetheless. Vampire folklore is the same—thrilling, vaguely accurate accounts of my race's history.

Dr. Adair himself was far less interesting, as such people usually are. A round little man with a shock of white hair, his saving grace as a speaker was his passion for his subject. Even Brittany stopped squirming after a few minutes. By the end, she was so enrapt that as others rose to leave, she still sat there, leaning forward, hoping for more.

"That was actually interesting," she said as we pulled on our leather jackets. "Like history and mythology and science all mixed together."

"If you enjoyed it, I could introduce you to an anthropologist," I said. "He's a werewolf."

"Oh?" A slight arch of the brows, a blasé gesture that I'd learned, in teen body language, marked genuine interest. Brittany had never met a werewolf. They were almost as rare as vampires, and there were none living in Toronto.

"His mate's a delegate on the interracial council."

I got a "Seriously?" and a genuine grin for that. I was going to have to remember to name-drop more often. She checked her school calendar to see when we might be able to squeeze in a werewolf visit. I didn't mention that her parents might not let her go off to New York state with me. She wouldn't ask; they wouldn't care.

"Miss?" called a voice as we crossed the front of the room. "Miss?"

I turned to see Dr. Adair waving me back.

"Uh-oh," Brittany whispered. "He's made you, Zoe. You're in trouble now."

I rolled my eyes, though I'll admit to a spark of concern as I walked to the podium.

"Do you know a good place to get a drink?" he asked.

"Drink?"

"Oh." He flushed and looked from me to Brittany. "I'm sorry. I thought you were old enough. My mistake."

"Believe me, I'm old enough."

I glanced at the crowd of people streaming past. Seemed odd to single me out. I look like a typical college-age girl. Maybe that's why he was asking—horny old guy hoping to hook up with a fan.

"What sort of bar are you looking for?" I asked.

He leaned over and lowered his voice. "Not one most of these folks would frequent."

I glanced at the attendees again. Lots of Goths and vampire wannabes.

"Ah," I said.

"Yes. You looked...normal."

Brittany choked on a laugh.

I gave him directions to a neighborhood pub that profs frequented. As I wrote it down for him, a waiting girl in a leather corset and black lipstick sighed impatiently.

When Brittany and I left, Goth Girl muttered, "Finally. Fucking mundanes. Aren't you missing *American Idol?*"

"Aren't you missing the muzzle to go with that dog collar?" Brittany shot back. "Better yet, do us all a favor and get one that covers your whole face."

I took her by the arm and steered her out as Goth Girl shouted profanities.

"Did you hear what she called us?" Brittany said. "Mundanes. Do you know what that means?"

"People who are not members of her subculture. Which we are not. Unless you want to be part of a group that thinks fishnets go well with army boots."

"She's not going to leave that poor guy alone, you know," she said as Goth Girl tagged along after Adair. "She'll be on him like a leech for the rest of the night. We can't let that happen."

"Yes, I believe we can."

"We shouldn't. It's wrong."

"All right. We'll follow them as a stalking lesson. But no fighting. If she won't leave, I'll cut in and distract her, and you'll lead him away."

Brittany sighed. "You know, for a vampire, Zoe, you can be killer dull."

"So I've been told."

As we stalked Adair and Goth Girl, I pondered the political correctness of that label. Did they still refer to themselves as Goths? That seemed very 1985. I was sure the terminology had changed. I'd have to check up on that. If you're going to blithely slap labels on people, you should at least know the right ones. For now, Goth Girl she was.

She wasn't pestering Dr. Adair overly much. Just walking with him, asking questions, which he seemed happy enough to answer. There's a certain ego appeal to having someone hanging on your every word. It didn't hurt that—once you got past the bad dye job and worse fashion sense—the girl was actually cute. Not my type—I prefer blond hair and pink lipstick—but I couldn't blame Dr. Adair for enjoying her company. I had a feeling she'd be joining him for that drink. Maybe more. Whatever the end result, Brittany was getting a hunting lesson, and that was always worthwhile.

Goth Girl and Dr. Adair were heading for the parking building, where he said he needed to drop off his bag. The girl suggested a shortcut, in a way that had him trotting eagerly after her.

I tugged the back of Brittany's jacket. "You're too young for that kind of lesson."

"I'm seventeen, Zoe. I know all about sex."

"Sex, yes. Screwing behind buildings with strangers, no."

"I'll stop when clothes start coming off."

Considering Goth Girl was wearing a miniskirt, the removal of clothing would not be necessary in this instance. But before I could say so, Brittany took off, creeping along as Goth Girl and Dr. Adair cut between two buildings.

"Can I ask you a question about the list?" Goth Girl's voice drifted back.

"Of course."

"Why didn't I get on it?"

"Hmm?"

"I sent you my qualifications. You rejected me."

"It's not a rejection, my dear. There are very strict criteria for the list. While there are thousands of adherents to the basic tenets of vampirism—avoiding the sun and drinking blood—the list only contains those who are medically—"

"I sent you a doctor's note."

"And I'm sure I attempted to verify it. Having met you, though, I'm happy to review—"

"I want on that list, Doctor. I'm a vampire. And I can prove it."

Adair shrieked. Brittany was already running. I raced after her. Goth Girl had Adair up against the wall and was going for his jugular with her fangs. Fangs that flashed silver in the moonlight.

Brittany charged and hit her in the side. Goth Girl went flying. She hit the ground and lay there in a huddle, whimpering. I motioned for Brittany to watch her as I helped Adair to his feet. He'd slid to the ground when the girl released him and sat there, staring in shock. As I bent over him, Brittany turned her back on her opponent. Before I could say anything, the girl yanked a knife from her boot.

Goth Girl leapt at Brittany. I shoved my protégé aside and told her to get Adair out of here. I kicked Goth Girl's feet out from under her. She stumbled, but didn't go down. When she spun, knife out, she nearly nicked Adair. That got him moving. Got Brittany moving, too, hustling him to open ground.

Goth Girl ran at me. I waited until the last second before spinning out of the way. My jacket caught on the tip of her blade. Put a nice hole in the leather. I stopped playing then, and took her down with a high kick to the chin. Another kick sent the knife flying.

When she fell, I pinned her. She snarled and thrashed and tried to bite me with a set of really awkward silver teeth.

"I hope you didn't pay much for those," I said.

"It's not fair," she howled. "I belong on that list."

"Yeah?" I curled back my lip and let my fangs extend. "Well, so do I."

I didn't hurt the girl. No reason to. I wasn't hungry. I gave her a stern warning about curses and revenge and the incredible psychic powers that would tell me if she spoke of this to anyone or contacted Adair again. Total bullshit, but if you're crazy enough to believe in vampires, you're crazy enough to believe that crap, too.

She ran off after that. Probably to change her panties. The smell was...not good. I got the idea she'd had enough of unholy bloodsuckers to last her a lifetime.

Next I found Brittany waiting with Adair at a bench. She mouthed an apology and I made a mental note to add "keeping your attention on your opponent" to her future lessons.

For now, it was Adair who got the stern warning. If he was going to work in this field, he needed to be more careful about following people into dark alleys. A canister of pepper spray might be wise, too.

"Y-you're right," he said, as he rose unsteadily from the bench. He looked around, blinking. "Now I really need that drink. Do you know anyplace quiet? Out of the way? Where I won't bump into anyone like..." he shuddered, "that?"

"I know just the place," I said as I took his arm. "In fact, the bartender is the one who told me about your lecture. Huge fan. You'll have to tell him all about your work. He *loves* meeting new people."

"Rudy *hates* meeting new people," Brittany whispered as she fell in step beside me. "Especially mundanes."

True. Which meant, when I left Millers tonight, I'd be the one laughing.

Kelley Armstrong is the author of the *Women of the Otherworld* paranormal suspense series, *Darkest Powers* YA urban fantasy trilogy, and the Nadia Stafford crime series. She grew up in southern Ontario where she still lives with her family. A former computer programmer, she's now escaped her corporate cubicle and hopes never to return.

Nosangreal

By Ivan Dorin

If she had begun her death spiral, its completion was years away. She was about seventeen, a little overweight by modern standards, and plain to view at a glance, like the prairie itself. I could see her married and running a farm like her ancestors might have done. She just couldn't be a farmer in Nose Hill Provincial Park, especially by gazing out over the lights of the city at three o'clock in the morning.

"Heritage Park is that way," I said, walking up in front of the bench, then pointing south past the downtown skyscrapers.

"Do I look lost?" she asked.

"Only misplaced," I said. "You just seem like such good farming stock. It would be a shame to waste the look."

"Well, I never was one for being on display."

"Neither were they. Have you seen how the old pioneers looked in pictures?"

She smiled at that. "And where do you belong?"

"I'm still trying to figure that out. In the meantime, I walk around here. I'm a sort of self-appointed, unofficial guardian, I suppose."

"Of what?"

"Not of. From. Not that it's that dangerous, of course. It can take years before a threat gets serious, but it can creep up on you."

She nodded and motioned for me to sit down next to her.

"It's so quiet," she said, "like perhaps everyone in the city has vanished and I don't know it yet. The cars could be driving themselves, the traffic lights changing color automatically, but when I get back everyone could be gone."

It was a strange sort of rapture to hope for, wanting to be the one left behind. "Just don't make a habit of coming here, especially at night," I said. "I don't want to see you become one of those people."

"Those people?"

"People who gaze into the lights as if there were one person they needed to find, and they could reach into the city and pull out that person by staring long enough. People who lie down in the grass, thinking they can draw strength from the earth. People who talk to the wind, because they have something they need to confess and can't go to church."

"We're natural rivals."

"You and the church?"

She nodded.

"The park isn't any better," I told her. "People may say they love it, that it's beautiful and worth preserving, but coming to a park won't make them treat anyone like they're worth preserving. This place can anesthetize you, suck the life out of you, just as surely as the government, the corporations, the financial system, even sheer force of habit, or our national insect."

"Our national insect?"

"The mosquito."

"I've known a few people like that too," she said.

"The individuals aren't so bad," I told her. "People who go around sucking the life out of other people, they don't last. They gorge themselves to death or get swatted. It's the institutions they serve that advance, that evolve, while the people suffer and die. I heard a radio phone-in not long ago where they seriously discussed putting reflective dust into the atmosphere to blot out the sun. Who would pay people to come up with a scheme like that, and seriously discuss it on public radio? Who could devote their time to creating a country of people so mind-controlled that they're scared to see the sun come up?"

"It's a deeply rooted fear," she said, "the fear of living. Institutions have exploited it for centuries."

"But how? An institution can have hypnotic appeal and many servants, can wield both natural and bureaucratic powers and appear in corporeal or incorporeal form, but it's also vulnerable. It loses much of its power if you refuse to let it into your home, it can be burned by the light of truth and, in the case of this park, it can't cross water. So how does an institution keep people in thrall without being demonized or exposed as a monster? By masquerading as its own enemy, the monstrous individual."

"And you're one of them? One of these mythical monsters?"

"Do I look like one? You tell me. If I were a mythical creature, which one would I be?"

She turned and looked me up and down, taking in my face, my shoes, my clothes, as if for the first time. "Narcissus," she said. "Good looking, graceful, impeccably dressed, alone. I could see you hypnotized by your own reflection."

I laughed out loud at that one.

"Am I far off?" she asked.

"Well, it's hardly very Canadian, is it? To have a reflection is to have an identity, and that's the number one thing Canadians are supposed to lack."

"And yet we have a third of the world's fresh water surfaces," she said, a teasing lilt to her voice. "Strange how we never look down and see ourselves reflected in them."

"Some do, in the end. Some of the favorite Canadian places to commit suicide involve a plunge into water: Niagara Falls, the Lion's Gate Bridge. Seductive, romantic places, where one might go with a lover to enjoy the view, or go without one to fall fatally for oneself at the last moment."

"Calgary's hardly the setting for fatal seduction, is it? No dramatically high bridges, no big lakes, no water more menacing than the drowning pool below the irrigation weir."

"And they got rid of that," I reminded her.

"So here you are, in Nose Hill Park, all flowers and no water, surrounded by what you could become and safe from becoming it. Narcissus turned into a flower in the end. You could still be shaped by what you fear."

"Do you think our fears define us?" I asked.

"They can if we let them."

"And what are you afraid of?"

She shrugged. "Living. Dying. Killing. Myself. The usual."

The lady doth protest too much, I thought. "It's not usual to be that aware."

"I've never been the sort of person that people notice. I've made a career of observing other people, trying to understand them, living vicariously through them."

"Or dying."

She paused and scrutinized my face again. "Is that what you've done?"

"No, I'm a cautionary tale. I came here too many times on my own at night. I try to steer people off the path I took myself. If they continue coming here, becoming more lonely and desperate, at least I provide them with company. When the time comes for them to end their lives, some allow me to be with them. Then, if they slit their wrists, I drink their blood. They die knowing they at least gave a little life to someone."

"Being a vampire is socially acceptable now, isn't it?" she said. "Is it comforting for you, drinking despair, knowing that there was nothing you could have done to save them?"

"Now that's the question of someone who dies vicariously," I said. "Even as an animated corpse, I can see that what I do is unhealthy. My existence will end more slowly than that of those I fail to save, more quickly than those I frighten into saving themselves. But in the end, there's no treatment for suicide, only palliative care. Perhaps I'm a monster for believing that, but at least we've established what sort of monster I am. I'm the scapegoat servant of a vampiric institution. I divert attention away from the greater monster, a park that provides seductive comfort to those who feed it with a belief in its sacredness and the money to maintain it. Meanwhile, the park quietly waits for them to give up their lives. The question is, what sort of monster are you?"

"I don't know." She stood and paced back and forth in front of me, alternately blacking out and revealing the brightness of the cityscape. "Maybe I'm an advanced version of you, but here's what I'm not: There's a story about a policeman who drove with his partner toward a high, windswept bridge where he saw a young man preparing to jump. His partner stopped the car. The policeman leapt out and grabbed the young man just as he jumped. He started falling over with the young man, and would have plunged to his death if it hadn't been for his partner, who arrived in time to pull the two of them back. People asked him, themselves and each other the same question over and over: *How could the policeman have hung on for that moment when it seemed certain that he would die? How could he sacrifice his life, his hopes, his dreams, his career, and his ties to his family, and everything else he had ever held dear for the sake of a total stranger?* The policeman said, 'If I had let that young man go, I could not have lived another day.' In that moment, he saw himself and the young man as one and the same person. That's what a good, moral person, a hero, is supposed to be.

"Now, what if it became possible for me to say to myself, 'I'm not going to die. Not now. Not ever.' Where's my oneness, my connection to everybody else then? I lose the one thing everybody alive has in common. If I can choose to live forever, everyone else who can't do the same becomes suicidal to my eyes. So maybe I'm the kind that sees bridges and people jumping off them no matter where she goes, the kind that doesn't have to stalk her victims, the kind that could truly save people if she were willing to choose who lives and who dies. Maybe I'm the kind that refuses to make those choices, kills everyone without even lifting a finger, and refuses to die with them. But I must be some sort of monster, mustn't I? What else could I be?"

For years I'd held back, warned people away, provided final company to those beyond hope, never once fed on them until they took their lives, but I'd never witnessed someone on the brink of such an outpouring. She was babbling, bubbling, filled to bursting with life and words and ideas and blood. I could feel the pressure within her. I'd known only dwindling puddles of humanity, and she was, by comparison, a nascent geyser. Her need to nourish, to be drained and redistributed, was more urgent than any I'd known. It was intoxicating, terrifying, and irresistible.

I sprang from the bench, seized her by the arms, and sank my fangs into her neck.

She struggled at first, but then she reversed, and seemed to strengthen rather than weaken. She didn't moan so much as coo, and then sing, and then squeal. In the noises she made, there was no pain, no surrender, no craving for dissolution. My hollow insides filled like a cactus in a monsoon. The more joyful she became, the more absurdly I craved her; the more I craved, the deeper I drank, and the deeper I drank, the more I sank. All that saved me was that I'd been vertical and my legs stopped holding me up. Before I slumped back onto the bench, I felt a great surge of sympathy for mosquitoes that get pinched and then can't stop feeding.

"Wow," she said. "I want to sign up with a blood bank. I never knew donating blood could be so fulfilling."

"Well, I certainly feel full and filled." I felt like the blood expanding inside me. I expected something more vital than usual, since I hadn't ever fed on a living person, but I was still shocked at how rich this food was. I could hardly move.

She, on the other hand, could hardly *not* move. "So how does this blood-drinking work?" she asked animatedly. "Is it like a sexual thing? Do you have a refractory period?"

"I couldn't suck another corpuscle," I groaned. "What are you, the mainline from the Athabasca Blood Sands? You should have been a shriveled husk by now."

"Sorry," she said, embarrassed. "I didn't know I had to be gentle with you. This was my first time."

"I know it might sound like a standard male lie, but nothing like this has ever happened to me either."

"Maybe my technique was off. Or yours was. I've never really seen how sucking on someone's neck could be sexy—well, I've seen it now, in my case, because it stimulated me to produce blood faster than you could drink it, and the production is exciting—but that's anti-vampiric, isn't it? Normally, orgasm requires a pooling and release of blood in the pelvis. That's tough to do by taking blood from the neck. The destination hardly seems right either. Pumping blood into someone could do wonders in the right spot, but blood wouldn't get there from the stomach. Do you even have a stomach?"

Her last babblings resulted in me feeling bloated. "Could you talk about something else for a while?" I pleaded. "Preferably something off my menu?"

"Well, I've wondered for a while whether I might have certain—abilities. I think my body can remake itself, re-grow any cells it needs to, very quickly." She reached down and broke off a stem of native grass. "I think I can grow things outside my body too." She closed her hands over the stem. When she opened them again, the grass was headed out, full of seeds.

"You're the holy blood and the holy grail," I marveled. "How many?"

"How many what?"

"How many seeds did you make? Give them to me. I have to count them." I took the grass from her, took off my jacket, spread it on my lap, and picked the seeds one at a time, taking care not to risk spilling them on the ground.

"That's all you can do at a time like this?" Her voice sounded far away. "I show you healthy eternal youth, and you retreat into your vampiric shell."

Mercifully, she stopped talking until I was finished inventorying the seeds and could put them safely in a plastic sample bag.

"So are you really the manifestation of a soul-sucking bureaucracy," she asked, "or do you just have a garden variety case of obsessive compulsive disorder?"

"Don't play Buffy the Vampire Therapist with me," I told her. "There are serious issues at stake here. You could have introduced an invasive species with that trick."

"And you could be one."

I sprang from the bench, or tried to. The blood spread into my bones and tissue, but I felt like the heaviness from my stomach went with it. I twisted back and forth on the bench, wondering if she'd multiplied me as easily as the seeds, scanning the fields for twins of myself before finally coming to my senses.

"That's ridiculous," I told her. "I have the least impact of anyone who's ever come here. I'm cold and dead and pure."

"I suppose that's why I ended up talking to you," she mused. "You're the only one I feel safe with. Would this spread if I had sex with a live person, or just told a live person what I've told you? What if I can do more than make blood and seeds? What if I can give other people the ability to make blood and seeds?"

My bones groaned at the thought. "Now that's just cruel."

"I suppose you're right," she admitted. "I could divert you all night by making seeds, but you can't get any sort of nourishment from them, can you?"

"I think seeds are supposed to confound vampires because they're symbolic of the early Christian church. Jesus was talking about spreading the smallest seeds of spiritual nourishment that would be the hardest to stamp out and grow into the biggest church. I think I want to count them just to keep track of the competition, the way one political party conducts polls to find out how much support the other one has, but all our political parties are fundamentally vampiric."

"Stefan's Law doesn't apply to liquids," she said.

I had no idea what Stefan's Law had to do with the point I was trying to make. But I did know that if she didn't have the sense to stay away from me, I could still wring her neck, right then and there. And might, as soon as I could figure out what the hell Stefan's Law was.

I reached to my pants pocket for my smart phone and couldn't get my hand *into* my pocket, since my legs seemed to have swollen up, so I took my pants off. It wasn't like I needed them for warmth anyway, and mosquitoes never bit me, either because of my undead skin or from professional courtesy.

I did a search on the 'net.

"I'm such an enabler," came her voice, but she sounded far away. "I hope I haven't overdone it. I don't know which is more incredible: that vampires exist, or that they could survive the advent of the 'net. I suppose it shouldn't surprise me, though. You're not just socially acceptable, you're a model citizen. You're passive, compliant, a consumer, a blood recycler, and you give me a safe outlet for my creative powers. You make me feel like it's a crime to duplicate my own cells, that it's evil to exhale, that the only good Canadian is an undead Canadian."

Stefan's Law was an equation stating that the intensity of radiation given off by an object is proportional to its surface area, its efficiency at taking in and letting out radiation, and especially its temperature, which was so important that they multiplied it by itself four times, just for emphasis. I couldn't find any mention of it not working for non-solids, though. This was going to be a tough search. I tried to roll up my sleeves, found that they bunched more than I'd expected, and took off my shirt.

In the meantime, the background voice droned on. "There were times when teenagers were rebels. Maybe everyone has always hated us for being younger and more alive than they were, but at least we fought back. Now we're fed an empty, self-destructive mockery of real youth and life, and they've got us believing it's cool."

It turned out that the sun was considered cool because of Stefan's Law. You could take a satellite measurement of the intensity of sunlight above the earth, trace its path back to the sun, figure out how much more concentrated it would be there, and calculate the sun's temperature. The funny thing was that the outermost part of the sun was supposed to be millions of degrees, while the lower surface where our sunlight came from was supposed to be only a few thousand, which seemed to violate another law saying that something farther from a heat source can't be hotter than the source itself. It was all very vampiric, like blotting out the sun with math. I wondered if I could take some night courses on it.

"Strictly speaking, I'm not a teenager," said the voice. "I've been away from high school for a few years. I still feel like one, though, and I think my abilities have made me a biological teenager again, although I wasn't old enough to see the difference when it happened. Everybody's adolescence is longer now; we go from high school to university to apprenticeship. Why shouldn't we always feel like we have a future ahead of us, like we could go on learning and trying new things and improving ourselves forever?"

On earth, though, the equation was full of fear. Sunlight warmed the ground and the ocean and caused them to give off more radiation, which warmed the air so that it gave off more radiation. This heated the ocean and ground some more, so they gave more radiation back to the air. It was like sunlight could multiply, feed on itself and burn us all to a crisp.

I went on searching for quite a while. I couldn't guess the question behind the answer she'd given me. I couldn't even find the answer. All the while, the ominous radiation seemed to build within my mind, not only from the material I was reading, but from some other source I couldn't quite identify. I became aware of my unwitting donor again, attributed my fear to her and accused her of cheating.

"Search for 'The Little Heat Engine,'" she said.

I found the article and read it. It talked about how a solid has to radiate much more when it's heated, but liquids and gases don't, because their atoms have more freedom to do other things.

"You can't do the same heating job twice with the same unit of energy," she said. "Even if the air made energy and sent it back as radiation to heat water, hot water just flows more freely; it doesn't give off any more radiation than cold water."

"That sounds like more than one answer," I said.

"There are about twenty more like that."

"So you've given me the total." I smiled inwardly.

"Actually, those are just the contradictions of basic physical laws. The contradictions also contradict each other."

My bones rumbled, and I swelled some more. I tried to go back to my keypad, but my fingers were getting too fat to punch the buttons. I felt dizzy and had to lie down on the bench.

"I'm trying to reenact *Nosferatu*, the silent movie about a village plagued by a vampire, but with a healthier ending," she said. "In the old *Nosferatu* movie, a young woman saves her people by making love to the vampire all night, delaying him until the sun comes up. In my version, I prepare the vampire to see the sun come up and live. I'd call my movie something like *The Vampire Who Drank from the Holy Grail*."

"Why are you making me ask all these questions?"

"I never used to be the monster-attracting type. The vampire in the movie got the prettiest girl in the village, and he was just a shriveled old corpse. I assume you have a reputation to uphold."

"Why didn't you just have sex with me?" I wanted to ask the question in present tense; I hadn't been interested in her at first, but now I was bloated, oozing from my ears, and about to die. My standards were dropping fast. Or maybe they were just changing. She could do some unique things with blood flow.

"Maybe it won't be like in the movie," she said, almost pleadingly. "No sex, no death. Maybe this could be an opportunity for personal growth. You could embrace your inner child."

I could only scream. My 'inner child' went through a pulse of growth, increasing the pressure on what surrounded it. I felt as though I grew a new heart, gut and lungs that joyously heaved and throbbed, limbs within limbs, bones within bones, a new penis inside the old. One hot, self-creating, multiplying mass pressed outward on the cold dead shell in expansive waves, with no canal to carry it to birth. I was ecstasy wrapped in torture, a scream in stereo surround, a singing kidney stone.

"I'm sorry. I know you're in pain. Try to breathe. Breathe and push. I think my cells can teach yours to make younger versions of themselves. Imagine the new life copying and flushing out the old necrotic tissue."

This was hardly welcome advice, since I considered necrotic tissue to be the only kind I had. "You sadistic raping bastard!" I shrieked. "You did this to me!"

"You did it to yourself. You called yourself a vampire, identified with your vampire oppressor. Maybe I should have called you on it sooner, but if you hadn't identified yourself as a vampire, I wouldn't have opened up to you."

It was easy for her to say. She wasn't the one being pushed open from the inside. I wanted to tell her to put a stake in me, just to relieve the pressure. I tried to say as much, but my lips and tongue had swelled too; it was getting too painful even to talk.

"You can live and stay young and healthy, or you can die, but you can't try to do both anymore. I needed to spread what I have. Biting me wasn't evil; it was brave. You acted like a one-man government, only better. An institution can take from one person and give to another, but an institution fears self-sufficiency above all else, because making everyone self-sufficient would make it unnecessary."

She leaned over me and looked straight into my eyes, but she seemed to be farther and farther away. I had two sets of eyes, one growing beneath the other, both buried deeper and deeper by my swelling face. I looked up out of myself as if from the bottom of a well.

"You can get through this," she told me. "You can be more alive than you ever were. But you have to want to live. You have to try."

I could feel my very thoughts being copied, washed away, replaced with living duplicates. I saw more and more of the flaws in my old undead way of looking at the world. I was frightened to think of them and pushed them down, then felt them resurface, at shorter and shorter intervals. At least thoughts could be hidden. There were organs forming within me, layers of new skin beneath the giant blister I'd become. A body didn't build things it didn't intend to use. When my inner self was complete, the blood might wash away the outer self as well. How could I walk among people who thought and acted like vampires if they couldn't see me as one? I'd be utterly vulnerable.

"There's no morality without choice, and no choice without life," she said. "You didn't kill for me, or die for me; you risked living for me, when that was what scared you most. No lifeless idea or faceless organization could have done that. You're beautiful, and precious, and you deserve to live, to breathe, to own yourself and be your own creator. I've given you all I can, and now I have to go. It's better that I don't know if you survive so that if I'm caught, I can't tell on you. We live in a country where life is illegal, but life will find a way. Spread life, and leave no trace, and one day there'll be too many of us to drain away."

Then she ran. She ran from me, from herself, from the sunrise and from those who might hunt us when it rose. If I'd been wretched, emaciated, a bringer of disease and death, she would have stayed, and feared me no more than she had all night.

No Sangreal, she could say, *no holy blood, no holy grail. The transfusion can't be substantiated.* The question of the holy vampire wouldn't even be asked.

The sun hit the Rockies first, then the foothills, then the ski jump at Canada Olympic Park. My outer self gasped like a bureaucrat with an unspent budget. The light hit me; I smoked and sizzled. My inner self cringed in anticipation of its coming exposure. I thought for a moment that I'd never realized how much internal pressure blood could exert. My outer skin burned, thinned, and then gave way.

From the outside, I disintegrated. From the inside, I watched myself explode.

The blood consumer died; the blood producer was born. I tried to convince my new, living, fangless self that I could still pass as a vampire. Trying to drink one's way to youth was passé; blood would never have kept me young because it was the result of my youth, not the cause. Self-sufficient youth could still make me hated and hunted, probably more than I would have been before. Maybe I'd heal and replace my blood too quickly to slit my wrists and be drained again by the grassland, the true vampire, Nose Hill Park, the *Nose Feratu,* but—

I realized that I'd never quite been able to name my master. I'd never been a full-fledged vampire, only the individual decoy to the institutional real thing, the park that drank the blood of a suicidal young man. True vampires let their lackeys do the biting.

I lay on the bench for a moment, silent, breathless, unwilling to acknowledge myself, to accept that my womb was gone. Maybe the bright harsh world would go away. All around me was still—

Except for a faint, irritating whine.

It grew louder and louder, then stopped.

I felt a burning itch.

I slapped my hand to my neck, jumped up, and pulled the dead offender away. Then I gasped at the sight of the crushed insect body, full of my blood.

Crying, throbbing, bloody, and shivering, surrounded by my own smoking remains, I gathered up my clothes. In the glassy panel of my phone, shocked, I saw my reflection, younger than my vampiric self had been, young as the teenager who'd been bled to death by the park. It didn't fascinate me; if I'd ever been narcissistic, her influence had prepared me to give up that vampiric defense.

I found the plastic bag and closed my hand over the seeds she'd made. When I opened it I found their numbers doubled.

I looked around me at the pattern of the blood burst I had left on the ground, spread out like the petals of a flower.

Something would grow well there.

Ivan Dorin says that many influences contributed to his story: the Calgarian practice of memorializing the dead with plaques on park benches; the Canadian ban on cloning and chimerism under the Assisted Reproduction Act; the high concentration of mosquitoes that thrives in the long grasses of Nose Hill during damp spells; a series of stories about contagious (but anti-vampiric) eternal youth which began with "Little Deaths" in *Tesseracts 13*; and the opportunity to extend that series in this anthology. Ivan Dorin's work has aired on CBC Radio, and in print has appeared in *Alberta Rebound, On Spec, Greatest Uncommon Denominator,* and *Vox.*

A Puddle of Blood
By Silvia Moreno-Garcia

Six Dismembered Bodies Found in Ciudad Juarez.
Vampire Drug-wars Rage On.

Domingo reads the headline slowly. Images flash on the video screen of the subway station. Cops. Long shots of the bodies. The images dissolve, showing a young woman holding a can of soda in her hands. She winks at him.

Domingo waits to see if the next news items will expand on the drug-war story. He is fond of yellow journalism. He also likes stories about vampires; they seem exotic. There are no vampires in Mexico City: their kind has been a no-no for the past thirty years, around the time the Federal District became a city-state.

The next story is of a pop-star, the singing sensation of the month, and then there is another ad, this one for a shoulder-bag computer. Domingo sulks, changes the tune on his music player.

He looks at another screen with pictures of blue butterflies fluttering around. Domingo takes a chocolate bar from his pocket and tears the wrapper.

He spends a lot of time in the subway system. He used to sleep in the subway cars when he was a street kid making a living by washing windshields at cross streets. Those days are behind. He has a place to sleep and lately he's been doing some work for a rag-and-bone man, collecting used thermoplastic clothing. He complements his income with other odd jobs. It keeps him well-fed and he has enough money to buy tokens for the public baths once a week.

He bites into the chocolate bar.

A woman wearing a black vinyl jacket walks by him, holding a leash. Her Doberman must be genetically modified. The animal is huge.

He's seen her several times before, riding the subway late at nights, always with the dog. Heavy boots upon the white tiles, bob cut black hair, narrow-faced.

Tonight she moves her face a small fraction, glancing at him. Domingo stuffs the remaining chocolate back in his pocket, takes off his headphones and follows her quickly, squeezing through the doors of the subway car she's boarding.

He sits across from the woman and is able to get a better look at her. She is early twenties, with large eyes that give her an air of innocence which is quickly dispelled by the stern mouth. The woman is cute, in an odd way.

Domingo tries to look at her discreetly, but he must not be discreet enough because she turns and stares at him.

"Hey," he says, smiling. "How are you doing tonight?"

"I'm looking for a friend."

Domingo nods, uncertain.

"How old are you?"

"Seventeen," he replies.

"Would you like to be my friend? I can pay you."

Domingo isn't in the habit of prostituting himself. He's done it once or twice when he was in a pinch. There had also been that time with *El Chacal,* but that didn't count because Domingo hadn't wanted to and *El Chacal* had made him anyway, and that's when Domingo left the circle of street kids and the windshield wiping and went to live on his own.

Domingo looks at her. He's seen the woman walk by all those nights before and he's never thought she'd speak to him. He expected her to unleash the dog upon him when he opened his mouth.

He nods. He's never been a lucky guy but he's in luck today.

Her apartment building is squat, short, located just a few blocks from a busy nightclub.

"Hey, you haven't told me your name," he says when they reach the fourth floor and she fishes for her keys.

"Atl," she replies.

The door swings open. The apartment is empty. There is a rug, some cushions on top of it, but no couch, no television and no table. She doesn't even have a calendar on the wall. The apartment has a heavy smell, animal-like, probably courtesy of the dog. Perhaps she keeps more than one pet.

"Do you want tea?" she asks.

Domingo would be better off with pop or a beer, but the girl seems classy and he thinks he ought to go with whatever she prefers.

"Sure," he says.

Atl removes her jacket. Her blouse is pale cream; it shows off her bony shoulders. He follows her into the kitchen as she places the kettle on a burner.

"I'm going to pay you a certain amount, just for coming here. If you agree to stay, I'll double it," she says.

"Listen," Domingo says, rubbing the back of his head, "you don't really need to pay me nothing."

"I do. I'm a *tlahuelpuchi*."

Domingo blinks. "You can't be. That's one of those vampire types, isn't it?"

"Yes."

"Mexico City is a vampire-free territory."

"I know. That is why I'm doubling it," she says, scribbling a number on a pad of paper and holding it up for him to see.

Domingo leans against the wall, arms crossed. "Wow."

Atl nods. "I need young blood. You'll do."

"Wait, I mean…I'm not going to turn into a vampire, am I?" He asks because you can never be too sure.

"No." She sounds affronted. "We are born into our condition."

"Cool."

"It won't hurt much. What do you think?"

"I don't know. I mean, do I still get to…you know…sleep with you?"

She lets out a sigh and shakes her head. "No. Don't try anything. *Cualli* will bite your leg off if you do."

The kettle whistles. Atl removes it from the burner and pours hot water into two mugs.

"How do we do this?" Domingo asks.

Atl places tea bags in the mugs and cranes her neck. Her hair has turned to feathers and her hands, when she raises them, are like talons. The effect is disturbing, as though she is wearing a curious costume.

"Don't worry. Won't take long," she says.

Atl is a bird of prey.

The first thing Domingo does with his new-found fortune is buy himself a good meal. Afterwards, he pays for a booth at the Internet cafe, squeezing himself in and clumsily thumbing the computer screen. The guy in the next cubicle is watching porn; the moans of a woman spill into Domingo's narrow space.

Domingo frowns. He pulls out the frayed headphones wrapped with insulating tape and pushes the play button on the music player.

He does a search for the word *tlahuelpuchi*. Stories about gangs, murders and drugs fill the viewscreen. He scrolls through an article which talks about the history of the *tlahuelpocmimi*, explaining this is Mexico's native vampire species, with roots that go back to the time of the Aztecs. The article has lots of information but it uses very big words he doesn't know, such as hematophagy, anticoagulants and matrilineal stratified sept. Domingo gives up on it quickly, preferring to stare at the bold headlines and colorful pictures of the vampire gangsters. These resemble the comic books he keeps at his place; he is comfortable with this kind of stuff.

When an attendant bangs on the door, Domingo doesn't buy more tokens. He has more money than he's ever had in his life and he doesn't know what to do with it.

It is nearly dusk when he finds his way to Atl's apartment. She opens the door a crack and stares at him as though she's never met him before.

"What are you doing tonight?" he asks.

"You're not getting any more money, alright?" she says. "I don't need food right now. There's no sense in you coming here."

"You only eat kids, no?" he says, blurting it.

"Yeah. Something in the hormone levels," she waves her hand, irritated. "That doesn't make me a Lucy Westenra, alright?"

"Lucia what?"

She raises an eyebrow at him.

"I figure, you want a steady person. Steady food, no? And... yesterday, it was, ah...it was fun. Kind of."

"Fun," she repeats.

Yeah. It had been fun. Not the blood part. Well, that hadn't been too awful. She made him a cheese sandwich and they drank tea afterwards. Atl didn't have furniture, but she did have a music player and they sat cross-legged in the living room, chatting, until she said he was fine and he wouldn't get woozy and told him to make sure he had a good breakfast.

It wasn't exactly a date, but Domingo has never exactly dated. There were hurried copulations in back alleys, the kind street kids manage. He hung out with Belen for a little bit, but then she went with an older guy and got pregnant, and Domingo hadn't seen her anymore.

Atl lets him in, closing the door, carefully turning the locks. The dog pads out of the kitchen and stares at him.

"Look, you've to get some facts straight, alright? I'm not in Mexico City on vacation. You don't want to hang out with me. You'll end up as a carpet stain. Trust me, my clan is in deep shit."

"You're part of a clan?" Domingo says, excited. "That's cool! You got a crest tattoo? Is it hand-poked?"

"Jesus," Atl says. "Are you some sort of fanboy?"

Domingo shakes his head. "No."

"Why are you here?"

"I like your dog," he says. It is a stupid answer. He doesn't have anything better. He wonders if she'll go with him to the arcade. He went there once and drank beer while he tried to shoot green monsters. It would be cool. Maybe she is too old for arcades. He wonders what she does for fun.

"It will bite your hand off if you pet it," she warns him. "I'll give you a cup of tea and you leave afterwards, alright?"

"Sure. How come you drink tea?"

She doesn't reply. Domingo is about to apologize for being crass, but he isn't up to date on *tlahuelpocmimi* diets. Except for the kid part.

A knock on the door makes them both turn their heads.

"Health and Sanitation."

"Open it. Don't tell them I'm here," she whispers, moving so quickly to his side it makes him gasp.

She goes towards the window and jumps out. Domingo rushes after her, pokes his head out, and sees Atl climbing up the side of the building, her shoulders hunched and looking birdlike once more. She disappears onto the roof.

Domingo opens the door.

Three men waltz in, faces grim.

"We have a report there's a vampire here," one of them says.

Domingo, with the experience of a master liar and a complete indifference to authority, shrugs. "I don't know. The guy that's renting me the place didn't say nothing about vampires."

"Look around. You, I'm going to check you, give me your hand."

Domingo obeys. The guy presses a little white plastic stick against his wrist. It beeps.

"You're alone?" the guy asks him.

"Yep." Domingo takes out a chocolate bar and starts eating it. The dog is sitting still, eyeing the men.

"What are you doing?"

"Sleeping."

Domingo can hear the other two men opening doors, muttering between themselves.

"It's all empty," one of the other men says. "There's not even clothes in the closet. Just a mattress in there."

"You live here?" asks the first guy, who hasn't moved from Domingo's side, carefully cataloguing him.

"Yeah. For now. I move around. Been working for a rag-and-bone man lately. I used to wash windshields and before that I juggled balls for the drivers at the stop lights, but this guy I worked with beat me up and I've got the rag-and-bone gig now."

"Just a damn street kid," says the man, and Domingo thinks he must have an earpiece on or something, because he sure as hell isn't speaking to Domingo.

The men leave as quickly as they've come. He locks the door, sits on the rug and waits. Atl doesn't fly in—not technically—but she seems to jump in with a certain grace and flexibility that is birdlike.

"Thanks," she says. The feathers disappear, leaving only pitch-black hair behind.

"How'd you do that?"

"What?"

"The bird thing."

"It's natural. We all do it after we hit puberty."

She goes into her room. Domingo stands at the entrance, watching her pull up floor boards with her bare hands, taking stuff from under there and tossing it into a backpack. She rips the mattress open and begins to throw some money and papers in the bag.

"It's been nice meeting you. I've got to find another place now."

"What sort of trouble are you in? What do those guys want?"

"Those guys aren't the trouble," she says. "That's just sanitation. But if they got word there is a vampire here, that means the others aren't far behind."

"Who are the others?"

Atl gives him a narrow look. "One month ago my aunt's head was delivered in a cooler to our home. I left Ciudad Juarez and headed here before I also ended in a cooler."

"Who killed her?"

"A rival clan. It's part of our territory fights. We were trying to kill a certain clan leader and botched it. She's got a big scar across the middle now, and she's mighty pissed at us. I hope you can appreciate the situation," she says, zipping her jacket up.

It sounds very exciting to Domingo. He's only seen the gang fights from afar. Mexico City has managed to insulate itself through the conflict, partly because it keeps the vampires who are waging the wars out of the city limits, and partly because it is so damn militarized. The drug dealers in Mexico City are *narcomenudistas*, petty peddlers, small-scale crooks focused around Tepito and Iztapalapa. If they kill each other, they have the sense to do it quietly, without attracting twenty Special Forces ops who are ready to put a gun up your ass and shoot before bothering to ask for identity cards.

Atl goes down the stairs. Domingo follows her.

When they reach the front door she turns to look at him and he thinks she is going to tell him to beat it. Her hands tighten around the dog's leash. She takes a step back.

Thirty seconds later Domingo is in a comic book.

Half a dozen men pour in. The dog growls. Somebody yells, "Stay the fuck still. Stay the fuck still!" Big bubble speeches.

A guy grabs Domingo by the collar and drags him out, pinning him against the ground and putting a plastic tie around his wrists.

Domingo doesn't know if these are cops, or sanitation, or narcos. All he knows is he can hear the dog barking and he is being dragged against the pavement, and then kicked towards the trunk of a car. They're trying to stuff him in the trunk.

Domingo panics. He tries to hold onto something. The guy punches him and Domingo folds over himself.

It doesn't really feel like he thought it might feel. Action. Adventure. Comic book manic energy.

The guy pulls Domingo by his hair and Domingo gets a glimpse of teeth, half a smile, before Atl pulls him off Domingo with a swift, careless motion that breaks his bones.

Domingo, on his knees, looks up at Atl. She cuts the plastic tie and the dog comes bounding towards her.

She's got three sharp needles sticking out of her left leg. Blood puddles next to her shoes.

She vomits. A sticky, dark mess.

The dog whines.

"Come on," he says grabbing her arm, propping her up.

He tries not to look at the bodies they leave behind. He tries not to wonder if they're all dead.

If this is a comic book, then it's tinted with red.

She's awake. He knows it because the dog raises its head. Domingo looks at her. Sure enough, her eyes are open, though he can't make her expression.

"How you feeling?" he asks.

Atl looks down at her bandaged leg. He knows he didn't do a great job, but at least he took out those weird needles.

"My bag. Do you have it?"

She clutched it all the way there. There was no way he could have left it behind. Domingo nods.

"There's a blue plastic stick in it. Small. Hand it to me."

He does.

She presses it against her tongue and shivers. Then she unwraps the bandage around her leg. The skin looks odd. Blackened, as if stained.

"What's that?" he asks.

"Anaphylactic reaction from the silver nitrate. Lucky for me they didn't want me dead yet."

Domingo blinks.

"It makes me sick," she explains.

"You've been out for about an hour."

Atl brushes the hair back from her face. She looks around at the little room and the piles of old comic books, hybrid personal protective clothing, and all the other assorted junk he collects and sells together with the bone-and-rag-man.

"Where are we?"

"My place. It's safe. We're in a tunnel downtown. It's very old. I think the nuns used it. There was a convent nearby. Benito Juarez closed it fifty years ago."

Atl chuckles. "Juarez is the 1800s. That happened nearly two centuries ago. Jesus!"

She gives him a funny look. Domingo frowns. He doesn't know lots of stuff and obviously she does. He doesn't like it when people make fun of him. It's unpleasant. Even Belen was rude at times, though there was no reason for that.

"It's cool," she says. "This works. It was smart thinking."

She opens her arms and the dog rushes towards her, pressing its great head against her cheek. She scratches its ear and smiles at Domingo.

"How come your dog's so big?" he asks.

"*Cualli's* a special breed. He's an attack dog."

"Were those the gangsters?"

"Those were freelancers. Health and Sanitation must have tipped them off that there was something odd going on. Or somebody else did."

"You were fast. Like really fast. Are all vampires like that? I've read a lot about the European ones and the Chinese, and how there's all the infighting with them up north and if you go to Mexicali it's like all run by the Chinese. But they say they're all stiff, no? *Jian shi* and they can't really be green, can they? I don't know much about your type. Funny, it's probably—"

"Please. Stop," she says, pressing her fingers against her temples. "I don't want to talk about vampires. Or gangs."

"What do you want to talk about?"

"Nothing."

Domingo wants to talk about everything. He sits in front of her, brimming with questions as she curls up and closes her eyes.

This is how a vampire sleeps. Not in coffins. Curled up, with a dog by her feet and a boy watching her.

He gets up early and goes above ground. It's raining, so he ties a plastic shopping bag to his head as he heads to purchase food. He buys bread, milk, three cans of beans, potato chips and pastries. He feels very happy as he pays for the stuff, like it's Christmas.

On the way back, he scans the screens at the subway in search of news. There's nothing about the confrontation of the previous day.

As he stands in the subway car, listening to the tired music on his player, he conjures a story in which he's making breakfast for his girlfriend, and she's real pretty and they live together. Not in the tunnels. In a proper place.

When he returns to the tunnel he's humming a tune.

She's sitting, back against the wall, browsing through a bunch of magazines. When she looks up at him, the tune dies on his lips.

"Where did you go?"

"I went to get us breakfast."

"I don't need breakfast. It was stupid of you. Someone might have seen you."

"Sorry," he mutters and then, tentatively, to diffuse her anger. "How do you like my collection?"

"It's great," she says, quirking an eyebrow at him and jumping to her feet, showing him the cover of a comic book. "Not a fanboy, huh?"

It's an old-style thing with a guy in a Dracula cape. She picks another one. This is a recent clipping from a magazine he stole a few weeks before. It talks about the narco-vampires in Monterrey.

He wets his lips, struggling for words. "Why are you angry?"

"I am not a goddamn hobby."

"Who's talking about a hobby?"

She shoves the magazine against his chest, pushing him back. "Do you like vampires? Huh? You like reading about them? You like looking at the pictures of dead vampires?"

"Yeah, well...it's exciting."

"Do you know how long my kind can live? Three-hundred years. You know what's the average lifespan of my kind? Thirty years. Do you want to know why?"

Domingo does not answer. She grabs him by his shirt, holding him up, his feet off the floor.

"Because we're all getting massacred. Before I arrived in Mexico City, I was at the market in Ciudad Juarez. The decapitated body of a vampire bled onto the pavement, right next to a food stand. People kept eating. They bought soda. They were more bothered by the heat than the corpse."

She lowers him and his feet touch the floor.

"I'm going to be a puddle of blood."

He's scared to say a thing. She sits down, folding her legs and staring at the wall. Eventually, he sits next to her.

"What are you going to do?" he asks.

"Hell if I know," she whispers. "I need to eat. I need to sleep. I need to think."

He pulls up his sleeve, offering his arm to her. She smiles wryly.

"You're going to get hurt one of these days," she tells him, "if you keep helping strangers like me."

"It doesn't matter," he replies.

She presses her mouth against his skin.

Domingo is groggy when he opens his eyes. Atl's still asleep. He doesn't try to wake her. He flicks a battery-powered lantern on and looks at his magazines, feeling odd when he runs his hands across the vivid picture, the splashes of red.

The dog growls. Domingo lifts the lantern and listens. He doesn't hear anything. The dog growls louder. Atl shifts her body, fully awake.

"What is it?" he asks.

"People," she says.

He still can't hear anything. Atl grabs her bag and pulls out a switchblade.

"*Cualli*, stay," she tells the dog, then raises her eyes towards him. "Don't move. The dog will keep you safe."

"What are you doing?"

"I'm going to take a look," she says.

She runs out. Domingo crouches next to the dog, trying to listen for anything odd. The tunnels are quiet for a bit, and then he hears loud sounds. Might be gun shots. The sounds seem to be getting closer. He's nervous, heart beating very fast. He twists the dog's leash between his hands.

Atl returns running and her face is very tense.

"Lead me out of here!" she says.

Domingo scrambles ahead of her, holding his lantern. He turns left and finds himself face to face with three people wearing masks and goggles. They raise their guns. He blinks and is yanked back, thrown against the floor. The air is knocked out of his lungs.

Bullets zing; the loud blast of a shotgun. Domingo covers his ears. One of them lunges past Atl, towards him. Atl plucks him back. The man tries to escape. Her claws and teeth tear the protective mask apart and she bites into his face like he is a ripe fruit.

The dog is also biting, tearing.

Domingo looks dumbly at all the blood.

"The place is crawling with them," she says, angrily. "They must have followed you back. You've got to lead us out."

"We've got to keep going straight," he mumbles, picking the lantern off the floor.

The light illuminates a shadow, the figure of another man with a mask coming just behind Atl.

"Look out!" he yells.

The man's head rolls onto the floor.

Atl's fingers are stained crimson. Brains are splattered over her jacket.

It's Domingo's turn to vomit.

Dozens of *mariachis* in *charro* costumes litter Garibaldi Plaza. They're waiting for someone to hire them to play a song and do not pay attention to two dirty beggars with a stray dog. That's what Atl and Domingo look like, covered in grime and dirt after running through the tunnels.

"I'm heading to Guatemala, kid," Atl says, her bag balanced on her left shoulder.

"Do you have friends there?"

"No."

"Sure. I'll go," he says.

She stares at him.

"You're going to need to feed," he says. "You'll need someone to watch your back."

"I don't need help."

"I can shoot a gun," he blusters.

"You've almost died twice in less than a week."

"The life expectancy of a street kid isn't much higher than yours," he says, knowing he's got nowhere to go. There's nothing but forward.

She smirks. "Find another way to commit suicide."

She slips a couple of bills into his hand.

"Atl," he says.

"Keep the dog," she replies, handing him the leash. "It'll slow me down."

She takes a couple of steps. The dog whines.

"Stay with him," she orders.

"Atl," he repeats.

She walks away. She doesn't turn her head. He tries following her, but the square is crowded at this time of the night and he loses her quickly. She must have flown away. Can vampires fly? He'll never know.

She's gone.

A trio sings *"La Cucaracha"* while the rain begins to fall. He sniffles, eyes watery.

Domingo pulls his plastic bag from his pocket and ties it above his head. He's out of chocolate. He's out of luck. He pats the dog's head.

Silvia Moreno-Garcia's stories have appeared in publications such as *Fantasy Magazine, Tesseracts Thirteen* and *Shine: An Anthology of Optimistic Science Fiction.* She is the owner of Innsmouth Free Press, a micro-publishing venture specializing in horror and dark speculative fiction, and through Innsmouth she has co-edited the anthologies *Historical Lovecraft* and *Candle in the Attic Window.* She has written a couple of stories set in a near-future Mexico where vampires are real and hopes to write a novel which takes place in the same universe.

V-Link

By Eileen Bell

I love Vlad the Impaler!

The words floated in, a warm spot in Roslyn's mind. It was Gina, with information.

Roslyn pretended to pay attention to Dr. Erickson, who was standing right by her bed. She watched his lips move as Gina's voice crawled around in her head, giving her the up-to-date about the U-Link implant patients. Everybody was getting weaker by the day. Roger and Cassidy were still off the grid. In other words, no good news.

She muttered "uh huh," like she was listening to the doctor, then felt the small warm spark in her brain as she responded to Gina.

Can't talk long, Erickson's here. Who's Vlad?

Original vampire or something. A real bad ass, apparently. But anybody with Impaler in his name couldn't be all good, now could he?

Gina was being held in a university and actually had access to a library, so she could look stuff up. Dead tree technology, but at least it was something.

The rest of them were in hospitals all across the country, with no access to the outside, or to each other. At least, that's what the doctors believed when they shut down the wireless network to disconnect everyone fitted with Version 1.0 of the U-Link implant.

U-Link. Before their surgeries, Roslyn and the rest had been told it would be the next great networking system.

Roslyn touched the IV cannula sprouting from her chest, into which would soon spew the latest chemical stew, and wondered if maybe this time she should have waited for Version 2.0. The one that *didn't* shut down all your internal organs one by one until all you had left was your brain.

Dr. Erickson grabbed her foot and she jumped. Not that it hurt—it didn't, her nerves didn't carry pain messages the way they used to—he had just surprised her. She cut the connection to Gina and glared at him. "What?"

"Are you having difficulty focusing?" He looked anxious. "Maybe another CT scan—"

"No," she snapped. "My brain's not shutting down. I'm ignoring you. I only ever asked for two things, Dr. E. Saying no about the blood, all right, I get that, but no computer? That's BS and you know it."

She almost added that the V-Link—the name Gina had coined when the U-Link patients spontaneously reconnected—wasn't enough anymore. That she missed her old friends, and her mother, and her life. But she clamped her mouth shut before those words slipped out. He didn't need to know about the V-Link. That was *their* little secret.

His expression went from anxious to almost angry. "Those are the rules. You know them as well as I do. Now, pay attention, please. We are going to change your regimen—"

"Again?" she whined, hating the weak sound of it. "Why?"

"Remarkable advances were made at the New Hampshire facility—"

"What advances?" Roger and Cassidy were in New Hampshire.

She clawed at the blankets until Erickson helped her sit upright. "Have you been out of bed today?" he asked.

"No. Tell me what happened in New Hampshire."

"You must exercise." He pointed to the hated walker, the scorch mark visible on the side. "Your muscles are atrophying—"

"Thinner's better," she quipped. When he didn't laugh, she went serious, too. "I'm not taking the chance. Not after Melissa."

"You don't have to go outside. Just up and down the halls."

"But I have to do it during the day, when the physio staff's here. You know that, Dr. E."

She closed her eyes and saw Melissa stepping out through the front door of the hospital like it was happening at this moment and not three months before. The late afternoon sun touching her. Igniting her. Her screaming and screaming as Roslyn fell backwards into the safety of the shadows. And then Roslyn screaming as Melissa finally fell, finally silent, to the sidewalk, and burned to ash. "I'm not doing that again."

"But you have to walk."

She shook her head. "Tell me what happened in New Hampshire."

For a moment she thought he wasn't going to answer her.

"Please?" She let her voice wander up to little girl young, because it worked on him sometimes.

"They removed the implants from two of the patients there," he finally said.

A chill, like a puff of winter, and she pulled the blanket up to her chin before she realized it was fear and not cold. "Successfully?"

"More or less."

The chill trickled over her like ice water. She shuddered. "What does that mean?"

"The good news is, both survived, this time. And it appears that some of their internal organs are regaining viability." He smiled. "We are very hopeful."

"Their hearts?" she asked.

"No. The appendix. But it's a start."

"And the bad news?" There was always bad news.

"There was some loss of brain function—"

She touched the scar that ran along her hairline. "How much?"

"Some cognitive ability, and for some reason, scent recognition." He shook his head, as though that was the real puzzler. Then his eyes slid from hers and settled on the thin blanket covering her belly. "They only lost a few IQ points, though. Nothing to worry about."

"How many's a few?"

"Not many." Erickson's eyes did not leave her midsection. He was lying. "The results were positive enough to warrant phase two. A slight variation on the chemical mixture. And then extraction."

"So, who's your next victim?"

Erickson's face tightened and his eyes swung up to hers.

"Not me," she whispered.

"You don't have a choice."

"But that's not fair!" Roslyn looked around the room as though trying to find something in all that sterile white with which to protect herself. She clicked on the V-Link and thought/screamed *911, 911, 911,* as if it would do some good.

"We'll start the next round of chemical therapy tomorrow night," Erickson said. "It's for your own good."

The V-Link came alive. Through the noise of everyone asking what was wrong, she tried to focus on him, on his words.

"I don't want to die," she finally whispered. "Please tell me I'm not going to die."

"We won't let that happen, Roslyn." He smiled, and she tried to smile back. "I won't see you until the day before the extraction, but I want you to be brave. Think of it. You're about to get your life back."

He patted her hand and walked out of the room. As the door swished shut, she was left alone with her own thoughts and those of the twenty-eight people left of the Link experiment. She was so afraid; all she could do was cry like a little girl.

She was next. They were going to disconnect her next.

Before she was hooked up to the blood/heart machine to pump the new chemical stew through her system, some of the other Link patients almost convinced her that having the implant taken out could be a good thing. If she went through with this, she could go back to normal. So what if she lost a few IQ points, and the only organ working in her body was the hugely useless appendix? She could go back to her life. Her friends. Maybe even her mother.

The machine clicked and slurped to life beside her and she tried to hang on to that thought. Then the toxic liquid boiled through her veins and she couldn't think anymore. All she could do was scream.

After the nurses disconnected her and wheeled her back to her bed, she struggled against her tightly tucked blankets until Gina's voice rippled through her consciousness.

How do you feel?

Weak. She tried to pull her arms out from under the blankets, but couldn't. *A lot weaker, actually.*

We were strong before they started all this. Very, very strong.

I know. But we can't go back to that. It's against the law.

The laws need to be changed.

Roslyn snorted laughter. *Yeah. I'll get right on that. Maybe run for office—if I could get out of bed!*

I'm not kidding. Gina's thoughts read deadly serious. *They shouldn't be treating us like this. We are real.*

Of course we're real. Roslyn thought about disconnecting. Gina was going to go into one of her conspiracy theory rants, and she didn't feel up to it. Not after the blood-heart machine. Not after the screaming.

Don't shut me down! Gina's thoughts slammed into Roslyn's head, bringing more than warmth. Heat—almost pain. *I found an article in the New England Journal of Medicine. They are calling what happened to us an unintended side effect of the Link implant.*

You think?

Just listen. Somehow the implant flipped a switch—a genetic switch in all of us. I don't know how—hell, I don't understand half the words they used. But that's what all the experimentation is about. They want to make the Link work, without turning the users from human to—whatever we are. That's why there are only twenty-eight of us left.

She wished Gina would shut up. She was too tired. *The others aren't dead or anything. They just disconnected from the V-Link when the implant was removed.*

I think we got that wrong. In the article, they talk about brain biopsies after extraction. Brain biopsies, Roslyn.

Roslyn shuddered. Gina was lying. She had to be. *They're trying to save us!*

I don't think so.

Roslyn fought against the blankets, listening to her choked gasps and wondering if her lungs, somehow, had restarted. She was, for the first time, afraid it was all a lie.

We need to get strong, Roslyn. That means getting blood. Real blood. Not this plasma shit they've been feeding us.

She stopped fighting. Stared up at the ceiling. *I won't kill anyone.*

Probably be better if you didn't, Gina replied, and laughed her smoky, angry laugh. *But we need to build our strength. Blood's the only way.*

Are you sure?

Yes. Gina broke the link, and Roslyn was alone.

She wriggled one arm free and pulled the sheets back from her body. Exhaustion overtook her, and she almost gave up, but then mentally kicked herself. Get up now!

She pulled herself upright, then grabbed her right leg and swung it over the edge of the bed. She almost fell to the floor, but gained control. She grabbed the other leg and moved it next to the first, like so much dead wood. Focusing on her legs, she tried to convince them to move. She couldn't tell if she felt more like cheering or crying when she saw her right foot twitch. And then another twitch. And then, almost without thought, she was standing beside the bed, staring through the gloom at her walker. So far away.

"I can do this," she whispered, hoping she wasn't lying to herself. She shuffled forward a step. Her eyesight darkened, but she waited it out. Another step and another, clutching first the bed, and then the chair no one ever used, and then the cupboard that held everything she had left from her other life—the clothes in which she had been caught. She wondered if they were still covered in Terry's blood and tried not think of that. Two steps. She grabbed the walker and clung to it like an old friend. After a pause, she wheeled herself to the door and opened it.

A chair sat empty beside her door. The guard was no longer needed because she was no longer a threat. She hadn't been out of that bed for months. She wheeled past it, away from the nurse's station—she didn't want to attract their attention.

Her feet tangled and she almost fell. She clutched the walker and glared down until both feet faced forward again. She had four doors to check. Just four. If she didn't find a way to feed on this floor, she was done.

She pushed against the first door and glanced into the room. Two males. No one was being given blood. The door snicked shut as she shuffled to the next room. A woman, alone. The wonderful metal smell of fresh blood wafted over Roslyn. She checked to make certain no one saw her, and then walked through the door, pushing it closed behind her.

The woman was hooked up to every machine known to man, as far as Roslyn could tell. Her eyes, half open in her badly beaten face, looked more dead than alive.

"Hi," Roslyn said, ready to back out and find another room if the woman answered.

The woman didn't react.

Roslyn shuffled up and reached out a shaking hand, touching the IV bag that hung from the stand by the bed. Full of blood.

"I'm just going to borrow a bit," she said, as she disconnected the plastic tubing from the woman's arm. When a small drop of blood fell, her mouth flooded with saliva and she rammed the plastic tube between her lips, closed her eyes and sucked, sighing as the blood touched her tongue then flooded her mouth. Her gums felt warm, and then began to ache. She groaned, sucking and swallowing, feeling warmth slide down her throat into her belly, then expand everywhere inside her.

With the warmth came strength. Her arms and legs stopped feeling wooden. She knew if she drank it all she'd be caught. She took one more long pull on the plastic tubing, filling her mouth before she reconnected the tube to the woman.

"Thanks." She grabbed the walker and tugged it behind her as she headed out the door and back to her room.

Gina. It works, she chortled as she jumped into bed. *It works way better than I would have believed.*

We all need to do this, and then get out, Gina replied. *Find some place to hide. All of us, together.*

Roslyn paused. She didn't know if she wanted to run away. Maybe some of what Erickson told her was the truth. Maybe she could still have her old life back. Maybe, for her, it would work.

I just want to go home, she thought.

Don't we all. Gina's thoughts were filled with such remorse, Roslyn wondered if she had kids. She didn't ask. Nobody talked about the family they left behind.

Every night Roslyn went to the woman in the coma, stealing sips of blood from the plastic tube. Then she walked, to rebuild her strength. At first all she could manage was the hallway, but soon she tackled the stairs. Up to the roof, and then down to the basement. She moved more and more quickly, taking the stairs two at a time, running up and then down them as though she was on flat ground. It felt glorious.

The second night on the stairs, she went on the roof. She stood in the cold dark, drinking in the sight of the stars and the swollen harvest moon and wishing she could just fly away. She said that to Gina, who replied flatly, *We can't do that.*

How do you know? She stared longingly out over the parking lot. Just one step. That's all it would take.

Raymond couldn't.

Oh. Roslyn backed away from the edge of the roof. Raymond had been the first to disappear, even before the artificial Link had been disconnected. Before they'd all been caught.

He'd jumped off the roof of his apartment building when the police came to pick him up. Splattered his brains all over the sidewalk in front of his condo. And they'd all seen it. Felt it. Roslyn shuddered.

Did you ever figure out why he did that?

He killed his wife. Felt bad about it.

Her thoughts touched on Terry, then skittered away.

You do realize you weren't the only one, right? Gina said. *We all killed someone.*

Roslyn stared out at the cold starlight. They'd never talked about it, but it made sense. Funny she'd never connected that particular dot before.

The media dubbed us vampire killers.

But we don't kill vampires—

It's not funny, Roslyn. We have to be careful when we get back out in the world. That's all I'm saying.

Roslyn stared up at the stars, feeling a twinge of anger. That was probably why her mother left. Hadn't had anything to do with Terry at all. No, dear old Mom wouldn't have been able to stand the embarrassment of media attention.

Thanks for looking out for me, Gina, she thought, impulsively. *You would have made a good mom, know what I mean?*

Gina broke the connection without answering, leaving Roslyn alone, staring at the cold stars, impossibly far away.

Gina did not communicate with anyone for three nights. When Roslyn felt her thoughts finally curl into her mind, anger and relief washed over her in equal measure.

Where were you? Everybody thought something happened. They're all acting crazy. Are you all right?

I'm fine. Gina sounded strong, blood strong, and relief flooded through Roslyn. *Did you know Erickson and the rest were coming here? To the university?*

Roslyn frowned. *No. Why would they do that?*

They're having a frigging symposium. Trying to figure out how to deal with the Link issue. Gina laughed, smoke angry. *We're an issue now.*

Roslyn kicked her legs to loosen the blankets and got out of bed. *So what are they going to do?*

They've decided to speed up the experimentation. It's not just you next. They've chosen ten of us. Same 'therapy' they used on Roger and Cassidy.

Because it's working? Hope touched her faintly.

No. I saw Cassidy's autopsy report.

But Cassidy survived! Roslyn felt sick and wished she could puke. *Erickson told me she survived.*

He lied. They're killing everyone. Everyone. We have to escape. Go somewhere safe.

Roslyn heaved once, but there was nothing to vomit and hadn't been for months. She padded back and forth between the door and the foil-covered windows, feeling like a caged animal. *Where's safe?*

Gina was silent so long, Roslyn was afraid she'd disappeared again. *I don't know yet,* she finally thought. *But soon. I'll find someplace soon.*

Roslyn reached out and touched the foil over the window, felt warmth, and knew the sun was just on the other side, ready to burn her to a crisp. *Just don't leave me.*

I won't.

Promise? She pulled her hand away from the foil and looked down at it, half expecting to see blisters. There was nothing.

I promise.

The woman in Room Three died, but it was all right, because Roslyn didn't need her anymore. She moved around the hospital silently, feeling like a ninja or something, taking blood where she found it. She felt stronger with every sip, and chafed against being trapped in the hospital. But Gina said she had to wait until they were all strong enough to leave, so she bided her time, and continued to work out.

Up and down the stairs she ran every night, reveling in the return of her strength. She moved more quickly, taking the steps two at a time, then three, then four. Leaping and landing, light as a jungle cat.

"I think Gina might be wrong," she whispered. She tried jumping a flight of stairs. Landed. Took the next flight, laughing joyously. "I bet we can fly, if we try hard enough."

She turned to head back down the stairs, and leapt. Her toe caught on the top step and she fell, crashing down the whole flight and half of the next before she finally stopped, stunned.

She heard a door swing open on the floor above her and knew she had to move or she'd be caught. She opened her eyes, and then slammed them shut as the staircase whirled around her.

Steps, slow at first, then a quick rat-ta-tat down the stairs to her side. "Are you all right?" a man's voice asked.

"I slipped," she whispered, opening one eye and then, carefully, the other.

A janitor stood a step up from her, staring stupidly. "Maybe I should get a nurse."

The last thing in the world she needed. She shook her head, and then slowly began to move body parts to see what damage she had done to herself.

"I'm all right," she said. "Really. I just slipped." Everything seemed to be in working order, except for one broken toe. It hurt like a bitch.

"Are you sure?" the janitor asked. He still didn't look convinced, so she pulled herself to her feet and smiled, even though the pain was horrendous.

"Absolutely! Sorry if I frightened you."

She walked down the stairs until she heard the janitor leave the stairwell, then groaned and hobbled back to her room, feeling like an idiot. Flying was definitely out.

Her head started to ache as she climbed into bed and attempted to contact Gina. She didn't feel the usual warm click, and frowned. "What the hell?"

Tried again. Nothing. She felt the first flicker of panic, but steadied herself and tried again. Still nothing. She touched the scar and felt a spot of pain where she'd obviously hit her head.

"Oh my god!" she whispered. Almost without thinking, she grabbed the emergency button clipped to her bed and pressed it over and over again, as though it could do some good. She'd disconnected herself from the V-Link! She was all alone.

The nurses added sedatives to the chemical stew they pumped into Roslyn's body and for days she couldn't pull it together enough to even get out of bed. The truth was, she didn't know if she wanted to. She couldn't hear a whisper from the Link.

"I've lost everything," she muttered.

"What was that, dearie?" A nurse stood on the other side of the room. Roslyn hadn't realized she was there.

"I think I'm going to die," she whispered.

"Oh no, dear," the nurse said. "Just three more days and you'll be right as rain."

"Three more—"

"Your procedure, remember? We had to wait for the swelling in your brain to ease."

Roslyn closed her eyes and swallowed. Her throat hurt. How long had it been since she'd fed? Then she frowned. "Swelling?"

"Why yes. You took a tumble. Hit your head. We had to put off your procedure until the swelling eased." She walked to Roslyn. "Can't you remember?"

Actually, she couldn't, but she was not letting the nurse know that. "The drugs are muddling my head," she replied, using the young girl cadence in her voice that seemed to calm all meat. "But I remember now."

"Just rest," the nurse said. "Soon, you'll be back with the rest of us. Dr. Erickson is a miracle worker."

"Yes, I'm sure he is." Roslyn muttered, trying to keep the smile on her face until the nurse finally left the room.

As soon as the door clicked shut, she kicked off the blankets and got out of bed. She was weak, but not debilitated. And her foot didn't hurt anymore. Healed. Maybe her head had healed too.

She closed her eyes and focused on connecting. She tried not to think how much she needed it, just cleared her head and waited for the warmth. She thought she felt something, but couldn't be sure; her head was still fuzzy from the drugs.

Anybody there?

Is that really you? The thoughts winding into her head were so weak she barely believed they were real. But they had to be.

Yes, it's me.

A flood hit her. Thoughts, from all over the country. All of them saying, *Thank god you're back! We can't lose any more!*

Gina? Roslyn hadn't felt her thoughts in the cacophony. *You there?*

The sudden silence made her panic. Had she been cut off again? One small taste, then back to black?

Are you still there? she thought-screamed. *Please be there!*

Finally, a Yes, but it sounded like Mandie Lee from Spokane.

Where's Gina? More roaring silence, and she thought-yelled, *What the hell is going on?*

She's dead, Roslyn.

Roslyn felt as though she'd been caught between two breaths, felt the moment stretch and become impossibly long.

She can't be dead, she finally thought. *She's just hiding again. Spying on the doctors.*

No.

Maybe her implant was removed.

No! Stronger this time, but still Roslyn refused to believe.

How can you be so sure?

We watched. Her husband killed her.

She was married? Stupid thoughts jumped into her head, but all she had were stupid thoughts. Gina was dead.

Yeah. Mandie's thoughts rolled through Roslyn's mind like a flood. *She was caught spying on the doctors and they put her on the extraction list. She begged them to let her see her husband before they took out the implant. Said she had to make him understand that it wasn't her fault.*

What wasn't her fault?

She killed her kids.

There was nothing more to say. It was like Gina had said a million years before: they'd all killed somebody.

Roslyn looked down at her hands and her feet. They felt like wood again, and she didn't know if she wanted them to come alive this time. Gina was dead.

We've all decided something, Roslyn.

What?

We're going to get strong and get out, just like Gina wanted. She was right. We have to stick together.

Their collective thoughts warmed Roslyn, and she sat up, clenching her hands before slowly pulling herself to her feet. Gina was dead, but Roslyn wasn't alone. She had the rest of the Link patients. She wasn't alone.

Dr. Erickson walked into her room just after sunset on the night they had all decided to leave. She stared at him for a long cold moment, as though trying to remember exactly who he was.

"What do you want?" she finally asked.

He looked taken aback, and she realized she'd forgotten her usual questions about blood and a computer.

"Tomorrow's your procedure," he said. "We need to talk about next steps."

"Oh." She'd forgotten that, too. "Yeah."

"There will be changes, after the extraction." He looked so small, so weak. "Once you're stabilized, you'll be moved to a different facility."

"Really? Where?"

"It will be…more secure."

"Like a prison?" She smiled. "Or where Gina is?"

"Gina?" His voice flattened. "Do you mean Gina Wilson? She… didn't make it."

"Is that so?"

His face stiffened and he took a half step away from her bed. He looked afraid, like meat should look, and she hoped he'd run. It would be more fun if she could get him to run.

"You're upset," he said, and she smiled. He was the one who sounded upset. She could almost hear his heart beating in his chest. "A sedative will calm you."

He took another step toward the door and she caught a whiff of iron. Her mouth flooded and she kicked the blankets away. "Did you cut yourself shaving?" she asked. "It smells like it."

He gasped and ran, tripping over the walker and falling heavily to the floor. Before he could kick himself free, she was on him.

She tried to think of something memorable to say before she pulled his head back and bit out his throat, but nothing came to mind.

She didn't completely drain him, though. She stopped herself while he was still moving, though she figured he wouldn't last long. Not with his throat shredded the way it was.

She grabbed him and easily swung his body up over her head, slamming it down onto the IV pole beside her bed, giggling when the curly metal ends sprouted from his mouth like grotesque, dripping flowers. He tried to scream, but produced only a faint whistle through the jagged hole she'd ripped in his neck.

"I am Roslyn the Impaler!" she laughed, and linked with the rest.

I'll be with you soon, she thought as she watched the doctor's feet, barely touching the floor on either side of the stand, jerk spasmodically, like he was trying to run away.

Just one quick stop to make, she told the V-Link. *I want to say good-bye to my mother.*

Eileen Bell lives in Edmonton, Alberta. She won the 2010 Aurora award for her novella "Pawns Dreaming of Roses" in the *Women of the Apocalypse* anthology published by Absolute XPress, and has had several other short stories published. Her inspiration for "V-Link" was twofold. She wondered whether future vampires would fit into society or revert to their roots, and she had nightmares about online networking. She is happily at work on several other projects, and when she's not writing, she's living a fine life in a round house with her husband and her daughter's cranky cat.

Six Underground
By Michael Lorenson

"We owe respect to the living;
To the dead, we owe only the truth."
—Voltaire

At a command from the bailiff, a door slid into the wall with a soft hiss and the jurors filed into the deliberation room. Connor noticed that there were no other exits in the room and that the far wall was solid stone, rough and brown, flaked with black. This room was at the back end of the courthouse, which had been built into the very edge of the underground. Connor imagined that he could feel a kilometer of metal and rock and people pressing down on him from above. After forty years of this life the depth still caused him to panic at times. Unless you were born to it, you never got used to the feeling of living underground.

Overhead lamps flooded the room with soft white light, and a blue glow emanated from the outdoor view displayed on the false window in one wall.

"All right, let's get this vote done with so that we can all go home." The foreman handed out pencils and small slips of blank paper. He hadn't even bothered to wait until all the jurors had taken their seats.

"Why the rush?" Connor asked, taking a seat at the opposite end of the long table from the foreman, his back to the false window. "The trial only started this morning. Shouldn't we discuss the evidence before we vote?" Connor examined the pencil he'd been given. All the pencils on the table were shorter than his thumb and about as sharp, as though they'd had problems before with violence in the deliberation room and weren't taking any chances. Connor wasn't inclined to complain over the lack of long, pointed bits of wood, but he thought that bolting the table and chairs to the floor was a bit excessive.

The foreman paused in his distribution of writing materials and looked at Connor without raising his head. "Let's vote first. If we're not unanimous, then we can discuss the evidence. Everybody write either guilty or not guilty. No doodles, no knock-knock jokes, no yes or no. When you're done, fold it up and put it in the bowl."

The jurors silently obeyed their instructions and deposited their folded votes into the stainless steel bowl in the middle of the table. It wasn't bolted down but it didn't look extremely heavy. Connor guessed that any past violent confrontations in the deliberation room must not have involved the blunt object or it would have been replaced.

The foreman collected and unfolded the ballots, dealing them like cards, all but one into a single pile. "One guilty, and eleven for acquittal. All right, which one of you is the hold-out?"

Eleven faces turned towards Connor, clued in to his vote by his suggestion that they examine the evidence. He had hoped that he wouldn't be the only one to vote guilty. This would be difficult.

He leaned back in his chair, bringing one ankle up to rest on his other leg. "I voted guilty because I believe that they are guilty. And if we vote again, then I will vote guilty again."

A collective groan filled the room. The juror three seats to his right was the only one who seemed sympathetic, and she was the first to speak. "The prosecution didn't prove their case at all. Their closing arguments just went over the evidence of the beating, they didn't even address any of the defense's claims. You can't tell me that there's no reasonable doubt."

Connor tsked at the woman, but was happy to hear that at least one person was open to discussion. He had heard all their names, but after such a long life he found names difficult to retain. He preferred to name people himself, because the ones he made up for people were more likely to be remembered, and he decided to refer to this one as Mrs. Rational. "The prosecutor was a robot," he said. "Each side thought they had the case in the bag so they agreed to an expedited trial and that meant the government wasn't going to assign a flesh and blood lawyer to the case. I have to say, though, the defense didn't prove their case either. Those boys admitted to beating that girl. There's video evidence of it. We can watch it again if you want." He pointed to the wall behind him, occupied almost entirely by the false window.

The woman's expression soured. "No thanks, once was enough."

The man to her left cleared his throat. He was very large, with no neck. "But she was found, exactly where they left her, dead with clear traces of vampirism in what little blood she had left."

"And some serious drugs, too," said Connor, "but yes, death by blood loss. None of that means that she was a vampire when they beat her."

"No," agreed the other juror. "But if we're not sure, if there's any possibility that she was already dead when they got to her, then we have to let them go free."

"Those boys beat her to death for absolutely no reason," said Connor. "It shouldn't matter whether she was already dead or not."

"The judge disagrees with you," said the foreman. "And so does the law. If she was a vampire when they beat her, then she was already clinically dead and she didn't have the same rights as you and me. If she was a vampire, then they were within their rights to defend themselves."

Connor spun his pencil on the table. It stopped, stubby point facing him. He left it where it lay and crossed his arms across his chest. "So that's what we're deciding, then. Not whether or not those boys beat her, but whether or not this girl was a vampire when they did what they did."

"You got it." The foreman nodded.

Connor wasn't certain if that would make it easier or harder for him to win them over.

"Okay, so what do we know about vampires?"

"Oh God," said the foreman. "We know whatever we know. We know what that expert witness told the court. Weren't you there for that?"

Connor spun the pencil again, this time with more force than he intended, and it skittered over the edge of the table and into his lap. "Of course I was there. I heard the same things all of you heard. I just want to go over it again, see if we can spot any holes."

"The only hole here is the one in your head," said the juror to Connor's left, sounding agitated. "Did any of us really need an expert witness to tell us that vampires are dead, strong, fast, and that they drink blood? Why do you care so much about this girl anyways?"

"Because we're here to do a job and I'm going to do it right. Why *don't* you care about this girl?"

"Because my brother was turned into a vampire. Drove him crazy until he lit himself on fire just to die, said he didn't want to live that way and couldn't understand why anyone else would want to." The juror leaned back in his chair, took a deep, sighing breath. "There was nothing we could say that would convince him otherwise. He knew that he was a monster. He knew that he didn't belong with real people anymore and some monster forced it on him."

Connor stared back at the man, trying to judge his age. The body was fifty-ish, but that meant nothing. All through the trial this juror had maintained an angry expression, and it hadn't faded in the deliberation room. "Well," said Connor, "I'm sorry for what happened to your family, and I can understand the kind of pain this trial brought up for you, but I have no doubt in my mind that this girl was not a vampire when those boys did what they did. In a trial like this, both sides probably glossed over details. I think we need to go through the evidence that was presented and look for any mistakes."

Again a collective groan. Again Mrs. Rational spoke up. "Isn't that the prosecutor's job? To go through the evidence and challenge the defense's claims?"

"Again, the robot?" Connor slammed his open palm onto the table. "It's a court-appointed machine. It knows the law and presents evidence but it can't play the jury's emotions like a real lawyer can, and because of that it can't fight fairly against the defense when they use those tactics."

"You're saying that the prosecutor didn't do the same kind of job that a paid lawyer would have?"

"That's exactly what I'm saying," said Connor. "And any one of you who thinks a real person wouldn't have challenged the defense's claims is deluded."

Lips were chewed, pencils were drummed on the table, and there was a lapse in verbal communication.

"So, what do we do now?" The foreman was folding and re-folding one of the small slips of paper. "There are eleven of us who think there's a reasonable doubt, that these boys should walk, and you're the only one who says they shouldn't. I don't think anybody's going to convince anyone else they're wrong."

"I'll tell you what," said Connor. "I think a lot of the evidence presented would have looked different if the prosecution had actually done its job, but I won't waste your time just for me. You guys vote and I'll abstain. If the vote is still eleven for not guilty then the boys can walk. If at least one of you agrees with me that the robot could have done better, then we look at some of the evidence again."

Ten faces were turned down to their papers so Connor locked eyes with the only juror who was looking in his direction—a muscular man to his left, halfway between himself and the foreman. He held the stare for a moment but broke it off, not wanting to make the man uncomfortable. Connor turned and paced to the corner of the room while the others voted. He took great pains not to look at any of the jurors, and instead stared into the fake window—a viewscreen recessed into the wall which showed a scene of a sun-drenched corn farm, thin clouds floating through the clearest of blue skies. 'Windows' like this were a staple underground where there was no sky.

There were nine guilty votes and two in favor of reviewing the evidence. Most of the nine cursed. Some threw up their arms in exasperation. Mrs. Rational and Mr. Muscles looked calmly at Connor. At least now he knew who his potential friends were.

"Thank you," he said, waving a hand at the viewscreen. The sunny vista disappeared, replaced with a menu listing all the evidence of the case. "I just want to make sure nothing was overlooked. This doesn't have to take long. I know some of you have things to do."

Mr. Angry rose from his seat. "I can't believe two of you fell for this garbage! We could have been out of here by now. These are good kids, they thought she was a vampire, and it turns out she was!"

"They were dead quiet when they were first interrogated," said Connor. "Check the timeline of the evidence. They only said they thought she was a vampire after they heard from their lawyer, and that was after he had seen the coroner's report."

"That doesn't mean they didn't know it beforehand."

"No, but it means that they might only have gotten the idea from their lawyer."

"You're full of shit. These are good kids who've never been in any trouble. Their moms were sobbing on the stand when they were testifying."

"And right beside them were the sobbing parents of the victim, so what does that prove?"

"That girl deserved what she got," said Mr. Angry. "What was she doing in a dump neighborhood like that if not looking for trouble? She was six levels underground, only the worst of the worst spend any time down there."

Connor brought up a still image of the location where the attack had happened. The courthouse's level was a kilometer underground, with so many twists, turns, and elevators between it and the surface that it would take almost a full day to navigate to ground. A billion people lived this way; many of them were born and died without ever seeing sunlight. Lack of sun was why there were so many vampires underground, where the government had all but declared open season on them.

"Six-Underground is only one level down from this courthouse. And she ran into your *good kids* in that neighborhood, didn't she? If it was such a trouble spot, what were they doing there?"

Mr. Angry didn't respond.

There was silence around the room as Connor took his seat, shaking his head with disgust. "Nobody deserves what this girl got."

"Okay," said the foreman, "so maybe their lawyer told them to say that they thought she was a vampire. It doesn't change the fact that she *was* a vampire."

"She was a vampire when the coroner got to her, that doesn't mean she was a vampire when the boys got to her." Connor gestured at the listed evidence. "Look, here's the blood test we saw in court, the one from the morning before the attack, taken when she applied for a job. That test was negative for vampirism."

"So you think a vampire saw what happened to this girl and turned her afterwards? What for?"

"To stop her from dying, I guess. To save her life."

There was a laugh around the table.

"Great," said Mr. Angry. "Now we have compassionate vampires, biting people in the neck so they won't die. You know what he *could* have done to keep her alive? Call a fucking ambulance!"

More general laughter, of approval.

Connor stared at the man until the laughter died down. He stared until the silence grew uncomfortable. He had no problems making Mr. Angry squirm. He knew that he could convince some of the other jurors through logic, some through charm, and some would follow like sheep. He knew that some would need to be humiliated or berated. What Mr. Angry needed was to be afraid, to understand that there was one in this room who was bigger and fiercer. Connor waited until the man swallowed and looked away. "Do you know so much about vampires?" he asked. "Do you know that one of them wouldn't have behaved that way?"

"They're monsters," replied the man. "I've seen it firsthand. They don't feel anything. They're not human anymore, that's why they don't have rights."

"Then maybe this vampire smelled blood and got hungry, I don't know, but I bet that they feel more than you think," said Connor. "And the expert who testified agrees with me. Nobody knows exactly how vampirism does what it does, but victims respond normally to most lines of questioning even if they're clinically dead."

"And then they grow ridiculously violent and the cops have no choice but to put them down for good. They can't even be sedated."

"That's right," said Connor. "Sedatives don't work and neither do stimulants, but this girl had drugs in her system. If she was a vampire, what would be the point? As for the violence, how would you react if they locked you in a cage without food but you could never die of starvation? What would you do if they left you there for days or weeks until the hunger was the only thing you could think about, until it had torn you inside out, and then they had you interrogated by a giant hamburger, or whatever your favorite food is? You'd lose it, too."

Mr. Angry had started to sweat, and he loosened his shirt collar with a finger. "We can't prove whether she was a vampire when they got to her. Nobody can. But we know that when her body was found that she was a vampire. That's enough doubt for me to say that maybe the boys aren't guilty."

If Mr. Angry was starting to argue using logic, then Connor was winning. He turned to the foreman. "Can we do a quick vote? I think I've put a small hole in the 'good kids' argument, and I've given a couple of explanations besides the one where this girl was a vampire before the beating. I'd like to know if we're going to keep going through the evidence or if nobody agrees with me."

There were four votes out of eleven to continue re-evaluating the evidence.

"Maybe we should order some food?" The foreman leaned back in his chair, patting his stomach. "It looks like we're going to be here for a while."

Connor startled at the mention of food. He hadn't eaten since the previous day and the hunger was becoming hard to push aside. It was easier to keep at bay when nobody spoke about food. "I'll pass," he said. "I had a huge breakfast, and I doubt they have anything here that I'd find particularly appealing." He waited until all the others had indicated their preference for food and the foreman had given the list to a guard outside the door.

"Okay," said Connor. "Let's forget who was good and who wasn't. Aside from the coroner's report, what evidence do we have that the girl was a vampire before she was attacked?"

Mrs. Rational chewed her lip, staring at the viewscreen. "The girl finally stopped fighting back when the boys stabbed a piece of wood through her heart. That's a vampire thing, right? The expert witness talked about that."

Connor stared at her for a moment, and then leaned over to pick up a pair of pencils from the table, placing them end to end in his palm and closing his hand so that two inches of wood protruded from the top and bottom of his fist. He looked at the woman's eyes, then to the center of her chest, then back to her eyes. "It's not exactly 'a vampire thing'."

"Yeah," she said. "I see your point."

The juror to Mrs. Rational's right looked thoughtful. "We really only have the testimony of the boys, I guess."

Connor nodded. "They said she attacked them, but video evidence only shows her standing on the corner while the boys approached. She certainly didn't back down from them, but she didn't make the first move."

"The boys said that she threatened them, and fought like a demon, strong and fast."

"Strong and fast compared to what?" asked Connor. "People have been engineering their kids' genes for almost fifty years. Everybody's strong and fast—bones like titanium, muscles like Atlas. People are living so long that we don't even know what the life expectancy of a human is anymore! What do vampires have that humans don't?"

The foreman raised a hand. "Are we sure she was engineered? I don't remember hearing about it at the trial."

Connor menued through the options on the viewscreen, stopping at the victim's basic information. After her name was the indicator M01FF. The last two letters meant that she had been born female and was still female. The *em* meant that she was modded—genetically modified. The numbers indicated that she was first generation modded—that her parents had not been engineered.

The foreman nodded. "They said she was stronger and faster than 'normal', that they hit her as hard as they could and she wasn't going down, not until after a long time."

"The video shows that," agreed Connor, "but if she was still a human, that could have been the drugs. The footage shows the boys dragging her body into the alley just before they left. The coroner's report says that the girl's death was caused by massive loss of blood. 'Near-complete loss of blood' was what he said. And yet the police didn't find all that much blood at the scene. That's another argument for her being attacked by a vampire *after* she was attacked by the boys. A vampire might have tried to drink what was left inside her."

"The shopkeeper whose sidewalk it happened on hosed a lot of blood away before the cops showed up because he didn't see a body anywhere," said Mrs. Rational. "The police had no way to measure how much blood was inside or outside her body when the boys left."

"I know that," said Connor. "But bodies don't bleed out *all* the blood inside them, no matter how badly you cut them. You'd have to run them through a blender. There must have been some blood left when she was dragged into the alley."

"So you think a vampire got to her in that alley, sometime between the point at which she was beaten to death and the time the police arrived?"

"That's what I think could have happened, yes."

Connor noted six heads nodding at his assessment. With any luck, he now had a majority. Having numbers on his side might even swing some additional votes his way, especially if some were more interested in leaving early than in seeing justice done.

"But you're not sure?" asked Mrs. Rational.

"How can anybody be sure?" asked Connor. "But the prosecutor-bot sure didn't bring it up, and it should have."

"So let's say," said the woman, "for the sake of argument, that she wasn't a vampire when these six guys beat the tar out of her."

Connor nodded.

"And let's say, for the sake of argument, that a vampire got to her in the alley after she was dumped there, and it drained all her blood, which turned her into a vampire, but then she was too weakened so it didn't stick and then she died..."

Connor nodded again.

"If that's the case, then these kids are still not guilty of murder. Some vampire killed her." She leaned back in her chair, waiting for Connor to come up with a valid reply. There were murmurings from almost every other seat.

"We don't have to find them guilty of murder," said Connor. "At that point we could return a guilty verdict for a lesser charge like attempted murder."

"But that's a lot of theory," said Mr. Angry. "There's still reasonable doubt that the girl was already dead before they got to her. We have to find them not guilty."

Mrs. Rational nodded. "It's not that I disagree with you about vampires; I think we as a society could, and should, find a way to integrate them, but that's not our job here."

Connor stared back at her. If he lost her support, then there was no hope for a guilty verdict. Was it enough that he had convinced one person that vampires deserved equal treatment? He had come to see justice done for a girl whose only crime was to have been bitten in the neck, could he live with having altered one person's perception towards the undead?

No.

"God damn it!" Connor stood up so quickly that he strained the bolts which held his chair to the floor. "Don't you even care about doing what's right? Doesn't it matter to you that these kids beat a girl for no good reason, maybe beat her to death? They punched her, they kicked her, they threw her down, and they beat her with a piece of wood they'd been carrying around since they found it at a construction site. When it broke they jammed it into her chest!"

Blood rushed to Connor's head, but the flow left him unsteady. He was running out of energy and he could feel his rationality being pushed aside by instinct. He forced down the feelings of confusion and hunger as best he could.

"The girl was a nobody!" Mr. Angry stood too, his face red. Connor could see veins straining against the skin of the man's forehead, could almost taste the pulse of the arteries in his neck. "And if she was a vampire then she was less than nobody! I'm not saying these kids are angels, but we're here to uphold the law, and the law says that if she was a vampire then they aren't guilty. I don't know that she was, but she might have been, and if we can't prove for sure that she wasn't, then we have no choice! It's not our damned fault that there isn't enough evidence!"

He swept a hand across the table, sending his pencil flying as he sat back down, one hand rubbing the left side of his chest, under the armpit. "Fuck the girl *and* the piece of wood to the heart. All of this yelling is making *my* heart hurt."

Connor stared at the man, forcing aside thirst and focusing on one coherent thought. "That's not where your heart is," he murmured.

"What?"

"I said, that's not where your heart is." Connor walked over to the viewscreen in the wall and ordered it to show him the evidence menu again. He selected the video footage of the beating, obtained from a security camera. He skipped to the point where one of the boys thrust the shaft of wood into the girl's chest. It penetrated on his third attempt.

"You sly bastard," he said.

"Who's a sly bastard?" asked the foreman.

"The defense attorney." Connor jabbed a finger at the image of the girl lying on the bloody pavement. The action brought up a menu with her name and a list of the evidence attached to her.

"When he was questioning the expert witness about vampires, he asked him what was the effect of someone slamming a piece of wood, a stake if you will, into the heart of a vampire. The expert said that that was one of only a few ways of killing a vampire, the others being fire and sunlight. The attorney asked if a stake to the heart would explain someone's sudden lack of movement when they had withstood a massive amount of damage without falling down, damage that should have been enough to bring down a normal human. He asked if that was a good indication that someone was a vampire."

"What's your point?"

"He never once showed the witness the wounds the girl suffered. Not the video, not the coroner's report, not even the weapon. He never once asked if *her* wounds were consistent with what was required to stop a vampire."

Confused faces turned to face him, and they were all starting to look the same to him. He was losing control. A voice in his head told him that he had been stupid to worm his way onto this jury, that he had taken too great of a personal risk. He repeated silently to himself that he needed to finish what he had started. He closed his eyes and steadied his pulse.

"Listen, we know the girl was modded, like most of us are. Her bones were engineered from before she was born to be denser and stronger than normal, many times more so. There's no way anybody anywhere is driving a piece of wood through engineered bone. That's why the boy with the wood had to try three times and eventually..."

Connor called up the evidence of the girl's wounds. Zoomed to her chest. Zoomed to her left breast where a ragged wound was visible between her ribs, to the left of her sternum. To the description beside the wound stating that it did not extend to any vital organs but had severed an artery. Death by blood loss, not by heart trauma.

"That piece of wood never went through her heart. If she *had* been a vampire, this wound here wouldn't have stopped her. She just went into shock. She was just a girl. That weasel made sure never to specifically mention in court that the stake went through her heart, meaning that the prosecutor-bot wouldn't object to the evidence. Everything he said was a fact, but he twisted everybody's perception so that we would draw our own conclusions and that damned robot was too prehistoric to reason it out."

He looked at the faces around the table. A few had the decency to look ashamed.

"The prosecutor saw a wound," said Connor. "The defense saw an opportunity."

Connor stepped out of the courthouse onto a poorly lit sidewalk. There were few people about and he could hear the constant hum of the underground city's air circulation system. Someone placed a hand on his shoulder.

"Hey," said Mr. Angry. "Guilty for murder. I never would have thought."

Connor nodded. "Well, it was you who pointed out that by abandoning her, the boys were accountable for any attack she sustained afterwards. Are you okay after what happened in there?"

"Yeah, I'll be all right." The man's shoulders drooped as he thrust his hands into his pants pockets. "It just brought up a lot of memories I thought were long gone. Ancient history, you know?"

"I understand," said Connor. "I'm sorry about your brother."

"Don't worry about it," said the other man, withdrawing a hand from his pocket long enough to gesture dismissively before hiding it away again. "Ancient history, like I said. You should have met my brother. You remind me of him a little, just a bit smarter than everyone else around. Ever thought about becoming a lawyer?"

"Thanks, but no." Connor could feel his canines pressing into his tongue. His stomach knotted and his vision was shrinking to a tunnel. He knew that he wouldn't be able to hold out for long. "Hey listen, I need a drink like you wouldn't believe. You want to join me? You won't have to pay a thing."

Michael Lorenson was born and raised in Montreal where he still resides with his wife, two sons, and cat. He recently rediscovered a love for writing after a long hiatus. His work has recently appeared in the *Tesseracts 14* anthology of Canadian speculative fiction, and he is looking forward to many more years of letting his imagination carry him where it will.

Outwitted

By Sandra Wickham

I wake to pain in my arm and across my chest that makes me want to scream and curl into a ball, but I can't do either. Panic rushes through me as I try to open my eyes. They don't respond.

"It's the drugs," a woman's voice says, close to my ear. "Just relax."

Relax? Why can't I move? The words are only in my head, I'm unable to speak. I'm lying on my back. Was there an accident? I can hear other people moving around me but no one speaks to me again. I feel something pulling me under, the pain or the drugs. The sounds fade.

I'm with my family, in the house my brother, sister and I grew up in. It's spring. Today is warm, sun kissed with the promise of summer.

My sister and I are laughing and playing with our dolls in the backyard, trying to sit them on the swing so we can push them. My Dad and brother are in the driveway working on their bikes, fixing and adjusting, acting like mechanics.

Mom isn't home from work yet, but she'll be back soon and we've planned a family barbecue.

Something pierces my arm and the vision of my family spins away. This time my eyes snap open but I see only a yellowish blur.

"It's awake again." This, a man's voice.

My eyes won't focus and my mind feels trapped in a heavy fog. My senses seem cut off, dulled. I know someone is laying fingers on my arm at the wrist, but their touch is cold.

"We can't keep her like this." It's the woman from before.

There's a loud click, then a filtered voice fills the room. "I don't need to remind you how important this is. Keep it under until our colleagues arrive." There's another click.

Keep me under? I fight to move any part of my body, anything at all, but it's useless.

"We've taken as much blood as we can," says the man close to me.

Click.

"Then we wait."

Click.

My blood? Is there something wrong with my blood? Sounds and feelings slip away from me once more.

I'm in the cafeteria, eating an overflowing sandwich with one hand, holding a highlighter over a text book with the other. Lettuce falls onto the book and I set the sandwich down to pick it off. I look up and see a male student crossing the room. He catches me staring and I quickly look down at my text. It's too late, he's coming my way. I know I'm blushing, I can feel the heat in my face. Why is he making me feel this way? I've never even seen him before. He's at my table so I have to look up.

"Hi," he says. "This seat taken?" I shake my head and he sits down, throwing his backpack on the chair next to him. He holds his hand out across my book. "I'm Tom."

I take his hand and swallow the last bit of food in my mouth. "I'm Sarah."

"Nice to meet you, Sarah."

Before we know it, we've both missed classes and have talked non-stop for nearly three hours. After exchanging phone numbers and email addresses, we agree to get together again soon. It seems corny, but in my gut I know this could be the beginning of something amazing.

This time it's my dry, swollen throat that brings me back. I feel I'll choke if I don't get something to drink. I cough, and then realize I've made a sound. "Water, please," I manage to say. I don't know if anyone is around me to hear. I open my eyes, but my vision is still blurred. "Hello?"

I can't move my head and my heart clenches. Am I paralyzed? Maybe I'm dying. Someone lifts my head and places something against my lips. My vision goes from blurry yellow to blobs of white and blue. I can make out the shape of my own body and an arm by my face as I feel water pass into my mouth. It hurts to swallow, but I take in all I can. It doesn't seem to help the thirst. My head is lowered back down.

"This will all be over soon," the woman whispers close to my ear. "They're filing to their seats. Then this whole thing can be finished."

Who? Finished, how? I cough again. "Where am I? Where's my husband?"

"It's delusional." The man's voice is close and assertive. "It'll be pointless if it's incoherent the whole time."

I spiral downwards again.

We're on the beach at sunset, Tom, Vanessa and me. It's like something out of a movie, Vanessa giggling with delight as her father chases her along the water's edge. I have our dinner laid out on a blanket, the one I was so excited about finding online. Grinning, I take video of my husband and beautiful daughter with my phone.

Click.

"Then revive it so it can speak," the voice commands.

"But sir—"

"It's drained of blood and restrained, what's it going to do? We need it to speak."

Click.

More needles poke me and gradually I can feel my body again. I feel weak, but my mind is clearing.

I can smell them. The woman is young, healthy. The man is older and has a taste for wine and illegal cigars. I can hear their hearts beating, his, a regular rhythm, hers faster. She's nervous. The last of the drug-induced confusion dissipates like an extinguished candlewick.

No! My entire being screams it again and again. No, I want to go back. I *need* to go back. Let me stay with Tom and Vanessa. A tear threatens to slide from my eye. The pain in my heart is greater than anything they could inflict on my body. I haven't cried in many decades.

At first I'd cried every day, even after seeking out and killing the one who changed me. It didn't ease the pain of having to leave my family. If I'd stayed close, I would've killed them too. They smelled too enticing, as though my love for them sweetened my desire for their blood. They thought I was dead, killed by the one who attacked me. At least, for them, there'd been closure.

I continued to exist in utter loneliness, long after my grandchildren's children would have died. I found no solace in finding others of my kind; around them, my instincts were like those of a wild animal—kill or be killed.

I hear the click again. Whoever is giving the orders is tucked away somewhere safe, not in the room with me. "Welcome, Doctors, Honorable Officiates and Hunters. We will now begin."

Click.

I know that voice. He is the reason the others are gone. For years he has organized those who hunt and kill us, campaigning

over the Net Waves, encouraging government officials to give
them access to the latest technologies in order to wipe us off the
earth. After almost a hundred years of being the hunter, I became
the hunted when the human population banded together to exterminate us. But, I'd avoided the riots and the wars. Until now.

"Yes, thank you, Ambassador." The man in my room launches
into a well prepared speech, congratulating himself and his team
for my capture.

He outlines their plans to discover how I was able to survive
while most of my kind were not. Most. So I am not the only one
left. That would explain the Hunters.

The man relays the findings of their tests and experiments.
My chest feels as though it's been stabbed repeatedly, my arms
and legs are restrained by straps and some sort of energy field.
There are several needles in my veins. I feel like I haven't fed
in weeks and I can tell they've taken almost all blood from me.

I doubt this is a human hospital, more likely an isolated facility
to house the dangerous. Me. I'd thought my latest sanctuary
secure, that I wouldn't be discovered. They must have sent more
advanced machines to track me, ones I couldn't detect. They'd
swarmed me—I remember now.

According to the man's speech, there's nothing about my blood,
tissue or brain that would indicate I am any different from the
others. He intends to interrogate me, though, for answers to his
questions.

Bring it. I know one thing: they've underestimated my strength,
drained or not.

Ironically, survival of the fittest meant more to me once I was
dead. While others of my kind lived for the moment, I learned to
be the fittest, the fastest, the deadliest. Never again would I be
the victim, or so I thought. Once the Hunt began, it took everything I had to deal with the Hunters and the machines. Most of
the others had grown delusional, believing themselves gods to
be feared and worshipped—they had died first.

I open my eyes but remain silent, keeping my recovery to
myself. My vision clears. The yellowish blur above becomes a
paneled ceiling with powerful lights which cause me pain at first,
but I've trained myself to adapt to pain. In my peripheral I can
see the man, dressed in the blue uniform of the human doctors. I
can't see the woman, but I can tell from her scent she isn't far. The
table I'm on hovers at the height of their waists. Several machines
are close to the table, silently scanning and analyzing my system.

Click.

"Ask it where it got the technology to deceive the machines."

There are voices in the background coming through the intercom. The Hunters want to know how many of their number I've killed. I suppress a smile. I lick my lips.

The man comes closer and bends over me, holding a precision laser tool. "We know almost everything about you. But there's more to learn. Tell them what they want to know or this is going to get very unpleasant for you."

Every part of my being wants to break free of my bonds and rip out his throat. "You humans are quick to advance your technology," I say, loud enough for them all to hear. Without moving enough for their eyes to see, I test my restraints. "But you fail to think things through."

There's laughter from the Ambassador through the intercom and others join him. "We have you. *You* are the one who failed," he says.

I wait for the laughter to subside. "I, however, think things through. For example..." I lower my voice to a whisper.

"What's it saying?" The viewing room is anxious. I can feel it. The man leans in closer. "Speak up, beast."

In one movement I snap the alloy restraints on my right arm and punch through the energy field to grab the man by the throat. I pull him toward me. The woman screams.

"For example," I snarl in his ear, "I've trained for capture and blood loss."

Fangs find flesh and I drink sweet life force. It charges my body like an electrical current. Energy returns to my muscles.

Click.

I feel panic from the viewing room and it heightens my senses. I drop the man to the ground, dead. With much less effort I pull my other arm free. I realize they've strapped me down with a row of silver spikes in my chest. One smooth motion rips the strap with the spikes free, tearing flesh with it, but I don't cry out. I rip the needles from my arms, kick my legs free and am on my feet.

"Please..." The woman backs up, away from me, reeking of terror and panic. "I have a family. A daughter. Like you did once."

I tilt my head and step closer. "Then you should have thought of that before getting involved."

I lunge and stop, fangs inches from her face. The clearest image of Vanessa I've seen in over eighty years flashes before me. I laugh. "Fine, my little one. I will spare her."

The woman cries hysterically and falls sideways onto the floor, curling into a ball. I grab her up with one hand and set her on her feet, bracing her against the wall. "Tell the humans it ends here or more will die."

I turn to the viewing deck and see the humans fighting each other to get to the door. There is only one who remains where he is and our eyes lock. In a fluid motion, I jump onto the hovering operating table, bend my legs and spring before he can even blink.

My forearms hit the glass first, shattering it and forcing him to fall back. Glass shards slice my arms and legs but that doesn't stop me. I tuck and roll to standing. Jumping over the ones still clambering for the exit, I slam the door shut and destroy the door controls with my fist.

The three Hunters reach for their weapons: an old fashioned crossbow, a plasma gun, an energy-enhanced sword. I launch at the one holding the plasma gun before he can pull the trigger and burn me to death. He needs both hands to hold the weapon which leaves him vulnerable. My hands grip his head and I snap his neck.

The one with the sword is skilled and fast, but it's a dance I've executed before. The secret is in knowing how to control the choreography and I outmaneuver him with only a few steps, and then move in for the kill.

A wooden missile hits me from behind, but not close enough to my heart to matter. I turn and rush the Hunter as he works to reload the crossbow. Grabbing his throat, I lift him off his feet and smash him against the wall; he dies on impact.

The others in the room—the bureaucrats—crouch together in terror in one corner. I turn away. I'll get to them soon enough.

The Ambassador is on his feet.

"You see," I say as I close in on him, his fear tickling my nostrils with the red promise, "your kind never thinks things through."

He opens his mouth to speak and I dart forward, clasp one hand over his mouth and grab the back of his head with my other hand. "It's not your turn, it's *mine*."

His eyes remain wide as I tilt his head back. Careful not to kill him too quickly, I tear bits of flesh from his neck. He is alive as I bite again and again. When he is near death, I release him to die in a painful, crumpled heap, alone.

Most of the rest scream at my approach. Feeding without mercy, I leave none alive.

The night welcomes me in a cool embrace and I don't look back. I will withdraw to a new sanctuary to heal, then will seek out the few of us remaining.

My kind must survive. It's time to put aside natural instincts and band together. Leaders will teach survival skills, and how to fight back. Makers will build our army, our new family.

Humans will continue their attempts to exterminate us, but the past is gone, for them, for us. For me. They are strong, but we are stronger—we think things through.

Born and raised in Ontario, **Sandra Wickham** now lives in beautiful Vancouver, British Columbia with her husband and two cats. Sandra has been a coach and fitness trainer for over twelve years and is new to the writing world. Her friends call her a needle-crafting aficionado, health guru and ninja-in-training. Sandra's story "Mama's Boy" appeared in the anthology *Evolve: Vampire Stiroes of the New Undead*, and was her first publication. She's thrilled to be included in this new vampire anthology and hopes this means she'll get to dress up as a vampire again.

Toothless

By Peter Sellers

Hot. Sunny. No chance of rain even though it always felt like I was walking through a fish tank. It was the same forecast as yesterday. For that matter, it would be the same for tomorrow. They tell me that weathermen used to get it wrong more often than not. Now they're always bang on. Everyone hates people who are right all the time.

I was working days for the third week running. I hated days. Every cop did. Only a few more shifts, though, and then the switch to blessed nights, with temperatures that we'd all conned ourselves into believing were cool.

There were still a few people around who remembered what it was like before the meltdown. Most of them worked in the suicide clinics. If you were feeling down you went in and they'd talk about how it was and show you photographs, or maybe a film. If you were lucky you got slides—those had the best resolution. After seeing that presentation, people went out and threw themselves off bridges. A lot of people I used to know had killed themselves but, bad as things were, I figured what came after just might be worse.

I'd even heard that once upon a time cities used to send out tanker trucks full of water to wash down the roads. Such profligacy made me shake my head. They tell me it isn't like this in Scandinavia. But I haven't seen for myself, and no one I know can afford the flight either.

When I got off shift I headed to Alan's place. There were eight of us staying there this time. Couch surfing was a way of life for most people these days. The government turned on the air conditioning by zones, one week at a time. So every Sunday morning you saw people clutching toothbrushes and sweat-stained pillows and moving from an apartment in one zone to an apartment in another. Most people had worked out a sharing arrangement among a group large enough to make sure you could sleep with air every day, but not too large so as to become unwieldy. Of course, you had to have a couple of spares so you could kick someone out if he became too obnoxious or smelly.

Police work was not much about deduction and forensics and solving baffling crimes anymore. Mostly, we protected property: water, zinc and Vitamin D. Zinc was the only thing that really worked to keep the sun from turning you into a walking tumor. Needless to say, it got expensive and that made it a popular item for theft and lucrative for black market sales.

The meltdown had hit everybody hard. But to the vampires, it was like a crucifix to the nuts. It took the night away from them. Science is not my strong suit, so I may have got some of this wrong, but here's how I understand it: When the ozone burned up, the radiation that hit the earth pervaded everything. Turns out it wasn't sunlight that made vampires fall apart like lepers on fast forward, it was the radiation, and all of a sudden radiation was everywhere. Even at night, vampires were no longer safe. The radiation after dark wasn't strong enough to kill them but it sure made them sick. They went from invincible to weak, ill and tired most of the time. That was no different from the rest of us, of course, but for them it was one hell of a come down. They went from social paragons to pariahs overnight. Needless to say, this decline stripped them of their charisma. There's nothing charming about an emaciated vampire bent over and coughing up blood in an alley.

The effect of radiation combined with the fact that the quality of blood was poor. With depleted D levels, human blood was not as nutritious as it had once been and vampires began to suffer from malnourishment. With their exotic appeal gone, there wasn't much left. Vampires weren't used to working for a living and resented having to do it, kind of like exiled royalty. They tended to take a lot of sick time, which made employers hesitate hiring them. Some vampires took night jobs, like driving cab and waiting tables. A lot of them, though, became hookers, drug mules, petty thieves—anything to find the money to afford the high-priced artificial plasma that, like margarine, was not the original but would do in a pinch. From a cop's standpoint it was a good thing because there were a lot of snitches around, too. A desperate vampire would sell out anybody for a pint.

For those of us who'd spent years exposed to microwaves, phones and mp3 players, the levels weren't high enough to kill quickly. But during the day, any kind of skin exposure brought up blisters in minutes and tumors shortly after that. It didn't take many of those episodes to add up to bad news.

It was one of those low rent blood fiends that we found that morning. He was tucked away in a basement that we'd been told was a warehouse for stolen water, which turned out to be untrue. But, in scouting around, Kelly found the body in a dim corner.

"I've got something you have to see," he said.

It was a dead vampire. Nothing unusual there. We found them all the time, OD'd on hits of fake plasma cut with cleaning products, melted candle wax or radiator fluid. What made this one different was the blood around its mouth. With vampires, there's always some, but this puppy looked like he'd ripped into a full unit of O Positive. "Whose blood is that?"

Kelly reached down and pulled back the upper lip. The absence struck me immediately. "Well, well," I said. The usual startling whiteness was missing. The vampire's fangs were gone, probably ripped out by the roots with a pair of pliers.

"Nasty," I said. "What do you think happened? Bad trick?"

"Gambling debt?" Kelly said.

"In-law trouble?"

We both laughed.

Maybe someone had taken the fangs and made a necklace like people did with shark teeth. Neither of us cared. All we had to do was drag the corpse into the sunshine and in a few minutes the problem would disappear.

But there was something that nagged at me; no sign of shoot-up gear. When we flipped the body over, just in case he'd fallen on his kit, we saw that his head had been beaten in. That was something new.

Two days later, we found another one. Head bashed in and teeth ripped out. Even though cops aren't called upon to do much detection anymore, by the time the fourth toothless vampire turned up I was starting to sense a pattern.

We filed reports, but nobody cared about dead vampires. But the incidents nagged at me; what was the defanging about? I ruled out the obvious right away: Revenge for a child or loved-one bitten and turned. Revenge for one of the blood infections vampires so often spread, despite all the hype about safe biting. Neither felt right.

I went to a peeler bar for a drink. Strip joints had become increasingly popular in recent years. With the necessity of keeping every square inch of skin covered up all the time, the opportunity to glimpse bare flesh in public was precious.

Maybe it was all the toothless vampires I'd seen the last few weeks, but before I looked at anything else, I found myself watching the strippers' mouths as they danced. I saw the same thing over and over: a fixed smile, like a rictus. And then one of them flashed something different, a gold tooth. She was leggy and not overly emaciated. But what struck me most was that her left fang had been replaced by a golden one. I knew it couldn't be real gold because that baby would have bought enough plasma to feed her for a year. Either that or someone would've ripped it out of her head, and that would've been a crime that made sense.

"I want to see her," said the floor boss.

Guillermo looked doubtful. "There are better," he said. "Much better, special for cops."

"I want to see her. In a private room."

Guillermo opened his mouth and I got the sense that he was going to say something else, but what came out was, "Of course. This way."

I was only alone for a couple of minutes. "What happened to your tooth?" I asked as soon as she closed the curtain behind her. I was never one for prolonged romance.

"You like it?" She touched the tooth with her tongue.

"I don't feel one way or another about it. Just want to know where it went."

"Why?"

"Tell me or I'll keep you up past your bed time." Funny that no matter how bad it got for most vampires, they always choked on the idea of dying for real. Me, in their situation, I'd be outside waiting for dawn with open arms.

"I lost it," she said.

When she got up off the floor, I asked her again. "Keep lying to me and you'll lose the other one, too."

"I sold it."

"Why?"

"This guy wanted it."

"What guy?"

"I don't know. Never saw him before." That smelled like the truth.

"You're still doing this, so he can't have paid enough to change your life." I handed her some cash. "Doesn't it affect chow time?"

"For the better. It's like using the cutlery you keep for special guests." She looked me up and down. "Or, in your case, using cutlery at all."

Toots was playing at a basement joint called *Bloody Sunday*. He was a jazz harmonica player who had a way of covering holes with his fangs so he could play three notes at once. If he hadn't been a plasma junkie, he could've been famous. He also knew most of what was going on in the vampire world.

Toots limped off stage to indifferent applause. I took out a bag of China Red and put it on the table in front of him.

"What'll that cost me?" he asked.

"I got dead suckers turning up with their big teeth ripped out. You get wind of anything like that?"

"Nothing else done to 'em?"

"Isn't that enough?"

Toots grunted. "There's a rumor. Not saying it's true, but it's what's in the wind. They say someone's collecting teeth and using 'em."

"Using them for what?"

"Grinding 'em up is what I hear."

"Go on."

"Grind 'em up, mix 'em with blood."

"Why?"

"Don't know more than that. Just that there's a market for fangs. Lowlifes are on the hunt to collect the bounty."

"Who's paying?"

"Folks I don't want to meet."

We heard muffled screams, as if from a mouth partially gagged, and moved cautiously towards the sound. One of the first things they teach cops is never to rush in. Most of the time it isn't worth the effort. Better to get there too late than to wind up in a situation.

Then I thought about the fangs and who and why and I started moving quicker than usual. Kelly grabbed my arm. "What're you doing?"

"I want to check this out."

"Let's wait'll it's over."

The screaming became more shrill and insistent. It didn't sound like there was much time. "I'm going now."

"What the hell," Kelly said and, though he probably didn't want to, followed.

As we went down the alley the screaming grew agonized. A piercing wail got me running. Two men held a writhing vampire while a third reached forward with a pair of bloody pliers. Blood streamed from the vampire's mouth.

I could see one fang gleam but only darkness where the other should have been.

"Stop," I yelled. "Police!" To make sure they understood, I shot the man who held the pliers. The other thugs dropped the vampire and ran. Kelly and I shot them, too.

With the vampire alternately screeching and sobbing behind us, we searched the bodies. In the pocket of the one with the pliers I found the missing incisor, some cash and a business card. I took them all.

Before we walked away, Kelly looked at the vampire. "There's nothing we can do for him."

"Put him to sleep," I said.

When I got up the next afternoon, and everyone else in Alan's apartment was gone, I looked at the tooth. I'd never examined a vampire fang up close. It smelled slightly rancid, and was not as sharp as I would have expected. But beneath the coating of dried blood, the tooth was the same vivid white as all vampire fangs. No matter how bad their health, those teeth never yellowed or decayed.

The cash amounted to all of sixty bucks, just enough for a couple of imported beers. All the business card said was *Clive— Collector*, and gave a text address. I sent a message. "Need sum1 2 c my teeth."

All the reply said was, "I'L bite," plus a time and a street corner.

The car pulled up in front of me right on time. "You got something to show me?" the driver asked.

I held up the fang, shining in the twilight. The car door opened.

The man sitting in the back wore dark glasses, and his head was white and smooth. "Show me," he said. I got in and the door closed.

I held out the fang. The man took it between thumb and forefinger. He twisted the tooth around, gazing at it intently, then, placed it between his teeth and bit down gently. "Where did you get this?" he asked.

"At a crime scene. I'm a cop. What's going on with these?"

"This was stolen, then, from its previous owner?"

I explained the circumstances and the fang was handed back. "It's a lovely specimen that I would like to have, but I must return it." He reached into his coat pocket and removed a small jar. "All of these have been obtained through legal means."

"Yeah, well, the guy who had your card had just ripped this out of a reluctant vampire's head, so you may not want to be so trusting in future."

Clive smiled and held the jar up and the teeth inside it shone like precious stones. He shook the jar and the sound was a tinkle, like bells.

"Why did you buy those?"

"Once upon a time people believed that rhinoceros horn, ground to powder, could cure impotence. The same was thought to be true of a bear's gall bladder."

"People believe weird shit when they're desperate."

"True enough. However, sometimes folk remedies have substance." Clive shook the jar of teeth once more. "It's amazing how white they stay, no matter what."

Suddenly the car door opened. I had the feeling that he'd told me something significant, but I knew I wasn't getting it, and I wasn't getting any more information, so I got out. I spent the rest of the night visiting strip clubs and looking for peelers with missing teeth, to no avail.

Two days later I got another message from Clive. We met at the same intersection as before.

"You were right," he said. "I was too trusting and now I've been robbed."

"That's too bad, but it happens."

"I want you to find them and retrieve what they stole."

"Why should I?"

"You're a cop." He sounded serious.

"Sorry for laughing, but there has to be a better reason than that."

"If you do this, I'll give you something that will change your life." He sounded serious about that, too.

I spent the rest of that night sitting in bars and listening. Thieves tend to have trouble keeping their mouths shut, and when one of them scores off someone as uptown as Clive, silence would be impossible to maintain for long. But I heard nothing until I went back to see Toots.

"I think I got your tooth thing figured out," he said as he sipped some high-grade synth that I'd slipped him. "Somebody's making sunblock. Stuff that really does the job. I'd say hit the streets looking for chicks wearing tank tops."

The only place you saw tank tops these days was in the Museum of Daylight, along with the croquet sets and lawn chairs and other relics of more moderate times. If anybody had a secret sunscreen that actually worked, he was smart enough to keep it to himself.

"How do you know this?"

"Couple guys shooting their yaps about something they claim they found."

"And it works?"

"Man, they say it works like it's nineteen fifty."

The thieves were not hard to find once we knew where to look. Kelly came with me but I had told him nothing. We went to a small bar where the two idiots were laughing and shouting.

"What do you want?" one of them demanded.

"We'll discuss that outside." Kelly and I were holding our weapons.

The thieves reached for their sun gear. "You won't need that," I said.

The taller of the two looked confused. "It's noon, man," he said, as if he assumed I was reasonable.

"Too bad for you. But if you're using what you stole, hey, no worries." We pushed them out the door.

The sun hit them like water on the verge of boiling. They whimpered as their skin turned pink and then reddened. We just stood and waited. In minutes, blisters bubbled up on their faces and necks.

"Please," the tall one said, eyes closed against the ravaging glare. He stopped talking when the sun caught the exposed tip of his tongue. Bending his head down to protect his face, his neck erupted in sores that soon turned black and smelled of roasting flesh.

"Give me what you stole," I said, "and you can go back inside." That was all it took. He reached into his pocket and handed me a small container. Kelly knew better than to ask.

"I'd get that seen to before it turns into something nasty," I said.

The two men crawled towards the door of the bar like roaches scuttling for a dark crack.

In the back of his car, Clive opened the container. The oint-ment inside was creamy and pink.

"What is it?"

"It's freedom," he told me. "Have you ever felt the sun on your skin?"

"What are you, nuts?"

"Here," he said, closing the container and handing it back to me. "Try it." He told me what to do and it sounded impossible.

"From blood and fangs?" I asked.

"More or less, if correctly mixed. Try it. If you like the results, let me know. We can work something out."

It took a lot of self-persuasion before I worked up the guts to do as Clive had suggested. I pulled my shirt back to reveal a small patch of shoulder, bone white and freckle free, and rubbed on a tiny amount of the thick pink cream. I had no idea how much to use but, given the amount of SPF 500 we'd all taken to slathering on before that stopped working, I went over the area again and again, until the cream was invisible. It was slightly gritty when first applied but, once rubbed in, left no trace, no residue, no greasy sheen.

I stood by the door, took a couple of slow deep breaths and then I slipped outside into the sun bathed yard. When I was sure no one was looking, I took in another breath and peeled back my sun suit, exposing the cream-coated shoulder.

The sun felt wonderful, warm but not hot. There were no instant blisters, black and oozing where the rays touched. It felt so impossibly good I almost laughed but caught myself. It was seldom good to be overheard laughing.

Inside, I sent Clive a text. Then I went out and bought some pliers.

Peter Sellers lives in Toronto. He occasionally writes short stories. Several of these have been published in *Ellery Queen Mystery Magazine* and *Alfred Hitchcock Mystery Magazine*. His dark fantasy work has appeared in the *Northern Frights* series, edited by Don Hutchison. In addition, he has edited thirteen crime fiction anthologies.

Symbiosis
By David Beynon

Damp gravel crunched beneath the soles of a shuffling set of ragged New Balance running shoes. The upturned collar of his denim jacket did nothing to keep the constant drizzle from crawling down his neck, biting him with an unaccustomed chill.

There was a time when his eyes would have burned in this near darkness with unparalleled clarity. Not now. Now he squinted like a feeble myopic old wretch, struggling to focus on his hands eighteen inches from his face.

They were ghastly, skeletal things, his hands. Gaunt and pallid, the skin hanging from his long, brittle fingers glistening in the drizzle like the belly of a frog. He tried to steady them, but they trembled and with each tremble, each stuttering tremor, he could feel his life slipping away.

Starvation.

Oh, he'd known hunger. Many times. Hunger and Ray were age old acquaintances. He well knew the gnawing, persistent ache, the yearning in his jaw, the burning of his throat, the coiled tension in the pit of his stomach. These he knew well and could deal with.

But starvation... Starving was another beast entirely.

Ray touched his face, his fingertips navigating an alien landscape. His eyes were sunken into pits with harsh, sharp edges. His cheekbones were a pair of mountains that descended into valleys etched deep into the sides of his face. Beneath cracked lips, he could feel receding gums set against a wall of loosening teeth.

This can't be how it ends.

Ray looked up. To his left stood a wooden post crowned by a white mailbox. Stenciled in black paint: "A. and B. W. Smith".

He peered down the driveway into inky blackness. He caught a pang of something down that darkened drive that was both compelling and forbidding. He breathed deeply through his nose, exhaled a staccato whimper and made a decision.

At the end of the driveway stood a neat, well cared for house with white siding and black trim. Ray's gaze drifted to the porch steps, then higher to the unadorned front door. He tilted his head and sniffed the night air.

No dogs, he thought, and then looked above the door. *No sentry lights, either.*

Expending a staggering amount of effort, Ray climbed the three steps onto the covered front porch. He began to run his fingers through his tangled hair, abandoning the effort when he encountered hopeless tangles.

Gaunt, bony knuckles rapped against the wooden door.

He heard a host of sounds from within the house: A rustling, the snap of newsprint being briskly folded, the scrape of a chair against the floor. There were footfalls beyond the door, then a click; the porch light sprung to life. Ray winced, turning his face away from the dim illumination.

Beyond the door, Ray heard a man clear his throat. A deadbolt shifted and the doorknob turned.

The man framed in the doorway looked Ray up and down, then opened the door completely. "You don't look too well," he said. "In fact, no offence, you look like shit. What can I do for you tonight?"

Ray sniffed, rubbed his face, and then spoke in a raspy voice. "I guess…I guess I'm here to beg."

The man closed his eyes and gave his head a gentle shake. He raised his left hand. Ray saw that he held a long, metal flashlight.

"Two things, friend," the man said in a voice sounding older than he looked. "First—I'm not going to need this, am I?" He inclined his head toward the flashlight.

Ray shook his head, his eyes darting from the flashlight to the man's face. "No… No, sir."

"Good. I am really, really glad to hear that. Second—I'll have no one beg on my doorstep. If you're so inclined, I'll invite you in out of the cold. Then we can talk about what you need."

Ray hesitated. He looked down at the threshold, then back at the man.

"My name is Barry, by the way," he said, extending his right hand. Ray, dumbstruck, shook it. "I know what you are, but I don't know *who* you are. How about you come in so we can both find out?"

Ray stepped through the door. As his foot lighted on the rubber "Welcome" mat, he noticed that Barry's gaze had drifted to Ray's filthy shoes.

"Can you do me a favor and slip your shoes off by the door?" Barry said. "They're looking a bit muddy."

Ray kicked off his runners, regarded his equally dirty socks and peeled them off, too. Barry held out his hand.

"Pass me your jacket. I'll hang it here to dry."

Ray snaked out of the soaked denim. Barry's eyes registered the line of ribs beneath the white cotton of Ray's threadbare t-shirt; they looked like a strip of corrugated roofing. He grimaced at the emaciated state of his guest's arms, but, carefully keeping his voice neutral, simply tilted his head and said, "Kitchen's this way. It's warmer in there."

Ray followed his host along a short hallway. Hanging along the wall were framed photographs. One showed a teenage girl holding a Holstein cow by a lead, a ribbon affixed to the halter. Another photo showed a much younger-looking Barry standing next to a massive tractor. Yet another showed Barry, the girl and an older woman, presumably his wife. All smiles. All looking carefree.

Ray looked ahead. Barry's shoulders were slumped. His gait was that of a broken old man. He glanced back at the photo. The man who had invited him in was a washed-out shadow of the happy family man, the proud tractor owner. The photos were clearly pre-Pandemic.

The Pandemic had changed everything for everyone. Ray could hardly believe it had been less than two years since humanity was devastated by the most virulent flu the species had ever encountered. The death toll was staggering. The planet reeled, mourned, and then took precautions for the future.

Thermal imaging began in a nightclub in Singapore. Cameras mounted at the entrance measured body temperature in order to keep out patrons running a fever. Soon, Public Thermal Imaging was installed in airports, shopping malls, everywhere.

A security person routinely scanning a line up at a Frankfurt nightclub pulled a woman out of the line. He had noticed that she was a full eleven degrees centigrade below normal. As she attempted to flee, she was apprehended, held until morning when someone from public health could assess her. During the night, she paced the cell, rattling the bars and begging to be released, her agitation mounting with each passing hour. As the first rays of daylight spilled through the barred windows, she momentarily glittered, then burst into flame. It was all captured on closed-circuit television, the graininess of the image somehow making the scene all the more horrific. The footage went viral on YouTube before lunchtime.

Humanity now knew without a doubt that there was another enormous problem to contend with—vampires. In the course of a single day, vampires had lost their greatest predatory attribute—they could no longer blend seamlessly among their prey.

Barry walked into the kitchen and crossed to a round oak table surrounded by four matching chairs. His footsteps skirted a cut out patch in the linoleum; a rectangle measuring three feet by four framed with a greasy black stain marring the exposed floorboards.

"Mind your step there," he said as he pulled one of the chairs out and turned it invitingly toward Ray. "Take a load off."

"Thank-you," Ray whispered as he sank into the chair.

Occupying the table was a half-empty cup of black coffee and a stack of neatly piled daily newspapers. A news section lay on its own, folded in front of Barry's usual chair. Barry placed his flashlight on top of the stack of newspapers, retrieved a silver percolator pot from the stovetop and filled his cup.

"I'd offer you some coffee," Barry said, "or something to eat, but the papers tell me that regular food and drink just pass right through you folks. Can make you sick, too. Is that true?"

Ray's eyes lingered on the flashlight.

It had taken all of two days after the YouTube video saturated the internet before someone had seen what a UV flashlight could do to vampiric flesh. At that point, Ultraviolet flashlights had been relatively weak, the tools and playthings of miners, gemologists and crime scene investigators. It took little time for engineers to increase the wavelengths and efficiencies and for manufacturers to move to production. Vampire Protection Kits flew off the shelves.

Barry noticed where Ray's attention was focused.

"You're wondering why I would just put it down like that?"

Ray nodded.

"There's a few reasons. Let's face it—if you were going to go for my throat, I imagine it would've happened while I had my back to you in the hallway. Besides, it's been my experience that someone hell-bent on murder doesn't knock politely at the door."

Barry slid into his chair opposite Ray with a sigh. "So, how much do you need?"

Ray's gaze moved from the flashlight to Barry. "How much?"

"Listen. It doesn't take a genius to see that you're hurting. And I don't think I'd be too far wrong to say it looks like you're starving. Am I right?"

Ray's eyes dropped and his head gave the slightest of nods.

"The way I was raised, if you see someone in need and it's within your means to help…well, you lend a hand. You're obviously in need. How much, you know, to take the edge off?"

Ray's tongue crept out to moisten his parched lips. "Very little, really." His voice sounded like a rusted hinge. "A teaspoon or two would be a banquet to me."

"Honestly? So little? Would that really be enough?" Barry leaned forward, his elbow on the table, his chin in the palm of his hand. "No offense, but from the way you look, I would've thought you'd need a lot."

Ray answered by way of a quick little shake of his head.

As Barry sipped his coffee, he let his fingertips wander across the bristles on his chin. He rose from his chair and walked over to the white-painted cupboard over the stove. Opening the door, he took out a cream-colored eggcup.

"I could use a shave," he said as he walked past Ray to the hallway. "I always bleed like a son-of-a-bitch whenever I get rid of my whiskers. Excuse me for a few minutes, will you. Make yourself at home."

Ray listened as the stairs squeaked with each step Barry took. A door above clicked shut and the sound of running water surged through the house's pipes. He looked again at the forgotten flashlight perched on the stack of newspapers and shuddered. Something so innocuous to them, yet so gruesomely lethal to his kind. And how easily the humans wielded them—the flashlights and, worse yet, the automatic sentry lights fitted with UV bulbs. Silent killers lurking beneath the eaves for the unfortunate or incautious vampire who strayed close enough to trigger them.

His eyes drifted from the flashlight and newspapers to something he hadn't noticed before. Casually leaning against a cupboard, its shortened barrel nestled in the slot between two doors, was what Ray assumed to be a shotgun. Ray started to rise to take a better look at the gun, but his thighs trembled and his strength deserted him. He settled back down.

A scent reached Ray's nostrils and he shuddered: the delicious coppery scent of blood mixed with a hint of iron-infused well water. His eyes brimmed with tears and his tongue swept longingly around the inside of his mouth. The sound of running water ended, accompanied by the spin of a toilet paper roll. The upstairs bathroom door creaked open. Each stair announced that Barry was drawing closer to the kitchen and with him fresh blood.

Barry, sporting three folded over tabs of toilet paper on his face, each with a crimson blossom spreading to its edges, walked into the kitchen carrying the eggcup in one hand and a stack of clothing and a towel in the other. He watched Ray's eyes track each scrap of bloodied toilet paper, finally settling on the eggcup.

"Well, I told you I bleed like a bastard when I shave," Barry said. He placed the eggcup in front of Ray. "I figure there's a little over a teaspoon there." He crossed to the stove and made a production of fiddling with the coffeepot with his back to Ray. "Let me know when you're finished."

Ray glanced furtively from Barry to the eggcup. Pooling in the bottom was the difference between life and death. His nostrils flared. His fingertips trembled as they found the edge of the porcelain. He looked from the blood to Barry, back at the blood and sobbed.

"Everything alright?" Barry didn't turn around. "It's okay, isn't it? Is it enough?"

"It..." Ray shuddered and exhaled. "No one...no one has ever offered it freely."

Barry shifted uncomfortably from foot to foot.

"Like I said—simple hospitality. Drink up," he said, "then we can talk."

Ray's gaze dipped to the eggcup. It didn't look like much, that shallow layer of crimson pooled at the bottom, but to him it was everything. As far gone as Ray was, the offering in the cup wasn't just a meal. The cooling, congealing mass oozed with potential vitality. It would sustain him, make him whole.

Ray looked up at the worn-down, slumped shoulders of the total stranger who had just handed him back his life. The tired, broken farmer who had opened his door and let him in out of the cold and the rain. Wasted, trembling fingers raised the cup to his lips.

The scent filled his sinuses. His head spun. The blood slipped between his lips, along his tongue, cascading down his throat. Lifeforce rolled through him. Atrophied muscles sprang to life. He gasped, a drowning man breaching the surface for a second chance at life.

"Are you okay?" Barry asked, not turning around.

"I'm...much better, thanks," Ray said. "I'm...I'm finished now. And thank you for not watching."

Barry turned with the coffee pot in his hand and topped up his cup. He lowered himself into the chair. His eyes widened.

"Wow. The change is...well, it's extraordinary. And about turning my back... I figured it was the decent thing to do. I figured...you know...feeding might be a private thing for you."

"It is a private thing."

Barry took a sip of coffee. "No one's ever offered you blood freely before?"

Ray buried his face in his hands. He shook his head.

"Never."

"Then...how do you get what you need? I mean, I read a lot of newspapers and listen to the radio and TV but there's not a lot of mention about how a vampire leads his day to day life. Well, I guess in your cases it would be night to night. Do you usually take what you need by force?"

Ray's eyes were moist when they met Barry's. He nodded.

"The worst possible force. You must understand. We're no stronger than you are and not really any faster. Our greatest advantage is our senses. We see and hear and feel and smell and taste so much more than you do. And we have another, beyond your five."

"Like what? Some kind of ESP? Can you read my thoughts?"

"No. Something much more basic...more primal. We...we are able to feel your emotions, especially your fear. And...when we get one of you alone...we can amplify your fear...until you're paralyzed."

Barry shifted uncomfortably in his chair. "Paralyzed with fear? Well, I guess that would certainly get the blood pumping."

"Please understand. Most of us take only the small amount we need. A miniscule minority give us all a bad name."

"Does it cause trauma, this fear your people can project?"

Ray looked away. "Very much so. Our donors are so traumatized that the truth of our feeding is often repressed and misinterpreted as something mundane, easily explained or understandable."

Barry tilted his head. "I try not to judge, but I think 'donor' is a pretty liberal euphemism. I think a more accurate word might be 'victim'. No offence."

"I think..." Ray said. "I think the manner of our feeding might be why we have no reflection."

Barry looked over at the kitchen window, then back at Ray.

"What are you talking about?" he asked. "I can see your reflection in the window just fine."

Ray nodded. "But I can't. I think it must be some kind of defense mechanism. If you had to terrify and traumatize someone every time you had to eat, you wouldn't be able to look at yourself in a mirror, either."

"So you really can't see yourself?"

"No."

Barry took another sip of coffee. "You know, you're not the first vampire I've encountered."

"Really?"

"A couple of weeks back. It was around this time of night. Chores were all finished and I was going through the papers like I always do. We dairy farmers are by necessity creatures of habit. Anyway, I'd picked up that flashlight there from the hardware store with a few other things the previous week. I don't really know why. I guess the stuff I read in the paper. Hardly a day goes by that there isn't a story about some poor bastard with his throat torn out and not a drop of blood to be found."

"As I said," Ray said, one hand raised defensively, "those monsters represent a tiny minority of my kind."

"And I believe you. You wouldn't have known it, though, from the man who came running through that front door over there, fangs bared and growling like an animal. Everything was pure instinct. The flashlight was sitting next to my coffee cup. It was in my hand and turned on before I really knew what was happening. The man skittered to a halt just there—" Barry gestured with his cup toward the patch of removed linoleum. "—and he flamed and blistered and melted."

"You can't be blamed for defending yourself," Ray said, catching the grief in Barry's voice.

"No. And if it happened again, I figure it would end the same way. You notice I answered the door tonight with the damn flashlight in my hand. No—it wasn't killing him that upsets me, though that in itself was upsetting. What really bothers me is what happened after."

"After?"

"I called the police and told them what happened. You know what they said? 'So why are you calling us?' That's what they said. They claimed I hadn't killed a person, I'd exterminated a pest. I told them he certainly screamed like a person. They said it wasn't their concern. I asked them who I should contact regarding the charred remains on my kitchen floor and how the body would be disposed of. The cop on the phone told me once more it wasn't a police matter and most people were depositing remains in garbage bags and dropping them off at the dump. The dump, for Christ's sake. I told her I had never been more ashamed to be a human being. She hung up on me."

"You...you didn't..."

"Hell, no. I did need to cut the linoleum to...well, to get him off the floor but, no—I didn't take him to the dump. He's buried in the side yard. I planted a tree over his grave. There was no ID or anything, no name to put to the man. I had no idea if he had a religion or not, what kind of a marker would be appropriate. I figure you can't do much better than a tree as a grave marker. Universally non-offensive, a tree."

Barry took another sip of coffee.

"We've all changed, you know," he said, "since the Pandemic. We've grown mean and petty and lost any sense of what it's like to be a good neighbor."

Ray tilted his chin toward the cupboards by the sink. "Is that what the shotgun is for? In case some of your fellow humans are less than neighborly?"

Barry's answer was all too matter of fact. "The shotgun is for me."

"For you?"

"Every night I come in here after milking and chores. I make a pot of coffee and read the papers. I read all four, cover to cover. I try to make sense of what's happened to our world. Everything's so hopeless. The world is this giant mess. Then we—humanity— discover we're co-existing with another intelligent species and what do we do? We make lethal flashlights, UV Laser pointers and sentry lights called Vamp Zappers that you can buy at your local Wal-Mart for $32.99. And that, compounded on everything else that happened, is why the shotgun sits loaded by my sink."

Barry reached back, grabbed the gun and laid it across the table between them.

"I took a hacksaw to the barrel," he said, sliding his fingertip along it. "Now it's the perfect length to wedge against the seat of my chair between my legs so that it nestles firmly under my chin. I can't tell you how many times I've felt that rough sawn edge under my jaw."

"Jesus..." Ray whispered.

"And the only thing that keeps me from pulling the trigger, the only thing that keeps my brains from being splattered all over the ceiling is my goddamn cows."

"Your cows?"

"Goddamn cows need to be milked. Nowadays the milk truck only comes every three days. Cows can't skip a milking. If I'm not there to take care of them it could be three days—six milkings—before the truck comes and the driver discovers me sitting in here. Do you have any idea the agony a Holstein would endure if she missed six milkings? So, as I'm sitting here, thumb on the trigger, shotgun under my chin, I think if I just let the cows loose in the barnyard one of my neighbors will notice and take care of things. And that's true. But, by the time I get to that point, the despair is so bleak I just can't muster the will to go all the way out to the barn and turn them out. So the shotgun slides out from under my chin, gets put back by the counter and I slink over to the daybed and cry myself to sleep."

"And yet," said Ray, "even with a despair that I could sense at the end of your driveway—even with all that you've personally lost—even after you've been attacked in your own home by one of my kind—you open your house and your...hospitality—" He lifted the empty eggcup. "—to a stranger. To a vampire."

Barry shrugged. "It's the way I was raised. What can I say? I guess I look upon vampirism in the same way I view homosexuality or vegetarianism."

Ray laughed. "How's that?"

"I don't really understand any of them. But, just because I don't understand them, that doesn't really give me a right to judge, does it? They're all just different ways of getting by in the world."

"And that's what it's all about nowadays, isn't it? Getting by? For your people...and for my kind."

Barry looked into the bottom of his empty coffee cup. "You know," he said, "until that vampire came running through my front door, I never really gave your kind much thought. Afterwards...well, I got to thinking on how difficult it must be...how desperate your people must be getting. And how unfriendly it is out there for you."

"Is that why you let me in?"

Barry considered this for a moment. "Nah. You had the decency to knock. You needed help. Really, what else could I have done? How are you feeling, by the way?"

Ray's hands came up from the table and he turned them. They had lost some of their pallor. The skin seemed less loose. His fingers no longer shook. "I don't know what to say. You've given me my life back. How can I repay something like that?"

"You can't and you don't have to. I had a little something you needed and it didn't hurt me any to give it up."

Ray sat contemplating as an awkward silence filled the room. Finally, glad to feel that strength had returned to his legs, he rose to his feet. "Will you let me try to repay you for everything you've done?"

"There's no need."

"Do I have your permission to try?"

"I suppose. What do you have in mind?"

Ray moved to Barry's side of the table.

"Should I get up?" Barry asked.

"No," Ray said. "Seated is better, I think. Remember what I told you about how we can dial up someone's fear."

"Yeah," Barry said with a hint of uncertainty.

"Well, I've never tried this before. I doubt anyone ever has, but as I sat there across the table, I got to thinking: What if I could dial it back?"

"But I'm not afraid."

"You're telling me. You don't have a hint of fear about you. I suppose after the worst thing imaginable has already happened, there's not a lot left to fear. But I'm not talking about fear."

"What then?"

"Your despair. You have so much. What if I could take some of it away, even if for just a little while?"

"I'd be a fool to say no."

Ray lifted his left hand. "I'll need to touch your face." Barry nodded. "Remember, I don't know if this will work."

Ray's fingertips came to rest on Barry's cheek. At first Barry felt them as icy yet clammy, but after a few seconds they seemed to warm.

Ray breathed deeply and concentrated. Instead of projecting a wave of anxiety, he focused on Barry's overwhelming despair. For just an instant Ray felt the entirety of Barry's loss, the sum of his suffering, the depth of his loneliness. His knees grew weak until finally he broke the contact and staggered back to his chair.

"Jesus," Ray whispered. "How do you cope?"

Barry gave his head a shake. "Most days, not very well."

Ray waded through the lingering effects of Barry's grief, rubbing his hands over his face, and then said, "I'm sorry it didn't work."

"Don't worry about it."

With a crestfallen shrug, Barry nodded at the bundle of clothes he'd brought down after shaving.

"You look about my size." he said. "There's a bathroom and shower just off the living room if you'd care to get cleaned up. I need to say goodnight. It's getting late and 5:30 is chore time. I don't know if you're planning to move on tonight, but you're welcome to spend the day here in safety. I've got a root cellar and a sleeping bag. It's not much, but it'll be dark."

"I am in your debt."

"Think nothing of it. You may not have been able to siphon off any of my sadness, but I am genuinely glad to have made your acquaintance. Which reminds me...I never did catch your name."

The vampire extended his hand.

"My name is Ray."

"And I'm Barry," said the farmer. "I'm really pleased you stopped by."

David Beynon is a writer of speculative fiction who lives in Fergus, Ontario with his wife, two kids, a Golden Retriever and what increasingly appears to be an immortal cat. David's novel, *The Platinum Ticket*, has been shortlisted for The Terry Pratchett Anywhere But Here, Anywhen But Now First Novel Contest. *Symbiosis* is his first published story, about which he says: "*Symbiosis* arose from a news story about thermal imaging used to screen for spiking fevers of clientele at a nightclub in Singapore. I wondered what they would do if they discovered someone registering as room temperature."

POST-APOCALYPSE

Forest-Bathing
By Heather Clitheroe

The rule was that the person who shit in the bucket had to empty it. The piss could collect in the bucket, but once somebody pinched off a loaf, it had to be dumped. That was the rule. Otherwise the stench would go from bad to worse, and it was already pretty disgusting. Everybody was holding it as long as they could, hoping that somebody else would get to the bucket first and carry it out to the gutter behind the embassy wall and dump it down the drain. It was easier, so much easier, to empty the bucket if it was your own shit in there. If it splashed on your shoes, well, at least it was yours. The kids never had to empty the bucket, but they held it too—you could see them jumping from one foot to another, jiggling their legs and dancing around. Nobody liked using the bucket. But there wasn't enough water. There hadn't been any water pressure for days, and nobody was really certain if it was about to crap out—oh, the pun—altogether, and since the electricity was off, they expected the water would be gone soon, too. They had to save what they had.

Jake hated the bucket. There were nineteen of them camped out in the lobby, and another fifteen in the reception area, where they could look out the windows at the green grass and the gardens that lay within the long, white walls and the iron fence. The gates were closed. Nobody was coming or going. They didn't go outside. Too dangerous; the virus had gone airborne, but nobody knew *how* airborne, and the trips to pour out the bucket were accomplished as quickly as possible, with mask and gloves. That was the other reason to hold it for as long as you could—to make as few trips outside as possible. If you didn't shit in the bucket, you didn't have to go outside. Better to stay inside, just in case. It felt safer inside, away from the sky and the quiet, and the virus that hung in the air, invisible and deadly. It was too late to go anywhere else. And anyway, there was nowhere left to go.

Traffic had vanished. The streets were silent, in a way Jake had never seen—not even early in the morning. The embassy was closed, the phones were silent, and all they could do was sit and watch the news in the employee lunchroom. The news broadcasts were terse, the official messages nothing more than instructions. *Stay indoors. Go to quarantine centers if you show symptoms. Watch for fever, headache, and bloody discharge from eyes, nose, or mouth, in urine or feces. Isolate victims. Place bodies in a cool, dark room and wait for collection.*

The stateside casts were worse. More ominous. Rioting, looting. Images of people sitting in quarantine tents and clinics, blood running down their faces, more talk of the spread of the hemorrhagic fever and less of the survival rates; a person wouldn't live long once they'd contracted it. Once *it* started. There was discussion about that, in the lunchroom, but when the power went out the ambassador's assistant told them that they had to conserve the diesel fuel for the generators, so they could only watch television for a couple of hours at night, after the kids had fallen into an exhausted stupor. The ambassador was already dead.

When it had seemed that the excrement was hitting the ventilation system—Jake's expression, not really a pun, but had seemed funny at the time—he'd left his apartment and headed for the embassy. He thought he'd catch one of the last flights out, because he'd heard that they were evacuating Americans. Taking them to a hospital ship sitting out in the Sea of Japan, or to one of the carriers. Taking them home. The airports and train stations were closed and commercial traffic grounded. The only chance he had of making it home, before the bug came to Tokyo, was the embassy. But by the time he'd made it inside the gates, it was too late. They told him to sit and wait. Then martial law was declared by the prefecture, and a curfew. He couldn't leave if he'd wanted to. He hunkered down in the lobby and, one by one, the people inside got sick. Then they died. He helped wrap the dead in plastic and carried corpses down to the basement. He soon figured out that nobody was coming to pick up the bodies. Transports had stopped. You couldn't call for help—hospitals weren't answering phones; maybe nobody was left *to* answer the phones. So they continued to take the bodies down to the basement, and then close the door. Jake didn't mind carrying them. When the power went out and took the water pressure and the flush toilets with it, hauling bodies became preferable to emptying the shit bucket.

Just how many people were dead? How many people were sitting in tenements with *obasan* wrapped in a quilt and left in the stairwell? How many *gaijin* were freaking out in neighborhoods where nobody else could speak English? Jake didn't know. Nobody really knew. What they said on TV wasn't necessarily the truth, and the main networks were down, only the emergency station broadcasting. He couldn't get to Twitter. He couldn't email. Couldn't Skype out to find out what was really going on. Like the others trapped in the embassy, he sat and waited. Waited because it was somehow better to wait inside, with people who knew where you were from and why you wanted to go back there.

But the talk:
We're not getting out of here.
The radio is dead.
Not dead, nobody's broadcasting.
Same thing.
It's all ending.
What's ending?
Everything.
The world.
All of us.
We're all going to die.

Just like that. The world, ending. With a whimper instead of a bang.

Jake carried the bucket to the door, opened the door, walked outside down the cement path and carried the bucket to the gutter. He poured the contents down the sewer drain, stood and looked around. The gates were still closed but not locked, though the guards were long dead. The sky was overcast, the color of an old bruise. The world was silent and felt damp. He stood for a moment, listening to the peculiar silence that hung heavy over the gardens. Tokyo was dying. Dead, really. The embassy was a mausoleum. *We're all going to get it. We're all going to die.* There was food enough and bottled water. The paranoia of the embassy staff—the great fear of terrorism—had left a larder well-stocked with meals, ready to eat, and tins of fruit cocktail. Even a handy supply of toilet paper, and the bucket. The damn shit bucket. He laughed, a sound like a sob. Lots of food, but only one decent sized bucket for shitting in. No foresight. It had been the janitor's bucket, a big heavy one with wheels and a wringer for a mop. When you crouched over it, you had to jam the bucket against the wall and lock the wheels with your feet so it didn't scoot away at a critical moment.

He scratched the back of his leg with his foot and shrugged. *Might as well stay out here and wait,* he thought. He was tired of the arguments inside, the endless poker games to pass the time, the whining of people's children. He put the bucket down, carefully, and walked away from it.

He strolled the gardens like a man without a care in the world, straightening his shoulders and tipping back his head to take in a deep breath of air. *Throw caution to the wind,* he thought. The gardens here were still neat, still immaculate, and without the hum and rush of traffic just beyond the walls, he could imagine himself back in Georgetown on a Sunday morning. If the breeze hadn't shifted and brought with it the stench of decay and rot, the fantasy would almost have worked.

Jake held his breath. Waited. The breeze died, the smell faded. Almost. What he'd give for a breath of fresh air. Real, fresh air. He sat on a bench, stretched his legs out and folded his hands in his lap. Behind the clouds he felt the sun climbing higher in the sky. Still morning. He wondered if he ought to be doing something. If there ought to be something for him to think about. If there ought to be something to worry about in the headache that had started that morning. The pain had settled in behind his eyes with a bothersome throb, now accompanied by shooting pains in his neck and shoulders. Tension? Tension headache? Tension headache and a stress fever?

He began to laugh then, softly at first, and then louder. *Yeah, right.* He thought about the metal bucket, the one he'd taken to the gutter to empty, and how there was probably somebody waiting impatiently to use it. He laughed harder, and then coughed. He looked at his hand, and saw the blood. *Let them come out here and get the damned bucket!*

Perhaps then he should have been afraid. The sight of blood in his hand should have brought a thrill of fear to him, a quickening of the pulse, a sharply indrawn breath. It should have. But didn't. He was tired of waiting. Tired of waiting for *it* to happen. Tired of waiting for somebody to wrap him up in a plastic sheet and drag him down to the basement with what was left of the others. He shook his head and bent to wipe his hands on the grass.

When he sat up, a woman stood before him. *That* made him jump, startled him so that his heart skipped a beat and his breath caught. He coughed again and choked on something salty that he was afraid to spit out.

The woman stared at him, and cocked her head. Said something to him in Japanese.

"*Watashi wa nihongo ga hanasemasen,*" he said. 'I don't speak Japanese.' He'd learned it from a phrasebook. That and 'Want to have a drink with me?' Now he wished he knew how to say something more, like 'It's a charnel house in here. Go away.' Or 'Stay back.' He shook his head. "I don't speak the language," he said.

She sighed, and he saw how truly beautiful she was: a lithe, small woman, with hair dark and glistening, dark eyes that looked out from under a slightly furrowed brow as she gazed at him. Then she smiled. Her teeth were small and even, her lips extremely red. He thought she looked like a girl he would have wanted to know, before. Before the shit bucket days.

"English," she sighed.

"Yes."

Her clothes were old. She wore a kimono, but not the kind he'd seen the girls in the neighborhood wearing. Maybe it was silk? It was the color of moss, subtle and faded, but when she moved it seemed that the color shifted with her, moving slightly as she cocked her head to the side, again, and looked at him.

"I'm not well," he said. "Don't come near me." He coughed again, and touched his forehead. "I have fever."

"Ah, fe-ever," she said. She shook her head. Her hair, loose around her face, mesmerized him. He thought, slowly, that it would shine if the sun were out and the sky not overcast, if the mist would clear and the blue sky were visible above with all the buildings crowded underneath...

"I'm sick," he said again.

"Yes," she said.

It wouldn't take long for him to go. The others went quickly. Once the coughing started, it got worse. Once the headache started, it got worse. It would all get worse. An hour, maybe more. But this woman, this impossibly beautiful woman...she should not be so close.

"Please, stay away," he said, and he tried to push himself up, thinking that he would walk away from her, but strength seemed to have left him.

She narrowed her eyes. "No," she said.

He felt pinned to the bench, held against the concrete and wood like a butterfly pinned to cork.

"I stay," she said. She took a step towards him, and smiled. He saw now that her teeth were not just small, but small and pointed. Sharp. He stared up at her in confusion, wondering why he could not move. Why he could not stand.

A bird fluttered suddenly and her gaze shifted, her head swinging around as an animal's would, and he thought of a fox scenting prey. And as her head moved, he found his strength and scrambled to his feet. He stood, chest heaving, head filled with blinding pain and an urgent throb that kept time with the thumping of his heart.

She turned back to him, her eyes pinning him. "Sick," she said.

"I've got the bug," he said.

"Oh, yes." she said. She blinked slowly, and then took a step towards him. "You are sick. All men sick."

"Don't come near," he said, but once again found himself rooted to the ground, held in place by the force of her eyes. Her eyes...her eyes were dark. Hell, all Japanese women had dark eyes. But the woman in the green kimono, with the hair that fell around her beautiful face like a curtain of ebony and silk, who looked at him this way and that...her eyes were not dark but darkness. Black. Matte black, no pupils. No whites to her eyes.

Very long ago, when he had first come to Japan, he had known a girl from Canada who had come to work as a translator, who had gone with him to the temples and the museums. She had been a tall girl, who walked with long strides and wrapped long legs around him when they made love. Once, in the summer, when they lay sweaty and tangled in bed, listening to the rain falling on the pavement outside the window, she told him stories of the demons that the peasants feared. The demons that walked the earth and brought the end times with them, that soared in the sky on scorching waves of heat, or walked through the forest and carried death with them. The demons that stood between this world and the next. The ones with the black eyes. They walked through the forest on this side, in this world, she'd said. On the other side lay death. Or eternity. Something like that. He didn't quite remember.

He wanted to cough, but found he couldn't. He wanted to look away, but couldn't. She was even closer to him now. She smiled and said, "All men die. The world dies." She reached out and took his hand, holding it in her cool flesh. She looked at his palm, at the streak of red there and on his wrist, and bent her head towards the blood.

That girl from Canada—he'd liked her. But she went missing. They said she went crazy and ended up dead in some forest near Mount Fuji. Sometimes that happened to people...they came to Japan and freaked out. She'd never seemed to be one of those, but...

The woman's tongue touched his palm. He felt the rough tongue licking his skin and he felt weaker.

Jesus, he thought, why can't I move?

Her hair had been the color of wheat, the girl from the prairies. A girl who talked about legends and demons, about the *kitsune* that fed on souls, that moved between this world and the next, guarding the way between but feeding on the bodies of the helpless. *Just like a vampire,* the girl said. *Every culture has a vampire story.*

The woman stared up at him, smiling. "All men dying," she said. "You, too."

Sometimes the demons will eat people, the girl had told him. Sometimes they suck the soul out and the blood. *Sometimes they strike bargains—they can help people, if they feel like it.*

"I'm sick," he said, and his voice sounded impossibly weak and thin.

She shook her head. "Not die sick. I save you. You want?"

He thought for a moment that she was crazy. Some chick walking around in her *obasan's* best *kimono,* out for one last spin around the neighborhood before the whole fucking world came crashing down around her. But as she gazed at him, he found himself lost in those black, black eyes. And instead of the fetid smell of shit and rotting bodies, he thought he smelled the prairie girl's perfume. The fragrance of jasmine came flooding back to him. He closed his eyes. He wanted to remember her perfume as long as he could, wishing that the memory would last, would overtake the smell of the shit forever.

"I don't want to die," he said, the memory of the tall girl with the legs still drifting through his mind. She'd been found in the forest; he'd heard about it from somebody who knew her. She'd taken the train and headed out to Mount Fuji and wandered into the forest to die. The people here had a thing about walking through forests. *Shinrin-yoku*. Forest bathing. Something about getting out into the forest air for a walk. He'd always thought it was crazy—hell, the people here were half-crazy. Back home, people went for hikes. None of this forest-bathing shit.

Shit. He thought about the shit bucket—just for a moment—and the people huddled back in the lobby of the embassy. The stink of the place—the foul, fetid smell of the shit, the sweat and the vomit. The odor of blood so thick he could taste it when he inhaled. It hung all around him, was embedded in his clothes. *I wish I'd left*, he thought. *I wish I was in a forest right now*. He wished he could wash himself clean, bathe in clean air and walk through the trees. He thought about how badly he wanted to go home, to be in his own bed, be near his family and friends, and as he thought of this, the woman nodded and sighed again.

"Nobody wants," she said. "Nobody wants, but all men die. The world dies. Then I die." She lifted a hand to touch his face. "No men, I die. No people, I go, too. From this place to the other." She smiled wanly, with a tired half quirk to her lips that he thought must mirror his own. "We go now? To other place. I take you. Not stay here."

He felt the release in those words, and found himself nodding. "I'll go."

"Oh," she said. And she nodded, too. Then she leaned in close, touching her face to his neck, and he felt the warmth of her lips. "I take you there," she whispered. "I help you."

The sharp sting was blazing heat and white agony. He closed his eyes. The smell of shit filled his nostrils and mouth, so strong that he gagged and choked. Instead of pushing him away, she held him tighter. He opened his eyes and stared fixedly at the sky. The woman murmured something and the rank odor of rot and decay grew stronger, overpowering him. She lifted her head from his throat, her lips stained an even darker red. *Blood? His* blood, he realized, but he felt quietly numb. Dead inside.

"I bring the forest here," she said, "take you to the other place."

He thought he could hear the rustle of leaves and birdsong. She bent down again, and there was the pain, but with it came the fragrance of something sweet: jasmine. And then the smell that came just before the rain and when grass was freshly cut, of earth and damp moss. Then, wonderfully, blessedly, nothing more.

Heather Clitheroe lives and writes in Alberta, Canada. Her fiction can be found in *Hobart, Awkward Press,* and *Beneath Ceaseless Skies*. When she's not cubicle-bound in Calgary, she can be found on the banks of the Bow River or at the Banff Centre for the Arts, tucked away in a studio. "Forest-Bathing" is a continuation of the world created in her short story, "Come to Me", which appeared in the first *Evolve: Vampire Stories of the New Undead*.

The Deal
By Erika Holt

"Thanks for springing me." Tau slid the passenger seat in Linh's Hyundai Accent back and reclined with a jerk as they screeched out of the alley across the street from the Foothills Hospital.

"Here, put these on." Linh tossed him a bag of clothes. Naked, he'd draw attention. Especially with a bandaged, seeping wound on his upper thigh, where he'd been bitten.

"They tried to knock me out with morphine." Tau pulled a pair of shorts over his bandage, and then scrubbed his fingers through his woolly hair, trying to hold it together. "Felt a bit stoned, but that was it. Lucky for us though, eh? What would you've done if I was out?"

He didn't give her time to say she would've used a wheelchair or gurney, dragged him if necessary, all 104 kilograms, 190-some centimeters. They had a deal, and he would do the same for her.

"Guess they don't make allowances for experienced livers," he continued, rubbing his wrists where the restraints had chafed. He laughed, raw and forced, unlike his usual easy chuckle.

Of course, there were bound to be changes. Perhaps this was just the first.

"Okay, dude. You're free. Can we just talk about something pleasant?"

Linh didn't want to think about what would've happened if she hadn't found him in time. If the Containment Squad had transferred him to Zir Corp's lab where infectees, "Toxics," were kept in morgue drawers, the conscious ones thrashing against metal for twenty-four hours until their transformation, and then thrashing all the more when they realized they were trapped, would serve as specimens for experimentation, existing in some in-between state, unable to die, always ravenous. Still able to suffer.

No, Linh didn't want to think about this, or that her time with her best friend—safe time—was coming to an end. She glanced at the dash clock. 6:06 a.m. His toe-tag said he'd been infected around 11:00 p.m. Seventeen hours left. Max.

Linh clicked on the CD player. Heavy bass cut by angry, operatic wailing erupted from the speakers. Chaos Monkey, one of her and Tau's favorites. Too much. She pressed another button and the lighter strains of the Ambrosiaks took over. Good old-fashioned road-trip music. Better.

Nondescript office buildings passed in a blur and more cars appeared on the roads, mostly two-seater electric models. Linh's Accent was old by comparison, her mechanical skill and stockpile of parts allowing her to squeeze extra life out of the relic now clocking in at over 240,000 kilometers. Thankfully there were still a few other big gas guzzlers out there, so they wouldn't stand out too much. Anyway, "Midnight Gray" was the sort of color people forgot instantly.

Tau stretched to reach for a vodka Chill from the back seat cooler, in its usual place and stocked with Pomegranate Prodigy, his usual flavor. The least she could do was ensure he got one last, good buzz. A sharp pop as he opened the can followed by an eruption of fuchsia foam. Nothing the charcoal, fabric seats hadn't absorbed before.

"Shit shit shit!" then his mouth was over the hole, sucking down liquid.

Linh giggled. Pretty soon they were both laughing. Tau snorted Chill out his nose, causing fresh bouts of hysterics, even though it wasn't that funny. Sometimes there were other reasons to laugh. Like when you'd kidnapped an infected friend and were fleeing Calgary, hoping to avoid Containment Squads long enough to kill your best friend proper, and deliver his ashes to his Aunt Lesedi in Arborg, Manitoba. It turned out there was something insanely comical about this.

After a few, heady minutes joy evaporated and they both went quiet. Tau crunched the can flat and grabbed another. He offered Linh a sip and she took it, though she didn't like Chill. Had she thought of herself during last night's frenzied preparations, she would've brought a Coke bottle filled with Shiraz.

"You look hot, by the way," Tau said. "Never thought I'd see you in pastel flowers."

He grabbed her knee before she swatted him away.

He was always like that. Flirty. Not that anything had ever happened. It wasn't like that between them. He *claimed* he was bi, but that was only because he once banged some electrofunk slut when messed on crash. But he'd never had a relationship with a woman and out at clubs and parties Linh saw his gaze pulled exclusively towards men. Extremely slender, blond-haired men with multiple piercings usually, who at some point or other he proclaimed to love, attempted to date, and cried to Linh about after. He never chose a woman, only bad, blond boys who broke his tender heart.

But, that was okay; kept things between them less complicated.

"Wearing dirty hospital laundry is not my idea of 'hot,'" Linh said. "There's a blood stain—"

Blood.

She changed the subject. "Can you believe it actually worked? I mean, do I look like a nurse?" She twirled a finger in the long, blue hair of her dangling mohawk and smirked. "The only one who confronted me was some ancient janitor. Told him I was from the Rockyview, covering someone's shift. Ha!"

But of course it worked. No one wanted to go *near* Toxics, let alone *help* them. Guards were unnecessary. Left unsaid were thoughts of what would happen to the janitor if the Containment Squad found out.

"That's my girl." Tau grabbed her pale hand on the steering wheel and enclosed it with his much darker, much larger hand, causing the car to swerve momentarily. "I never had a doubt you'd pull it off, if it came down to it."

Intense camaraderie flared then faded out. Again, silence.

When they'd made plans for what to do if one of them ever got infected, she'd never thought it would happen. Just one of those silly, late-night discussions you have while high. The odd Toxic was around, of course, sneaking into seedy after-hours clubs or costume raves, but avoiding one wasn't difficult. Just don't go to *those* parts of town. Don't associate with people with the telltale pale, starved look; the perfect, pointy-white smile. And if you felt an irresistible pull, *run like hell*. Easy. But Tau must've gone. Why?

Those weren't his types of places. Of course, he *had* been with Chen, and Chen was bad-ass. Not even the fact that it'd been Chen who called to say Tau had been hospitalized, and his attacker beaten to death by a mob, could raise her opinion of him. It was Chen who'd once dragged an intoxicated Tau to a scarification shop and convinced him to get a unicorn outline burned onto the pristine, black flesh between his shoulder blades. Somehow she was sure it'd been Chen's idea to go to some freaky fetish club.

If only Linh hadn't been with her sister last night.

She didn't bother asking questions. Nothing Tau said now would make a difference.

9:40 a.m. They were out of the city and traffic was light. Hardly anyone traveled by highway anymore; there were better ways and the scenery was depressing. The occasional mega grain terminal or reeking livestock complex distracted from endless fields of dull green or faded yellow, overarched by rolling metal contraptions, alternately spraying pests, irrigating, or fertilizing, depending on their programmed schedule. Best to keep the windows closed.

Tau slept. Seven crushed cans littered the rubber mat at his feet and a dense, alcohol fog permeated the close air. He didn't snore—never snored—so Linh waited until his breathing took on a rhythmic pace and his lower jaw drooped, before reaching into her pocket. Capsules rattled against a plastic container. She shot a glance his way. Still out. She couldn't so much as take an aspirin without sharing, let alone something stronger. But she didn't need him hopped up on drugs just now. Not these drugs. She summoned spit in her dry mouth and shook two amphetamines onto her tongue. The sticky things skidded down her throat. Tau wasn't the only one who was tired.

A yellow sign with flashing lights advised of the last convenience hub for 400 kilometers. Linh slowed to take the exit. The change in pace woke Tau.

"Where are we?" he muttered groggily, yawning. "Oh, good. I've gotta go."

Linh eased into a parking stall just outside the store and Tau jumped out. Once he disappeared, she popped the trunk, assembled the spout mechanism on a full jerry-can, and lugged it out to pour a bit of gas in the tank. Not too much; she wouldn't have time to fill it before he got back. Her hand shook with the beginning of drug-induced jitters.

Through the window she saw Tau emerge. Hastily she screwed the gas cap shut and re-stowed the jerry-can. She slammed the trunk lid before Tau looked inside.

"You brought your own gas?"

And other things. Things he didn't need to think about right now.

"Uh, didn't want to use my fuel card. CS might figure out that I didn't show up at work today. Could trace me. See I'm out of town.

Might put two and two together." A weak story. Containment Squads were undermanned and overworked, unlikely to throw resources after a single, escaped Toxic—at least, not right away, not unless they had a reason. But she hoped he'd buy it.

Tau considered this a minute then nodded and grinned. "Got you something yummy!" He tossed her a pack of Sweet 'n Sours. "Jesus it's hot."

Linh noticed soaked circles around Tau's armpits.

The question she was about to ask—How did you pay for these?—died on her lips. He didn't have any money. He stole them. And it wasn't hot, though the fresh adrenaline radiating from her stomach could've tricked her into believing it, too.

"Yeah, stifling," she lied. "I'm just gonna run in for a sec. Why don't you turn on the air conditioning?"

"Naw, I'll come with you. We should eat. Might be a while until we get another chance."

A long while. Never.

"Yeah, sure. Sounds good." Linh's stomach churned at the thought of food.

Rather than circling around the outside in the *heat*, they went back into the store and followed the curved hallway of the complex through a casino, salon, and an arcade before arriving in a dumpy, retro pub appropriately named *Culture Shock*. Three patrons occupied its gaping hollows. Linh wondered how the place stayed in business—any of these places. Government subsidies maybe. Preservation of small towns and rural life or some BS.

The place *smelled*. Wafts of stale cooking grease briefly masked the sour aroma of spilled beer and the trio of customers all puffed away on cigarettes—former ex-smokers, she assumed, celebrating last year's cure for cancer. Linh and Tau grabbed a corner booth with red vinyl seats that hadn't been wiped in her lifetime.

The menus were paper in plastic, not the computerized touchscreens they were used to. A real-live-waiter approached to take their orders. He was slight. And blond.

"My name's Gary and I'll be serving you today. What can I get you?" Somehow he managed to say this like it wasn't scripted. Like he hadn't said it a hundred times before.

Linh looked around the nearly empty space; maybe he *hadn't* said it a hundred times before.

"I'll have the crispy noodle rolls with corn and olive salad," Linh said. "And a liter of your house red."

Gary raised a brow and recorded her order. Cute little dimples pressed in his smooth cheeks.

Linh glanced at Tau.

"Triple vodka press, neat. What do you recommend for food, Gary?"

It was his cute voice. His vulnerable, oh-my-God-I-love-you-and-want-to-buy-you-a-house voice.

"I eat pretty plain," the waiter replied, jamming a hand in his jeans' pocket. "The potato and venison pie's good. And you can't go wrong with the lamb cannelloni."

Tau studied the menu and nodded. "Bring me one of each. I trust you." Smile.

Gary beamed back and collected the menus, hand brushing Tau's—on purpose?—before he hurried off to input their orders. Or pass the cook a hand-written note, or just tell him there were suspicious people out front.

"Close your mouth," Linh said. "And, you *do* realize you just ordered two meat dishes, right? What's up with that? We haven't eaten meat for twelve years!"

"Yeah, but I'm *ravenous*. Veggie quiche just isn't going to cut it, you know? Did you *see* him? I mean, what are the chances? We stop in some nowhere place and I meet the world's hottest farm boy! Almost makes me believe in God or karma or—" He stopped.

An awkward moment as they both contemplated Tau's fate and whether or not God gave a shit.

"I've always thought it would be cool to live in the country, you know?" Tau continued softly. "Sit on a veranda, swing on one of those swings, look out at my...goats or whatever."

Linh giggled as expected but inside her heart tore. She wanted Tau to snuggle on a swing with Gary; wanted to hang out with the two of them on a hot summer day, drink Ruby Red grapefruit punch, and barbecue vegetable skewers—normal people things.

"You'd go nuts. I mean, this is it, the heart of the action." She gestured to their dim surroundings. The jukebox played *John Denver* of all things. "Gary would probably bore you in five minutes." How she wished he would've found someone boring earlier; found Gary.

"What's that?" Gary approached with a tray balanced on his shoulder. "Did I hear my name?"

Tau snorted at Linh then said, "Just saying how cute you are."

"Oh!" A dark blush bloomed on Gary's face and crawled down his neck in shades of purple. He fumbled with their drinks, the wine carafe rattling dangerously before arriving on the table. "Well, thanks!" He darted a look at Tau, then scurried off.

Shit. She hadn't counted on Gary being smitten, too.

"You can't do this."

Tau ditched his red straw and gulped down half his drink. "Do what?"

"This. Gary. Flirting. It can't...go...anywhere."

"Oh really? Thanks for reminding me. It's not like this bite on my leg is driving me *fucking insane* or anything. I kinda forgot for a second." His features were suddenly sharp, eyes hot.

Is he going to cross the table? Linh sipped her wine and resisted the urge to back away.

Tau chugged the rest of his drink. "God, sorry. Just ignore me, Linh." Under the table he clamped his thighs around one of her knees and squeezed. "You know how I get when I'm hungry."

Not like this.

Linh rubbed her foot against the back of his calf.

After Gary returned with their orders, she picked while Tau scarfed, shoveling in food so fast Linh was surprised he could breathe. Sweat dripped from his forehead onto his plate but he didn't seem to notice. His lips, usually a deep, black-brown, were pale tan.

"Uh, all done there?"

Gary was back.

"I'll just clear those dishes for you." He stacked plates on the next table. "Um, anyway, I...well, um, here." He handed Tau a neat square of paper. His cell number or email.

Tau clenched the note in his fingers like a prize, a brief flash of joy crossing his face as he looked up at Gary. Then he slumped. Vomited. On the floor. On Gary's feet. Food, vodka, all that meat, spewed, spattering the waiter's white runners. Too late, Gary jumped back. "Uuuuh!" He shook his foot as though the liquid paste would fall off like dried mud.

Tau stood, stumbled, pushed past Gary for the washroom.

"I'll clean this up," Linh mumbled, mopping ineffectually at the puddle with her napkin, smearing it more than anything. After a useless moment she threw the thing down and went after her friend. Everyone stared.

The reek of urinal pucks and mint assaulted her. Tau had smashed the plastic display window on a wall-mounted vending machine and was drinking packets of mouthwash. His face and shirt dripped with water from splashing himself.

"God dammit!" A wrenching sound and then he couldn't talk; he supported himself on the cold edge of the sink.

She went to him, wrapped her arms around his waist, and rested her head between his shoulder blades, where his unicorn was; she could feel the bumps against her cheek. She held him as he sobbed.

He spun to return her embrace and she was wrapped in hard muscle, his strength, as though he were comforting her and not the other way around. They stood, locked tight, hearts thrumming unnaturally fast, hers from the uppers, his from whatever was going on inside, until he pulled back, grasped her cheeks and slammed his mouth to hers; those pale lips, burning hot, a taste of mint and salt and bile.

They parted. She wiped her mouth; checked for blood, *her* blood. None.

"Come on," she said. "We have to go."

On their way out she tossed bills over her shoulder.

Someone yelled, "Hey, stop! What's wrong with that guy? Is he—"

Tau turned and screamed, an enraged, rasping bellow that raised the blood vessels on his face into prominence against the bone beneath. He upended a table, knocking over chairs in a clattering heap. Linh grabbed his arm. He whirled, teeth bared.

"Tau! It's me!"

Fury drained from his face and his lips curtained teeth now whiter, now sharper, than before.

Linh dragged him to the door. Together they half ran through the parking lot to the car and didn't look back to see if anyone followed.

Four hours and thirteen precious minutes. The sun hung low on the dusty horizon, giving up its fight against the somber gloom of approaching night.

Tau wasn't drinking anymore. Instead he stared out the window. Or at her. She could see him in her peripheral vision. Once, she tried staring back; saw that he wasn't blinking and his irises had deepened to black soulless pits against his dusty brown-gray skin. And he didn't seem to register her. She poked him and, after a moment, his eyes shifted back to the scenery. For a minute or two.

Run like hell, her instincts screamed.

But she couldn't run. They were running together. She couldn't just abandon the plan, her friend, even if he wasn't quite himself anymore; even if she no longer trusted him. But she had to do something. The quiet had become predatory.

There were trees now. Clumps of verdant bush dotted the rolling landscape, hiding rusting pump-jacks, abandoned farm equipment, a deer. Linh watched the ditch alongside the road and, when it deepened, pulled to the shoulder. Thick weeds and tall grass brushed the underside of the car.

"Need to stretch my legs," she said, puncturing deep silence. "Why don't you stretch yours?"

Tau didn't reply but obeyed in a robotic fashion, pulling the door handle, half falling down the slope. When Linh pulled the door shut behind him from the inside, he was too low to see in the window.

From beneath her seat she retrieved a flat box, what might be called a "rape kit" if she were a sexual predator or serial killer. She tucked the contents in her waistband and pockets—easily reachable places—and exited the car. Tau stood in the ditch listing like an unmanned boat.

"How're you feeling?" Linh asked, tone light, hand at the ready behind her back.

"You're my best friend, Linh. I...I love you. Just wanted to say it."

The words pierced her heart as surely as a well-aimed arrow.

"Don't do it. I can control it. I *can*. Just hide me. Please. I can do it. For you."

Tau's pleading eyes focused on her, *really* focused, for the first time in hours. The weight of their shared history, his plea, pressed on her lungs. Her hand fell to her side, empty. She could almost believe him. That he'd master the sickness in ways other hadn't. Hide him in some crumbling barn and everything would be okay.

Movement across an open expanse of field snagged her attention. A vehicle, a *van*, vivid chartreuse, the color of warning, still discernible in the disappearing daylight, on a road parallel to their own. Just a glimpse, then her view was blocked by a tree stand.

Containment Squad.

Gary.

Gary, or someone, must've reported them.

Linh whirled back to Tau, still standing with a lost puppy look. She whipped her police-surplus taser from her waistband

and zapped him. He dropped, thrashing and screaming. The front of his shorts darkened as his bladder emptied. From her pocket she withdrew a syringe and a vial containing dissolved sleeping pills. Her hands trembled as she struggled to fill the fragile thing and jam it into Tau's massive, jerking thigh. At this new pain, this further betrayal, he lurched up and grabbed for her, but she jumped back and his fingers grasped only air. After what seemed like an hour but was only a few seconds, his chin dropped and he slumped to the side, rolling a bit more down the steep embankment. Linh scrambled after him while fishing hard plastic zip-ties from another pocket. She looped them around his wrists, linked in a figure eight or symbol of eternity behind his back, then tried to do the same with his ankles, but the ties weren't long enough.

She hiked back up to the road and scanned the horizon for more brightly colored vehicles. *Any* vehicles. But the roads were empty. She wasn't sure if they'd been spotted; it was hard to tell at a half kilometer distant. Thankfully she'd turned off the car so there weren't any lights to attract unfriendly notice.

She popped the trunk and transferred the jerry-cans, blow torch, and axe to the floor in the back. Leaving the trunk open, she half-slid back down the hill to retrieve the barely conscious Tau. Unlike the hospital staff, *she* knew just how much it would take to sedate him. But it wouldn't last long.

It took every ounce of her unimpressive strength to drag him from the ditch, inch by slow inch. Dirt and grass clung to his hair and his ankle scraped raw. The sight of pale pink flesh beneath his dark skin, his blood, red and flowing, nearly brought Linh to tears. His body still struggled to live.

No time for weakness.

She cursed to dislodge the lump in her throat then dug-in her heels, threw herself back, and hauled his dead weight the last bit of the way up onto the lukewarm asphalt, rivulets of salt-sweat blinding her.

She lugged his torso up onto the bumper then lifted under his legs and pushed him into the trunk, cringing as his head slammed into the floor, the blow softened only slightly by the comforter she'd placed there. She arranged his prone form into what she hoped was a comfortable position and brushed debris from his cheek.

Before closing the trunk, she paused.

She could do it now. While he wasn't awake, couldn't look at her accusingly, was unable to beg. It would be so quick; so *humane*. But...no. She wouldn't take these, his last hours, from him.

She slammed the lid, enclosing him in darkness for a moment. She flipped down the back seat behind the passenger side to open the trunk pass-through, now separated from the car's interior with hastily welded basement window bars. He'd still be able to breathe freely and see out. Talk to her, if he wanted; if he could.

Linh jammed the car into gear and they were on the move. No music played. She needed to be able to hear.

An hour passed, every second marked by the blinking dash clock. A groan and then, "Linh? Linh. Linnnnnnh!" An anguished wail.

Any relief at the sound of her friend's voice was short-lived. A loud thump-thump-thump as he used his unrestrained legs to kick violently against the trunk hood. Linh swerved to throw him off-balance.

"Tau! You have to stop doing that! It'll...be okay."

He didn't answer but complied at least. Linh adjusted her rear-view mirror to see the back seat. Tau's livid face pressed against the bars, eyes bulging, lips pulled back in a snarl.

Linh stifled a scream.

"Tau, please. I'm just doing what you asked! What we agreed! You don't want to end up in one of those labs. Or loose, infecting and...*feeding* on people. Or shit-kicked by thugs! Think of your Aunt—"

She risked another glance. He'd retreated.

But it wasn't long before Linh wished she'd given him more drugs. Or just finished things. He alternated between kicking—forcing her to swerve ever more wildly, tricky on the now-pitch black roads—and wailing, a high-pitched sound straight out of hell. Linh wasn't sure if he was in pain or just wanted to torture her with the only means available.

Distant headlights—three sets—appeared in her side mirror.

"Oh fuck."

Tau wailed again.

"Shut up! Just shut up!"

Linh wrenched the wheel back and forth wildly to send Tau tumbling around the trunk compartment.

She waited until they rounded a corner then killed the lights and slowed. After a couple of painfully long minutes her eyes adjusted and she scanned for side roads under the glow of a half moon.

Please God.

On the next straightaway she saw lights again in her mirror, closer, but still a ways off. They wouldn't be able to see her anymore but that wouldn't stop them from following. If anything they'd come faster now that their prey had gone dark.

The road continued with no sign of an intersection, gravel offshoot, or even a deer track.

"Dammit!" she whispered.

Then she saw something, veered onto a barely visible ATV path, so narrow that sharp branches screeched against the car as they claimed paint. They flew along the trail for a few minutes before Linh wrenched right into a field, jerking and bumping over heavy ruts. They crested a hill and came to a sucking stop in thick mud. She stomped the gas but the wheels just spun. She turned off the engine.

For a minute they sat, Linh with her forehead on the steering wheel, Tau eerily quiet in the blackness of the trunk.

Then a weird whining. She stilled, listened.

Tau sang. Or hummed. She couldn't tell. She didn't recognize the song, if it was even a song.

She breathed but couldn't pull air deep. It just swirled shallowly at the top of her lungs and seeped back out. She had to do it now.

The axe felt heavier than it did last night, more unwieldy. She hefted it over her shoulder and pushed the trunk button on her remote, prepared for Tau to spring out.

He didn't.

He remained sprawled in the twisted knot of comforter humming idly to himself, snatches of a tune, like a radio station with poor reception. She couldn't see him well but dark, wet spots glistened on his forehead and chin; injuries from his wild ride with no hands to brace himself.

Linh tensed, axe ready, but was unable to move. She couldn't just... A sob escaped her throat and she blinked furiously to clear tears.

"Don't cry. It'll be okay," he said, mimicking her words.

Or, maybe not. Maybe a lucid moment. It was just like him to try to soothe her.

His humming resumed, then, "I know the plan, Linh. It's okay. But...come here first. Last time." His voice purred, soft and deep. Just like Tau of old. More.

The axe head thudded to the ground and the handle came to rest against the bumper. Longing flooded her; a needful throbbing. There was something wrong; something alien in her attraction to him, but she ignored it, heard herself moan, but was still aware enough to feel embarrassed. Didn't care. Climbed onto the bumper, one knee inside the car, one out, hands on Tau's chest, his hard pectoral muscles straining against the bonds behind his back. She pressed her face to his.

He met her insistent desire with tenderness, seduction; nothing like the intense moment in the pub bathroom. Their lips melted together and the soft motions of his tongue tickled out more tears, this time of bliss. She'd wanted this so for long.

He bit. Pain seared through Linh's lower lip. She tasted iron, felt him drawing on her, sucking deeply. Numbness. She started to sag.

Tau's lips had been warm. These were icy cold. *Tau's gone.*

"No!" The word came out half-formed, her bottom lip still his. She punched his temple and ripped free.

She grabbed the axe. One swing and the blade sunk deep into his collarbone. He screamed. She rocked the blade to loosen it then swung again, a sickening crack as head separated from body. Not stopping, she doused the trunk, the body, and the seats with gas, emptying the cans, then ignited the blowtorch and tossed it in. Wild flames exploded.

"I'm sorry." Nothing else to say. No one to hear.

The bonfire burned, fuelled by gas, plastic, and her friend. Aunt Lesedi would have no ashes to mourn.

Orange flames reached ever higher into the black sky, a beacon for searching eyes. She swallowed the blood pooling beneath her tongue, knowing she should throw herself on the flames, too. No one would cut off her head. She stepped closer and heat seared her skin. She couldn't. Only one choice then.

Run like hell.

Erika Holt writes and edits speculative fiction and has stories upcoming in *Shelter of Daylight* and *Tesseracts Fifteen: A Case of Quite Curious Tales*. Recently she co-edited *Rigor Amortis*, a flash fiction anthology of zombie erotica, and her current anthology project, *Broken Time Blues: Fantastic Tales in the Roaring '20s*, is now out. She also interns for award-winning anthologist Jennifer Brozek, reads slush for *Scape*, and contributes to the Inkpunks blog. Born and raised in Calgary, Erika has included a few local landmarks in "The Deal." This story was inspired by two songs from the quintessentially Canadian band *The Tragically Hip*, namely, "At the Hundredth Meridian" and "Locked in the Trunk of a Car."

Homo Sanguinus

By Ryan T. McFadden

The walls of the army cargo truck vibrated under the impact of thrown bottles and rocks. The mob hurled insults in a language Remmy didn't recognize, maybe a Balkan language, and he closed his eyes, wishing that he could just wake up back in the compound. He didn't like encountering the survivors. These accidents brought out the worst in Homo sapiens—looting, raping, and murder. And yet they feared him and his kind.

It will be dark soon, his internal voice taunted him.

The human soldiers in the truck fidgeted with their automatic rifles, faces hidden behind gasmasks. Remmy wasn't sure if their nervousness was from the angry mob or from sitting so close to him—a Homo Sanguinus.

Remmy's Handler, a man named Okami, checked his timepiece, then startled as a particularly large projectile dented the metal wall near his head.

"It's going to be dark soon, isn't it?" Remmy asked.

"I'll take care of it." Okami's voice filtered through his gasmask. He stumbled along the hanging hand straps to the back and glanced out the reinforced tailgate window into the wake of locals, most not wearing environmental suits.

"We've run out of time, Corporal," Okami said, voice muffled from the mask. "Fire a warning shot above their heads."

"Sir?"

"We're late. Does that mean anything to you?"

The soldier glanced back at Remmy, then nodded.

Remmy's stomach coiled painfully but not because he wasn't wearing a gas mask to filter the heavy concentration of chlorine or phosgenes. His last infusion had been two days ago and already his hands was so tight that his fingers curled into claws.

Okami unlatched the window and the soldier took his position. He fired a quick burst along the horizon. The crowd fell back, momentarily.

"Jesus," Okami muttered. "I said *over* their heads."

"Sir—"

As Okami fought to fasten the window, a flaming bottle sailed past him and exploded on the metal floor, spraying liquid flames across the hold.

A soldier yanked one of the fire extinguishers from its bracket but fire roared up his leg and he dropped the cylinder. The truck jolted, gears grated. It slammed to a sudden stop and Remmy pitched forward. Another flaming cocktail burst against the back window. The fire spread, black, oily smoke pouring up the walls. The soldiers would be suffocated within moments.

The truck rocked. *They're going to tip us,* Remmy realized. He wanted to hide, to curl into a little ball and tuck himself away. Even as the flames burned hotter, he was paralyzed with fear; beyond the flames were the locals and beyond them the deepening night.

Okami threw open the tailgate. The soldiers dove from the truck into a wall of people. The crowd boiled over them with tire irons, two-by-fours, axes. Okami, too close to the edge, was dragged under. Brief machine-gun fire colored the night sky but that only emboldened the crowd.

Remmy huddled at the front of the cargo hold, preferring to face the fire than the mob. The black smoke hid him. And while he didn't need to breathe, the flames would soon cook him. He tried to peer through the smoke, hoping that Okami had escaped and taken control of the situation, because that had always been Okami's job.

He's dead. So are the soldiers. Only we're left now, his inner voice said.

Even if he got past the mob, he had nowhere to go. He'd be lost in the dark. *The dark.* He had never been alone and never without his Handlers. He wondered if perhaps burning here was a better alternative.

You're not going to die here. Run! Run!

Before he could reconsider, he ran and leapt from the tailgate, sailing twenty meters past the front ranks of faces bearing startled looks. Then he was running, fear pushing him faster than he had thought possible. Their surprise was temporary and they gave pursuit.

Remmy ran through petrified trees twisted upon themselves like broken skeletons. Flashlight beams bobbed around him. He didn't know if the pounding in his ears was from fear or from his hunger. Even when he lost sight of them, he kept running despite wanting to hunker down in a crater and wait for the Handlers to find him. Remmy stumbled onto a roadway that was no more than two hardened ruts. His stomach contracted with such intensity that he collapsed. He beat his hands on the ground and screamed at the sky because he knew he wouldn't survive the night.

A sound broke through the pounding in his head. A truck.

He stood, turned into the headlights of a pickup.

The front bumper folded around him, launched him flying and he landed with a crunch then tumbled along the hardpan. He managed to raise his head and stare into the lights. A door opened and Remmy realized that the humans had caught him.

Then nothing.

He wakened to the smell of chlorine-laced lavender—not a wholly unpleasant scent. He thought he was back in the compound because that's where he woke every day. The Handlers liked to keep things predictable. And for a brief moment, he felt calm. Then memories hit him like a spike to the eye: the headlights, the crack of impact, flying through the air.

Military hospital? Impossible. The bedroom was decorated in soft purples and violets, an over-stuffed duvet and frilly pillows piled high. Candles burned on a wooden nightstand adorned with porcelain and ceramic trinkets. Not a hospital—a house.

Then he remembered screaming into the night, his body wracked with spasms as it tightened upon itself. Remmy inspected his hands. His nails were long and the skin a pasty white. Normal. Someone had given him an infusion.

He pulled back the covers and winced. Thick, white bandaging cocooned his midsection. He swung his legs over the side of the bed, his feet registering the cold of the worn floor boards. The floor vibrated, perhaps from a generator hidden somewhere in the house.

Remmy's overalls had been replaced with tattered track pants. He inspected the faded pictures on the walls, and then quickly sorted through a dresser full of sweaters and pull-overs. He glanced out a greasy, double-hung window. He was on the second floor of a farm house overlooking wilted fields that a week ago would've held thick stalks of corn.

He heard someone humming downstairs and froze, weighing his options. He contemplated breaking the window and escaping into the cornfields, and he expected his internal voice to agree with that plan, but it was strangely quiet. Maybe because whoever was humming was probably the one who bandaged him. Maybe they weren't going to hurt him.

Remmy opened the door and winced when the hinges squeaked. He padded down the stairs, following the humming, fighting against his instincts that screamed *run, run, run*. He stood at the entrance to the kitchen.

A heavy set woman, grey hair tucked into a bun, waddled from oven, to counter, to toaster. The frying pan sizzled and she moved it to a back burner. She turned and smiled.

"You're up. Good to see." She glanced down at his midsection. "I did a nice job on the bandaging." She looked old. Harmless.

"Are you going to kill me?" Remmy asked.

"I rescued you."

"You hit me with your truck."

"Sorry about that. But you didn't look like you'd listen to reason and I didn't have time to explain."

"Explain what?"

"That I'm your friend. I know what those people are capable of."

Remmy thought he saw a flash of anger cross her face, but then it was gone and she was smiling again.

"People are afraid of me," Remmy said.

"Should I be scared?"

"No. Homo Sanguinus are incapable of harm."

"That's a clever name," Molly said. "Do you know what it means?"

"No." When it was apparent she wasn't going to tell him more, he asked, "Where are we?"

"Twenty-file kilometers from the epicenter."

Twenty-file kilometers? The danger zone for humans was triple that. "You're not wearing a suit," he said.

In response, she took a cigarette from a pack and slipped it between her lips and lit it with a match, inhaled deeply, then exhaled through her nose. "Guess I don't need to worry about cancer then, do I?"

He calculated that she had two weeks to live. She'd be feeling the symptoms soon if she didn't already: distorted vision, vertigo, nausea. The end would come with a sudden and massive bleed out.

"I never smoked, you know," she said. "Ben did, but not me. Two packs a day which I guess means I was probably huffing a pack myself. Made it easy to start, being the end of the world and all." The smoke created a haze around the naked light bulb dangling from the ceiling.

"It's not the end of the world," Remmy said. He had been involved with four emergency protocols in his lifetime. Each was horrific, but like this one, isolated.

"I wasn't talking about the accident," she said. "What's your name?"

"Remmy."

"That's a strange name. Mine's Molly." When he didn't respond, "This is when you say 'Nice to meet you, Molly'."

"Okay," he said. "Are you here by yourself?"

She smiled sadly, stepped too close to him, her breath stinking of cigarettes and coffee. Remmy preferred the chlorine. She put her palm on his cheek. The warmth of her skin was comforting against his cold flesh, her pulse beating beneath the tissue-paper skin. Thum, thum, thum. A beautiful sound like the first summer rain.

"God brought you to me. Ever since Ben..." Belief in a god was a tough concept for someone like Remmy. "I wish Ben were here to show you. He was involved with your project, you know, back in the beginning. It's funny that they blamed him. Just like they always blame you, don't they?"

"I don't understand."

Molly ignored the comment, tracing a line along the side of his skull. A scar with surgical straightness. *The saw whined, bits of bone dust sprinkling the air and stinging his eyes. The doctors had cut a window into his brain.*

"Don't," he said, blinking away the memory, but she continued to trace the pink ridge.

Remmy snatched her hand and she startled. He was crushing her wrist, her bones crunching beneath his grip. Her expression never faltered but her face paled.

He released her, suddenly afraid, and confused over his reaction. What was that? *Anger.* Now she would turn him over to the mob, or worse, tell his Handlers.

She shouldn't have touched us, that internal voice said, but it was faint, like an echo across a vast canyon.

Molly cradled her hand to her chest. "You see," she whispered. "You're still in there."

"I need to contact my Handlers," Remmy said. He had to leave. Now. He couldn't trust her and worse, he couldn't trust himself. "Do you have a short-wave radio or satellite phone?"

"You need to eat first," she said.

"I don't eat."

She placed a tea cup before him with a shaking left hand. "That's what kept you alive. That's what keeps the hunger away."

He smelled the pink liquid. "What is it?" His stomach clenched, not with pain but with desire.

"You're going to need that if you're heading out."

She fixed herself a plate of bacon and eggs. She sat across from him but never ate. Instead, she smoked cigarettes.

Remmy tentatively placed the teacup to his lips, spilt most of the first sip. But the taste. Oh the taste! The liquid flooded his mouth, warmth spreading from his core to his fingers and toes. A shiver of pleasure energized his nervous system and his muscles quivered. He didn't just want more, he needed more. His gaze flicked to Molly, his vision focused on the beautiful pulse along her neck.

More.

He clenched too tightly, the glass exploding in his hands, the remnants of the liquid dripping from his chin. His muscles twitched as the lust receded. He wanted to grab that feeling, to never let go, but the more he tried, the faster it faded.

"What...was that?" Remmy asked though he already knew.

"Milk. And lamb's blood."

"Blood?" The familiar pang of fear. Blood was forbidden. "This is wrong," he said. "The Handlers told me—"

"They've been lying to you, Remmy."

"I must..." He stood and his legs wobbled. "Wha—?" he said, words slurred. He grasped the edge of the table to steady himself. Molly took him by the arm.

"You're frightened. I'm sorry. I really am. The muscle inhibitor isn't permanent, I promise."

Muscle inhibitor?

He wanted to break away from Molly but every step was more difficult than the last.

"I have to show you something, Remmy. I'm afraid this is the only way." She led him to a door off the kitchen and when it swung open, the blackness pulled at him like the sucking maw of a vortex.

"No," he grunted, but Molly was strong and he was weak. His fingers unable to find purchase on the door frame, she pushed him into the darkness. The void. Falling...

His shoulder hit the fourth step. The wood cracked, and then he bounced, crumpling. He came to rest in a heap on the concrete landing. He tried to cry out but only managed a pathetic clicking with his tongue. His consciousness receded until the whole world was Molly standing in the doorway.

"Just because we created you doesn't mean we can control you," she said. The door swung shut, a meager sliver of light at the bottom, then that too disappeared.

The dark.

It took him over, pressed upon him so he was unable to move and he wondered if this was what it felt like to suffocate. Tears slid from his eyes. The paralysis became so complete that he couldn't move his tongue, swallow or blink. Remmy wondered if he was even awake.

He smelt the dampness in the basement, the punky wood and the mildew-soaked walls. Smelled the crap of the small scavengers surrounding him. Felt their tiny paws on his legs as they scurried over him, whiskers brushing his neck. Their teeth devoured tiny chunks of his flesh. Time poured over him like water—and the tighter he tried to grasp it, the more it drained away. Then, even the little animals left him. Gasping, he soon wished for their return. His memories overpowered him: scenes from the accident, of pulling bodies from wreckage. Of the purebreds throwing eggs at him, spitting at him, blaming him for their errors.

And there was that distant call again, like someone locked inside his skull, pounding to get out. But he couldn't hear what that voice was saying.

Remmy realized he was sitting. Somehow, he had righted himself and was leaning against the wall. He wiggled his toes, moved his hands. Slowly, movement returned to his limbs. How long had he been down here? Hours? Days?

The light under the door returned. After several attempts, he finally managed to drag himself to the stairs, that sliver of light drawing him like a beacon. He took each step carefully as his gross motor skills returned slowly. He collapsed next to the door.

"Molly?" he said, hysteria fraying his sanity. "Please, Molly. Let me out." He scratched at the old door, splinters tearing his nails and chewing away skin. Molly hummed on the other side,

the clink of dishes in a sink. The louder he cried, the louder she
hummed. He pressed his mouth against the crack of light. He
huffed at that opening and Molly fell quiet.

Why was she doing this to him? Maybe she was locking him
down here until the mob arrived. He gazed back into the dark;
a shiver swept down his spine. Wait. If he concentrated hard
enough, focused, rough images coalesced: the stairway, a railing, a cracked stone floor. Had light somehow filtered in or had
his eyes adjusted?

As the hours passed, his sight improved until there were no
shadows and no darkness.

There is no dark, not for us.

He had worn his fingers to the bone trying to get through
the door. The gnawing in his gut felt like the teeth of the ver-
min—and as he remembered the sweet taste of Molly's drink, the
pain intensified. He had to find his Handlers before the pangs
of starvation overwhelmed him.

Perhaps there was another way out. Maybe basements had
windows.

He padded down the stairs, hearing the rats scurrying at his
approach. They gazed at him with dark eyes, then turned tail
and dashed into their holes.

The basement was a maze of tiny rooms and hallways. He
found no exit, only endless spaces filled with oily machines and
abandoned lab equipment. He spent hours picking through the
junk, hoping to find something to aid his escape.

The hunger hit with a sudden burst of pain and he stumbled.
He gasped for breath, not because he needed oxygen but because
of a human response hard-coded into his genes. *Except you're not
human,* that voice said. The hunger didn't relent and it overpowered his rational mind. He clawed at the walls, shrieked at the
ceiling, smashed equipment, and raged through the basement.
The pain rippled, his skin tightening around his bones, making
it crinkle as if crusty and burnt.

The beating hearts of the rats drew him to his hands and
knees to sniff along the walls. That sound of blood surging in
their tiny veins made him mad with desire. Remmy reached
into holes in the walls, frantically trying to grasp their scaly
tails to draw them out so that he could crack open their chests
and suck out their life.

Madness! That voice, becoming braver. Taunting him. *Is this
what we have become?*

"What would you have me do?" Remmy asked.

Live.

"I don't know how."

He blinked and in that microsecond between reality and darkness, he became lost.

A halo of lights shines in my eyes but I can't close them. A saw motor hums followed by the sound of metal teeth biting into bone. My skull—they're cutting into my skull. The doctors wear white environmental suits with positive-flow masks and breathing tubes hooked to oxygen tanks.

I hate them. I want to break my bonds but my body is inert. Useless. Frustration so powerful a tear rolls down my cheek. The saw screams as it cuts my skull and though I rage, I cannot yell. I want to twist their limbs and pull them from their sockets. Their hearts beat so loudly: Thum, thum, thum.

The sound of the saw fades and the doctor holds a set of surgical snips. They consult amongst themselves while I imagine ripping out their throats and tasting a splash of blood on my tongue like the first snowflakes.

They begin the procedure while I lie helpless.

Snip. The anger disappears, disconnected.

Snip. The frustration, suddenly disengages.

Snip. Desire, gone.

More snips and they cut away my emotional self like trimming back an overgrown bush. They leave one emotional connection: fear.

I shiver because I am afraid...

The door unlatched and a sound drifted though his fever-hunger. He savored the last vestiges of the memory—the hatred, the frustration. But the more he tried to focus on those alien feelings, the more they became vapor drifting through his fingers.

"Molly?"

He heard a grunt, and then a body tumbled down the stairs. Remmy pulled himself from his knees and shuffled to the landing. The door closed and was re-latched.

The body lay crumpled at the bottom, smelling of sweat, rubber, chlorine, and blood. The man wore a gasmask with the eye holes shattered. Remmy heard the rats in the walls, but his presence kept them away.

The man groaned, shifted.

Remmy moved closer, observing, his skin tingling like he had touched a live copper wire. He breathed deeply of the scent and his vision brightened, a white halo forming around the bleeding man as he focused on the soft spots—the wrists, the thighs, the throat.

Just a taste.

Remmy took a step back, no longer trusting himself or his instincts. The Handlers had taught him that he would be punished for taking a life; his insides would boil and fester.

Lies.

The man startled awake and gasped for breath. He glanced around wildly, scrambled backwards like a crab until he hit a wall. He tore off his gasmask.

"Who's there?" he stuttered.

Remmy sat on his haunches, watching as the man fumbled about in the dark, cried at the door just as Remmy had earlier. Occasionally, the man turned, gazing into the black before renewing his efforts at the door.

Remmy's hunger pains had settled into the hum of anticipation.

What you were meant to do.

When the man returned to the bottom of the stairs, Remmy padded soundlessly behind him, arms encircling his torso, teeth sinking into his neck. The man cried out, then relaxed. Remmy suckled, pulling at the wound, worrying it wider with his tongue and lips. His tongue searched, wiggled deeper and the taste sent a beautiful orgasmic wave through him.

Soaring through the night. Feeling as large as the heavens. The wind whistling in the ears.

The sky turns orange. The world freezes. The air shatters as if made of glass.

Darkness and suffocation. Hunger so limitless, it is a line that stretches past the horizon.

The wall that separated the voice inside of Remmy burst apart in a torrent of blood. Electrical impulses jumped across the incisions in his brain. Old, dead tissue sparked with electrons, reborn with the infusion of blood. Bridges were reconnected, pathways rebuilt. Like the building pressure of a train through a tunnel, the emotions amplified: Hatred for the doctors and what they did to him. The hatred made him clench the man tightly, his embrace snapping bones like kindling. The man's only defense was a pitiful gasp.

Remmy sucked and drank until the body was a dry husk, the heart sputtering then dying.

The corpse slid from his arms and Remmy shivered with the aftershocks. Through this haze of swirling emotion, he heard the door unlatch and smelled cigarette smoke drifting through the crack. He made his way up the stairs letting his fingers trail along the rail as if experiencing touch for the first time. The whorls and imperfections in the wood sent shivers along his spine.

He opened the door.

Molly sat at the table, good hand holding a smoldering cigarette. His vision focused on her heat. He smelled her fear and it tingled in his groin. And yet, he felt something new: gratitude. Molly had done this. For him.

"Molly. Dear Molly," he said.

"Are you leaving now?"

"Do you want me to?"

"You know I don't." She stubbed out her half-finished cigarette.

"Tell me what you want," he said.

He saw her pulse quicken and his senses sharpened. Crystal, another layer of magnification. If he focused, he could hear the earthworms tunneling, the piercing sonar of the bats outside— but none of it mattered except for the thrumming of her heart.

"You're playing games with me now?" she asked.

"Isn't that what all of this has been? A game?"

"Not a game."

He moved so swiftly that she startled when his hands touched her neck, flowing down her shirt. His breath was cold and goose bumps flowered on her skin. Remmy wondered if it would excite him more if she resisted. *Not with Molly.*

She exposed her neck for him. Her breath fluttered when his mouth touched her throat, her good hand clenched in a fist. "Molly," he whispered, then punctured her with a swift stroke. Blood squirted to the back of his mouth, flowed over his tongue and he swallowed. His veins filled and his heart pumped as he gorged on her life.

The perfect softness of holding hands.

Klaxons. A crush of people, so many they push him down, trample him as he gasps for breath. She cannot reach him. The air distorts from heat, smells of chlorine. His hand is empty as she takes it. Bitterness, like a mouthful of diesel fuel that she cannot spit out.

He heard a truck with an over-loaded suspension bouncing down the laneway. Headlights shone through the window, Remmy staring into their brilliance, Molly holding the back of his head in a lover's embrace, fingers entwined in his hair.

"You know what you have to do, don't you, Remmy?" she whispered.

He licked the slowing wound and pulled away. Molly sat with half-lidded eyes and he crouched to her level. He stroked her hair.

"I know what I will do."

"Thank you."

He kissed her on the mouth, delicately painting her lips red with blood. He heard the mob outside: car doors closing, muffled laughter, the clink of metal on metal.

"You've come this far…" she said, her hand pulling him toward her.

He returned to her throat, worried the bite wider and sucked until her heart gave a final, weak pulse. When he pulled back, her eyes were closed and he marveled how beautiful she looked. He wanted to stay with her but the voices were outside the door now.

You know what you have to do.

"Yes."

Remmy left through the back door and stood in the shadows away from the brilliance of the headlights. His gaze shifted from person to person, at the way they laughed nervously, at the way they looked over their shoulders waiting for the inevitable attack. Despite their weapons and numbers, they were afraid. Terrified.

And so they should be. Molly had shown him the truth: he didn't have to fear the dark. They did.

Ryan T. McFadden is an award-winning fantasy/SF author in London, Ontario. He has several short stories published and his novella, *Deus Ex Machina* was part of the Aurora-winning *Women of the Apocalypse,* published by Absolute XPress. He is busy working on his next project in the always popular Neo-Noir Supernatural Crime Thriller category. The story "Homo Sanguinus" (rough translation: *Bloody Man*) began from two desires. The first, to never say the word 'vampire' (an idea given to him by Kevin Nunn), and the second, to place the vampire protagonist as the oppressed rather than the oppressor.

Out with the Old
By William Meikle

From the journal of John Sharpe—April 3rd 2062
Although we had manned the barricade all winter, this was
the first day I felt tense and on edge, the first day I really *believed*
that danger might be imminent. There was something in the air
that spoke of a possibility of spring. Not that anyone would
notice much. We've been under the same grey cloud for two
years and more now, and there hasn't been a sign of any sun in
all that time. All of us *hope* that this year things will be different, that this year will see us turn the corner. None speak of it
though, for that might jinx the thing entirely.

There was also something else with us this morning besides
hope. Bill Davis actually cracked a smile when the light changed
from a murky gray to a slightly less murky gray, and Harper
Lodge sang "The Spring's a Coming", so off-key that we *all*
laughed. The jollity had a forced note to it, though. You don't
come through a winter like this one without it affecting you. All of
us have been touched by standing too close to cold death. We've
had thirty-five bodies to burn out back of Mifflin's store, and I
know I'm not the only one who's laid awake at night thinking
about their dead eyes.

I haven't been doing much writing. Not doing much of anything besides dying slowly and watching this old town fade away.

We're down to fifty-five souls, sinking fast. We won't make it
through another winter. We all know it, but nobody will speak of
it, a huge elephant in every room. Actually, an elephant wouldn't
be a bad thing. At least we could eat it. The last of the deer meat
went this week, and we'll be lucky to see any more. Grass doesn't
grow real well under this cloud, and the wild animals aren't any
better off than we are.

There's not been fuel for automobiles or tractors for three months now, and nobody's volunteering for a trip to Edmonton—the last four we sent never came back. I'm guessing it's the same all over.

Weren't any one thing that caused the world to go to shit so fast…just a lot of things at once: war, warming, pollution, and too many folks chasing too little water. That, and the weather deciding to throw everything at us all at once for five years in a row, and we're left where we are now—no infrastructure, no food, and damned little hope.

A fine start to spring!

The morning's brief flirtation with a lift in the gloom soon faded as the clouds fell down from the Rockies, slate gray and flat like a giant tombstone just over our heads, getting ever darker as the sun went behind the mountains. I was just starting to look forward to the thin gruel that would pass for supper when Harper cocked his rifle.

"We got company," he said.

Suddenly the day felt a lot colder.

The three of us stood at the barricade watching a vehicle close in on us along the highway, the headlights too bright in the gathering dark.

I was thinking how unlucky I am. I'd been there on the road the last time too, when the three bikers came along shooting and hollering. I'd stood alongside Frank Brookes when he took a shot in the chest and died gurgling at my feet as I pumped round after round into the bikers, and I'd helped burn the bodies later that day.

I never want to smell flesh burning like that again.

Maybe I'm afraid I might start salivating. Ha! Morbid humor.

Anyway, there's not much chance of a repeat of that gunfight. We're down to twelve rounds between the lot of us, and we really should be keeping them for hunting game this coming summer. They might be all that stand between us and starvation.

All those thoughts were going through my mind as the vehicle approached. Whoever was driving, they didn't seem to be in a hurry. It was a pickup truck, sleek, black and cleaner than anything I'd seen for years now. It could have come straight from a showroom. It came to a stop ten yards from the barricade and when the driver cut the engine I heard warm metal *ping* as it cooled rapidly. The door of the pickup opened.

"Let's see your hands," Harper shouted, his voice high and whiny with fear. "Right fucking now!"

A pair of pale hands rose above the door. There was no sign of a weapon. Bill Davis covered me as I walked up to the pick-up, knees like jelly and a stone brick in the pit of my stomach.

As I approached, the door opened further and a tall man stepped out. He showed me his palms, which looked almost white in the gathering gloom. When he looked into my eyes my stomach turned to ice, and I was sore tempted to just drill him there and then.

It was something in those eyes that did it. They reminded me of a time before the darkness, and a bar fight in Boston with a man who didn't care how hard you hit him, a man who just liked to fight. This newcomer gave off the same aura, and that was trouble I didn't want to know.

He smiled, and that put paid to any idea I might have of shooting him.

"Hello," he said softly. "As you can see, I'm not armed. I'm here with a proposition."

Harper was having none of it. "You can take your proposition and shove it where the sun don't shine."

He'd come up to my side and aimed his shotgun straight at the newcomer's nose. If the stranger was intimidated, he didn't show it. Ignoring Harper's gun completely, he stepped back and patted the tailgate of the pickup.

"You'll want to see what's in here," he said.

And he was right. He drew back a tarp and showed us what he had under there. When I stepped forward I did indeed start to salivate.

The stranger...he said his name is Josh Prentice...brought us enough tinned food, liquor and smokes to see us through a month at least.

We've just had a town meeting. He's promised to share it all, if we let him stay.

Mine was the only dissenting vote.

From the journal of John Sharpe—June 12th 2062

I still haven't taken to Prentice, but I can't deny he's made a difference. Three times now he's gone out in that big pickup of his, and three times he's come back with supplies—less each time, but still enough to keep this town on a borderline subsistence.

It's better than dying, that's for sure.

And he's certainly been putting in the work up at the Avery place. Nobody's lived in that big house for three years and more—

it's too far out of town and too high up the slope in winter for any of us townsfolk to care for it. But Prentice says he's doing just fine. Most days we hear the sound of chainsaws and hammers echoing down the valley. Bill Davis is the only one who's been up to see. He took the deeds of the house to be signed.

"Just 'cause the world's gone to fuck don't mean we shouldn't keep the law here in town," he said. When he came back down he was quiet, and it took a few beers to loosen his tongue. Even then, he refused to be drawn, beyond a single phrase that he would repeat when asked what he'd seen: "He's building a fort up there."

Prentice has sure made himself useful. Apart from bringing in food, he's also done his shift on the barricades, volunteering for night duty where nobody but the stupid would stand. Most nights there's just me and him there. He doesn't speak much, but his eyes scan the horizon continuously, like an eagle watching for a rabbit.

Haven't learned much about him. Says he came out of Vancouver, and it was bad. I can tell that much from his eyes and the way his hands tremble when he speaks. But he won't give away specifics, and when pushed his eyes get that hard look that reminds me never to get him riled.

He said something that's got me thinking, though: "We need to go back to the old ways."

When I pointed out to him that maybe it was the old ways that got us into this mess in the first place, he said something under his voice that I almost didn't catch. "'Old' depends on how far back you want to go."

From the journal of John Sharpe—August 17th 2062

Fall's going to be here soon. The sense of trepidation in the town is palpable. If it weren't for Prentice I'm sure we'd have a few suicides on our hands by now. He's stopped taking the pickup to Edmonton. He says there's nothing left there to scavenge but rats, and even they're having trouble hanging on.

That news, brought two weeks ago, hit us hard. We'd grown accustomed to the supplies he was bringing—especially the liquor and the smokes.

But meat is what we mostly crave. I can't count the nights I lay awake listening to my stomach do impressions of thunderstorms and thinking about burgers, and sausages, and rib-eye steaks with all the fixings. While we still had some smokes I managed to keep the cravings at bay, but I figure it's going to be another long protein-free winter.

Until Prentice made one last trip out.

Our summer hunting has yielded nothing but a pair of coneys and a maggot-ridden coyote. But the stranger—I still call him that—thought he could do better.

He called a town meeting yesterday to set out his plans. We yielded the floor to him and he stood up on the stage in the school hall and looked down at us as if he was the headmaster and we were recalcitrant pupils.

"Look at you," he said. His voice sounded soft, but it carried across the whole hall even though it was several years since we've had power for a microphone. "There you sit, preparing for death, when you should be preparing for life. You don't know how lucky you are."

A few snorts of derision rang through the hall, but nobody spoke up. It seems I wasn't the only one who'd recognized the look in Prentice's eye.

"You're all worried about the coming winter? And well you should be, if it is anything like the one I spent last year. But I can ameliorate the situation. I can bring you what you need."

Bill Davis joined me in *snorting* at that one, but everyone else seemed rapt.

"What can *you* do that we can't do for ourselves?" Bill shouted.

I was sitting close to the front so I caught the angry glance Prentice shot Bill's way. All everybody else noticed was the harsh laugh.

"The world has changed. I am adapting," Prentice said. "How many of you can say that?"

He let us chew on that for a while before continuing. He repeated what he'd said earlier.

"I can bring you what you need. I can guarantee survival. In return I will ask you for something. Maybe not this week, this month or even this year. But the time will come when I will ask. And I will expect it to be given...with no questions."

He left us to mull that over for a while too, but there was very little discussion. Everybody had already benefitted from his trips to the city. Everybody knew he was a man of his word.

"Besides," Marion Larkin said, "we ain't got much to give him, no matter what he asks for. What have we got to lose?"

The vote was near unanimous again. Bill Davis stood with me in the nay saying, but no one else was listening. We got Prentice back in and agreed to his terms. He left looking like the cat that got the canary.

He came back tonight with three large moose in the back of the pickup. I was the only one who got a good look at them before Taylor Bishop's truck hauled them away for carving up, but they sure didn't look like they'd been shot to me.

They looked like something had *torn* their throats open. Damned near took their heads off.

We have enough meat to see us through months to come.

But at what price?

From the journal of John Sharpe—October 10th 2062
Heavy snow today. Winter is almost here.
God help us.

From the journal of John Sharpe—November 18th 2062
The men who came along the road last night were desperate. They had to be to brave the passes on foot in this weather.

Damned near caught us by surprise, too. We'd given up expecting any more marauders, not this late in the year. But hunger drove them out of wherever they'd been holed up, and set them straight at us. We must have looked like a target.

I counted twenty of them in the pack that tried to sneak around our defences. Mangy beasts they looked, and as disease ridden as the coyote I shot in the summer. But their guns were filled with ammo, and that put them one up on us even before we started in to the fighting.

Harper Lodge took one in the chest that's looking to put paid to him before long, and I felt a bullet graze my temple. We used up the six rounds we had left in the first assault, putting down three of the attackers. Then we were down to hand to hand fighting at the barricade.

The one that threw himself at me was more animal than man, a snarling beast with ropy drool hanging from his chops. He had a knife in his left hand and his right was little more than a mass of pulpy tissue, grey and full of pus. I smashed my rifle butt against his jaw and three teeth flew in a bloody spray. It hardly slowed him.

I was aware of fighting all around me but I couldn't take my eyes off the attacker. Once again he threw himself at me and his weight took us both to the ground. We rolled, clawing and scratching like kids in a playground.

Suddenly the weight lifted from me. I looked up just in time to see Prentice snap the man's neck, as easily as if he'd been tearing a sheet of paper. He left me lying there, mouth agape, and moved along the line. Everywhere he went attackers fell before him. He moved smoothly, fluidly. They shot straight at him but he never slowed. He weaved and bobbed, lighter than any fighter I've ever seen, leaving a trail of dead behind.

By this time I had got myself to my feet. I moved to Prentice's side and put a hand on his shoulder. He stood over the last of the attackers. The man lay broken like a wooden doll smashed to splinters. Prentice looked down at the body that was panting like a hot mutt. At my touch he turned and looked me in the eye. By reflex I went for the rifle— I knew that look all too well.

Once again he smiled at me. "Do you still think you'll make it without me?"

I already knew the answer to that one.

He didn't hang around to help us with the bodies, but that was fine by me. Like the bikers before them, we burned them at the back of Mifflin's store, and I made sure I stayed upwind of the smell.

It was only later that I realized I had missed something important, something I had better write down here before I forget. I counted twenty marauders coming up the road. But we only burned eighteen bodies, and I'm damned sure nobody got away.

While writing this, I hear a scream, high and thin, come down from the Avery House, but I'm not daft enough to go and check it out.

From the journal of John Sharpe—January 12th 2063

I was summoned to the Avery House last night, the first time I've been up there since he moved in, but I fear not the last.

Bill Davis came to my door after nine o'clock. It was bitterly cold out, and he was wrapped up so that only his eyes showed. "He wants us."

He didn't have to say anything else. I knew who he meant well enough, and I'd been waiting for this night since the attack on the barricades. A favour was about to be called in, and I knew for certain that I wasn't going to like it.

I kept Bill waiting for a minute as I fetched a long hunting knife and hid it inside my parka. If he saw me do it, Bill said nothing.

It was a long walk up that hill, made longer by the foreboding that had settled in my spine. Bill didn't speak, and that was fine by me. I concentrated on putting one foot in front of the other, trudging through the peculiar grey snow that had been falling for the last week or so. By the time we reached the turnoff to the Avery place, I felt like a Popsicle. Even then, I wanted to turn back to town as soon as I saw what he'd done.

The perimeter of the property, which once had a facade of a pretty white picket fence, was now a wall of thorn bushes, thick, black and strangely alive. Inside that, where there had once been lawn, was now an expanse of concrete, weathered and broken so as to resemble old stone.

The old house had also been transformed, reinforced with more stone and concrete that made turrets and balconies that towered above. I remembered Bill's words from the summer.

He's building a fort up there.

This wasn't a fort. This was a *castle*.

The main door to the property was a thick piece of oak that looked like it had been there for centuries. There was even a bell chain to pull.

A fucking bell chain!

I felt like screaming as Bill Davis pulled it while we waited freezing on the doorstep in the increasingly heavy snow.

Finally the door swung open and we stepped into a sauna. At least that's what it felt like at first. I saw the reason soon enough. A huge fire blazed in a solid stone fireplace big enough to walk into. Overhead, three chandeliers hung, each festooned with twenty candles, all burning. At the far end of the room, across a floor constructed of concrete blocks made to look like flagstones, Prentice sat on a large, throne-like chair. He showed no sign of getting down to greet us. Instead we walked forward.

There was no preamble.

"I want a girl," he said. "A virgin preferably, but I know how hard that can be these days. A young girl will do—no younger than fourteen, no older than twenty. I'll leave it up to you to choose."

Bill moved before I could. He too had come prepared. He had a knife out and thrown before I registered it. Prentice scarcely flinched, just plucked the blade from the air like he was catching an apple falling from a tree.

Bill leapt forward, fists flying.

Prentice stopped him with a single backhand blow that sent Davis sprawling and sliding across the floor. I was still struggling to get my knife out from the folds of my jacket as Prentice came down off the throne and bent over Bill's prone body.

For the first time he let me see his fangs.

"Is this what you want?" he said, looking straight at me. "I can take the whole town tonight...if that is what you want?"

He smiled. He knew he had me.

He moved away from Davis and sat back in the chair.

"This is how it will be," he said, in a voice that would brook no argument. "I will protect you and feed you. The town will survive."

"And in return?"

He smiled again. "In return, I will ask you for a favour now and again, a token of your goodwill. And you will send any travellers that come this way to see me first. As I have said already, the old ways are sometimes the best."

Bill and I took the message back to the town and called for a meeting. And once again, it didn't take long.

We gave him Becky McKenzie.

It's better than dying.

But not much.

William Meikle is a Scottish writer with ten novels published in the genre press and over 200 short story credits in thirteen countries. He is the author of the *Watchers* series among others, and his work appears in a number of professional anthologies. His ebook *The Invasion* has been as high as #2 in the Kindle SF charts. He lives in a remote corner of Newfoundland with icebergs, whales and bald eagles for company. In the winters he gets warm vicariously through the lives of others in cyberspace.

Chelsea Mourning
By David Tocher

Stooping low in the darkness, Chelsea Mills clutched her bleeding palm and peered at the Montreal ruins through the grimy window of an abandoned pub.

Thick dust clouds and debris smudged the sky, and Chelsea thought it'd probably been months since any living thing had seen sunlight. Montreal had become a disemboweled corpse, stone and steel guts scattered amongst the bones of its streets and avenues. Skyscrapers and cathedrals no longer blocking the view, the landscape offered her a panorama of the distant St. Lawrence River, a rippling expanse of black, swirling with cross currents.

Chelsea listened to the wind, high and keening, as it rushed through the crumbled framework of buildings, spinning eddies of ash and debris into the air. She also heard the voices of *the others*. Fleeting words. Sentence fragments. A mostly incoherent drone.

Since childhood, she'd called them *think-voices*. Hearing them now, Chelsea knew she wasn't the only person above ground; there were others nearby. Those disembodied whispers kept her pinned inside the dark building, unwilling to show herself. Of this earth, but not human—that was how the think-voices *felt* against her mind.

As the pain in her palm dulled from searing to a bitter throb, she considered the think-voices—how they seemed like one thing, but were really another. That reminded her of something from childhood: She'd dug a hole in her backyard with her plastic shovel. When she thought she'd uncovered a rock, she pried it out from the soil. But, unlike a rock, the object had some give. Movement. When she realized she'd unearthed a large beetle and saw its legs scrabbling at the air, she had screamed in horror.

Chelsea noticed three shadowy figures emerge from the remains of a nearby building.

She sucked her breath in and held it, afraid to make a sound. *Don't be silly,* she thought. *The think-voices, of course they're human. What else could they be?*

But she didn't convince herself. With good reason, too. After the world went to hell, she had seen things she could never un-see. Mummified corpses scattered in the streets. Bodies motionless, decayed clothing fluttering with the wind. Each time she pointed her flashlight at one of their faces—leathery skin stretched taut on skull, eyeless sockets, yellow-toothed mouth howling soundlessly—she saw a deathmask swimming in a sea of darkness.

What frightened her even more were the fresh bodies. The people who'd come above ground before her. She'd counted ten pale, lifeless forms, all with large puncture wounds in their throats, legs and stomachs. *If those are teeth marks,* Chelsea had thought, *then they're not human teeth. Animal?* She doubted it.

It was as if someone had driven railroad spikes through the skin. Smeared dried blood formed straggly patterns, like brushstrokes of abstract art, the canvas their rotting flesh. It was their faces, though, that horrified her most—frozen contortions of pain that screamed a warning: *Run! Get away from here! Now!*

That dreadful *someone's-behind-you* feeling struck like a fist. The city's ruins came to life, taunting her. Wind-tossed newspapers scraping pavement became dragging feet; the clatter of distant rubble, a shout. She spun in circles, gasping, looking everywhere, her flashlight drawing zigzag patterns in the dark.

She couldn't think straight. She had to find someplace to hide until her courage returned. She'd run down an alley, crawled through the transom above the pub's backdoor, slicing her palm on a shard of glass jutting from the frame.

Now, as whispers clamored in her skull, Chelsea watched the three shadowy figures outside. She squinted, struggling to see details from the darkness. Suddenly, what she saw made her skin crawl. Not one particular thing, but a bunch of slight irregularities that, when added together, made each of their three forms seem...*offish.*

The backs of their skulls were bulbous, slightly larger than normal. One turned in Chelsea's direction. She made out the eyes, bulging from their sockets. Another was female by the flare of the hips, tapered legs, rounded chest, long hair—the jaw opened wider than normal when she spoke.

But when one of them raised his hand and pointed at another, Chelsea's crawly feeling was replaced with fascinated horror. The thumb extended past the fingers and curled into a talon. She examined the hands of all three and saw that they were the same.

Their think-voices were a cacophony of words and phrases she couldn't string together. But after watching how they interacted, it became clear that the female was the leader.

Chelsea fine-tuned her mind to the woman's think-voice. The others faded to faint whispers, but the woman's echoed even louder.

Stop bleeding humans! It's been two days since we've found any. We're taking the next one we find back to the colony. Maybe they'll know where we can find more.

One of the men barged towards her, raising his taloned fist in protest. Instantly, the woman's arms shot out and seized his throat. She heaved him off the ground. He kicked and twisted. Chelsea wished she could hear more than one thought-voice at a time.

I'm the leader of our colony, so I'll be giving the orders. If we don't find more, we won't have enough blood to feed our weaker ones.

From where Chelsea squatted in the darkness, she sensed waves of power emanating off the woman. A feeling of excitement flared inside her chest— *I want that power! If I'd had that kind of power…nobody would've ever been able to hurt me. Or Brian.*

At his name, her throat constricted. She touched the friendship bracelet on her wrist, the only thing she had to remember him by. He'd been the only man who'd ever—

Footsteps behind her. Hands seized her by the shoulders and flipped her around. She struggled in his steely grip until she saw his face. Bulging eyes. Bulbous head. Trembling, she looked at the large, taloned thumbs clutching her upper arms.

"You shouldn't have cut yourself, girly. I could smell your blood on the wind," he said. "If it weren't for my orders, you'd already be dead."

He raised one hand above his head. It swept down and struck Chelsea's face.

Everything went black.

When Chelsea came to, she was lying on the floor of a wide cement room, torches fitted into the walls. The air, thick and clotted with burning oil, made her stomach clench. She fought back the urge to gag.

Dark shadows flickered in the orange glow. People surrounded her in a loose circle, their features offish.

The room also had a coppery smell. It vaguely reminded her of pennies, or rain, or blood. *Blood!* Her mind screamed the word, conjuring up the memory of a night, five years ago, when her father raped her.

On the night it had happened, she was fifteen. Chelsea, lying on her back, awoke in the darkness to her father's hand over her mouth. Booze on his breath. His other hand roamed places on her body where no father's hand should ever roam. His fingers probed a place no father's fingers should ever probe.

She thrashed and kicked him where she knew it would hurt. He snatched a handful of hair and smashed her head into the wall, knocking her out.

She awoke to the smell of copper. Pain throbbed in her skull. Her father looked down at her. She heard a whisper in her mind, her father's voice. Except his whisper said different things than what came out of his mouth.

What now? How will I tell her I'm sorry? How will I make her trust me again? Brenda can never know.

Chelsea wondered how she was able to hear his think-voice. She touched her sore head. She felt the bandage. Understanding descended.

"I can hear your think-voice, Daddy," she said, and then, in a forceful whisper, she mimicked the tone of his thoughts: "What now? How will I tell her I'm sorry? How will I make her trust me again?"

She caught an image inside herself. A mere husk of a girl, alone, buffeted by winds of rage and hatred swirling in the emptiness.

She stared at her father and hated him.

She had wanted to drag him into the black, swirling chaos and let the rage and hatred tear him to pieces.

In the coppery, torch-lit room, Chelsea felt panic well in her chest. She was surrounded by hideous offish-people, staring down at her with bulging eyes.

She closed her eyes and remembered what Brian had taught her, months ago, when they'd taken shelter beneath the city, on that day the earth was scorched.

When you're afraid, when you're in danger, you have to go somewhere in your mind. The Place of No-Hurt. It could be a memory, a fantasy. Whatever makes you feel safe and strong.

Chelsea, trembling, turned within her mind.

She went to the closest thing she'd ever had to a Place of No-Hurt—a revenge fantasy. She imagined herself swinging a baseball bat, smashing her father's face to a pulp. His screams and the sound of his splattering blood were music to her ears, a soothing ointment to her hurt and fear.

The whirlpool of reality drew Chelsea from the placid waters of her mind and back into the swirling madness of the waking world.

When she came to again in the torch-lit room, the think-voices were faint and jumbled. Her mind was weak, unable to decipher their whispers.

Her eyes opened as narrow slits and her head tilted sideways. She saw that her arm had been raised. Her eyes followed her arm to the wrist where one of the Offish-people had his mouth clamped. Blood ran down her forearm. It looked black in the firelight. The friendship bracelet, woven with green and red chevron patterns, was still on, stained. Relief washed through her. If she was going to die, she'd prefer to go out with the only object she cared about, one that helped her remember Brian.

After the night she had been raped, her father never touched her again. His glances, though, remained eager. Furtive. Sometimes her mother noticed. Why didn't she do anything? Six months later, Chelsea ran away from home and hitchhiked from Ottawa to Montreal. She met Brian at a homeless shelter.

Frightened and alone, in a city where people spoke a language she didn't understand, she was standing in line at a soup kitchen, her hands red and shivery from the nighttime cold.

"Hey, you look like you could use these," a voice said.

She turned her head; he held a pair of gloves out towards her. Short and stocky, with a shaved head, he looked about seventeen. He wore green cargo pants and a black hoodie.

"What do you want me to do with those?" she asked, refusing to make eye contact.

"Take 'em. If you want."

Chelsea listened to his thoughts: *Looks like a nice person. Afraid, though. Hope she lets me help her out. These streets aren't the place for this one.*

Unlike most men she'd met, his first thought had been directed at her body. She knew his concern was sincere. But no matter how much Chelsea wanted to accept the gloves, she couldn't.

Even her father had been capable of showing love. That hadn't stopped him from hurting her. What would stop this stranger?

She crossed her arms over her chest. "Did I ask for your help? Now please, fuck off."

His mouth dropped open.

As she watched him walk away, anger and sadness twisted her up inside. If only she could dare to accept someone's kindness, let someone come close to her. At that moment, Chelsea became painfully aware that the walls she'd put up to protect herself had become a prison.

Chelsea rushed out of the line-up and sprinted towards him. "Hey. Wait! I'm sorry."

He smiled.

She had taken the gloves. "Thanks. My name's Chelsea. Wanna wait in line with me?"

The memory made Chelsea ache inside. Brian had taken care of her, had shown her how to survive on the streets. He was the only man she'd shared her body with that she'd trusted. And now he was gone, shot in the head because he'd caught a fever.

"We can't let him make the rest of us sick," they'd said. That happened after The Scorching, while people struggled to survive below the city streets, in the metro stations and tunnels.

She'd fled to the streets above, feeling powerless and hating herself for it. She had roared, wept, screamed, and begged whatever was out there—God, the universe, the devil, she didn't care—to give her the power to repay them, all of them for what they'd done to her, to him.

Now, as Chelsea grew faint from blood loss, she looked away from the mouth clamped on her wrist. She heard someone groan. Before she could register it as her own voice, she slipped back into her Place of No-Hurt.

She holds a rifle. She fires it at the man who shot Brian. The bullet takes off half his head, spraying skull fragments and grey brain into the air. But in this fantasy, he does not die. Blood washes over what remains of his face. He begs her to stop. She aims at his stomach, fires. Guts splatter. But in this fantasy, he doesn't die. He screams, waving his hands in surrender. The sound of his pain is soothing music to her ears.

She feels a hand—

—patting her cheek, jerking her out of her fantasy.

Chelsea opened her eyes and took in the Offish-people, their strange faces highlighted by the glow of the torches, and creased with flickering shadows. She was in an armchair. The same woman she'd seen outside sat opposite, patting her cheek. Chelsea waved the hand away.

"Wake up, sugar," the woman said.

"I'm awake, I'm awake!"

Chelsea saw the bracelet, still on her wrist. A cloth was tied below it, serving as a bandage. The blood had been washed away.

She looked at the woman. What she'd imagined to be a long coat was actually a pair of wings, thickly webbed with veins, and attached to the hooked thumbs. Chelsea thought of a bat. A *vampire* bat.

"I know what you are," Chelsea murmured.

"Do you now, Sweetie?" asked the woman. She tilted her head, smiling, but her eyes stared coldly.

"You're the Offish-people."

The woman arched an eyebrow. "What?"

Chelsea thought, *Let her be confused.*

"Desmond," the woman said, "get her some water."

A moment later, the same man who'd knocked her unconscious held a cup to her mouth. Chelsea finished the water in one gulp.

Offering her hand, the woman said, "My name is Jessica. And yours?"

"Chelsea." She looked at Jessica's hand with a mix of horror and disdain and didn't take it. Jessica withdrew it.

"Fine. Let's get down to business. As you've probably already guessed, we're a colony of vampires. The way we work is, we hibernate for twenty years, then hunt and feed for one. We don't have to do this. We chose to when your kind began hunting us back. We're a young colony, most of us less than two-hundred years old. We've followed this pattern for all that time. When we woke up yesterday, though, we encountered a problem."

Yeah, I bet you encountered a problem, Chelsea thought. *A big fucking problem.*

Chelsea tried to hear Jessica's think-voice. It was no use. Though she felt much better than the last two times she'd awoken, she lacked the strength to tune in. She figured she was too weak from the blood they took. "I guess you didn't hear about The Scorching?"

Jessica's cold stare remained unchanged. She clapped her hands together in a let's-get-started manner. "Now, this is exactly what we need from you, Chelsea. Information. So please, tell us about The Scorching."

"How come you never asked anyone bef—?"

"Why we do things isn't your concern," Jessica scowled, and leaned forward into Chelsea's space. "When we awaken, our first priority is taking care of the weakest in our colony. That answer's free. Any more questions you want to waste my time with?"

Chelsea thought of the reason Brian had been shot. She compared that to the vampires' priorities. Though she felt a chasm between herself and them, she also felt a reluctant respect.

"The Scorching, that's when an asteroid hit Earth. Before it struck, the news said it might be coming. Most people thought it would be a false alarm. Nobody was prepared."

"So, how come you're still alive?" Jessica asked.

"Some of us got some supplies together and went under the streets, into the Metro stations and tunnels."

"We've been down there. There are only bodies."

"A lot of people died from radiation, and starvation. A lot were murdered. Like my boyfriend."

Jessica leaned forward. "Help us find them."

"Why should I help you?"

"What choice do you have?"

"I'm not afraid to die."

"Who says we'll kill you? We can do a lot worse than that. In two-hundred years, we've had a lot of practice making people suffer."

Chelsea's will hardened. Suffering didn't frighten her. Suffering defined her. "You're gonna have to do better than that if you wanna scare me."

Jessica's hands balled into fists.

"Want my help? Fine. There's something you gotta do for me."

Jessica gave a tight-lipped smile. "You're hardly in a position to negotiate."

"Make me one of you," Chelsea blurted out. "Turn me."

Jessica threw her head back and laughed. "You think you can handle immortality? Once you realize you can't be in the sun, that you can't contact loved ones anymore if you want the colony's protection, you'll commit suicide like most of the ones we turn."

"I have no friends or family. And I hate this world and the people in it. They're selfish. They're *evil*. If I would've had your power—"

Jessica raised a hand. "Okay, okay, enough. If we turn you, you'll help us?"

"Yes."

"If you don't help us, or if you create problems, you'll be killed for treason. I'll cut your head off myself."

Murmurs and nods of approval.

"So," Chelsea asked, "how does it work? Does someone have to bite me?" Chelsea tilted her head to expose her neck.

The group burst into laughter. At that moment, her confidence shriveled. There was a fierceness, a *knowingness* in that laughter.

"No Sweetie," Jessica said, setting her hand on Chelsea's thigh, "that's not how we turn you. You've watched too many movies. And a Vampire 101 lesson for ya—we're not mind readers, and stakes through the heart don't work."

You aren't mind readers, Chelsea thought, *but I am.*

"Then what do you do? Or...is it something I have to do?"

Jessica stroked Chelsea's thigh and gazed into her eyes. "For you to become a vampire, one of us has to impart to you their being. Make himself one with you."

Chelsea's face scrunched up. "I don't get it."

More laughter.

"Sex, sweetie," Jessica said, her hand stroking slowly and sensuously now. "One of us must have sex with you." She waved her hand and the one that had knocked Chelsea out came over. "Desmond, please oblige the girl."

At the word *sex*, Chelsea felt like a trapdoor had opened beneath her. A falling sensation filled her chest and she found it hard to breath.

Desmond rushed forward. He seized her by the throat and shoved her to the floor. Pain exploded in her skull. He straddled her, knocked the air from her lungs. Chelsea struggled, twisted her body, clawed at his hand.

Finally, she realized he'd been still the whole time, patiently waiting for her surrender. Up close she could feel his hot breath. His piercing stare filled her with dread.

He spread her legs and the reality of what was happening crashed down on her like water breaking through a dam. It drowned her mind, soaking her thoughts with bloated images and Desmond's features turned into her father's.

A scream welled inside her. He pressed a hand to her mouth. She steeled herself as he seized a handful of denim and tore. One pant leg came off with a quick, dry raspy sound. Goosebumps prickled her leg as her body trembled. Her throat constricted. And tears gushed from her eyes. He snatched the crotch of her panties and ripped them off too.

"You're such a brave, brave girl," Desmond said. It sounded as if there were two voices speaking through the same throat—the above voice a normal person, the underneath voice composed of millions of swarming, skittering insects.

His eyes changed. The irises spread like ink stains until there was only blackness.

His face changed too, blanching, then webbing with purple veins. Features reshaped themselves as seamlessly as liquid metal—his face elongated, extending his eyelids to droop like hound dog eyes; his nose flattened into double-slits on wrinkled flesh; a snout emerged, as if molded by invisible hands; lips blackened, stretched up to the ears and fangs, dripping with saliva, sprouted from his gums. She realized that the offish features were a disguise for his true form: *vampire bat.*

He roared. That skittering insect sound became the top-voice. Chelsea now understood humanity's instinctive loathing for insects. The sounds they make—sizzling maggots, chirping crickets, skittering cockroaches, buzzing flies—pronounce the names of demons. These are the creatures that can articulate the names and the voices of the dead.

Chelsea screamed. Her head beat against the floor as she thrashed. Desmond guided himself inside her, writhing and slithering like a snake. The horror plunged her to the rim of madness. If her father had shattered her, then this undead thing was grinding what remained of her soul to dust.

He clutched her head and forced her to stare into his black eyes. His mouth opened and his red tongue, tapered to a point, slid out, stretching longer and longer until its slimy wetness touched her face.

He grabbed her hair and jerked her head forward so she could see her belly.

She screamed, *"NO! NO! NO! GET IT OUT OF ME!"*

She saw her stomach distort. She screamed for oblivion, desperate to un-see, to un-know, unable to do so.

In her mind she raced towards The Place of No-Hurt. Where was it? She couldn't find it!

The colony of vampires gathered around them in a circle chanting, their voices rising, becoming one, the howl of a demon. They were chanting a name of the dead. *Her* name!

She awoke changed. She was filled with a power that had eluded her. Until now.

In the wide, torch-lit chamber, the new Chelsea propped herself up on her elbows. Desmond no longer seemed a monster to her. She felt a strange kinship with him now.

The friendship bracelet was lying on the floor, a broken chain that released her from her former life.

Desmond knelt before her, spoke to her in tender tones. "I must feed you. You're weak because you're young. Soon you'll have the power to hunt on your own. I'll teach you how. Colony law says if you turn someone, you become their protector."

"You were so fierce. You hardly seemed—"

Desmond put a finger gently on her mouth, silencing her. "Shh. You're weak. You need your strength. I was fierce because you were my prey. I was a hawk staring into the eyes of a rabbit. Things are different now."

He put his face over hers. "Here, I must feed you. Look up and open your mouth."

She obeyed.

His jaws opened wide. With a guttural retching sound, blood spilled from his mouth and into hers. Warm and hot and delicious. It coated her mouth and throat and ignited her fragmented soul with a rippling current of black life.

She hungered for the blood. Lusted for it. She moaned and shuddered as she rose up and kissed him hungrily, deeply. They were one now—the same.

She laid her head against his chest and trembling, clutched his body against hers. Clutched him with her new hands, with long taloned thumbs.

She could hear every think-voice in the room. Each one was clear, sharp. None of them had her ability. In fact, when it came to telepathy, they were...

...*blind as bats.*

I'm a new kind of vampire, Chelsea realized, the revelation calming her. *I have more power than any of them, than all of them.*

She considered the desolate landscape of the city and the refugees that hid beneath it, starving, desperate as the vampires that surrounded her now.

The world is mine, she realized. *I will rebuild it.*

I will have revenge.

Born and raised in Northern British Columbia, **David Tocher** now lives in Montreal, Quebec, where he's currently at work on a novel. He appreciates literature which explores the paranormal and the dark side of human nature. He also loves heavy metal music. He is a member of the Horror Writers Association and International Thriller Writers. You can find his recent short story, *Letters from a Dead World,* in the *Dreamspell Nightmares* anthology, published by L & L Dreamspell.

Blood That Burns So Bright
By Jason S. Ridler

Knuckles? What Ned taped together was closer to jagged turtle shells hiding under torn, red calluses. Sakura's hand remained calm and still in his palm while the tape made its long way around.

"You shouldn't have called time out," she said, voice a thin mist in the fetid air. "I had him."

"Deep breaths," Ned said. "Remember to breathe." She complied while he pulled out another a stretch of tape. "Fine, my bad. Make him eat my words when you get back in the cage."

"Tighter," Sakura said, legs dangling over the edge of the ancient massage bench, body still and poised despite the agony. It made Ned's silent heart ache. Chains of sweat dropped from her chin, past her boots, and turned the dirty floor into a fresh mess. Each drop hit with a rusty echo. This was the change room for a slaughterhouse, once upon a time. Fitting, Ned thought.

Down the hall around the killing room floor, the frenzied crowed hungered for the last round.

"You want a little flexibility," Ned said, as the tape made another lap. "So the impact has somewhere to escape besides your wrist. And you need a grip to grapple."

She exhaled hard now, controlling the pain. Crooked fingers flexed like a dying critter. "Thumbs are all I got that work on their own. Tighter."

He chuckled. "Fine. Full mummy treatment, minus the thumbs. You know he'll try a submission now."

The tape did another lap around her tortured hands. "Try and fail."

He forced a smile. Outside the deadbloods howled from the stands as the time-out burned like a fuse. "You should be proud, child. Those boos? That's a kind of cheer. They hate that one of us is getting beaten by one of you. But they love a good fight.

And loud as they boo, the cheers in the Scrum amongst your kind must be shaking the roofs. Turncoats will be having their hands full tonight!"

"Only if I win," she said, chin dripping, voice clearer. "Any bets on that happening?"

He stopped taping. "I never bet on my talent until they win one, so you should feel righteous for making me lose. Sure you don't want to grapple?"

Sakura's glare was steady as a cat's, and just as heartless. He'd hurt her. And it twisted his guts, wishing he'd believed in her then as he did now. "Then make a fist," said Ned.

Trembling, her fingers tried retracting into the knuckle-bombs she'd dropped on every deadblood she'd fought on her short rise toward arena glory, bombs harder than steel, enough to rupture a deadblood's brain stem.

Impossible bombs and speed for a brightblood.

And yet here she was. Still alive, but—

"Ned?" Sakura grunted. Her fingers shook like a dying spider. "I can't—"

"Easy, child."

Slow, strong, and steady, he taped her hand into a boney hammer. The pain had to be cosmic, but she just breathed in and out like a bellows. As he reinforced the tape at the wrist, his finger hovered above her vein. Her pulse shivered like it belonged to a meth head cornered in an alley, heart burning out and melting down at the same damn time.

He cut the stray tape with his thumb nail. "Give me your other hand."

She did. It was worse. God, they'd been pristine last week, when he'd watched her for the first time. Tough and strong, but healthy, like a deadblood fighters after they'd eaten their kills in a mob match.

But not Sakura. She wasn't like Ned, or the elders, or the monster Gregor starving for the last round, or even the chump-ass brightbloods normally torn apart by deadbloods. Whatever she was, she was—

"Ned?"

"Right, right." He began the wrap. Sweat hung off her chin. "Finish some water, but not too much. No sense fighting dry."

"Ned?"

He looked up.

Eighteen, she'd said. Eighteen and now with the face of a career grinder, starved of blood. He wrapped slow, head down. "Don't let him rush you," he said, "but if he does, keep the elbows hammering on the back of the skull, like you did yesterday."

"Who'd you bet on?" Sweat dropped.

"Child, you have two minutes before Gregor tries to eat your spleen while you watch. Focus."

She stole her hand back faster than he could sense it, she was that quick. "Damn it, Ned. Who?" she seethed, chin wet, body vibrating. "Who?"

He straightened the frayed lapels of his red sports coat, brushed the dust and stains off. Damn Wallace for shooting off his big, stupid mouth at the last fight. He knew it would rattle her cage. She needed an angry focus, but not on Ned. And he couldn't lie about it, like he had with Wallace. Just to make everyone feel good. Not again. "Child, either way I lose."

"Coward," she grunted. "You really think I can't take this fangjob out? That it?"

He took the slang-shot. "We wouldn't be here if you couldn't. And that's coming from a fangjob."

She slid off the bench, the white hammers at the end of her arms hung like a gunslinger's pistols. "Then say who you bet on."

Ned pushed his hands tight and down in his coat pockets. "You want to wail on me, spar on my mush, go right ahead, child. You hate us. You have every right to. We're butchers and slave masters and have turned your kind into chattel and chum. That hate has carried you a long way in a short time. From the first moment I saw you in the mob fights to the roar of that crowd out there. Hate's made you who you are. Maybe it will carry you all the way." He shrugged. "Maybe not. Unless you go in packing a little heat."

Sakura stepped back. "Don't even think it."

He ground his teeth. "Listen, child. It won't hurt, I promise."

"Don't say it."

"Just want to help."

The punch drilled him quick as a bullet and nearly shattered his skull. Ned hit the tiled corner like a heap of trash. Deadblood surged and mended the damage. Her gnarled hand snapped out of the tape, gripped his throat, and pushed him against the wall. "Help? You call turning me into a fucking fangjob help?"

He gripped her mangled fingers and squeezed hard.

She dropped his ass and backed up, pain coiling her face as she nursed her hand.

"Idiot move," Ned said. "Like we need to breathe? And if he knows your hand is busted, he'll tear it up like a rat on a bleeding baby."

Her back hit the bench. "Asshole!"

He stood, slow, sure, unthreatening, but his voice trembled. "Damn right, and you know why? Because I'll tell you the truth. Win or lose, you ain't coming out of that fight alive. We both know it."

She hissed.

"However you do what you do, it's being flushed out with every swing. Each fight, each victory, each miracle sucked out a few years here, a few years there. You only got one fight left." Nausea ran through him worse than hunger, one symptom that blood could not cure. "Don't you get it? I'm losing you tonight unless—"

"Ned."

She'd regulated her breathing. Forcing strong breaths in and out. Calm. Cool. Focused as a razor on a wrist. Maybe she'd heard him. "Yeah?"

She spit a pink stained gob on the floor. "You're right. About me…burning out. About the boos. About the cheers in the Scrum. Why they're listening. Because a brightblood is doing the impossible. Fighting back." She swallowed hard. "So this is what's gonna happen." She held out her exposed wrist, tape hanging off. "Ned?"

Ned's tongue rubbed his incisor.

"Tape me up."

His jaw clamped like a nail in soft wood. "Yeah, child."

When it was done, Sakura boxed the air faster than any human could, each swing with the force of a nine-pound hammer cracking into a spike. A buzzer sounded. The crowd's savage roar peaked.

"Time's up," she said.

"Sure is."

Her lip pouted out. "Last question?"

Here, on the wire, his resolve crumbled. He couldn't lie to her about the bet. Not now. "Ok, shoot."

"Why'd you decide to train me?"

He smiled. "I know a sure thing when I see it, child. Now go on. Your fans await."

She snorted, but smiled. And left.

He stood and connected the dots on the mildew-stained walls, sucking in the smell of old blood and the cool air of decay. She needed to walk out alone. When the boos pitched, he strolled to the door, heading for his place in the stands.

The stink of a familiar brightblood halted him, a strange mix of old smoke and wet sugar.

A Turncoat filled the hallway, long, black rain slicker too big for his frame, chewing gum. One arm was folded to make sure his lost appendage was clearly noticed, just as much as the giant pink scar on his neck and the red eye patch. "Howdy, Coach."

Ned removed his fists from his jacket. "You quit smoking, Wallace. Good for you."

The Turncoat chewed. "What was it you used to say? Be harder on yourself than your enemy, and over a thousand battles you'll be victorious. Too bad we both lost that bet, huh?"

"I don't have time to hold your hand down memory lane, Wallace. Get to the point, or get out of my way."

Wallace smiled, still chewing. "Easy, Coach. We need to chat."

"I won't miss this fight."

Wallace chewed. "Afraid the Lords disagree. Feel like you might try and play foul. Best to let the new girl meet her fate her own way." He chewed. "Not yours."

Ned scratched his face, hard. "How long you been listening?"

"Long enough. Trying to turn her before this big mixed-race fight? Jesus, the only reason anyone cares is because she's not one of you. Course, that's also got the Lords worried. Though, I must say, it made me wonder why you never made me this tasty offer. Unlike Ms. Sure Thing here, I sure could have used it."

Ned tightened his fists. "You were good, Wallace. And the day you fought out of the mob, you were great."

Wallace's smile flatlined, Adams apple caressing the pink wound on his neck. "And you're a sucker for a lost cause. I was feed compared to what your cherry bomb can do." He chewed until his smile returned. "Christ, hear that? Those fangjobs want her torn into gristle so fine it sluices through their teeth. You should see the Scrum. Brightbloods hovering over stolen laptops. Waiting. History in the making, they say. Revolution in the air. If she wins."

The boos and screams shook the air, filling the greasy halls and walkways of the old slaughter mill. She must be already in the cage.

"You always talked too damn much," Ned said. "What do you want?"

"Answers."

"Do I look like a fucking library?"

"About her."

"What difference does it make?"

"Lords don't know what she is."

Ned growled. "Bullshit. They tested her, prodded her, damn near committed her before agreeing she could fight our kind. All results came back. She's human."

"Bullshit." Wallace spat juice with his words. "We can't do what she does. If we could, you and every fangjob would be shrieking back to the dark side of the Balkans or wherever the fuck you came from."

"Jersey."

Wallace snorted, cheeks chubby, gum juice on his wet lip. "Funny man, that's our Coach Diamond. See, I think I know what she is. And why you're protecting her like a mother hen."

The crowd cheered and Ned wanted to die.

Wallace spat out his gum, peeled off the silver foil wrapper on a new piece, and shoved it into his mouth. After three long chews, a word fell out. "Bastard." He chewed hard, swallowing the juices. "Mutant, half-breed bastard."

Ned bristled, and a deeper pit opened in his stomach. "We can't carry your brood. And your kind die if they carry ours. Along with the babies." So all that's left is the daddy, alone and wounded and crushed with eternal memories of their passing as fresh as they day it happened, memories like a demon shackled to his heels. "It's impossible."

Wallace smiled, wet and big. "Ain't evolution a bitch, Coach? Try something a zillion times and all you get are dead, dead, babies. And then, one day, someone else tries it and… bang!" The word snapped out, wet and sharp. "Mutation! And a new happy family. Too bad the Lords don't like change."

Ned licked the sharp edge of his teeth. "No. She's just a kid. Just a kid from the Scrum."

Wallace shrugged. "You're a worse liar now than when I was your protégé, Coach. But fine, suck on the tit of denial if you want. Whatever she is, she's coming with me when the fight is done. I got a feeling that her blood work and heart look a little bit different than last week. Going to need a whole new set of tests."

"Only if she lives."

"Oh, she will. Gregor's playing ball. Going to knock her out cold. He's got enough chemical in his system to take on a hundred magic mutant girls. She's got a better chance of shooting eleven the hard way than winning, let alone dying. And you're coming too, Ned. We'll just be one happy family."

The crowd roared. She was losing.

Ned bowed his head in surrender, but the hands in his pockets were fists. "Then what harm is there in letting me see her fight?"

"You always said I got a soft heart, Coach. Might break it to watch you lose some replacement for a half-cast, still-born daughter."

Wallace's last word choked as Ned drove his fist into his solar plexus and his teeth through Wallace's neck. The Turncoat's death-gurgle was absorbed by the wail of the crowd. Sugar tainted the wet red rush into Ned's mouth, but he ate until Wallace defecated in his pants and expired in Ned's arms. He shoved the soiled husk aside as the Turncoat's heart link beeped.

Kill a Turncoat, Ned knew, they send in the Blackcoats. And even deadbloods never saw them coming.

He had seconds.

In the stands among the howling throng, louder than any alarm bells or whistles, legions of fans stood with arms in V formation as their hero stalked Sakura. She was broken, on her knees, swooning like a willow stalk. Her bandages were torn, ugly knuckles exposed.

"Come on, Child!"

Gregor wiped his sparkling ruby fist across his mouth, long and slow, licking every finger while the crowd ate it up.

"Sakura!" A black hand of steel clamped Ned's mouth while others gripped his arms.

The crowd's attention steered toward him. Their voices hushed to a hiss for the interruption. From the bottom of the pit, Gregor looked and laughed. He gripped Sakura's neck, turned her head to see Ned before waltzing around her for a choke. Her swollen, bloody eyes barely opened.

Ned ate through the hand on his mouth and it snapped away for a beat, long enough for him to suck in air and shout. "I bet everything on you!"

Everything tightened. Cold sizzles burned through his back and danced like barbed static across his eyes...but he kept them open, thanks to the fresh blood in his guts...the world slowed and silenced until all that Ned heard was the thud of a courageous heart, strong, fierce, and defiant.

Sakura still stared at him. She smiled, and snapped out her thumbs. Bullet quick, she drove them behind her and into Gregor's eyes.

Yes!

Gregor, hands on face, stumbled blind as Sakura rose from the bloody ground. Quickly, she wrapped her fist into a mangled morning star, knuckles big and rotten, and went to work.

Stars popped against the growing black in Ned's eyes, as Sakura's heartbeat slowed, racing toward its final thrum: elbows to the neck, kicks to the back of his skull, softening him up like an ax on an old tree until Gregor's neck was ripe...then a gasp, a stumble.

Breathe, child, he thought, head swimming with memories of a back-alley delivery room, and the breathless faces of a mother and daughter, still as the night, heartbeats lost...she never even got to, the tiny thing never got a chance to—

"Breathe!"

Sakura inhaled hard, the beats slowed, but her form was perfect—

The morning-star-fist launched, and a dying girl screamed with her last heartbeat. Gregor's head landed six feet from his body, but all Ned could feel was Sakura's heart burst, her body crumble, her pulse whisper to silence.

Pain engulfed Ned, a sliver of what was to come. But it couldn't shake the fresh memory of Sakura at her best, doing what she was born to do, and the spark she'd lit in the dark places of this world. A memory worth dying for.

Jason S. Ridler has published over thirty short stories in such magazines and anthologies as *Brain Harvest, Not One of Us, Chilling Tales, Tesseracts Thirteen,* and others. A former punk rock musician and cemetery groundskeeper, Mr. Ridler holds a Ph.D. in War Studies from the Royal Military College of Canada. About his story, he says, "'Blood that Burns so Bright' was inspired by the Joe Louis/Max Schmeling boxing matches of the 1930s, and how a single fight can encapsulate a moment and time of great importance. Plus, I'm a sucker for an underdog story. And who would be more of an underdog than a human fighter in a vampire fight circuit?"

Survival of the Fittest
By Leanne Tremblay

It took Kara Morales more than two hours to slow her breathing. Only then did she try to wipe the blood off. Killing Angeline had been surprisingly easy.

At first, she had sat on the floor beside the body, mesmerized. A cavity the size of a fist yawned in the chest. The pooled blood beneath the body had begun as red but had since turned black. Kara touched the tip of her tongue to the droplets adorning her wrist like a bracelet. Salty. Hesitating, she licked the rest of the blood off her arms and fingers and sucked at the matter congealed under her nails.

At some point during the afternoon, she left her office and activated the cleansing system. Thirty minutes later, she re-entered in fresh clothes. Her office, sterilized and lightly scented, showed no trace of blood. Looking at the body annoyed Kara, even though it had been scrubbed white as a china doll. She lifted it under the shoulders and dragged it out of sight behind her desk. The monitor blinked the time, just past four o'clock in the afternoon. Two hours until sunset. For now, she had to remain where she was, sealed inside the Institute. She'd just have to wait.

Kara's first surprise had been seeing Angeline in the examination chamber when she arrived at the lab. The woman had been laughing, sharing a joke with a figure already seated at a small metal table in the centre of the room.

"Angeline, what are you doing here?" asked Kara sharply. The woman's interference in her research was becoming endemic; always sniffing around. Kara put it down to a morbid curiosity in the research subjects. Homo sapiens were short, cowering creatures, dirty, malnourished and infested with parasites. She assumed Angeline wanted the thrill of proximity so she could pass along scintillating tales to her friends.

Secretly, Kara despised the woman's classic Vamparian looks: tall, pale, sharp features, red lips, perfect skin. She was the pretty, public face of the Institute, the PR voice that soothed and cajoled. Kara may not have inherited beauty but she did inherit the mind, the historic bloodline. That's what mattered.

"Kara, there you are! Charlie and I were wondering where you'd gotten to." Her canines flashed, the ridiculous diamond chips embedded in them winking under the fluorescents.

Charlie? Who? Confused, Kara blinked several times and halted mid-step.

"Ah, hello. That would be me," said the subject, getting up from his chair. He rounded the table in a few long strides and offered his hand. "Charlie Koop." He smiled.

Charlie—the second surprise.

Dazed, she took his hand automatically. Lord, he was warm! Even through gloves, her hand sucked up the heat from his fingers and an unfamiliar wave of perspiration pricked her skin.

Civilized social behavior, coherent speech—what form of Homo sapien was this?

Kara cleared her throat, hiding her unease. "Hello...I'm *Doctor* Morales. I run the Sapiens Outreach program."

"I was just telling Charlie about the Institute's mandate for hominid species preservation," said Angeline.

"What a relief," he quipped, smiling at Angeline, who'd hitched herself onto the edge of the table, letting one long leg dangle.

He turned back to Kara and frowned slightly. "You okay, Dr. Morales?" Standing at full height, he was as tall as any Vamparian male, but his face, brown and smooth as glass, betrayed a different ancestry. He was dressed oddly, in a high necked tunic made from some kind of dull brown fiber. His hair, so blonde it was nearly white, fell softly to his shoulders. With his height and healthy build, he could almost pass as Vamparian, if it wasn't for his skin. Burnished gold. Like sunshine, she imagined.

Flustered, she fumbled with her recording tablet. "Yes, um, I'm fine. I'm sorry, but where do you—"

"I live in a community about a hundred miles outside New Chicago."

Kara nearly choked. A hundred miles outside the Net? No one had lived that far from a Net city in centuries. "But the atmosphere... the heat during the day would... So, there are more like you?"

Charlie laughed easily. "Sure. We don't all live under rocks."

"But that's impossible!" she spluttered. This had to be a joke. Sapiens in the New World lived individually, not in groups. In fact, as a species they were becoming hard to find, hence her Outreach program. Her brain scrambled to assemble the possibilities. An entire community within a hundred miles of the Institute? If Koop was telling the truth, then she'd made the discovery of a lifetime.

"Isn't it just so lucky that we found Charlie," Angeline said, interrupting her thoughts, "before some nasty race mongers got their hands on him."

Starting, Kara looked at her and blanched, the threat underlying her statement all too clear. Angeline had no intention of letting her keep this discovery to herself. Kara sucked in her breath and gripped the recording tablet, her knuckles whiter than usual. She still hadn't turned it on. Charlie was unlike other Homo Sapien she'd ever encountered. She couldn't, *wouldn't* lose this opportunity.

Ignoring the smug look on Angeline's face, she tapped the tablet to activate it and gestured towards the chair. "I'd be interested in hearing more about your community," she said.

He smiled and sat, folding his hands loosely on his lap.

Kara drummed her fingers on the desk, keeping time with the flashing clock on the monitor. She thought it surprising how little she remembered of their conversation, although she and Charlie talked for at least an hour. She had a vague recollection of Angeline leaving during the interview, probably bored. The thought pleased her. One thing she did recall was telling Charlie about her father. Had he asked her about him? He must have—everybody did. Her father had been over four hundred years old when he finally died. She'd only met him a handful of times. The last time, he grabbed her chin, his yellow nails digging into her jaw, and forced her mouth open. Squinting, his rancid breath blowing up her nostrils, he ran a dirty thumb over her canines. They were like child fangs, no more than blunted points compared to the elegantly-tapered dentition of the devotees clustered around the sickbed. "Throwback!" he'd barked, and shoved her away. She never saw him again.

Kara glanced at the hole in the body where Angeline's heart had been. She studied the secondary and less obvious wounds, including deep slashes at the throat. She wondered suddenly if her father would have been proud of her. "Genetic throwback, my ass!" she snapped, swiveling back to the monitor.

Twenty more minutes. She inhaled, letting scented air fill her lungs, and ran her tongue over the enamel on her teeth. For the first time, her head felt scoured clean. All this from the taste of blood.

She considered the small bronze bust on her desk. Lord Darwin, the Father of evolutionary science, bald except for a bushy beard and hint of teeth barely visible below his moustache. In all his works, beginning with *Transmutation of Species,* he said the consumption of human blood was nothing more than a cannibal fantasy—a myth about bloodsucking monsters created by Homo sapiens because their species was failing.

Kara imagined Darwin fuming about it, striding across the lecture hall, spittle caught in his beard, eyes blazing. It's not a need for blood, he'd shout, that elevates Homo vamparians above their less evolved cousins, but plasma proteins. A superior food source, easy to manufacture in even the simplest lab. Blood was, well, crude.

But, she didn't feel barbaric. If anything, she felt stronger, healthier. She flexed her arm, feeling individual muscles lengthen and contract, and cocked her eyebrow at the bronze head. Could Darwin have been wrong?

She shook her head to clear it. No. She knew all his precepts by heart, drummed into her head before she could read. Darwin predicted that man in the near future, as measured in centuries, not millennia, would be a more perfect species. The failure of Homo sapiens and the ascension of Homo vamparians proved him right.

A low tone followed by rhythmic clicking snapped Kara's attention to the sealed windows. The shades began rising and moonlight flooded the office. Finally! She grabbed her recording tablet and pushed her chair back, bumping the body.

In the end, Charlie had made the offer to her, not Angeline. The study of this Homo sapiens community was just the beginning, she could feel it—the next important scientific landmark perhaps as heralded as the work of the venerable old man himself. Her name would be recorded in Vamparian history. It was her right. Her heritage. No one would remember Angeline.

As promised, Charlie picked her up in front of the Institute right on time in a black, two-seat rover. "You look a little, pale—" Charlie began, and then laughed. "But then again, all Vamparians look pale to me. Sorry. Everything okay?"

"Yes, fine."

"You'll need to use your palm chip to get us out of the Net. You know that, right?" He regarded her with interest.

Kara turned over her palm and rubbed the silver disk embedded in it with her thumb. A green pinlight pulsed gently in its center. She nodded.

At the checkpoint, a guard stared at Charlie and asked to see his chip. Before he could answer, Kara leaned across and explained that Charlie was one of her research subjects. She smiled, hoping she looked reassuring, and waved her palm at the sensor. The guard peered at the data coming up on his screen and scrunched up his face.

"Dr. Morales? Is everything all right here, ma'am?"

"Yes, fine, thank you."

"Okay, but be back before 0600. Sunrise is 0632."

She nodded at him but the guard continued to glare at Charlie.

"Absolutely. 0600," said Charlie.

The guard hesitated. Kara could tell he was thinking about giving Charlie a hard time, but then he waved them through. The rover eased into the tunnel. In seconds they were through the Net and travelling in the desert.

They made good time on the expressway, heading due west, straight as an arrow. Behind them, the gold dimpled bubble hovering over the city gradually receded and eventually disappeared from view. Without the Net's protective web, the moon, stars, and terrain appeared in unaccustomed focus; sharp, clean, and visceral. Fascinated, Kara held her breath, watching the landscape slip by, until she realized he'd asked her a question.

"Um, I'm sorry, what was that?"

"I said I was curious about your colleague, Angeline. Do you work together on this project?" asked Charlie.

"No! I mean, she's not a scientist. She works in public relations, recruitment, that sort of thing." The image of Angeline bent over the touch screen on her desk appeared suddenly in her mind, sending a pulse of adrenaline through her system.

Angeline had been trolling her office when Kara returned from the lab.

"What are you doing?" Kara stopped short in the doorway, her voice unnaturally high.

"Oh Kara, there you are." Angeline straightened and dropped her hands to her sides. "I've been looking everywhere for you." Again the smile. She came out from behind the desk.

"Is there something I can do for you?" asked Kara, consciously lowering her voice but keeping it even. Her eyes darted to the screen but she remained planted in the doorway.

"Yes, well. Oh, this is embarrassing." Angeline offered a tiny laugh and smoothed the front of her coat. "Just today, I was thinking that maybe this Sapiens Outreach project of yours deserves more resources. The Institute could benefit from the publicity. And Mr. Koop would be an ideal Homo sapiens specimen—I mean, just *look* at him. And your study would benefit too, of course."

"I see," said Kara slowly. Her body had gone rigid.

"Come on now Kara, you can't keep him all to yourself." Angeline winked and moved sideways to step around her. Kara didn't flinch.

Angeline frowned, the smoothness of her face momentarily distorted. She shifted her weight to the other hip. "Dr. Morales, let me remind you that your funding is coming up for review. The Director is ready to reassign resources. No one wants to pay for studies of under-evolved species, but you do things my way, and maybe I can change his mind."

"Charlie Koop is not under-evolved," snapped Kara.

"True." Angeline tapped her chin with her finger. "But, as far as the public is concerned, sapiens had their chance." She crossed her arms. "We weren't the ones who burned the ozone all to hell. We survived, they didn't. End of story. Besides," her voice turned silky, "sometimes family connections only get you so far. I'm throwing you a lifeline here."

"I don't need a lifeline from you, or a lecture on Vamparian science." Kara retorted. "Charlie is something different, something I…we…haven't seen before. If there are more like him, they have to be properly studied."

"Okay, let's say you're right," Angeline plucked at imaginary strands on her sleeve, "which is why the Institute needs transparency, Kara. The public wants, no, they *need* to know about our discovery. They'll want to see that we are handling the situation effectively, and that Charlie and his friends are carefully managed."

"By you?"

"If you like." Angeline looked smug. "The proposal to the Director is done anyway. I just needed a few more details," she gestured behind her at Kara's computer. "He should be pleased.

Don't worry, I'll make sure he keeps you on. Somebody has to count genes, or whatever it is you do."

Kara felt her cheeks burn. If Angeline wanted her share of glory, fine, but not by turning the research into some kind of freak show. Kara's eyes cast wildly about the room. She didn't want strings attached. To hell with funding. Charlie was her moment, not Angeline's.

Sensing her distress, Angeline tossed her hair and sneered. "What, Kara? Afraid of sharing? I'm not surprised. Like father, like daughter." She grinned maliciously. "I heard he was a bit of a control freak. Rumor has it he complained about siring a throwback or two."

Kara's vision bled white.

A different voice—male—penetrated her consciousness and the image of Angeline wavered. "Kara, are you all right? Seriously, what's wrong?"

Kara turned her head and Charlie's concerned face came into focus. Opening her eyes wide, she found herself leaning far forward, almost doubled over, all ten fingers digging into the dashboard. Gulping, she collapsed back into the seat and turned her head towards the window. Her chin and sweater at the neckline were soaked with saliva. Hastily, Kara rubbed her mouth with her sleeve and concentrated on breathing normally.

"Sorry Charlie. I'm fine," she stammered.

"Okay," he sounded doubtful. "Well, anyway, we're almost there. Then, we can get you something to drink."

The flats had given way to rolling hills, dotted with short thick-needled trees. The road, holed and littered with stones, wrapped around the base of a hill. When had they pulled off the expressway? Bewildered, Kara swiveled her head around.

"Where are we? Where is your place?"

Charlie brought the rover to a stop. "There. Don't you see it?" He got out and began walking towards the hill.

Disoriented, Kara stepped out of the rover and gasped, nearly falling. The heat of the unshielded environment took her breath away. Until now, she'd always been protected from a landscape that never completely cooled from the scorching it received every twelve hours.

Up ahead, Charlie waited for her. Behind him squatted a collection of dome-shaped dwellings arranged in two circles.

"Welcome to Saturna," he said when she reached him.

The rest of the night passed like a dream. Over the next few hours, the members of Saturna emerged from their homes, both males and females, each just as bronzed as Charlie. They submitted agreeably to her greedy rush of questions. How did they live? Where had they come from? What about their parents? What about water, food, waste...?

"Hold it, enough. I give up!" laughed Charlie at one point, raising his hands in surrender. They were seated inside the largest building at a long table covered with cloth.

"But, how...how do you survive out here? The heat..." Kara asked.

Charlie shrugged. "You tell me, you're the scientist. The heat doesn't bother us."

"But the UV—"

"Isn't an issue," interrupted a woman named Lola. She looked roughly the same age as Charlie and dressed in the same dull brown garb. Her hair was dark, though, like Kara's. Both hands were bandaged up to the elbow, which seemed strange, but Kara noticed others at the table bearing similar injuries.

Before she could ask about it, Lola continued. "Well, I should say, the UV's not as much of an issue. UV-C can cause just as much damage to our DNA as yours if we're not careful. We've just learned to...adapt when necessary, and now we're adapted at the cellular level." Her eyes flicked to Charlie. "But as for the rest of it—UV-A, UV-B—our skin doesn't burn like yours."

Stunned, Kara's mind reeled from the possibilities. How had Vamparian geneticists missed this development in Homo sapiens physiology? Before she had time to sort out the implications, platters of food appeared. Tentatively, she lifted a piece of something white and moist to her lips, first smelling then touching it with the tip of her tongue. Meat? She'd never tasted anything like it. Was this real protein, she wanted to know? Where did it come from?

Charlie winked and wouldn't answer. "Some secrets are worth keeping, Kara. But the wine's Vamparian. You'll find it more to your...taste, I think. Here," he reached over and filled her glass. Kara took a sip and relaxed, feeling the familiar blend of synthetic proteins slide down her throat. All this, she thought looking around, was almost too much to process at once.

After dinner, Lola took Kara's hand and examined her palm. "Let me see your chip. You must be at least Level 9?" Startled, Kara watched Lola press down gently on the implant and cover it with her thumb. The green glow of the pinlight showed through her fingernail.

Kara swallowed another sip of wine. "Uh, no. I'm Level 8. Level 10 is the highest." Charlie and Lola exchanged glances.

Thinking they doubted her, Kara blurted, "But, Level 8 is actually quite good. I have access to almost all Institute data collected since 1859." Her voice ran on, gathering momentum. In the six hundred years since Darwin, she told them, the Institute had sequenced hundreds of millions of genomes, genetic information of practically every species. She had access to it all, including rare clearance to travel between Net cities.

"That's impressive. I think your father would have been proud," said Charlie softly. Her father? Kara squinted at him. She was beginning to feel hazy. Yes, she thought she remembered telling him about her father, but wasn't it something unpleasant? She couldn't think clearly. She looked down at her palm. The green pinlight continued to pulse comfortably, but beside it, another tiny light shone a steady red. Kara frowned, her brain slurry. There was something important about red, a signal for...

"Wait. I can't..." she mumbled, "...something's wrong..."

Lola laughed. "Then no more wine for you. Come."

Before Kara could protest further, Charlie and Lola had taken her by the elbows and were leading her to the open area in the center of the ring of dwellings. They let go of her and she swayed. The wine? Was there something in the wine?

Charlie removed his shirt. He paused, smiled at her, and then stripped naked. Lola did the same. Kara's eyes widened as the other members of Saturna also took off all their clothing.

Kara laughed nervously. "I hope you don't expect me to do that."

"No, that won't be necessary." Lola's voice had lost its earlier friendliness. Kara felt a pang of warning run through her. There was something wrong here and her breathing quickened, while her brain fumbled to make sense of it.

"We recharge our bodies in full sun each day," Charlie explained. "We find dawn works best."

Dawn? Kara stumbled towards the edge of the circle. Wait. "What time was it? How long have I been out here?" Panic seized her. "It's sunrise? No, that can't be, Charlie you have to take me back. I have to go back *now!*"

Tightness built in her chest, a vice squeezing the air out. Gasping, she whirled in a circle, and then made an awkward charge towards the ring of naked bodies. Hands pushed her firmly back into the centre.

By now, the sky had lightened enough to turn the stars into weak beacons. Even the moon looked feeble. With each breath, she felt the temperature jump. The sweat forming on her face and arms evaporated as quickly as it appeared. Moisture fled her body, the air seared her lungs. Kara's eyes, burning in their sockets, scraped dry against her lids.

She turned to Lola, beseeching. "What are you doing? Help me, please." She grabbed her arm but Lola jerked away.

Lola turned to another man who carried a large metal case into the circle. "Quickly, it's almost time."

Dumbfounded, Kara watched while they lay Lola carefully on the ground and removed the bandages from her arms. On her upturned palms, Kara could now see deep, angry red cuts. The man knelt beside her and from the case withdrew a needle and vial. He wasted no time and injected her, rendering her unconscious in seconds. Charlie too knelt and with practiced ease, took a sickle-shaped blade and sliced open Lola's palm in two swift strokes, carving a bloody 'X'.

"What are you doing to her?" choked Kara, her heart beating painfully against her throat.

"Preparing her hand for the imbedding," said Charlie evenly. He didn't look up. Quickly, he placed a number of other unrecognizable instruments on the ground beside Lola's unconscious form. "The transfer of the chip must happen at the moment of incineration or else the Net believes the primary carrier is deceased and immediately deactivates it. It's why we couldn't just kill you earlier and take it." He said this with calm, matter-of-fact assurance.

Kara stumbled backwards, shaking her head, her voice a cracked whimper. "No, no, no..." This couldn't be happening.

"We've had a few near successes, but this time we're confident we've resolved all our past problems. With your chip and security clearance, we should have no trouble bringing down the Net. Then, we purge and repopulate. Genetic recombination of all species. Except yours, of course."

"What...what are you talking about?" she sobbed.

"Survival of the fittest, Kara." He stood and faced the east.

Escape. With every ounce of energy she had left, Kara flew towards the edge of the circle. Charlie stepped easily into her path and she slammed into him.

"Charlie, let me go!" She screamed and slapped his chest. When he refused to move, she hit him in the face.

He grabbed her and forced her face towards the distant hills. She didn't want to look, but her lids refused to close, all moisture in them gone. Horrified, she watched the first shard of fire pierce the horizon and a wave of light race down the hills and across the scrubby plain. Her legs gave way. At the moment of impact, her back arched.

Soundless white pain.

She crumpled and black smoking patches, like heat blossoms on paper, danced up her arm. She scrabbled at the ground and tried curling into a ball, but Charlie grabbed her hand and pulled her fingers open, holding her palm to the light. Black spots appeared between her fingers, spreading around her chip and into the meaty flesh of her palm.

"There, there, Kara," Charlie whispered, stroking her hair as it fell out in clumps and turned to ash in his hand. "It'll be over soon. Level 8, you said? Thank you, for that. Truly." He placed his hand on her forehead like a blessing.

The other man worked feverishly on the husk of her outstretched palm. Charlie leaned into her ear just as it curled around itself like a blackened leaf.

"You should know Kara, Darwin was mostly right. How did you say he put it? Ah yes: man in the distant future will be a far more perfect creature. But he was also wrong. What Darwin—your father—and all Vamparians failed to realize is, he was talking about...us."

Leanne Tremblay is a new writer of fantasy for children and teens. So far, the fanged undead have rarely made an appearance in her tales, but that could change. "Survival of the Fittest" is her first published story. She was inspired by the idea that history is largely written by the victors, not the vanquished. A graduate of the University of British Columbia and a long-time technical writer, she lives with her husband and two boys in a little seaside town near Vancouver, BC.

The Faith of Burning Glass
By Steve Vernon

I see the bottle glint in the distance long before I can ever hope to be sure.

I know it is out there.

That's what faith is all about.

Ask any television evangelist.

Not that there are many evangelists around these days. As far as I know they've all died and gone to heaven. I expect when the first big fire-blast hit the state, they clapped their hands together and peed their pants for joy. Cinder-fried into ashy cre-mains, one blessed-out, pissed-out rapture to go.

As for me, I'm burned dry.

My throat is parched like a two hundred mile crawl through a desert of pan-fried deep-salted squid. I see that glimmer up ahead. I see it reflect in the burning sunlight—tantalizing, transient, the wink of melting diamond.

I smell it.

I followed that glint of unbroken glass. It wasn't much as vectors went, but in this Gehanna-painted desert, it's a lot better than nothing at all.

The world has parched itself.

The world has smoked down like an ant under a burning glass.

How did it happen?

You could blame the nukes, but only in the round-about way that you would have blamed a zealous fireman for kicking down your burning door. The world was ready for desiccation long before the flying atoms ever got to it.

We did it to ourselves.

We emptied the sky. We poured it out like the last drop of cheap wine. That deodorized confidence that kept the earth safe, the Colgate shield that surrounded us, the ozone that distanced the earth from the sun's blind rape had swallowed itself down into nothing, leaving us naked to the burning eye of fate.

Bottles and cans and spray cylinders. We wrapped it all into neat double shrunk packages, everything but the world itself. Now it's all gone. Drained.

I understand this because of what I am.

A vampire.

I know what you read. I know what you saw in the movies. I know how you think we are so damned vulnerable. Sunlight will kill us. Garlic will kill us. Silver will kill us. Bible camp will kill us.

Forget that foolish prattle.

There is no race of vampires.

As far as I know, I am unique.

Alone.

I kept to the shadows for centuries—but now the shadows are burned away and I must walk. The steady beat of my footsteps is the only heartbeat I have.

It is slow going. I walk on sand glazed by heat. I feel each particle fused together like the icing on a funeral cake. The sun pours down on me like a white-hot acid bath. It doesn't kill me but it is damned uncomfortable.

I wish for a bottle of SPF sunscreen three hundred times strong but all I have is my cloak, a tatter quilt sewed from a dozen black "Keep On Trucking" t-shirts.

How's this for a slogan? *I Survived the Apocalypse and All I Got was a Dozen Crummy T-shirts!*

My jacket is leather, homemade, flayed from a biker's burned back. I wear high black riding boots, or they wear me. The damned boots rot to my skin. If I try to peel them off, I'll peel myself down to the bone.

I like my hat.

It's a large black sombrero, stolen from the wreckage of a tacky souvenir shop. The hat makes me think of Eli Wallach, in *The Good, The Bad and The Ugly*.

"Hey Blondie," I croak—a mouthful of razor and scorpion song.

At least I don't sweat. I don't need that kind of teasing, that kind of torment.

But I can't ignore the thirst.

Never mind. I'm focused on the glinting glass.

I am a walking shadow. I need no shade. I am a shambling darkled pocket of nothing, slanting through a wasteland.

Everything is dead.

Even the cacti are roasted dry.

I draw closer. Close enough to really see the burning glass. The light dances and tantalizes like the sharded mirage of a ripe-titted hooch dancer, shaking her naked juices at my sun-parched eye holes.

God, I am thirsty.

I want to lick my lips, but I resist the urge. A flick of my tongue will peel the dried-out membranes raw.

I plow ahead, immersed in the burning quicklime of want and my thirst for a glinting bottle.

What will it be?

A Pepsi?

A Perrier?

And then I see the actual bottle.

I pick it up. It's empty, of course. The black label compliments my pitchy cloak. It's square, like a miniature, transparent coffin.

I recognize the label.

Brother Jack Daniels, the patron saint of sun-parched sinners.

I glance skyward briefly.

"Are you up there, Jack Daniels?"

There is nothing but sunburnt sky. I haven't seen a cloud in a long forever. I slip the bottle into the pocket of my leather jacket.

Carefully.

I don't want to break it.

There is something else out here.

I can smell it.

It takes me two long thirsty days to find where it is hiding.

I count my footsteps, one to a second.

Habit or hobby?

Even the dead need something to do.

Here it is, or the face of it, anyway. A slab of concrete poured across a limestone cliff.

A gun slit.

I smell the life, hidden and cowering within.

"Hey," I call.

My voice surprises me.

"Hey in there."

Nothing.

Whoever is hiding is damned sensible.

They aren't peeking.

Maybe he'll go away, they are thinking. Maybe he's crazy, talking to the rocks. Maybe he doesn't know I'm hiding in here.

"I know you're in there."

I slide my hands over the rock, searching for any sign of a real opening.

"I can smell you."

It feels so good to touch something after acres and acres of nothing but sun and heat and lonely thirst. My fingers revel in the sudden rough gift of texture.

I find nothing.

The camouflage is perfect.

"I've got something for you."

I slide the bottle from my pocket.

Careful, now. It won't do to break the damn thing.

I tap the bottle against the rock. It sounds so loud. I hadn't heard anything for so very long but the wind and my endless lonely footsteps.

"Do you hear that?"

I clink it again, softly, letting the brittle ringing emptiness sound out.

"It's glass."

Clink.

"It's a bottle. Full to the brim. Anything you'd like to drink. Whatever you're thirsty for, that's what it's got."

Clink.

"Can't you hear it? Can't you taste it? That cool kiss of glass on your lips. Aren't you just aching for it?"

Clink.

"Don't you want to drink it? Taste it swilling down, like a laugh in reverse. Don't you want to swallow it right down to the bottom? That's always where the best taste hides, deep in the dregs."

Clink.

"That's what you remember, isn't it? The ease of refrigerators and the sound of ice cubes rattling in a glass. Good things, nothing but good things."

Clink.

"It hasn't all been broken. Not all the windows, and all the glasses, and not all the bottles. All those fine clear things you could see through. Not all of them were lost in that first great shock wave. Not all of them lost in that time of flailing around, throwing buckets of mass extinction at each other, trying to figure out how to kill the sun, not all of those holy transparent dreams were broken."

Clink.

I keep talking.

It might have been an hour.

It might have been a day.

Clink.

I keep talking, praying in the wilderness, until the rock swings open. The man inside the rock pokes his head out slow, like a sleepy turtle.

"Come forth, Lazarus," I husk out dryly.

He wasn't much to look at. Nothing more than a handful of bones and carcinogenized flesh. A desiccant tumor balanced on a fork of twigged legs.

I'm not totally inhuman. I give him time enough for a single croak.

It sounds like he might be saying What, or Where, or maybe Why. Then I bring the bottle down hard against the back of his skull. Bottle against skull. Bits of broken glass imbed in a shattered egg.

Then I use the edge of the broken bottle to open his throat. His flesh is putty soft, and no muscle tone to speak of.

The blood is paler than it ought to be.

But the blood is good.

I drink it down. I drain him dry. I suck each mouthful of salty goodness. I take it all in until my teeth sizzle around nothing but wet air.

I suck until even that dries up.

I let what is left of the man fall. The bones, no longer supported by the cushion of blood, make a rattling shatter as they hit open rock.

"Good," I rasp, enjoying the stolen fluid in my veins.

I close my mouth tight as a tomb. I don't want to lose anything to the wind, the evaporation from heat. I peer into the shadows of the bunker mouth.

It looks good and cool in there.

I could lie down and sleep the centuries away. Maybe the next wave of species that crawl across this parched-out madness might give me a little more sustenance.

I sniff.

Inhale.

Nothing.

I stare at the carcass. How long did he hide? What did he live off? A cache of hidden supplies? A scrapbook of faded paste memories? His family?

It doesn't matter.

He is empty and I am full.

I look at the bottle regretfully. I didn't need to break it. He was weak enough to take without the waste. But somehow there needed to be sacrifice.

Something had to be lost.

I turn from the bunker.

I sniff at the open air.

Nothing.

It doesn't matter. I am full for now. I can keep walking. I'll find something out there, sooner or later. There has to be someone left for me to drink.

But what if there isn't?

It doesn't matter.

I walk—a solitary speck of darkness enduring within a long and parched eternity of light. The bones behind me wash clean in the dust of burning forever.

Far off, long into that lonely gulp of horizon, I see a distant glinting.

I'm coming.

I know it is out there.

Steve Vernon is a Halifax, Nova Scotia writer and storyteller with nearly thirty years experience in the yarn-spinning business. He wrote "The Faith of Burning Glass" while in the heat of ship-in-a-bottle building entrapment. It took rescue teams nearly three hours of environmental lubricant, glass-welding techniques and applied snappy patter to talk Steve out from inside of that bottle. A much-altered version of this story appeared in an ultra-limited thirteen copy edition of his recent dark fiction collection *Do-Overs and Detours* (Dark Region Press). Steve has recently released his very first YA novel, *Sinking Deeper* (Nimbus Publishing), the saga of a young boy, a dying town, a sea monster and a caber toss.

NEW WORLD ORDER

Soulglobe
By John Shirley

"Even death has its fashions," said Tet, chuckling softly as he led Frank and Mella Zand through passage seventy-seven of the catacomb world. Frank thought the remark was pretty flip and insensitive, given that Mella was dying. But pushing his dark-eyed Iraqi wife smoothly along the stone passageway in her float-chair, he kept his peace. He'd promised Mella he'd accept Soulglobe, every last bit of it, including the morbid sense of humor sometimes displayed by its docents.

"*Soulglobe* is fashionable," the docent went on, in his silky voice, "but it will transcend mere fashion, that I promise you!" The docent was a tall, stooped, gray-eyed man, papery pale, with a tumble of curly flaxen hair about his shoulders; he wore a long white robe trimmed in gold and silver filigree; his feet were sheathed in spray-on gold shoes sharply outlining his toes. "This asteroid will survive for millions of years. Those laid to rest here will be safely entombed for all that long time. Memorialized in a work of art."

"I've got to wonder about that term, 'laid to rest'," Frank grumbled. "What with the drift coffins. The Ballet of the Dead..."

Mella glanced over her shoulder at him, her gaunt, reproachful face making his heart ache. Her raven hair had gone thin and white. At thirty-five, she was ten years younger than him—but she looked far older. "Frank...? Please?"

He sighed. "I'm not complaining, Mel. I just..." He couldn't say it. *I just don't want to think about your dead body floating through this place like a speck in a snowglobe.*

They were reaching the end of the passage; the docent, striding ahead, was framed against the semicircular opening into the Great Cavern. As they walked up to him, Frank noticed that the docent's fingernails had been replaced with long, sharp flattened crystals so that his hands sparkled when he gestured.

Why don't his fingernails grow and push the crystals out? Frank wondered. Had the guy gone to all the trouble to get genetically re-engineered for a fingernail effect?

"And here it is," Tet said, with a glittering flutter of his hand.

Frank pushed Mella closer—not too close—to the balcony's edge. They looked out over the great spherical chamber. A cold, fluctuating wind stung his cheeks. The Soulglobe was an asteroid, a nearly perfect sphere a little over a kilometer and a half in diameter. It was a gigantic, transparent bubble of crystal, with encrustations of scab-like rock making a rough mesh around the outside of the bubble; each rocky section was pocked with balconies like theirs. Shafts of light, curiously muted with a faint blueness, angled into the misty, spherical interior and bounced around inside, reflecting from glistening inner surfaces, shifting as the globe slowly rotated. It was difficult to see the stars from within the asteroid but floating close to one of the diamond-shaped transparent sections, an observer could see the distant sun. The sun was Sol; from time to time, in the right conditions, it was said that the planetoid Pluto and the nearby gas giant Neptune were visible as gemlike orbs against velvet black.

Frank shook his head in wonder. "You claim this thing is natural? That crust out there—the mesh pattern looks almost—"

"It does look almost artificial, at times, yes, though one can see the natural patterns of rock if one looks closely," the docent said, in his pompous diction. "We have plans to build artificial copies of this one, when we've reached capacity. Of course, the Soulglobe *could* be an artifact—it was found floating in the asteroid belt, then moved out to this safer location, and there is speculation that the asteroid belt was part of a planet that was destroyed, and that the sphere was a structure on the lost planet, artificial or natural. Personally I think it's a sort of giant geode."

"It reminds me of a Ramadan decoration I had when I was a kid," Mella said, her voice weak. "It was supposed to be a moon. I used to stare into it, imagine what it would be like to be inside it." Her voice was scarcely audible, trailing off when she said, "I feel like I'm inside it here..."

Sounds echoed across the vast interior space of the Soulglobe: a deep hum, rising and falling, the occasional rachitic metal clangor, the sigh of wind and a poignant sound that might be weeping.

The sounds made Frank think of that first battlefield pre-dawn on the terra-formed plains of Mars. He was Sarge for a relief platoon, defending Colony Three; wounded soldiers were calling from the dull red sands of the battlefield; crackly voices in transmissions carried thinly across the plains. The gusting of manufactured air— the artificial atmosphere of Mars—sighed as it lifted wraithlike curtains of red dust. Frank kept his platoon hunkered behind the barriers, waiting for morning, as per orders; the InstanStone the Orbital Army engineers had laid down for them was still soft in places. They'd deployed in a hurry, ready to advance with their night-seeing goggles—but it was the old 'hurry up and wait'. The sandstorm, and the procrastination of Command Center, kept them in their igloo-like shelter, peering out the stony slits. Their brothers, Rangers in the OA, were dying out there and they couldn't get to them.

For thousands of years, men on battlefields had groaned and died, their dying taking all night long, their cries unanswered; a soldier's life draining slowly away, as the hours of darkness passed. *Ought to be a better way to make war by now.* Three medical robots and a remote scoop had been sent to bring in the wounded, but the enemy had refused a medical truce, had slammed the rescue gear with seeker missiles, despite the fact that they'd have rescued wounded Orthos too. Frank and his men watched the fires of the rescue gear burning, the flamelight guttering along the crater rim; they'd listened to the screams, the begging. That night Frank had learned to hate the Russian Orthodox Army: psychological robots from the theocratic cult Russia had become.

A night of sighing wind, as if the darkness were weeping...

Something glossy-white swept by the balcony of Soulglobe passage seventy-seven, making Frank step back from the balcony, back into this melancholy moment with Mella and the gray-eyed, flaxen-haired stranger who called himself Tet.

"What was *that?*" Frank asked.

"One of our Guests," said Tet with a slight smile. "I just got a glimpse, but I believe it was a woman's body, sheathed in the new Mark Three coatings. Fixed in the cruciform position." He bowed slightly to Mella. "The posture was as per that lady's final request, of course."

Another of the dead swept by—this one carried in a glass coffin. The farther one went, away from the rotating shell of the asteroid and into the center of the globe, the weaker gravity became. Even here, in the enhanced gravitation of the shell, gravity was less than a quarter of Earth normal.

Tet reached into a pocket of his robe, pulled out a round, shiny golden object, and peered at it. When Frank looked at it quizzically, Tet smiled. "Oh this?" Even his smile seemed silky. "It's a 'pocket watch'. Nineteenth century vintage. Three hundred years old. A family heirloom. And it tells me that the Ballet of the Dead is about to begin...Ah! The first strains of Mozart's *Requiem in D Minor!* It's shortened a bit, adapted for ballet."

"Oh!" Mella said, as classical music skirled through the immense globular space with surprising fidelity.

Frank stared, as corpses danced by in the globe's hollow interior, moving precisely to the music: sheathed in translucent preservative material, fixed in a variety of dramatic poses, the bodies of all kinds of people, even a few children, flew into the near-zero-gravity core of the globe. Released from a circular opening below the other balconies, they were directed in their dance by pulsars at the extremities of the corpses; the dead were choreographed into a grand balletic display, first around the edges, close to the curved walls, then drawing in toward the center of the cloudy, light-shafted sphere. The music swelled; the corpses whirled, spun, arced up like droplets in a fountain, then spread out in choreographic symmetry, whirling like the dancers in a ballet.

"They'll all be guided back to their resting places," Tet said, soothingly, "when the *Communio* completes the Requiem."

"You see, Frank?" Mella said, raspily, gazing out at the Ballet of the Dead. "They're part of a work of art...a gigantic kinetic sculpture. I want to be part of it too."

Twelve hours later, Mella hadn't changed her mind. She signed the releases at the ship's computer interface. She signed the euthanasia release without a flicker of hesitation.

Hands trembling, Frank dressed Mella in the pretty ivory-white clingsuit that she'd picked for the occasion. He wore his ceremonial Orbital Army uniform. It was a tad too small for him, tight at the waist. He'd gained some weight since last time he'd worn it, at Lieutenant Bernard's funeral.

They took the shuttle from the space station to the Soulglobe hangar, scarcely saying a word, just holding hands. Neither one of them had bothered with breakfast. Through the shuttle viewport Frank glimpsed the finale of one of the ballets, seeing it from outside the Soulglobe, through the transparent panes: floating bodies, their small, distant outlines making him think of parading chromosomes, were silhouetted against the blue glow of the hollow sphere. Peering at the exterior of the globe he could just make out the clustered blackened carbonized steel tubes of the orbital adjustment thruster, fixed into the southern pole, the external part of the fusion engine that Transcrystal Inc had installed to move the Soulglobe to this position.

Frank was thinking, once more, of signing a euthanasia waiver too; of joining Mella in death. She was pretty much all he had in the world, except for the OA. He'd been a specialist in killing—and she'd been about life. She'd always been so lively, a believer in the beauty of living; she was his refuge from destruction. She was *his* center of gravity. He'd be like the moon without the Earth to orbit. And it didn't matter to him what happened to his body after death, though the Ballet of the Dead seemed ludicrous, even humiliating. Still, he'd killed too many men, seen too many bodies in his time to really care.

But they'd been all through it. She wouldn't hear of his joining her in euthanasia.

The Ballet of the Dead. Imagining Mella becoming part of that absurdity—it twisted his insides. He already felt responsible for her dying, though it hadn't been his fault the radiation shielding on the transport had been compromised. She'd been coming to share his furlough on Mars One, both of them happy—and then she started to shrivel up, even before she arrived. Interplanetary radiation poisoning was still being studied. No one knew exactly how uninsulated exposure led to Rapid Decline Syndrome, or why it resisted the cell reboots, the revitalizations that worked for so many other illnesses. But the doctors were certain that Frank Zand's wife was dying of the syndrome, with a great deal of suffering; that she was eligible for euthanasia.

It was natural, he thought, that she'd be attracted to the Soulglobe. She'd been an art history teacher—an activist in the Face-to-Face Teaching movement, insisting on human, in-person teachers in a time when most children learned via cognitive transfer and VR conditioning. She wanted to be an example to her students, show her commitment to art by donating her body to a work of art.

But there was something about the Soulglobe that alerted his protective instinct. And his instincts had grown keen on the battlefield.

"I'm sorry we didn't have kids," she whispered, as he eased her float-chair out of the shuttle, along the passageway to the Euthanasia Center. Ahead of them, a wizened, white haired man in an ochre clingsuit was riding an elderchair, heading for his own euthanasia.

Mella whispered, "I should've given you a baby."

"Not your fault, Mel," Frank said. "None of it was."

"You can still have kids, with someone," she said gently. "You *should*."

"Not without you, sweetheart," Frank said. "Anyway—I've got those green brats they send me for Mars Defense. Buncha kids."

She smiled wanly. "I bet you *are* a daddy to them, too."

"And I bet they sure as hell don't think of me that way."

Chit-chat—and she would be dead within the hour. They ought to be talking about something more serious. Maybe he should say something comforting about the afterlife, though he didn't believe in it. Maybe he should tell Mella, again, that he loved her, that he'd never marry again. Maybe...

But it all seemed all wrong, when he imagined saying it. Too staged. Like a ballet of the dead.

"This looks like the entrance..." she said. She seemed more excited than afraid.

"Mr. Jacobs and Mr. and Mrs. Zand," said the tonsured, silver-robed Guide, stepping through the arched doorway. Unlike the gray stone around it, the archway was carved out of pearlescent crystal; a relief sculpture of human souls intertwined in an eternal dance.

They went through the archway, and down the corridor that led to death.

The Soulglobe had started out as a gigantic catacomb, a final repository for the wealthy on the edge of the solar system. The galleries along the stone passage still contained the first interred here, thousands of mummified remains, a few little more than skeletons, in niches cut in the naked rock, the stone marbled with the crystal that became transparent panes in much of the outer shell. This section was not so different from catacombs Frank had seen on Earth, where ancient Christians had been deposited in Roman times.

He and Mella emerged into the stark, brightly lit contrast of the Soulglobe Transition offices, where Transcrystal Incorporated processed internees. The Guide took Mr. Jacobs into a separate receiving office for lower-income internment. Mella was greeted by a receptionist.

Soulglobe had used up all of Mella's savings, so Frank was glad to see they hadn't cheaped out on the receptionist—she seemed human. He was never quite comfortable dealing with androids and androclones, though they were often more polite and thoughtful than real people. The receptionist was a pale blond woman with Asiatic eyes; she wore a flowing white dress, her full, dark-red lips bent in a sweet, infinitely-understanding smile as she came from behind the marbled-crystal desk to bend over the float chair and take Mella's hands in hers. "You'll be Mella!" the woman said, her voice velvety. She gazed into Mella's eyes as she spoke. "I'm Sestrine. And look at you, smiling and ready! You look luminous!" She gently squeezed Mella's hands. "We'll check your DNA, and then you'll go right in...if you're ready."

And it seemed to Frank that Mella, frowning slightly, was about to ask a question—maybe she had misgivings, after all. But as Sestrine gazed steadily at her, Mella's frown vanished. She sighed and nodded. "Yes. I'm ready."

"It's painless, right?" Frank asked. "I mean—they *say* it is. But..."

Sestrine let go of Mella's hands, and gave her smile to Frank. "It's painless, yes—and quite pleasant, judging from the way people react. Now, if you'll come this way, we'll do the scan and then you can say your good-byes outside the transition chamber..."

Frank stood on the balcony of passage seventy-seven, and waited for the music to start. Mist swirled in the great globular chamber; a few other people could be seen, small and far away, in the semicircles of passage entrances across the blue-lit interior. A soft wind moaned; cryptic sounds echoed. And Frank ached inside.

He had been ready to take Mella out of there, back to the shuttle, right up to the moment they closed and sealed the door of the chamber. Watching through the window as Mella, in a wheeled bed, was being put to sleep with a colorless gas—and she looked, in fact, like she was sinking happily into a blissful sleep—Frank had felt numb, and unreal. The receptionist had stood by him, her hands clasped, offering silent sympathy.

After a few moments, as Mella succumbed, and the gas was cleared, the tonsured Guide entered the euthanasia chamber, and wheeled Mella's bed through a farther door. A gleaming silver door.

Lingering, trying to accept it all, Frank had asked the receptionist, his voice hoarse, "What's through that silver door? Some kind of...embalming?"

"We don't exactly *embalm* transitioners, Mr. Zand. Soulglobe is distinct in that we preserve the body perfectly, just as it is when the transitioner dies. The coatings do that. That's what takes place through that door."

"What if I wanted to go and see the place where they prepare the body?"

"No one is allowed in there, sir. We wouldn't want to violate the privacy of others being interred."

There was something in the way she'd said it. Something very still, and wary...

He'd felt very little, watching Mella go to sleep. It just didn't look much like death. But he couldn't quite accept that she was gone. Frank Zand was a soldier, he'd lost a lot of close friends— he knew about grief. He knew that often people don't feel much at first. Grief can gestate like an embryo inside you. Sometimes it shows up in funny ways, maybe in distraction, in a blanket of numbness—or in slow-simmering anger.

He was distantly aware that his hands had clenched into fists as he stood there, waiting for the first strains of Mozart. His main feeling, at that moment, was bitterness—the bitterness of a man who'd been cheated.

One good thing. That's all he'd had, that's all he'd wanted. Mella. And then...

And then the Requiem began to play. The music rose, and human bodies flew by through the center of the Soulglobe, neatly dressed corpses frozen in various shapes. The posed bodies made trails in the blue mist through the nearly zero-gravity space of the interior of the Soulglobe.

Frank watched and waited. They'd told him that if he stood exactly here, and tilted his head downward—

There she was! His heart caught in his throat as Mella came soaring up toward him, frozen in a dancing posture, arms over her head, one hip cocked; postured forever for some ancient dance of her Middle Eastern ancestors.

Frank drew his fone from a pocket, though it was against Transcrystal rules to use it here. He held it up as she drifted by, found her in the little viewscreen—it was already attuned to look for her—and pressed *binocular*. The outline of her floating body rushed to fill the fone screen, then her face was there, seen up close. She was still gaunt, but they'd done some cosmetic work on her, and her eyes were open as she flew past.

And her eyes moved—didn't they? They seemed to look around. Just a little. Looking for him.

Then she had passed upward, flown past.

Illusion. Had to be illusion. She was dead, she couldn't look around. There was something in the brochure about that kind of illusion. People supposing they see faces moving...bodies twitching with life...illusion of motion...

Why was it the contract had insisted that no digital recorders, no fones, could be brought into the Soulglobe?

Frank shook his head. He must have been mistaken. He'd seen an illusion generated by disguised grief, and denial.

But that nagging feeling, the instinct that had kept him alive all these years, wouldn't go away...

There were ways to be sure. *Why not?* Did he care what any of these funeral hucksters thought? He didn't. And now the choreography of the dead was bringing his wife's body back, circling her down and up again, returning her to his vantage. Closer... still closer...

What he did next simply happened—it was as if his body did it and his mind just went along. He ran to the edge of the balcony and leapt out into space.

He was Orbital Army. He had hundreds of hours of training, and experience, in low-G and zero-G deployment. His timing was right the first time.

The leap took him out past the pull of the shell's low gravity, into the nearly-Zero-G zone, toward the interior of the asteroid—he intercepted Mella, clasping her around the waist as if in a football tackle. Against his cheek he felt the soft envelope of transparent synthetic clinging to her. His momentum carried them both out of the dance line, toward the centerpoint of the spherical space. He wasn't moving very quickly; he was able to reach up to her shoulders, to pull her down so her face aligned with his. His eyes looked into hers. The transparent film around her face seemed perforated. *They gave her a little air. Why?*

As he watched, the pupils of her eyes contracted; her lips twitched as if she were trying to speak. She was cold to the touch—but not deathly cold. Her eyes moved, seeming to direct his gaze downward, toward her neck. He looked. There, two small red puckers, close together, one above the other. He got a better grip on her with his left hand; with his right he reached up and pressed through the plastic over the puckers, thumbed the makeup away from the skin of her throat. The pressure revealed two clear-cut puncture marks in her jugular. They'd said they didn't embalm, so why'd they puncture her?

To Frank, they looked like bite marks.

He looked into her eyes. "Someone's hurt you, Mella. Is that what it is? Can you blink once to say yes—twice for no?"

She looked back at him but there was no blinking. She didn't blink at all.

"I know you're alive, sweetheart," Frank said. "I'm here with you."

Then he felt the inner shift that announced he was past the midway point of the asteroid's interior, his momentum carrying him across the space toward the farther wall. The semicircular openings grew larger as he approached. He thought he saw someone in a gray security guard's uniform waiting on the balcony directly across from him. The man had a weapon in his hand.

Frank took a good grip on his wife, clasping her to him, and flipped himself, in a way that experience had taught him would change his direction in near-zero. They somersaulted together, and when he saw the openings again they were closer—and he was heading for a different one, relatively higher. His heart pounded; he could feel Mella, clasped in his arms, could feel the life in her— but it seemed feeble, like the last words whispered by a very old woman. *I'm alive. But I'm going...goodbye...*

"Mel! I love you, hon, listen, I..."

Then the farther balcony loomed up, and he had turned them both in the air so he could land on it feet first, skidding on the floor as he hit its stronger gravity. He was moving crookedly, and they stopped against a wall with a mild thump to his right shoulder.

Frank set Mella gently down on her back, close to the wall, and tore the plastic sheathing away. A chemical smell wafted up as he wadded the sheathing and tossed it aside. He rubbed her arms. He felt her wrist for a pulse. That *might* be one—faint and irregular.

He bent over her, blew breath into her lungs. He pumped her chest. One of her eyes fluttered. A creaking sound came out of her throat. After a moment he realized he was hearing his own name. "Frank..."

"You're alive!"

"Yes. Frank. They..." She gulped, spoke each word in a gasp. "Feed. Slow. Death. Frank. Get...away."

"Mel—hon, relax. Just relax, I'm getting you out of here, this wasn't how—"

"All visitors to the Soulglobe are required to evacuate." The voice boomed from hidden speakers. *"There is a terrorist element at large in Soulglobe. Return to the shuttle immediately. All visitors..."*

So that's what they were calling him. A terrorist.

He picked Mella up in his arms, and started down the passageway. A tram would take them to the shuttle. But there'd be security waiting there for him. Have to find a way around them.

Hurrying with long strides, he turned the corner—and caught the sizzling sound of a razorgun. He glimpsed two men in gray uniforms, teeth bared, smart carbines leveled from their hips. A squat, thick-bodied man was firing; the tall gangly one still fumbling with his gun. Razor rounds scored Frank's right side, and chunked into his left shoulder, a familiar sensation—the Orthos liked razor guns. They could be set to cause a lot of bleeding, and there was a lot of blood gushing—but it was mostly Mella's blood.

He stepped back, lowered her to the stone floor around the corner. Her blood pumped out from the razorgun gash in her neck. "Mel!"

"Frank." She took one long final breath. "Get...away."

Her gaze seemed to freeze in place, as if she were mesmerized by some sight seen in the beyond—her blood-flow slowed to a trickle. Her head drooped to the side.

She was really gone this time. They'd killed her, trying to get him.

Two long shadows stretched from the corner, growing longer. They were coming, whispering to one another. Neither was eager to be the first, not knowing if he had a weapon.

Frank didn't wait for them. Propelled by fury, he rushed around the corner, grabbing the muzzle of the nearest guard's carbine before he had a chance to react. OA training took over, and he used the quarter-gravity to good effect, slamming his shoulder into the man's thick gut as he wrenched the gun free. The guard sprawled backward; Frank went with him, reversing the gun as he went and firing point blank. Because this was the one who had killed Mel.

Frank's razor rounds cut through the stocky guard, slicing up from under his ribs, through his chest, his throat, up into the man's skull, out the top of his head in a jet of gray brain matter and blood. Two razor rounds sparked from the stone floor as the lanky one fired at him—Frank rolled, came up firing, aiming at the other guard's gun, pressing the charge button so each projectile carried a pulse of electricity. The guard's right arm splashed blood, and he staggered back, tendons cut, gun clattering to the floor.

The surviving guard was sitting up, shaking in a puddle of blood, groaning as the shock spasms left him. "Goddammit... fu-uck...whud I take this fucking job..."

"What's the deal with this operation?" Frank demanded, pointing the gun at the man's groin. "Why're they keeping euthanasia patients alive?"

"I'm...just a mercenary, I don't know nothing about what goes on back there. They won't let us back in transition, they got their own people to patrol it. I hate this fucking job..." He stared at the bloody corpse sprawled on the floor. "You kill Larry?"

"Larry killed my wife. What's your name?"

"Marv. *Ow.* Goddamn that hurts."

"Okay, Marv Ow, you're gonna get on that shuttle, and take any other personnel you can find with you. Evacuate all the employees. How many other mercs on this fucking bauble?"

"Just two others. We never had no trouble before."

"You talk them into going with you. You understand me?"

"Yeah, fine, just give me a chance to— *Shit* that hurts...Larry has the medic gear..."

Frank reached down, pulled a bloodstopper off the dead guard's belt. He sprayed his own light wounds with it, and then tossed it within reach of Marv's working hand. "Use that."

Marv sprayed the bloodstopper on his wound, shuddering with relief as the anesthetics took hold.

Frank spotted a concussion grenade on Marv's belt. "Pretty heavy ordnance for a security guard. Hand that little egg to me, very carefully, Marv—give me all your ammunition and your pal's too. Then get your people out of here. There's going to be real death in this place. Nothing but real death."

Stalking up to the balcony overlooking the great open space inside the Soulglobe, Frank remembered when he'd first seen Mella. That trip up the Tigris, thirteen years ago. *See! The new Hanging Gardens of Babylon! See! A re-enactment of the Execution of Saddam Hussein! See! Ancient Treasures and Glorious Executions!*

Frank had no interest in re-enactments of executions. He was ready to quit the trip, stupid idea doing a furlough there. Only, he had an interest in Babylon, the whole ancient Middle East. His mom had taken him to visit Cairo, Jerusalem, Istanbul. And he could count on peace in the Middle East—one of the most peaceful places on Earth, in the 22nd century. He wanted to be somewhere peaceful.

But here he was, in a deck chair on a tour boat listening to an android talk all breezily about re-enacting hangings. And there was Mella, handing out lunches to a group of school kids.

"Now that's something you don't see every day—face to face teachers," said an old tourist in a fez, winking at him. "I remember a few—when I was a kid. None of them that looked that good."

See! The girl you want to marry the moment you set eyes on her. Mella. Beautiful and apparently unaware of it; innately kind, as if it were the most natural thing in the world. Made you believe something good could come from people...

And now she was shot to pieces. He had to know if it was his fault she'd died this way...and if not, whose fault it was.

Frank stood on the edge of the balcony watching the blue mists rising past it; the angling light. The Ballet of the Dead was done for now—only a few glass coffins drifted around the edges.

But far away, in the middle of the open space, someone was waiting for him. A big, dark figure was floating there, in the center of the Soulglobe.

Frank didn't hesitate. He leapt from the balcony, pushing off hard, right for the man in the center. Everything about the stranger, his placement, the hunkered aggression in his stance, said this was an adversary.

The dark figure started toward him—it was like the guy moved through the near zero-G by his will alone. Frank couldn't see a jet pack, couldn't see him pushing off from anything. He went from motionless to flying toward Frank without anything propelling him.

They got closer to each other, Frank coming almost head first, like a diver, but flying horizontally across the space, propelled through the extremely low gravity by momentum. A hundred meters from his enemy; eighty, sixty, thirty. He saw that the guy had no weapons in his hands. But he was big, muscular, probably capable of killing without a weapon.

Closer. Wearing a black clingsuit, the man was pale, bald, with a big jutting jaw, craggy cheekbones, icy blue eyes, large hands opened to clutch. The stranger snarled as he flew toward Frank—were those *fangs* on his bared teeth? Not likely. Some kind of implants?

Frank had no desire to grapple with this hulking, toothy thug. He raised the razor gun, clicked the select screen up, used the ball of his thumb to tap the image of his target at the place he wanted to hit, modulating projectile configuration. He fired, the bullets flattening into the thickened razor shape he'd specified. Following the gun's directions the projectiles strafed across the target's chest—not much immediate effect. Maybe the guy had armor.

No—now his thick blood was splashing, spreading out from the dark figure's chest, blood globules blossoming like grotesque red flowers in the low gravity. A solid hit.

But the big guy didn't die. He just kept coming, grinning widely, displaying his fangs. Looming up. And the blood stopped coming out. The razor rounds hadn't stopped him. Was this some kind of androclone?

Then they closed, the stranger instantly clamping his fingers around Frank's neck. Squeezing. "I squeeze the blood out of your eye sockets," the big man rumbled. "I drink from these fountains..."

The two of them floated in lethal embrace in the center of the Soulglobe. The big man opened his mouth wide over Frank's eyes, fangs glistening. Choking, feeling blood forced painfully up into his head, Frank fired the gun almost point blank. The man only laughed. His fangs seemed to grow; his mouth gaped wider.

Frank's fingers found the concussion grenade in his pocket and he jammed it deep into a gaping wound on the big man's chest, shoving it in with all his strength, pressing the timer, jerking his hand free.

Frank's adversary roared, clutched at the invaded wound, the motion sending the two of them spinning apart...Frank lost his gun to centrifugal force—

A dull *thud* and an explosion of red—

Frank was slammed hard in the gut by the force of the blast, splashed by an expanding cloud of rancid blood and fragmented flesh, driven backwards toward the asteroid's shell. He spat blood and grabbed his knees, rolled up in a ball, twisting in an OA move, flipping to face the curved inner wall of the Soulglobe.

Something flew past him, trailing blood—a severed head. The fanged mouth still open, the eyes rolling, staring at him... then gone in the mists.

Frank was stunned, felt sick, disoriented by the explosion. *Part of the ballet of the dead myself, soon.*

A balcony loomed. He straightened his body, then brought his knees up sharply, changed angles so he was coming down feet first... The circular entrance seemed to widen, like a mouth opening to swallow him, then he was through, skidding, spinning—thumping hard against the wall, sliding, coming to a stop face down.

He lay there a long moment, spitting blood, not sure if it was his. His whole front was soaked in the dark giant's foul-smelling effusion.

Frank took a deep breath, his bruised chest aching, and got to his feet. He heard a clatter behind him and whirled. The razor gun, propelled by the explosion, skittering by itself along the floor, spinning as it went.

He ran to the gun, scooped it up, and turned to stagger toward the inner chambers of the Soulglobe.

Frank stopped about ten meters from her, and stared.

In a high-ceilinged stone room marbled with crystal, lit with soft blue light, the receptionist, Sestrine, was leaning over the body of old Mr. Jacobs, her hands pressed down on his shoulders. The old man was lying on his back on the stone slab. Intricate carvings, cryptic runes, etched the slab, and the wall beyond. Other bodies lay on shelves behind her, wrapped in plastic like flies in spider-silk bindings. Against the wall to the left were racks of pulsars, and remote control panels.

Frank watched as Sestrine bent over the old man. Her face dipped to his neck. He thought of a cat his mother had, its jaws on the neck of a dead bird.

A little blood trickled past her lips. The old man's fingers twitched but he didn't struggle. His eyes were glazed. Sestrine wore a cloth diner's bib, like something from a restaurant, so she wouldn't get blood on her gleaming white dress.

Frank remembered stories from old viddies. Horror stories. "So...you're real," he said. "Not just a story."

Sestrine straightened up with a jerk, staring at him, blood streaming down her chin, eyes alight with red fire. She swallowed a mouthful of blood. "Ah. Mr. Zand."

"You look kinda startled," he said. "Guess you never thought I'd make it past the bruiser. How long do you keep people alive, here? People like Mr. Jacobs there."

"Oh..." She removed the bib, used it to fastidiously wipe her face. She folded the bib, laid it neatly on Mr. Jacobs' chest. "Not so very long as all that. Long enough. They die in time. There are always new ones."

"Yeah. Like my wife."

"Yes. I shared the first taste of her with Tet. The radiation made her blood a bit thin." She took a step toward him.

He nestled the carbine against his shoulder, aimed squarely at her. "Uh uh. Stop right there. Answer my questions."

She paused, but she didn't seem frightened. More like—amused. She gave him the same sweet smile she'd given Mella. "You seem injured. I doubt you'll get much farther. You're lucky to have gotten past Karn. He was quite old and experienced and powerful. How did you manage it?"

"I'll tell you, if you tell me some stuff first. I'm gonna take a wild guess—you guys have found a way to make the radiation shields drop in transport ships. Maybe in selected spots. Provide more people inclined to euthanasia—"

"An intelligent guess. Essentially—yes. We needed to prime the pump." She started toward him. For some reason, he didn't tell her to stop.

"Is it all true?" Frank asked. He was fascinated by her fiery eyes. It seemed to him that he saw real flames flicker there. "The stories?"

"Oh, we don't turn into bats, and if you want to hear one of us laugh, just wave a crucifix at us." He was aware that she was gliding slowly toward him, but he felt a little sleepy, almost inclined to open his arms and welcome her, as she said, "We're not magical beings—we're simply an old race, with certain, particular needs. Not quite the same species as yours. It's true we don't like sunlight—the light in here is filtered. But we do have our special gifts..."

Frank. Was that Mella's voice?

Suddenly he could feel Sestrine's grip on his will. He realized the vampire was telling him things just to keep him from thinking too much. He felt the icy fingers of Sestrine's mind—being aware of her mind gave him the chance to resist it.

Frank backed away from her, shook himself, and squeezed off two shots from the razor gun. The rounds struck her right in the heart.

Sestrine stopped, shivered—then shrugged complacently. "There is something true in the old stories: It's very, very hard to kill us."

She grinned, and crouched—and he knew she was going to leap at him. But his fingers were already at work on the target selector. "You asked how I killed your friend..."

Frank fired, strafing the rest of the clip out all at once, the razor rounds following the directions the gun gave him, its expert program aiming with inhuman precision—to sever Sestrine's head cleanly from her body.

Her head simply tipped off the neck—spouting blood. The headless body seemed to hesitate, clutching the air. Then it toppled.

He walked over to the vampire's head, picked it up by her hair, thinking about Medusa. Her mouth gnashed convulsively at him.

He watched as her head bled out. "How I killed your friend is, I blew his head right off his body. Seems like separating a parasite's head from its body's a pretty handy way to kill it." He carried her head to a disposal chute, and tossed it in. "Works real sweet."

It worked on Tet, too, when he burst in through the silver door, a moment later. "Sestrine!" the vampire howled, staring in shock at her body, as Frank inserted another clip into the gun.

Tet whipped about, hissing in cold fury as he stalked toward Frank—but the gun already had its setting. Frank fired, and the razor rounds severed Tet's head from his body with almost surgical precision.

He went to Mr. Jacobs and patted his arm. "Almost over. You wanted to die, Mr. Jacobs, and I'm going to have to give you your wish. I don't have time to evacuate anybody myself. There'll be more of those bloodsuckers..."

Frank took an autotram along a back passage to the thruster casing. It wasn't far.

The thruster's engine room was a hangar-like structure, trussed with plasteel. On a metal table near the entrance to the control cockpit sat a coffee cup, the coffee untouched; near it was a half-used pack of Smoke Calms, and a clip from a razor gun.

Someone had left in a hurry. The other mercs had been here, guarding the engine, and Marv had gotten them out. With any luck, there should be no one but him and the vampires left on the Soulglobe.

"If you wanta call that luck," he muttered, climbing up a metal ladder, through a hatch to the screen-lined cockpit of the thruster control.

Frank dropped into the control seat, flicked the switches to manual, and sealed the doors to the engine area with a high security setting: *No entry under any circumstances.* The thruster was engineered right into the Soulglobe's stony shell—but if they tried to break into it, they'd risk an atmospheric breach. Maybe that'd keep them out. They'd bide their time, figure he was taking them to the authorities. They wouldn't be too worried about that. If they didn't get to him before then, they could tell the authorities he was insane.

Frank checked the surveillance screens—saw the shuttle was gone. Visitors and guards evacuated. They'd sent away the witnesses to his fight with the big guy in black. Figured they were safe to keep their operation going. Spin a terrorist story and send for some new blood.

He turned to the navigation screen. It was standard. Just pick the course, program it in, the ship did the rest. He used the locator, plotted the course, programmed the computer, and triggered ignition. The cockpit began to vibrate.

It would take awhile. He was tired, emotionally drained. If he was going to see this trip through, he'd need rest.

He leaned the control chair back and tried to sleep...

Frank was hovering over a river, looking down at Mella.

His wife was reclining against red silk cushions, on a long low royal barge painted gold and black in the Babylonian fashion. She was drifting down the Tigris away from him. She looked beautiful and young and strong, her hair shiny black, her eyes large and dark and luminous.

Frank—I want you to live. Mella's voice seemed to come from everywhere and nowhere. *Live, and find someone, and have children. That's what I want. You know it is. There's a time to go to death. This isn't it. Live for me, Frank...*

The boat spun about, caught in a whirlpool—and then suddenly sank away, vanishing like a chip of wood swirling down a drain, taking her with it...

From somewhere came a clanging sound...like a bell ringing in the depths...

"Mella!"

Frank sat up, sweating, hands clutching the arms of the control chair. His feeling of loss was gigantic, a thirsty void inside him; a vampiric suction.

Her body was still out there, lying on the cold stone floor.

The thruster hummed, the control room vibrated softly with it. They were still underway. He looked at the chronometer—he'd slept a long time. What had wakened him?

The clanging sound he'd heard in his dream—there it was again. He got up, climbed down through the hatch to the super-structure—and saw that the big metal door he'd sealed, across the big hangar-like room, was vibrating with the clanging. Shivering. Bits of powdered stone fell from the ceiling...

The vampires were breaking through. Maybe they'd worked out where he was going and they were risking the breach.

Frank shrugged, returned to the ladder, climbed into the control cockpit and checked the arrival time. Maybe they'd get through and stop him. Maybe not.

He removed the thruster control pad, ripping it from the console. The setting was fixed, now. He slid down the ladder, found another hatch in the back of the room, almost hidden in the deck. Another ladder here, down to another deck—he slid down that too, and located the lifeboats against the airlock.

Seven cylindrical escape vehicles—they were small, room for one passenger apiece.

Frank found a laser cutter, used it to slice through the propulsion packs for all the lifeboats but one.

That one was his. He opened it, climbed in—and hesitated. He didn't want to live without Mella.

Live for me, Frank.

Frank sighed. Feeling a deep twinge of guilt, he activated the lifeboat. The airlock door slid back; the lifeboat was propelled through the airlock.

Frank watched through the viewport as the hot-yellow energies from the thruster tubes pushed the Soulglobe down into the atmosphere of the eighth planet from the sun. The crystalline orb struck the outer atmosphere and began to glow. In moments it was wrapped in a corona of blue flame. But he didn't think it would burn up entirely.

It would fall into the churning storms of methane and ammonia. It would crash deep into poisoned plains, to be crushed by Neptune's powerful gravitation into a small fist of stone. It would be locked forever in ice.

He stared at the indigo orb of Neptune and thought it beautiful. Fourteen times the mass of Earth, it curved gigantically against the night, truly a god. Lit by starlight, it was a pearly dark blue, a perfect sphere. It was said to be mostly ice. Just ice and rock and ceaseless hurricanes of toxic winds. But from here it looked gorgeous, even elegant. A fitting tomb...

Frank Zand lay back in his recliner and activated the beacon that would transmit a subspace mayday signal. He would probably be found, and rescued. Maybe he would be able to tell them he'd escaped from some terrorist who'd destroyed the Soulglobe. Possibly they'd believe it. Could be he'd go free. He'd go on living. Without her.

Yes. He would probably survive. It was what she wanted.

But not dying just didn't feel right.

John Shirley's books include the novels *Demons, Crawlers, City Come A-Walkin', Eclipse, Cellars,* and *In Darkness Waiting;* his story collections include *Black Butterflies* (which won the Bram Stoker award), *Living Shadows, Really Really Really Really Weird Stories* and the forthcoming *In Extremis: The Most Extreme Short Stories of John Shirley.* He has had stories in two Year's Best collections, and is thought to be seminal in the cyberpunk movement. He was co-screenwriter of the film *The Crow,* and has written scripts for television. His newest novels are *Black Glass* from ESP, and *Bleak History* from Simon and Schuster.

Red Planet
By Bev Vincent

When Isaac awakens, he doesn't know where he is. In the distance, there's a muffled thrumming sound. Closer, an instrument chirps and a red dot blinks. It's the only light, but Isaac has no trouble seeing.

His mouth is parched and his back stiff, like he's been sleeping too long. He tries to sit up, but something is holding him down. Then it comes to him. For the past four months, he's been in stasis aboard the *Ferdinand*, bound for Mars.

Their sister ship, the *Isabella*, is behind them, on the same course. The media dubbed the mission the Hundred Years Starship, despite the fact that there are two ships, neither of which is destined for the stars. Nothing like it has ever been attempted before: sending people on a one-way trip to colonize another planet. Isaac and his colleagues are pioneers, en route to a brave new world aboard a nuclear-powered wagon train.

The austere federal budget of 2088 made it clear that this was the only way NASA could reach Mars in the foreseeable future. It's audacious and controversial, but the additional cost required to guarantee the safe return of the crew would eat up most of any other scheme's budget. This way, the ships are lighter and can carry more provisions. Disposable unmanned craft delivered sophisticated robots in advance to establish the base camp and set up a fission reactor for power. Other drones will bring supplies on a regular basis. Within a decade, they hope to be completely self-sufficient.

Eight candidates were chosen from the hundreds of applicants. All underwent physical and psychological evaluation to ensure they were healthy and up to the rigors of the mission and its implications. None left behind family—that was one of the main selection criteria. They also understood that they would probably live only twenty or thirty years on Mars due to celestial radiation exposure.

Isaac was subjected to short periods of stasis during training, but emerging from that was nothing like this. Air doesn't seem to fill his lungs when he inhales and he has a terrible thirst, unlike anything he's experienced before. It's specific and overwhelming: he craves blood instead of water. He also doesn't understand why his vision is so acute. In total darkness, he can see every tube running along his body, every needle in his wrists, every sensor affixed to his chest. Could these be unanticipated side effects of prolonged stasis?

Dyer, the chief medical officer, should be attending his awakening, but there's no sign that anyone else is up. For all he knows, he's only been asleep for part of the journey. Perhaps a malfunction awoke him too soon. If so, he needs to rouse Dyer to put him under again—but not before he does something about this burning thirst.

He closes his eyes and tries to sigh, but his lungs won't cooperate. He isn't breathing, nor does he have any discernable pulse. He allows his thoughts to drift, searching for anything that might explain what's happening. Some passing reference during their training—anything.

Instead, what flickers through his memories is a vision of frantic hands fumbling in a dark room. Clothing ripped off and cast aside. Passionate kisses. Groping. Teasing. Penetration. Blissful friction and release. Then nothingness.

He was supposed to be in quarantine, but it was his last day on Earth. Forever. His affairs were in order, his possessions sold or donated. The seven other people on the two NASA ships would be his only companions for the rest of his foreshortened life. After tomorrow, Earth would be nothing more than a minute speck in the sky, barely discernable from the stars.

Who could blame him for wanting one last fling? He was surprised NASA hadn't arranged one for them, considering what he and his colleagues were sacrificing in the name of science. He used the cash he reserved for just such a purpose to bribe one of the flunkies keeping tabs on them into letting him out of the compound for the evening. The closest bar was dingy and dark, which suited Isaac just fine. No one gave him a second look when he strolled in. After a few drinks, he targeted a dark, exotic beauty sitting at a table near the back of the joint. Surprisingly, everyone seemed oblivious to her presence. Anywhere else, men would be swarming her.

He had enough money left to treat her to anything she wanted, but the only thing she wanted, she said, was him. She had a place nearby. After that, the night was a blur. He staggered back to the compound less than an hour before reveille. During their pre-launch checkout, the NASA doctor noticed a gash on his neck. "Won't have to worry about shaving for a while, will you?" the man said with a snicker. The doctor also ignored Isaac's bloodshot eyes and the reek of alcohol that a shower and mouthwash couldn't eliminate. For all Isaac knew, his fellow crew members were in similar states. He hadn't been the only one about to be strapped into a rocket and sent on a one-way trip into space.

He slips one hand free of the restraints that keep him from floating around in his stasis chamber. Near the tube that runs into his neck, his fingertips encounter swollen flesh and the rough edges of broken skin. If he's been asleep for months, any injuries he sustained on Earth should have healed. Assuming he's not dreaming, he needs to figure out what's happening.

Isaac removes the mask from his face and the mantle of electronic sensors from his head, expecting alarms to go off.

Nothing happens.

The needles float away when he pulls the IVs from his hands. The monitoring equipment continues to chirp after he peels the patches from his chest.

He undoes the rest of his restraints and drifts to the entrance of his chamber, where he braces himself so he can open the door. There's a hiss when the seal breaks, but he doesn't sense any change in the air around him. He's neither warm nor cold, and he still doesn't seem to be breathing.

Shaking his head, he glides into the hall and examines the monitor outside his door. The mission clock reads T+128 days, which means they should gain Mars orbit in four days if they're on schedule. He's only a little early in waking. However, the display indicates that his vital signs all dropped to zero during the past twenty-four hours. He taps the monitor, but nothing changes.

Isaac floats up the corridor to the next compartment, the one containing Willows, the flight engineer. Her vital signs are normal. He peers through the porthole. Willows is on her back with her hands clasped across her belly. Peaceful. As he watches, he becomes fixated on the tube running into her neck. If he pulled it out, droplets of blood would appear at the puncture site and form perfect globules as they drifted into the air. He runs his tongue across his upper lip and discovers, to his amazement, something pointed at either end of the traverse. His incisors are pronounced and razor sharp.

Spinning around, he seeks the closest washroom, presenting himself to the mirror for inspection. Though the room is dark, he can clearly see, in its reflection, the metallic grey wall behind him. No matter how long he floats before it, the mirror remains innocent of his presence.

His scientific mind processes the facts and arrives at two possible explanations. He prefers the stasis nightmare option. The only alternative is too cruel. The woman in the dive. How the others shied away from her. They knew what she was—and said nothing.

The irony of his situation doesn't escape him—he's 200 million kilometers from Earth and his only source of sustenance is a handful of people. He's the first vampire in space, but he'll also be the first to perish in space unless he comes up with a plan—fast. Stasis must have slowed his transformation, but now that he's awake he needs to feed. Needs in a way he's never needed anything before. He flashes back to Willows, supine in her chamber, completely vulnerable for the next two days.

Then what?

He doesn't have time to take in the magnitude of what has happened to him. He's been altered, turned into a creature people fear and despise, but he can't dwell on that. His life expectancy may have increased from a few decades to forever, theoretically, but only if he can figure out how to survive. He can contemplate the implications later.

Time to put to use the problem-solving abilities that helped get him selected for the Hundred Year Starship in the first place. He sabotages his monitors to make it look like they malfunctioned, explaining why he's awake. Then he contemplates the food situation. There's blood in cold storage in the sick bay. How long will it last? Depends on how much he needs to survive. He's tempted to log a request for information via computer. What would they think at Mission Control if the first communiqué they received from the *Ferdinand* was a query about the dietary needs of vampires?

He navigates the narrow corridors by pushing off the walls until he reaches sickbay. The room is empty and immaculate. Isaac goes straight to the refrigerator. Rows of plastic bags of whole blood line several shelves. The crew has to be prepared for any eventuality. Almost any. No one foresaw what happened to him. He rummages through drawers until he finds a 14-gauge IV needle, inserts it into a bag, and drinks from the attached tubing. He knows the blood must be cold, but warmth permeates his body instead. He feels energized, powerful.

Dangerous.

When the bag is half empty, he stops. His thirst is quenched—for now. He reseals the bag and returns it to the shelf. This supply will sustain him for a while, but it will run out eventually. The others have provisions in the orbiting freighters, and the biosphere is already producing food. What's he supposed to do? Hitch a ride on the Russian ship that arrived before them? The Russians, who opted for a more traditional round-trip mission, are scheduled to return to Earth shortly after the *Ferdinand* arrives. Even if he could convince them to take him along, which he doubts, there wouldn't be enough blood for the journey. He needs to find a way to survive on Mars with the supplies at hand. That or perish.

He transmits a report to Mission Control, feeding them his cover story about faulty monitors. The response is a simple acknowledgement. It takes over twenty minutes for radio transmissions each way, so they can't exactly have a conversation.

For the next two days, Isaac roams the ship. His compulsion seems quelled for the time being, but soon, he suspects, the bloodlust will overtake him again. If he feeds from the others, he might convert them, too. The competition for their limited blood supply would be too much. He considers draining them mechanically, but that would be short sighted. Each holds about five liters but, unlike the storage bank, they can replenish themselves as long as they're properly nourished and healthy. He needs to keep them alive and producing, his own personal biospheres.

The main trick will be overpowering seven people, including the four aboard the *Isabella*. He can't do anything until they're on Mars—he needs them to land the ship. Will they notice anything about him when they awaken? Besides the whole lack-of-a-reflection thing, what might betray him—other than his compulsion to drink blood? A fact he intends to keep from them.

As he wanders the corridors, drifting past portholes that reveal blackest space outside and no hint of his reflection, he develops a plan. It will be risky, but it's the only way he can imagine surviving this seemingly impossible situation.

Isaac uses his time alone to make preparations and cover his tracks. He stashes the open bag of blood in his quarters in case he needs to feed again prior to landing. He then tinkers with the equipment the medical officer will use to check their vital signs so it will register his non-existent pulse.

When the rest of the crew wakes, Isaac greets them at their pods and explains why he's out of stasis early. No one questions his story or comments on his appearance. In the artificial light, they all look pale. Dyer's review of their vitals is perfunctory—after all, they've been monitored constantly since launch. Because they don't have a formal dining schedule, the others aren't aware that Isaac isn't eating or that he doesn't need to sleep.

After the *Ferdinand* enters Mars orbit, Captain Morrell gets the green light from Mission Control to begin landing manoeuvres. Isaac takes his place, strapped into his seat behind and to the left of Morrell. His months of training kick in, despite the change he's undergone, and he performs his assigned tasks as required. The *Ferdinand* breaks through the thin upper atmosphere at a predetermined angle of 14.8 degrees and, less than ten minutes later, they reach their designated landing zone near base camp.

The instant they touch down, Morrell flips the switch to kill the engines. While his fellow crewmembers are busy congratulating each other, Isaac produces three syringes filled with a powerful sedative he pilfered from sickbay. In quick succession he injects Willows, Dyer and Morrell through their flight suits. The drug acts so fast that no one has time to cry out. Their suits are designed to repair punctures automatically, so he doesn't need to worry about compromising them. The drug should keep them out long enough for Isaac to transport them into their new home. He has more syringes in his pockets in case the move takes longer than anticipated.

Briefly, he considers destroying the ship's com unit, but there are too many redundancies, including systems in the base camp and on the orbiting freighters. Instead, he sends a message to Mission Control and to the *Isabella* that cosmic radiation is interfering with communications. There's nothing the people off-planet can do, but the longer he can keep them in the dark the better.

He drags the three unconscious crewmembers from the *Ferdinand* into their base camp. It's hard work, but the reduced gravity—barely more than a third that of Earth's—helps. Once inside, he strips them of their flight suits and restrains them.

When he's finished, he returns to the *Ferdinand* for a well-deserved drink of blood. Apparently he can manage a few days without feeding, and he only needs a fraction of what he consumed after emerging from stasis. He files that bit of information away for future use.

For the time being, he decides to return the crew to stasis while he figures out what to do next. That way he won't have to worry about them getting free while he's dealing with the crew of the *Isabella*.

He transfers the equipment he needs from the *Ferdinand* and sets up a communal stasis center in what was supposed to be the biosphere's lounge. He's not a doctor, but he received medical training as part of preparations for the trip. While inserting IV lines into his crewmates' wrists and necks, he has to stop for another quaff of blood to allay the temptation to sink his teeth into their succulent veins.

The supply of drugs required to keep the crew subdued and nourished will last no more than a few months. That's how much time he has to come up with a way to keep them alive, restrained and docile for as long as possible. Though his muscles atrophied and he lost bone mass during the long trek from Earth, he feels strong. He's probably a match for any one or two of his former colleagues, but if they all managed to get free at once, he'd be in trouble.

The *Isabella* arrives on schedule. Isaac communicates with the ship sporadically after it enters orbit, allowing the link to go in and out at random, filling the feed with bursts of static.

His most interesting discovery over the past two days is the fact that he doesn't need to wear his flight suit outdoors—just his weighted boots to help keep him rooted to the planet's surface. Though atmospheric pressure is only a few percent of what it is on Earth, he doesn't require oxygen any more. An extra couple of hundred million kilometers apparently reduces his suscepti-bility to sunlight, too.

Without the suit, his mobility and range of vision are much greater than those of the arriving crew. He darts around their ship, hides beneath its struts and leaps out to overpower and sedate them one at a time. After they're all unconscious, he drags them into the lounge and strips the stasis equipment and blood supplies from their ship. Soon he has seven 'factories' lined up in a neat row. He strolls among them, admiring his handiwork.

The biosphere's computer has a database designed to supply the colonists with information. Though it can link to Mission Control computers, it needs to be self-reliant. For up to two weeks per year, communication with Earth will be impossible. He researches Total Parental Nutrition, the type of IV used to feed comatose patients. It requires inserting central lines into his subjects and maintaining the injection sites to prevent infection. He'll have to spend a lot of time in the lab preparing the solutions, as well as mass producing the drugs required to keep them unconscious. He's doomed to become both an extended caregiver to seven vegetables and a pharmaceutical factory. The life of a vampire never seemed less glamorous.

He remembers reading that pairs survive better in the wild. A companion would make his existence more tolerable. He has seven candidates, but he gravitates toward the one who tempted him first: former flight engineer Willows. He's not sure of the process involved in converting her into a vampire, though. Their computer database offers no help. All he knows is what happened with him on that surreal night at the bar, and much of that is a blank. Does he need to feed on her just once, or are multiple feedings required?

When science fails him, Isaac turns to their extensive electronic library of literature. Even that is contradictory and vague. If biting Willows on the neck and sucking her blood doesn't work, he'll have to force her to drink some of his blood.

He stops the flow of sedatives to rouse her from stasis. When she begins to stir, he brushes aside her auburn hair and sinks his fangs into the vein pulsing just beneath the surface of her neck. Thick, warm blood fills his mouth, mixing with his saliva. He swallows, more invigorated than after any of his blood bank meals. The sensation is electrifying. He feels intimately connected to her. Willows moans and arches her back, pressing her neck against his mouth, as if urging him to take more.

He does.

Then he waits. She lapses back into unconsciousness. Her breathing slows, then halts. The color fades from her body, though she still seems vibrant and alive. When her eyes open again several hours later, they are dark embers burning in the dim light. She turns in confusion until she finds him watching her. Slowly, she rises from her gurney, her features etched with hunger and desire. She moves toward the others, prepared to pounce, but Isaac stops her. "We need them alive," he says. "Take this instead." He offers her a small beaker of blood from the bank. She swallows it in a single gulp and holds it out for more. He refills the beaker. The second draught appears to satisfy her.

He explains his plan for their survival, but Willows has doubts. It will work in the short term, she says, but eventually these frail human bodies will fail. What will they do then? There will be other missions to Mars—the Chinese are scheduled to send a ship in a couple of years—but the radio silence from the biosphere may cause NASA to suspend operations.

"We have the Russians," he says. "They're scheduled to leave in a few days."

"Not enough," she says.

Before the Russian ship leaves, it attempts to establish contact with the biosphere on behalf of Mission Control. Isaac ignores their hails. The cosmonauts don't have time to send an exploratory expedition, however. Any delay would cause them to miss their Hohmann Transfer Orbit launch window and the next one won't occur for twenty-six months.

Isaac and Willows have all the time in the world, so long as they can keep their supply of blood going. It's definitely easier with two. They work in the lab together, and feed and care for their comatose patients the way they might tend a garden. They harvest and stockpile blood in cold storage, and sip beakers of blood in the terrarium like lovers on a date.

After two years, they initiate the second phase of their operation. They activate their rover, *Curiosity*, a vehicle the size of a car designed for both robotic and manned operation. It looks like a souped-up version of the old Lunar Roving Vehicle from the Apollo missions of the previous century. Willows and Isaac board it after tending to their human garden and set out across the red soil under a butterscotch sky.

The newly arrived Chinese explorers probably won't be watching for foreign incursions, but Isaac and Willows advance cautiously just in case, leaving the rover behind a rust-colored boulder and covering the last kilometer on foot.

Meant to last only a few months, the Chinese outpost is less extensive than the NASA biosphere. Two taikonauts are gathering samples when Isaac and Willows walk up to them without any protective gear as if they were out for a stroll. The Chinese astronauts are caught off guard, allowing Isaac and Willows to subdue them before they can send out a warning. Then the vampires wait for the others to investigate why their colleagues haven't returned and don't respond to their hails.

Within a few hours, Isaac and Willows have all six men bundled up on the back of the *Curiosity*, ready for transport to the biosphere. They raid the shelter's sickbay and the Chinese space-craft for supplies, especially reserves of blood. Every drop counts.

They've calculated exactly how much they'll need for the journey, factoring in two extra mouths. They need four people to handle takeoff and landing so they supplement their crew with an astronaut from the *Isabella* and the Chinese pilot, who is familiar with their craft and can communicate with their Mission Control. Willows' eyes gleam when she experiences the sensation of converting a living, breathing human. Isaac, too, basks in the warmth of fresh blood permeating his body.

Isaac shows the Chinese vampire how to jigger his radio so it manifests the same symptoms that plagued the *Ferdinand*. Over the course of several interrupted transmissions, the pilot tells his supervisors that the mission is proceeding according to plan, except for the persistent communication problems, which will also interfere with telemetry data sent back to Earth from the Chinese ship during their return flight.

Their blood factories continue to produce while they await their launch window. Six of them will go into the ship's stasis pods in case anything goes wrong with their reserves on the way back. The remaining four will be left behind to perish, the first people to die on another planet. Not that anyone will ever know.

The voyage back to Earth will be brief compared to the eternity they'll live when they get there. No one will be expecting a ship 'manned' by vampires. After being cooped up for months, Isaac knows that they'll be ready to celebrate, turning the blue planet red with the blood spilled from all those pulsing veins awaiting them.

Bev Vincent's most recent book, *The Stephen King Illustrated Companion,* was nominated for both the Bram Stoker Award and Edgar Award. He is the author of over sixty short stories, including appearances in *Evolve, Tesseracts Thirteen, When the Night Comes Down, Ellery Queen's Mystery Magazine, Cemetery Dance* and *Thin Ice.* He is originally from New Brunswick but has lived fifty miles from Mission Control in the U.S. for the past two decades. A scientific article about a NASA proposal for the Hundred-Year Starship was his inspiration for "Red Planet."

Beacons Among the Stars
By Anne Mok

Nocturne City, Chao Meng-Fu Crater, Mercury
Joshua strode through the riverside grove in the illusion of daylight, a thousand lanterns hanging from the trees like fruit. His blood still sang with warmth from the woman who had let him drink from her.

Here, the air shimmered like summer, but beyond the crystal-line dome ice lay scattered like diamond dust; and high above, the rim of the crater forever shadowed them in darkness.

Nocturne was a city where the sun never rose.

Joshua found Lucas sitting by the artificial river, arms wrapped around his knees. He seemed heedless of the children darting past, or the lovers strolling arm in arm. A faraway smile touched his lips as he gazed across the water.

"What are you looking at?" Joshua said lightly, settling down beside him.

"Earth." Lucas turned to Joshua like a sunflower. "The first starships will be finished soon."

His own smile died. "Are you still thinking about that?"

"Aren't you?"

When Joshua didn't answer, Lucas said, "You've never been afraid to tread new territory. The Far East. The New World. The Great South Land. So why stay here, clinging to the shadows of Mercury?"

Lucas had impossibly romantic notions sometimes. He had no idea what it was really like to launch yourself into the unknown. The terrifying struggle to stay alive and unexposed. "I can tell you now, if you get on that ship, you're on your own."

Lucas punched his shoulder. "Come on. You know if you stay behind, you'll always regret it."

They were both of them trying to make it light, but there was an edge to it.

Joshua drew him close, as though he could stop Lucas from slipping away. "We have a sanctuary here, for the first time in history. The rest of the universe is not so forgiving."

Lucas shook his head, eyes undaunted. "Just because we are what we are, does that mean we don't deserve to go to the stars?"

Two hundred years later

The blare of the emergency alarm shook Joshua awake. Cursing, he pushed open the lid of his sleeper, which clattered onto the steel floor of the cabin. Joshua crawled out and fumbled around in the puddle of yesterday's uniform until he found his commlink, just as the alarm cut out.

"Shepherd here," he said. "What the hell's going on?"

"Relax, the ship's fine." Zheng's voice buzzed over the commlink, an edge to its normal breezy confidence. "That was the proximity warning. You might want to get down here."

Joshua shrugged into a clean uniform and hit the switch on the synthesizer. It hummed as it warmed up and started processing. It was still set to the default: one liter, AB, 36.9 degrees. When it beeped to a stop, Joshua poured himself a cup of steaming hot blood. As he drank, his gaze fell across the chart pinned to the wall above the synthesizer: an antique map of the constellations as seen from Earth, faded and frayed at the edges.

The others were already crammed onto the bridge of the *Griffith* when he got there: Zheng in the pilot's chair, Arn leaning over her shoulder, Uresha and Kado squeezed in at the sides.

Joshua stopped in the doorway. "Hey, what's the emergency?"

"We reached the XDE system two hours ago," Zheng said. "Sent out a probe as usual. But there's already something out there." She pointed at the monitor.

The image on the screen resolved into a starfield, the XDE sun a bright glow in the distance, and in the foreground—

In the foreground, a hulking mass loomed, blunt as an ancient battleship, floating adrift in space. Joshua recognized it at once. One of the giant colony ships, slower than light, used in the earliest days of interstellar expansion. He had seen the first of them launch from Earth orbit, gliding out of spacedock like one of the tall ships of old.

"One of the Lost Ships." If Joshua had still possessed a heartbeat, it would have been accelerating. "Is it safe?"

Zheng nodded. "Phase engines are dead. I made sure to check."

"Poor bastards," Arn said, gazing at the wreck. Its hull gaped open, debris floating around the gash. "How many of those ships went out before they learned there was something wrong?"

"Nothing was wrong with phase theory itself—" Uresha began, and she and Arn launched into one of their frequent debates about engineering history.

"At least it would have been painless," Kado mused. "You go to sleep, dreaming about your new homeworld, and you just never wake up."

Joshua remained staring at the screen. "Zheng, I want to go over there."

She furrowed her brow. "What for? We'll put in a report with the Salvage Corps when we get back."

"I want to see if I can download the logs."

Understanding dawned on her face. "You still think his ship could be out there somewhere?"

"It's not impossible."

Zheng said nothing, only eyed him with worry. Eventually, she shook her head. "You be careful, okay?"

He flashed her an affectionate salute. "I've been crewing starships for longer than the rest of you put together. Besides, there's not much that can kill me."

The flitter touched down on the hull of the colony ship with a soft shudder. Joshua had picked a landing spot near the bow, furthest from the giant gash that opened the guts of the ship to space.

He powered down the flitter and swung out of the pilot's chair. Metal clanked as he moved—twin canisters of blood strapped to his back where oxygen tanks would normally be. These days, he knew better than to go anywhere without emergency supplies.

He waited until he stood inside the airlock to put on his helmet. All standard sanguinaire pressure suits had a titanium shield where a transparent faceplate should be, to protect against sunlight, and even though the helmet optics compensated, he didn't like having that physical barrier to his vision.

The airlock cycled and the outer hatch swung open. Joshua stepped outside.

The hull of the colony ship curved away beneath him to the horizon, its surface weathered by long exposure to radiation and micrometeroids. Even the letters on the nameplate had been all but obliterated. The sun was a bright yellow ball in the distance;

only a few centimeters of polymer separated him from incineration. But space was equally hostile to living humans.

We are all aliens out here.

The outline of a hatch was visible several meters away. Joshua shot a magline towards it; the grapple thudded home and he reeled himself in. He touched the controls beside the hatch, but they were dead. Fortunately, the manual release lever still functioned.

A ladder descended into darkness. He shone his wristlight down. "Heading inside."

"Roger," Zheng replied. "Reading you loud and clear."

Joshua propelled himself down the ladder, bouncing from rung to rung. It dropped him into a wide corridor that followed the long axis of the ship. The lights shining from his helmet and wrists cut circles from the darkness, revealing buckled walls and tangled metal struts. The damage looked bad, but even the most miniscule natural hyperfield could cause havoc if it intersected a ship's phase drive.

The door at the end of the corridor was stuck fast, frame bent out of alignment. He pulled hard, throwing all his considerable strength into it. It gave. A frozen body spilled through the open doorway. Joshua recoiled.

"Damn!" Zheng said in his earpiece. "That was nasty."

"Yeah." Gathering his composure, Joshua drifted forward and examined the body. Adult male, early middle-age, dressed in Expansionist Era clothes. His skin was tinged blue, and his swollen features were evidence of rapid decompression.

The dead were nothing to fear, Joshua reminded himself. He of all people should know better than that.

He pulled himself through the doorway and shone his wristlights across the vast chamber beyond. Row after row of cryocapsules, like glassy pods, lined the walls. Some were smashed; all were dark and lifeless. More bodies hung motionless in the vacuum—a silent, grim tableau.

His heart sank. No chance of any survivors in this wreckage. Not even sanguinaires, who could survive airless tombs, had an answer to hard vacuum. Even if he found who he was looking for, it would be a bitter outcome.

A second chamber lay beyond that one, in similar condition. But as Joshua approached the third door, he was startled to see a faint light emanating from its control panel.

He palmed the door open.

Air rushed out past him. He dragged himself inside and slapped his hand down on the controls and the door slid shut. His body lurched in midair without warning. Joshua realized he was falling a fraction of a second before he hit the ground, bones jarred by the impact.

The artificial gravity was working in here. Not only that, but his readings reported the chamber was pressurized and oxygenated.

Long rows of cryocapsules again dominated the chamber, frost spreading thin fingers across their surfaces. One cryocapsule drew Joshua's attention. It was open, its lid raised at a neat angle. Cautiously, Joshua peered inside.

Empty.

He swung his gaze down the row: at least a dozen cryocapsules in the same state, lids raised, all empty.

"Zheng," he said into the commlink. "I think there may be survivors."

Joshua opened the door to the bridge, his nerves taut with hope. It was irrational—there was slim chance that Lucas would be among the survivors, slim chance that he was even aboard this ship at all. It was a fool's hope, but better than no hope at all.

"The bridge is pressurized and oxygenated too," he said to Zheng. "And the artificial gravity is running. Residual power in the life support systems, maybe."

He went over to the computer, looking for the controls to power it up. The systems were antiquated, but he remembered when they had been state of the art.

"Zheng, can you look up the base codes for the Lateral 60 processors?" he said, hands roving over the control panel. He waited for confirmation, but there was nothing. "Zheng?"

No response.

Uneasiness crawled over Joshua. How long had the comms been down?

He looked up at the monitor again, still cold and black, reflecting behind him another face.

He spun around, and came up against the muzzle of a laser welder.

"Stop right there."

Joshua froze, staring at the woman who stood behind the laser welder. She stared back at him, eyes narrowed against the brightness of his wristlights. She wore smudged overalls and her blonde hair was hacked short. She might have been thirty, or older if she'd had rejuv. He couldn't remember if it had been made widely available before or after the last colony ships had gone out.

Slowly, Joshua raised his hands. "I'm not going to hurt you."

"Who are you?" she said. "Let me see you."

Moving slowly, Joshua took off his helmet. The air tasted cold and faintly chemical. "My name is Joshua Shepherd. I'm an astrocartographer." He watched the end of the laser welder carefully—he might be impervious to many hurts, but he could still die by fire. "I'm here with a survey ship. We found your vessel drifting in space."

"How do I know you're not a pirate or a scavenger?"

"I have ID." Joshua reached for his right wrist and unsnapped the disc fastened there. The woman's hand tightened on the trigger. Joshua noted that the safety was off. "This is my astro-cartographer license."

He tossed it to her. Just before she caught it, he remembered it listed his year of birth. But her face didn't change as she read it. Maybe it was all right. She couldn't know what year it was after all, with the systems down and no contact with the universe.

She tossed it back to him. "How do I know it's not fake?"

"How can I prove that it's real?" He jerked his head at the laser welder. "If you shoot me, how will you get off this ship?"

"I guess I would take your ship," the woman said flatly.

"I came here to help," Joshua said, in what he hoped was a reassuring voice. "You and the other survivors."

Her eyes flickered sideways and back. "There are no other survivors."

Joshua opened his mouth, and then closed it. She obviously didn't trust him yet, and she might well want to keep a few things back until she did. There were certainly things he wasn't about to tell her—this colony ship dated from before the Concordance, and she'd probably only heard of sanguinaires as myth or night-mare. In any case, it wouldn't help their fledgling relationship if he pushed her too hard now.

"I can get you off this wreck," Joshua said. "But we have to leave soon. My ship is on a mission, and we have a very narrow launch window to leave this star system."

He could see the conflict in her eyes. "All right," she said at last. "But stay where I can see you."

"Can I ask your name?"

"Sara."

"Sara. I'll get you to safety. And anyone else who—" He stopped. Around them, the computers were springing to life, rows of colored panels lighting up, the systems beeping in swift succession.

"Did you do that?" Joshua said.

"No. It's the engines coming online."

Joshua stared at her in disbelief. "The phase drive is dead."

She shook her head. "It powers up once a month to recharge the life support systems. But that's about all it can cope with."

He could hear it now, a dull whine rising to sharp pitch. "We have to shut it down, or we're all dead."

She stared at him like he had gone insane. "It's perfectly safe. I told you, it does this once a month."

"My ship is out there!" Seeing her incomprehension, he added, "My ship uses hyperfield technology. Hyperfields and phase drives don't mix."

Their gazes remained locked a moment more. Then a deep vibration resonated through the ship, sending his bones shuddering. The expression on Sara's face changed. She lowered the laser welder and pushed past him to the computer. "If this is a trick, so help me—"

But Joshua was already busy shouting into his commlink. "Zheng! Move the *Griffith* out! Stay out until the drive shuts down!"

Only static squealed from the comms.

The floor tilted. The walls warped. Joshua saw something bright and metallic hurtling towards him faster than he could even—

The world reeled as soon as Joshua opened his eyes. He let his lids fall closed again. Pain swelled in his chest, huge as a balloon.

With an effort of will, he forced his eyes open. The red glow of emergency lighting revealed a scene out of a nightmare. Above him, the ceiling had ripped apart, edges curled outward in frozen waves, exposing the bridge beyond. Twisted piping spilled like intestines from the walls. Fragments of metal floated around him, winking as they spun in slow motion.

Joshua looked down and almost passed out again. A jagged steel pipe, almost ten centimeters in diameter, protruded from his chest. He was impaled, a great gaping hole in the torso of his suit, seeping blood in a slow tide.

He let out a gasp, tinged with hysteria; the wound was a hairsbreadth from his heart. He tried to draw together shreds of calmness. He didn't have much time.

His hands felt like limp plastic, but he gripped the pipe with all his strength.

Counted to three.

Pulled.

The world turned white.

Joshua came to again, lightheaded, pain still radiating from his chest. Fat globules of blood hung in the air, gleaming like rubies.

Someone called his name in the distance. A shadow moved above, beyond the torn ceiling. "Hey! Are you down there?"

Sara. He mustn't let her find him like this. "Don't come down here! It's too dangerous!"

She shouted something back, but his awareness chose that moment to fade out again, and when sight and hearing returned, her shadow was gone.

Joshua reached behind him for his emergency canisters, fumbling in zero gee, the contortions almost causing him to pass out again. He finally managed to detach one of the canisters from its harness and unscrew the lid. He fastened his mouth over the nozzle and drank.

His throat worked as the blood poured into him, rich and nourishing, seeping into his cells, tanging in his nostrils with that sour metal smell. With the first canister drained, he started on the second.

The lights brightened to full power. The ship shuddered as gravity returned. Joshua experienced a moment of lurching freefall, and then crashed to the tiles. Twin bangs as the canisters hit the floor. Blood splashed like rain.

He lay motionless in the pool of blood, feeling himself start to knit together again, sensing the blood work its healing potency on him, knowing it wasn't enough.

"Hey!" Sara, on the other side of the door. "Can you hear me?"

"I'm all right!" He had to get his suit off. There was a bloody great hole through it. He undid the fastenings and crawled out of the ruined suit. He salvaged what he could—commlink, wristlights, magline—and shoved it out of sight behind some wreckage. Nothing he could do about the blood—the place looked like a slaughterhouse. He stepped outside and sealed the door behind him, hoping that Sara wouldn't enter the room anytime soon.

She had a cut on her forehead and stood with one arm cradled in the other. She stared at him. "You look like hell."

"Just a scratch. I'm fine." But his voice sounded hollow in his own ears.

The infirmary looked as though it had boasted enough medical supplies to tend an army. Sadly, it also looked as though that army had stormed through already. Burst bottles of antiseptic littered the floor, contents soaked up by long white streamers of unrolled bandages. The fuser still functioned to fix Sara's broken arm, but there was no familiar domed pillar of a synthesizer, or even one of the huge units from the early days. At the time this ship was launched, Talwar and Chang hadn't even been born, let alone thought about inventing a way to synthesize artificial blood.

"What are you looking for?" Sara asked, as Joshua roamed through the infirmary, opening and closing cabinets.

"Just taking inventory."

He ran the calculations through his head. He'd fed that morning. Only six hours ago. He should have been able to go a week without feeding again, if pushed, but he had lost a lot of blood. The two canisters he had drunk had helped restore him, but he was still running at a deficit. Hunger shock would set in soon unless he was replenished.

"We have to repair the comms," Joshua said. "Get in touch with my ship quickly. Within the next forty eight hours."

"What happens in forty eight hours?"

Good question, Joshua thought. "Let's try to get out of here before then."

Joshua lay on his back beneath the bridge computer, replacing the burned out circuits. It wasn't just the comms he needed to access, but also the database with the passenger manifest. Sara had left the repairs to go fetch extra parts from stores, evidently trusting him enough now to let him out of her supervision.

"Hey. This is for you."

Joshua pulled himself out from under the computer, prepared to make his excuses if it was dinner. So far, Sara hadn't offered him food, and he hadn't asked. He had rehearsed answers for all the questions she might ask, answers he hadn't had to use since the old days of pretending, of having to pass, and it was sad how easily it all came back to him, as though somewhere in his subconscious he had known he might have to do it again.

But it wasn't food Sara had brought. "I found some clean clothes. Yours are a mess."

She handed him a pair of overalls, neatly folded.

"Thanks," Joshua said. He shook them out, and found Sara watching him with an odd expression.

"They belonged to my husband. He was about your size."

"Was he aboard when—?"

Sara nodded.

"I'm sorry."

She shook her head, making a cutting motion with her hand. "It's past and gone. Only the future matters."

He looked carefully at her, but she seemed to mean it, fierce resolution burning through the shadow of grief. She would have had to be determined, to live on after all she had been through.

"Where were you going?" Joshua asked quietly.

"A yellow star out past Canis Major. One habitable planet. We were going to set up a homestead by the mountains. Farm wheat and barley. Grow peaches out the back." She fell silent for a minute, then said, "So. What are you doing out here?"

He had the answer ready. It was even true. "We're an astronomical survey ship for the Commonwealth of Worlds. Our mission is to chart new star systems and set up astrobeacons for interstellar travel and commerce."

"I got that before. I'm not looking for the official brochure. I mean, what are *you* doing out here?"

"Me?" Joshua had that answer ready too—exploring new worlds, making new discoveries, seeing all the wonders the universe had to offer. But it wasn't his answer, it was someone else's, the someone whose footsteps he was following in. "I'm looking for someone. Someone I lost long ago."

"And you were looking here?"

He shook his head. "I came here by chance."

"Lucky you." A twisted smile. But the first smile she had displayed.

He smiled back, feeling suddenly lighter. No, lightheaded. He blinked. Everything looked sharper and brighter, the colors more vivid, the smells more intense. Sara was saying something, but he wasn't listening. It was hunger, the onset stealing upon him, an aching sensation in his belly, fangs sliding forth from their recesses. He pushed them back in with his tongue, thought about snow, ice, the cold dark of space.

No good. The scent of blood filled his lungs; the pulse of blood filled his ears.

He leaned heavily against the computer and looked at Sara, whose face was registering alarm. "There's something I have to tell you."

She looked like she was deciding whether to support him or bolt for the door. "What?"

"I have a condition requiring regular medication, and I'm out. I may start to behave erratically, or even violently."

"What kind of condition? Like a mental illness?" Her eyes narrowed. "Is that what you were doing in the infirmary? Looking for drugs?"

"Listen. The important thing is to keep on with repairs and try to contact my ship. But I can't trust myself to stay in full possession of my faculties. Is there somewhere on this ship that can be used as an isolation room? Somewhere that locks from the outside?"

Sara nodded. "The upper cargo bay."

Joshua took a deep breath. "Lock me in. And then get back to work on the comms. Tell my crewmates you require urgent assistance, priority one. Wait until they get here. Until then, don't let me out."

"Even if you ask me?"

"Especially if I ask you."

Ten hours later, it no longer seemed like such a brilliant idea. Joshua paced back and forth in the aisles between towers of boxes, with nothing to do except brood on his situation, aware of the hunger yawning wider in his stomach.

His path took him in a wide circle, past the bay door that led to space at one end and the door to the ship interior at the other. "Sara?" he said into the wall intercom. "How are the repairs going? Any contact with my ship yet?"

"No," the curt response came. "Working on it."

"Well, work faster." He meant it to sound lighthearted, but it came out strained. Hoping to soften it, he added, "Please."

After a pause, Sara said, "How are you doing?"

"I'm okay." He gripped his arms and kept pacing. It had been a long time since he had last gone dry. So easy to forget, afterwards, how bad it got. He closed his eyes and leaned his hands against the wall.

He hadn't fed on human blood in over a hundred years. But how easy it would be, an inner voice said, if only he had the courage to ask. Sara would understand. She was a spacefarer, an explorer, a survivor. He should take her into his confidence. They could deal with the situation together. She could afford to help him a little. Just enough to tide him over until rescue came.

Joshua sank to the floor and buried his head in his arms.

After a long time, he unfolded and stood.

"Sara?" he said into the intercom. "If you're there, answer me."

"I'm here." Her voice echoed as though from far away.

"Any luck with getting a message through yet?"

There was a long pause, so long Joshua thought the intercom might have cut out. "There's not going to be a message, Joshua."

"What? Sara—"

"I found your suit."

Joshua stopped dead. He could hear her harsh breathing rasp over the intercom. "I can explain."

"Half stuck to the floor with dried blood—"

"Sara—"

"I could put my hand through the hole!"

Joshua closed his eyes for a moment. "I didn't want to scare you, Sara."

"It makes sense now," she cut in. "All the pieces that didn't fit. So the old stories are true. Monsters walking among us in the shape of men."

"The world has changed. There are things you don't understand—"

"I understand what you are! *Vampire*."

"We don't use that word anymore," Joshua said.

A strange sound came from the intercom. It took a moment for him to identify it as laughter.

"It doesn't matter what word you use," Sara said. "I saw your 'medical supplies'. Planning to restock?"

"It's artificial blood. We have machines that make it. If I meant to hurt you, why would I lock myself up?"

"I don't know what games you're playing, I only know you've been lying to me from the moment we met."

"Call my ship," Joshua said in desperation. "When my shipmates come, they'll tell you the same."

"How do I know they're not all like you? I'm turning off the intercom now."

"No! Don't!" He clutched at it in futility. Only silence. He pounded his fists against the door. "Sara!" The reinforced steel plating barely showed a dent. He struck it again in frustration.

Footsteps outside. He went on alert. Had she decided to confront him? An odd hissing noise. One edge of the door glowed with a line of light. He recognized the hum of lasers and stared in disbelief.

She was welding the goddamn door shut.

Joshua lifted the last of the crates into position, and then took a running jump and leapt on top of them. The tower of boxes rocked beneath his weight, but he could reach the air duct high up on the wall now. He took out his pocket screwdriver and began unscrewing the grill. His hands shook only a little.

The intercom crackled to life again. "I can see what you're doing."

Joshua didn't allow it to interrupt him. "They'll come looking for me, you know."

"I know. I'm not going to be here."

Joshua stopped, the implications sinking in. She was going for the *Griffith*. While his crew was over here, she was going to take their ship. With sudden desperation, he said, "Listen to me! Don't do this. You don't have to do this—"

"Yes, I do. There's too much at stake." The intercom cut out.

Joshua's mouth tightened. There were only two screws left in the grill. He forced himself to work calmly and swiftly.

The sudden howl of klaxons almost deafened him. He clapped his hands to his ears, the screwdriver slipping from his grasp. It fell to the deck, bounced twice, and went skimming towards the far side of the cargo bay. Other small objects joined it, his eye tracing their path.

With horror, he saw that the cargo bay door was rising, the black of space widening.

"Sara!" he bellowed. "What are you doing?"

No answer. She was beyond persuasion now, fixed on her course and accelerating.

The tower of boxes beneath him collapsed, pulled towards the open door by the vacuum of space. He was swept along with them, grasping futilely for a handhold, any handhold. But there was nothing to grasp, though he snapped his nails trying.

Then they were out past the door, floating in eternity.

Joshua flung out a hand and the magline unreeled, thunking home on the hull of the ship. He was yanked to a standstill, the magline at full extension. He hung from its end like a pendulum weight, suspended in a sky full of stars.

His head throbbed like it was trying to expand beyond his skull, and his skin burned with a thousand icy pinpricks. But it was not cold or lack of oxygen or depressurization that would kill him, but the sun, shining steadily just beyond the curve of the hull—the sun that would disintegrate him instantly into cosmic dust.

He imagined letting go, allowing himself to dissolve into a thousand motes of light. Maybe it would be painless; maybe Lucas would be waiting for him. It would be easy to let go, easier than finding a reason to go on.

But he reeled himself in, towards the open maw of the cargo bay.

Even if you didn't have a reason, sometimes you had to make one.

The corridors of the ship twisted like some nightmare maze, warped by flawed science and flawed engineering, and the laws of the universe enforced with a vengeance. Lights flickered with sudden power surges; intercoms hissed white noise like the whisper of ghosts.

Joshua stalked down the twisted corridors, intent on his goal. He had to get to the bridge before Sara did and finish repairing the comms. And heaven help her if she got in his way.

Broken pylons and collapsed walls blocked his path. He wrenched them aside like tinfoil, his fingers leaving dents in the steel. He knew this wild frenzy would slake itself, but right now it ran unchecked, this demon gale rising inside him, this raging flood that swept rationality away. The human race, including its many aberrations, had built civilizations spanning the stars, but their spirits were still yoked to their bodies.

"Sara!" he shouted, not knowing if the intercom was picking him up, or if she was even listening anymore. His voice crackled back at him from the speakers, cut to pieces by the static.

"You can't kill me. I'm still here! You need my help. And I need yours." His voice dropped to a whisper. "Do you know where the word 'sanguinaire' comes from, Sara? It means 'bloodthirsty'. I'm thirsty, Sara, so thirsty…"

He pushed open another door in his way, and emerged into the cryocapsule hub he had passed through when he had first come aboard the ship. Where were the other survivors, anyway?

He found himself staring at the cryocapsules cradling their precious cargo. A terrible thought entered his mind.

Drawn like a moth to a flame, he walked towards the nearest intact cryocapsule, blood pounding in his head. He would only be borrowing a little. He only needed a little.

The surface of the capsule was fogged with condensation. He wiped it away, hands shaking. The shape of the man inside became clearer. Joshua froze. The man was missing his arms.

There was no mistake. Each arm had been severed at the shoulder, clean cuts almost surgical in precision.

His gaze went to the opened cryocapsules. The ghastly realization dawned.

There are no other survivors, Sara had told him.

"You shouldn't have come here."

Joshua turned around. Sara stood in the doorway, laser welder pointed at him. Her face was white. "You shouldn't have seen." She fired.

Joshua dropped, the heat of the beam spearing over his shoulder. He rolled sideways as the beam tracked his path, lines of molten metal marking its wake. When he hit the base of a cryocapsule, he scrambled to his feet and ducked behind it.

"Sara, what have you done?"

"You don't know what I've been through. What it took to survive..."

Her footsteps approached. Joshua pulled away from his shelter and ran across to the next aisle. He swept his gaze over the rows of cryocapsules, realizing for the first time that the cables trailing from them were corroded, that their lights blinked in meaningless patterns.

"How many years since you woke, Sara?" he called. "Five? Ten?" Long enough for stores to rot, for hydroponics to fail. "How long have you been trapped here, alone with all the dead?"

"Shut up!" She punctuated her words with another blast of the laser welder. Joshua edged along the aisle towards the next. "I didn't have a choice. I tried to wake Robert. I tried to wake them all. But they thawed out dead. Every time. And then—" Her voice cracked. "And then the food ran out."

The final aisle. Sara was just around the corner. Joshua spotted a lone cryocapsule sitting a short distance from the others, cables attaching it to them like a long umbilical. Scant cover, but better than nothing. He made a dash for it, just as Sara strode into view.

"Get away from that!" she cried.

A lance of fire pierced his legs. He muffled a cry as he stumbled the last few steps, moving like a machine with jammed pistons, before collapsing against the side of the cryocapsule.

He looked up as Sara's shadow fell across him. Her eyes burned with white hot rage and grief.

"Who is it, Sara?" he asked. "Who's in this cryocapsule?"

She hesitated, chest heaving as she gulped down the stale air. "My daughter."

So that was it—the reason why she had chosen to live on despite the slim chance of ever being rescued, the reason for the desperate things she had done to survive. Because she wasn't alone. She had someone to live for.

"I'm going to take her, and get off this ship, and there's nothing you can do to stop me." She raised the laser welder, knuckles white around the grip.

"Sara, she's gone. What you're doing won't bring her back."

"Shut up." Her eyes were still hard, but they were bright as well, glistening with unshed tears. "You're lying."

"I'm not lying. You know I'm not lying."

"No!" Sara gestured with the laser welder. "You—you can bring her back! You can make her live forever!"

He saw the desperation in her face; he saw the hopeless denial. And he recognized it. A sense of vertigo assailed him.

You could cling to an illusion for a very long time. That was easy. The hard thing was letting go.

I'm sorry, Lucas.

I wish I had come with you then. But I can't unmake the past. And now you've gone where I can't follow.

Goodbye.

"I wish I could bring her back," Joshua said. "But I can't restore the dead to life. I can only help the living." Gently, he added, "She's gone on ahead. Let her go."

Sara stared at him for a few moments, her gaze darting about his face, searching for the truth. Then the laser welder dropped from her grip. She sank to her knees and wrapped her arms around the cold, lifeless cryocapsule.

"All I wanted was a new life with the people I loved. So what was it all for?"

Joshua pushed himself painfully to his hands and knees and placed a hand on her shoulder. Some fluke of the universe, some chance in a million, had spared her the fate of everyone else aboard, but that would not be any comfort now. "You still have a life ahead of you. It doesn't end here."

"I don't deserve to live!"

"That's not for you to decide." He watched her struggling with her despair, and remembered. "Do you think you're the only one who has ever committed terrible acts to survive? You can always redeem yourself. But first you have to live long enough."

He had survived the fall of Nocturne, lived through the internment camps, and witnessed the riots of '76. He had outlived more friends than Sara would ever make. But still he kept going. "It has to mean something. We're here, against all the odds. We have to make it mean something."

She turned her tear-streaked face to him. "What do I do now?" she whispered.

"I don't know yet," he said honestly. "But you'll find out."

"Look up there." Lucas pointed at Capella, winking in the distance; the bright blaze of Sirius; the warm glow of Antares; and behind them, the shimmering expanse of the Milky Way. "That's where I'm going. To the stars."

Lucas' eyes lit up as he spoke. All Joshua could think of were the vast dark spaces between, the immensity of distance.

"But the stars are suns," Joshua said. "You'll never be able to look on them up close."

"If you're talking about this sun, then yes. But we've never felt the light of a different sun." Lucas turned his face skyward. "There are a billion billion stars out there, Joshua. Who's to say one of them won't shine kindly on us?"

"Shepherd?" Zheng's voice crackled over the commlink.

Joshua jerked awake. His back creaked with stiffness from having fallen asleep sitting against the cryocapsule, head bent at an uncomfortable angle.

"Zheng! About time. Are you all right?"

"We had to swing behind the sun until the phase oscillations damped out, but we're all in one piece. How about you?"

"I'll make it. Just come pick me up."

"Did you find what you were looking for?"

"Not exactly. But I found what I needed."

"What about the colonists?"

He glanced at Sara, sleeping peacefully beside him. He didn't know what would become of her now, where she would go, or what her future held. But that would be for her to decide.

"One survivor."

Anne Mok lives in Sydney, Australia, where she juggles legal editing by day with fiction writing by night. She is a graduate of Clarion South. "Beacons Among the Stars" came from wondering about the lack of stories about vampires in space, and believing that they deserve to go to the stars too. She is currently working on a novel set in the same universe.

The Big Empty

By Thomas S. Roche

The things wait for Eve in the shadows of Paradise, at the base of the second set of spirals well past the desiccated sorghum stalks, the place where darkness claims the last pale whispers of the Level 85 grow lamps.

At least, that's what the stories say.

But, then, stories don't scare her. They don't scare any of her kind; Agarthans have very little fear and almost no imagination. Yes, there are stories in Agartha, like the ones of the things that live below Level 85. But there are not many of them. But Those legends are aberrations. 'Art' in the city of Agartha is the art of the well-delivered lecture on plant biology. Agarthans do not tend to conjecture. They do not react to speculation.

They respond to *evidence*, even when it is fragmentary.

So the Halloween tales of dark things that drink blood in the shadows don't worry Dr. Eve Mojica at all.

What worries her are the *lights*.

There's nothing growing on Level 85. Eve is given to understand that there has *never* been anything growing there, which is probably why someone many years ago thought up the story of the monsters to explain why there were grow lamps there.

Eve looks at the lamps as she spirals down past them on the death-black stairway built of carbon-fiber composite. There are ten full banks of glaring sun-spectrum lights exactly like what hovers over the now-dead fields on Levels 20 through 70—the fields that used to grow food for the 100,000 residents of Agartha.

So…why grow lamps on the big empty of Level 85?

Eve asks Gaardner, Captain of the Frosties.

He looks at Eve pointedly.

Eve doesn't like that. Eve doesn't like being looked at any more than the Frosties like being *not* looked at when someone is talking to them. Eve doesn't like eye contact.

Far worse, like all Frosties, Gaardner tends to forget that Agarthans like Eve have easily dark-adapted eyes. This was partially bred and partially genetically engineered, but for some reason the Frosties can't remember it. So whenever they talk to Eve, they blind her with those multimillion-lumen tactical flashlights, which he does when she asks him about the grow lights on Level 85.

Eve puts her hand up to block the beam.

He says, "Sorry." He lowers his light.

Eve repeats her question: "Why grow lamps on Level 85?"

"It's nothing. Superstition. It's just because of the stories. Stories. That's *all*."

Ondrusek overhears this. She's second in command of the once-frozen soldiers—a Lieutenant. But Eve's the lone Agarthan and the only plant biologist on this mission, so in that sense Eve outranks her as completely as Gaardner outranks Ondrusek. So if he won't tell Eve, he won't tell Ondrusek.

Eve opens her mouth to respond to Gaardner's dismissal; she thinks better of it and nods, even though she knows what Gaardner said can't be true. Every watt-hour counts; here are millions of them, slowly cooking rocks fifteen levels and four hundred fifty meters below the lowest hydroponics bays. What kind of sense does that make? And Agarthans don't do anything that doesn't make sense.

Ondrusek seems to think Eve understands what the Captain is getting at, so she looks at Eve, seeking eye contact.

Eve doesn't like her doing it any more than she liked Gaardner doing it.

Even though Ondrusek's face is savagely haloed in the blinding lights, Eve squints and tries to read her face. She can't. It's hard enough for Eve to deal with that. Like all the Frosties, Ondrusek has shiny, blotchy stains across her skin from her long sleep in liquid nitrogen. Eve finds it unsettling at a distance and repulsive up close. Agarthans have smooth skin and that's what Eve is used to finding attractive or even tolerable.

But that is far from the most unsettling thing about Ondrusek, or any of the Frosties. To communicate, they rely on facial expressions and eye contact. Eve can't read these facial expressions on the malformed faces of 21st-century humans. Specifically bred and engineered *not* to read expressions in faces, at least not naturally, Eve was also built not to react if she stumbles upon them.

Things are pretty cozy in Agartha; this helps keep everyone polite.

So Eve shrugs; it's a gesture the ancient humans do that means 'insufficient data', or something like that. Eve has been working on that gesture. She is not at all sure she does it adequately, but at least it gets Ondrusek to stop looking. Ondrusek looks away, in fact, with unsettling quickness.

Gaardner growls, "Let's keep moving."

The spiral stairway cuts through a smooth, ancient lava tube.

Eve and the others circle and circle and circle. They've much further to travel—*down*.

"Doctor, do you have a soul?"

This is Gaardner; he is given to such non-sequiturs during rest periods.

Eve says: "I'm sorry, Captain. I don't understand the question. You'll need to be more direct."

Gaardner says bitterly, "All right, I'll be more direct. At what point does a human cease to be a human? How's that for more direct?"

Eve says: "Not very."

Gaardner glares at her, thinking. "Let's try a different tack, then. Are we the same species?"

Eve can handle that question.

She says: "Captain, whether you or I could reproduce naturally and produce generatively viable offspring is entirely open. It wouldn't be allowed, and such an endeavor would be of no interest to any Agarthan beyond scientific curiosity. So it can't be settled whether we are the same species or not. Additionally, your sexual potency is at issue, given the cryosleep. It is unlikely you could even achieve sexual congress with *any* female, let alone an Agarthan."

Eve gets the sense her response hasn't gone over very well. She's never seen a Frosty's blotchy skin patches go so many shades of pink in the course of ten seconds.

Gaardner finally sputters, "You really *don't* have souls. What's inside Agarthans, Doctor? Just a big *empty*?"

Eve says: "I don't understand your question, Captain. Please be more direct."

He sighs. "You want direct? Here's direct. When I went to sleep I thought I was saving the race from extinction. They said, *When you wake up, you'll kill anyone we tell you to, capisce? I said, Hell, yeah. I'm saving the race from extinction, why not?* I woke up and they told me, *There's your enemy.* I was expecting to fight—I don't know. Aliens? Mutants? Monsters? That's not what I got. No, your forefathers pointed me at this pathetic band of surface survivors and told me to kill. Doctor, I don't know if you know much about what happened in the war, but it was *twenty years* after the solar flares. *Twenty years!* These scrappy little sons-of-bitches had survived as a society for twenty years! Not well, mind you—there wasn't much left—but they'd made it. They'd had children, they'd *raised* children; they'd lived through a scourging of the Earth unlike anything in the Bible or wherever. To them, Agartha would have been *Paradise.*"

He speaks with mounting animation, which makes Eve extremely uncomfortable.

So she says helpfully: "Yes. Paradise. That's what we call it. Colloquially, I mean—the way in your time this planet was called both Earth and The World. Historically, Agartha was a paradise at the center of the Earth—"

Gaardner ignores Eve and talks louder, trembling, panting slightly. "These were men and women I would have been proud to call brothers. Well, they found Paradise, all right. They found Paradise and asked to be let in. They were barely alive. They showed up in jerry-rigged tanker trucks, using hardware-store respirators, diving masks, buddy-breathing on old oxygen canisters—they had hunting rifles and crossbows and hatchets. They knew they couldn't last much longer, so they said *Save us.* My bosses said, *No, we don't think so.* The survivors fought their way into Level 0 before the City Managers—your, what, great-great-great-great whatever umpteen times grandfathers and grandmothers—they pointed us at them and said, *Kill.* So I killed. Life expectancy had to be like twenty-eight or thirty with the low oxygen levels and the lack of food and medicine and the new diseases. I killed *children,* Doctor. I killed lots and lots of children. I have to live with that."

Eve says helpfully: "Yes. You do."

Gaardner continues as if he hasn't heard her. "And a thousand years later I wake up and find you, Doctor, the precious seed of the human race, the fruit of my labors. And I don't even recognize you as human."

Discomfited by her inability to understand what Gaardner is trying to say, Eve tells him: "As I believe I implied earlier, you are arguably as inhuman as I. Had you the capability, I would suggest we mate and settle the matter, as revolting as that would be for me. But as I mentioned, you would be incapable."

Gaardner loudly talks over her. "What I'm trying to say, Doctor, is that if *you* had to pull the trigger on a hundred kids in dime-store respirators who wanted to come in out of the rain, would you have done it? And if you did, would it *bug* you? Would you be *haunted* by it, the way I am?"

Eve says: "Understanding your emotional makeup is well beyond me, but no, I don't believe I would have killed children. Even an order from the City Managers must be countermanded if it engenders the potential extinction of a viable species."

Gaardner makes a gasping noise. He looks distinctly like he has been struck with a club or a fist or an open palm—Eve has come to recognize at least that response.

She finishes her thought: "As I said, the question of whether you and I are the same species is sufficiently ambiguous that I would be forced to protest, even to my own sacrifice. I would not kill those children, Captain, and in fact I would physically defend them even against other Agarthans. To fail to do so would abdicate all the social responsibility that has been explicitly bred, engineered and trained into me over the course of a thousand years, specifically to prevent atrocities such as the ones you committed. Does that answer your question?"

Gaardner is trembling.

Eve says: "Captain, are you sick?"

His voice shakes as he says, "Yeah, I think maybe I am. You're saying that *I'm* the one who doesn't have a soul."

Eve says: "I'm sorry, Captain. You'll need to be more direct. I don't understand the question."

He says, "Yeah. There's a lot of that going around lately."

The party has passed below the brightly lit level 85 and is already descending the stairs between Level 88/89 when the first soldier goes over the edge.

Durgin is a big, hulking freezerburned brute. Eve is close to Durgin. Frosties have paused behind Eve to point out a glittering field of flowstone with their blazing lights. They're making cooing sounds at it. The Frosties ahead of Eve and Durgin are moving fast.

So Eve is stuck behind Durgin when he stops, leans against the railing, and lifts his shotgun. He aims the forestock tactical light out into the big empty black, and sweeps the beam around.

He says, "Do you see something?"

Then he's gone.

In the space between blinks of her dark-adapted eye, Eve sees the flying thing.

It's like a person with a flowing cloak. It's flying, or maybe rappelling down from a height, from a crane or some other support. Eve doesn't know. She just knows what she saw: A flying *thing*, shaped like a human but thinner, paler, sharper, scooping Durgin up in its long bony arms and sweeping him off the staircase, over the railing, into the big black empty.

In the split second it takes the creature to drag Durgin over the rail, Eve sees it illuminated in the blaze of Durgin's gunlight: naked, shriveled, sexless, sharp with bones jutting through starved pink papery flesh.

Durgin's face goes horror-distorted so clearly that even an Agarthan understands it. Durgin gropes and fumbles after his shotgun. His chest expands in the fragment of a second it takes his mouth to open wide as a human mouth can open.

He's going to scream.

He never gets to.

Before he can, the creature's long fingers slither across Durgin's face and jerk his head violently to the side.

A big mouth opens: red with sharp white teeth. It takes Durgin's throat; Eve sees his body jerk and twitch in midair and then his shotgun, with its forestock tactical light, spins free and falls.

The blazing light rakes her face. Ten million lumens: Eve is blind. She stumbles back against the far railing. She lands on her ass. She gropes at her scalded eyes. Eve tries to scream. She's not made for it. That part's been bred out of her, as it's been taken from all Agarthans. She tries anyway. Her mouth opens like Durgin's. All that comes out is a soft sickly *retch*.

Eve stares up into light-scoured blackness.

Someone says, "Durgin?"

Eve tries to say something; she can't. She waves her hands. Nobody notices.

Someone else says, "Durgin, where are you?"

Then the chattering starts, and Eve rocks back and forth.

Someone says, "What the hell happened?"

Someone says, "Dr. Mojica! Did you see it?"

Someone says, "Dr. Mojica! What happened to Durgin?"
Someone says, "Dr. Mojica! What did you see?"
A few seconds later, they wish they hadn't asked.

Gaardner listens patiently, and then declares a verdict. "I don't think so, Doctor. Durgin slipped and went over the edge."

Ondrusek says, "Captain...did you hear what Doctor Mojica just *said*?"

Gaardner replies crisply, "No offense, Doctor, but I think you're imagining things."

Eve says: "We don't really do that."

He says, "Well you did. I think Durgin slipped over the edge. That's tragic." He addresses all of them. "Don't let the next one be you, all right? We'll say some words in memory of him when we get to the next landing. Let's keep moving."

Eve says: "We don't imagine things."

No one notices.

The landing between Levels 101/2 hovers in a stretch of natural cavern, surrounded by big empty silence with the walls far away—a hundred meters in places, two hundred in others. The carbon-fiber strands and struts that support the landing and the spiral stairway alike extend almost entirely up and down; there is only minimal contact with the walls at strategic points.

As the expedition rests on the landing, some of the Frosties lower their lights.

By the time Gaardner realizes the lapse, it's happened.

Something brushes Eve's face. Wind hisses around her.

Someone's boots hit the railing very close to her.

Eve sees it again, closer this time: A swirl of white shrouded in black: an emaciated human form with what seems like a great black set of wings, allowing it to fly, which Eve knows should be impossible but isn't, based on what she sees. If it can't fly, how did it swoop down out of thin air and snatch a 200-pound soldier?

Again, it moves too quickly for Eve to get a really good look at it. But she sees more than enough. She sees the peeled-back, desiccated white lips of the thing. Eve sees the mask of sheer terror on the face of the Frosty—whose name she doesn't remember— a huge pale man of Northern European descent, blonde hair cropped close, face and neck and upper body lightly stippled from freezerburn and crisscrossed with war-era scars.

Eve again sees the long bony fingers of the creature fold over the soldier's mouth and across his big lantern-jaw, holding his head cocked at a soon-to-break angle. As that happens, a pale face, crazy with hunger, spreads wide around a big red-black hole; the mouth is red and wrinkled; the teeth are white and appear very sharp.

There is the wet, sickly, predatory sound of the mouth closing around the throat. There is the crack of the neck. The soldier blossoms at the throat, with the faint crunch of flesh and carotid and ruined, ravished trachea as the creature bites down.

Then more creatures flood in, like birds flocking. That's when the Frosties see them. They turn; someone screams, "What the fuck is that?"

Bony fingers tear in midair at the nameless soldier's clothes. Eve sees faces with paper-thin skin shot through with blue spiderwebs. She sees five or six red mouths open, sharp teeth tearing through military-strength fabric and into thighs, both sides of the throat, both sides of the belly—

Blood sprays freely.

Then Gaardner howls, "Lights around! Do a sweep! Head count!"

Lights sweep. Eve is blinded. She tries to scream. She gropes for something to lean against.

She hears a keening wail of blind terror coming from her own mouth.

Tangled in her lungs' fear-choked tributaries, her scream can't make it out. All it does for a moment is claw at her throat, and erupt as a vomiting sound.

Then a face comes out of the darkness for her.

Eve screams and hurls herself back; she doesn't know if she's falling or dying, and she doesn't care, because in that instant there's no room for anything but fear inside her. She may have gone over the railing; all she knows is she is screaming.

Eve gropes for the carbon-fiber floor and finds nothing.

She sees the face above her: masked with anger, furious: lips peeled back, teeth white, blood coming to his visage in great pulsing throbs. Gaardner reaches for Eve and screams, "Kill them!"

Screams burst all around Eve—everywhere.

Only *then* are there gunshots.

Gaardner throws himself on Eve, howling.

It all goes *dark*.

The caves are empty for a time; the space around Eve, beyond the spiral staircase yawns black.

Eve knows she's dreamed of faces in the darkness, white and bloodless. But she's not sure when the dreaming stopped; she's even less sure where it started.

Eve awakes and shivers herself upright with a start.

Gaardner's in front of her, sitting boots-apart, pistol in hand. Dazed, he stares at nothing, eyes wide and empty, mouth open: frozen in time.

The slide of Gaardner's pistol is locked open; smoke pours out. Bright brass cartridges litter the platform, alongside the empty brass-and-red-wax cylinders of spent 12-gauge rounds. There are also black pistol magazines, dropped shotguns, dropped lights, dropped pistols, dropped submachine guns. Many of the weapons have apparently not been fired.

Streams of white pour haphazardly from discarded flashlights. Bodies stretch on their backs, writhing. Eve realizes there aren't enough bodies. What began as twenty-four Frosties is now—maybe—eight. No, Eve counts nine of them.

With their respirators smashed or lost in the scuffle, the Frosties have to fight to catch their breath. The survivors haul themselves to their feet or their knees or to sitting positions. None of the dead are anywhere to be seen.

Her scream has left her throat raw; she doesn't like it. It didn't make her feel any better; she just didn't have a choice. Now a new sensation hits her. It's a desperate choking in her chest. It feels like she's about to vomit while being strangled.

She begins weeping. It's her first time.

Eve sobs: "Captain. What happened?"

He looks at Eve, obviously surprised to find her crying. "So you *do* have a soul?"

Eve sobs: "I'm sorry, Captain. I don't understand your question. Can you be more direct?"

He says, "I'm sorry. That was rude. Forget I said anything."

He ignores Eve and circuits the pistol through the envelope of darkness, stabbing bloody laser-sunrises into gunsmoky nothing.

Gaardner yells, "Head count!"

Eve has seen them do this before. It is useful when they are scattered up and down the stairway, because the matte black carbon-fiber structure twists in such a way that Gaardner can't see who's where.

They Frosties call out:
"Dentino."
"Hagler."
"Hunsley."
"Ondrusek."
"Verbasco."
"Tillett."
Eve's heard them do it a dozen times.

They always say them in alphabetical order.

There are always way more names—and no awkward silences between them while they wait for the names that never came: Dillard, Graleski, Haseman, Heiskel, Lintz, Menendez, Michalski, Weatherly, Yasso...

Gaardner says numbly, "Six. There are six of you left."

The sobs come at Eve hard. They take over her body. She can't control them. She doesn't like it. She screams: "I counted nine a few seconds ago!"

Gaardner growls, "Dr. Mojica? *When* did you count nine?"

"A few seconds ago!"

Gaardner pushes her away, turns around, sweeps the dark with his flashlight. Carelessly, he blinds Eve, which makes her sob harder.

"Where's Hagler?"

Five blank faces stare at him.

Ondrusek says, "She *just* called her name! I heard her!"

Gaardner snaps: "Anyone else?" He shouts. "Did you all hear Hagler's name a minute ago?"

Scattered nods answer him.

"Well, then, where the hell is she?"

No one answers him.

He loses it. "Keep your damn lights up! Keep your lights up! They're still out there!"

Someone, outraged, shouts, "They?"

Sobbing, Eve fumbles in the piles of spent cartridges. She finds an unfired pistol. She holds it and aims it into the dark.

Gaardner says, "We're aborting." He points and says, "We're going up, people. Up. *Fast!*"

Eve gets tired less quickly than the soldiers. She has less bulk to pull, and her lungs are made for low-oxygen subterranean environments.

The Frosties are all breathing hard, but Eve's not, when the seven of them cross the landing between Levels 93/4. That's when the light erupts. A bright flash from far overhead.

Everyone hits the deck.

The thundering burst is deafening.

Dust and gravel rains down around them accompanied by a wave of heat.

There's a big tortured sound like metal being ripped.

There's a hiss and a whistle.

Something sweeps past. Something *big*.

It is a very long time before Eve hears a scream, then a *Smack!* that echoes through the vast canyon.

More tremors, more dust, more gravel.

Gaardner yells, "Up! Up! Up! Go! Go! Go!"

He's *cursing* by the time they reach the jagged ends of the stairway.

The carbon-fiber steps have been sheared off by explosives at the landing between Levels 88/9.

Dentino is the one with the submachine gun and the field glasses. She looks through the latter and says, "Five levels at least."

Gaardner asks, "Damaged?"

"*Gone.*"

"That's impossible, Dentino! It's reinforced carbon fiber composite with an anti-brittling agent! They'd need high explosives!"

Dentino says, "Looks like they got 'em."

Someone howls, "They!?"

Gaardner says weakly, like a prayer, "It's carbon fiber! Carbon fiber!"

He looks at Eve blankly.

Eve makes eye contact, something incredibly weird for her.

He turns to his soldiers. "People, I need intel here. Tell me what you think you saw."

It explodes out of the five remaining grunts in delirious bursts while they wave their lights. Eve is totally blinded as she listens intently to the Frosties chatter:

"monsters—"

"—humans, but pale, flying—"

"—flying!"

"That wasn't rappelling, that was *flying*!"

"—*Mothman* or something—"

"—like demons—"

"—like the Devil!"

"—yeah, the Devil! Like medieval paintings—"

"I know I shot—ten, maybe? Twelve?"

"I shot some too! I know I hit them!"

"My shotgun hit one point blank. It didn't go down!"

"I saw them drag Dillard away in the air and—"

"I saw them *feed*."

"Oh, God, Eve saw that too? I think they—I saw them open his throat—"

"—her carotid—"

"—his femoral—"

"—this huge big gout of blood—"

"—teeth like knives—"

"Sucking blood. Sucking blood!"

Dentino shrieks, "Vampires!"

Everyone stops.

Someone says, "Dentino, are you *high?*"

Eve says: "What's a vampire?"

Everyone looks at her.

Eve doesn't feel the least bit gratified that she finally recognizes their expressions. They think Eve is crazy. She's getting used to that, but she'll never get used to being blinded, so she screams at the top of her lungs: "Get those fucking lights out of my face and tell me what the fuck a vampire is!"

They shy away from her as if slapped.

Dentino says, "You really don't know, Doctor? Don't you have *vampires* in Agartha?"

Eve howls: "How the hell should I know? What the hell are vampires?" She adds desperately: "Are they real?"

There's a big silence.

Someone says, "No."

Someone says, "Maybe..."

Someone says, "No..."

Someone says, "Then what the fuck were those?"

Someone says, "She's the scientist. *Could* they be real?"

Dentino shouts, "No! They're not. Vampires aren't real. They're characters from stories. Monsters."

Eve asks warily, like she has a hidden agenda—something Agarthans never, ever have: "What do the stories say vampires are?"

Everyone has something to add to the answer to that question. All of it comes in multi-voiced hysteria with the emphatic waves of a half-dozen ten-million-lumen flashlights.

Someone says, "Vampires are dead people."
Someone says, "They get bit by other vampires."
Someone says, "Then *they* turn *into* vampires."
Someone says, "And they live forever."
Someone says, "But they can't be killed."
Someone says, "They can be killed by sunlight, but not by bullets."
Someone says, "They feed on human blood."
Someone says, "On our blood."
Someone says, "On our *souls*."
Someone says, "Souls?"
Someone says, "Souls. That's how I heard it."
Someone says, "Dentino, are you *trying* to scare the doctor to death?"

Eve says: "They feed on your *souls*?"

"Well, they're fictional characters, so it depends who you— wait, Doctor. Did you say *your* souls?"

Eve looks at Gaardner, who sits, dazed and staring.

Eve says: "I don't have one, remember?"

Gaardner says, "I'm sorry, I didn't really mean that." He adds, "I guess you're learning about irony."

Someone says, "I always heard blood," but nobody wants to talk about it anymore.

Gaardner asks Eve, "Doctor, can we be rescued? By a rope ladder, crane, something from above where they sheared the stairway? Level 80, maybe, the last load-bearing entry point with granite?"

Eve says: "Of course. If we get the *seeds*."

"*If* we get the seeds?"

"If we get to the seed bank, I can send an ELF—extremely low frequency—transmission through the ground. If we have the seeds, they'll come rescue us."

Someone says, "We're closer to the top. We should go up, not down. We can send up flares."

Then, to Eve, someone says, "They'll come down and get us, right?"

Eve says: "Of course not. If we don't have the seeds, it wouldn't be worth the resources."

Someone, outraged, snaps, "Resources?"

Eve says: "Without the seeds, we're irrelevant to Agartha's survival."

Ondrusek says, "Great. So they'd just abandon us?"

Eve says: "I don't understand your question."

Dentino says, "Just like that? No guilt, and you think that's reasonable, Doctor?"

Eve says: "I don't understand what your question is."

Dentino growls viciously, "Does that bother you, Doctor?"

Eve says: "God damn it, I don't understand what you keep asking me!"

Eve is getting the hang of using profanity to indicate displeasure with their behavior; whenever she does it, it seems to shut them up quickly.

Ondrusek pushes through out of the blaze of five hot suns. She steamrollers over Eve and grabs Gaardner's shoulders. She asks, "Captain, what the hell are these things?"

In the darkness past the railing, something flutters.

Everyone backs away from the railing.

Everyone hoists weapons and aims at the dark—even Eve.

Her heart is pounding.

She doesn't like being scared; she hasn't been bred for it.

Blinded by the lights, she can't see much.

But she sees enough.

They move beyond the railings. Eve sees hints of *them*—cloaks, shrouds, robes, wings.

Then they're gone.

Eve says: "We have to get to the seed bank. I know what they are."

The Frosties gape at her, disbelieving.

Eve says: "I'll tell you while we go down."

Eve tells it in a spiral, fourteen booted feet tap-tap-tapping on the carbon fiber.

She says: "Agartha was built on the basis of limited biodiversity. They had about fifty years' worth of warning before the disaster happened. As with people, limited genetic lines of food crops could be brought underground and the crops tend to be vulnerable to the same diseases. That's why they built the seed banks. But they had limited time and resources. An elevator that size was power-prohibitive, so they built the stairway."

Someone says, "We know."

Eve say: "That's fact. Here's the story. When they built the stairway, they didn't have Agarthans yet—they hadn't bred us;

they hadn't genetically engineered us. In any event, if they had, we wouldn't have been good choices; we have too little upper-body strength and need too much mental stimulation to function optimally. The City Managers needed workers who could work in low light, without needing lights, in low oxygen without needing respirators, who would survive on very low protein diets. So they created them. This was in the early days. Genetic engineering wasn't as advanced. They were very short on time. They...they *improvised*. Radical modifications were attempted."

"At the end, the bureaucracy was confused and inefficient. There were contradictory orders. There ended up being thirty or forty different batches of workers. Some got away."

"Got away?"

Eve says: "Some went unaccounted for. Others vanished. Over the rails, off their ropes, out of tunnels. Sometimes witnesses saw them go—other times, they were just gone. Some were never found. Most were found...*drained*. Whatever did it didn't seem to like the light. So they built the grow lamps on Level 85."

Someone says, "How do you know all this?"

Eve say: "Everyone knows all this. They tell the story in Kindergarten. At *Halloween*."

"But you don't have *stories*."

Eve says: "We don't have *many* stories. But we have some. That's one of them."

Someone says, "Captain Gaardner, did you know this?"

Gaardner says, "I just knew there was a story. They told me it was *just* a story."

"Then why are there grow lamps on at Level 85?"

He says, "How the hell am I supposed to know? They didn't give me the details."

Ondrusek yells, "You're saying you didn't tell us crap that *Kindergartners* know?"

Gaardner snaps, "I didn't go to Kindergarten in Agartha. I went to Kindergarten at the Santa María del Cordero Catholic school in Vancouver. I'm from a thousand years ago, and I don't belong here anymore than you do!"

Ondrusek growls, "You don't know how true that is."

As the Frosties are distracted arguing, Eve's the one who sees what's coming.

Faces drawn and bloodless, lips pulled back to show fang-like teeth flashing deadly, naked starved bodies white with flesh stretched over sharp bones. The creatures have murder in their big open cat-eyes that blaze green-white at the faintest hint of illumination.

Eve screams at the top of her lungs, a real scream, so big it feels like she is turning inside out.

In an instant, the Frosties' panic-swept tactical lights and the vampire faces vanish into her blindness.

Then the lights start spiraling over the edge of the landing amid bleating howls and wet sounds and sprays of hot blood.

Eve raises her gun and starts shooting; hysterical with terror, she never stops screaming as she fires and fires and fires...

Eve hears her scream—fragmented, gone staccato between gunshots.

She's really getting the hang of this screaming thing.

Eve returns from the black haze of terror as if from dreamland.

She is on her back, legs cocked at an improbable angle.

The slide of her gun is locked open; it pours smoke. The thirty-round magazine is empty.

Sobbing, she feels in her pockets for the magazines she picked up after the second attack. They're all gone.

She can't see a thing. She gropes on the floor. She finds empty cartridges and shotgun shells—no fresh magazines, no unspent ammo.

Eve hears Ondrusek's voice in darkness, whispering, hoarse from screaming, "They got Gaardner."

Then Dentino, equally hoarse, much weaker, "They got *every-one.*"

Ondrusek says, "Head count."

"Dentino."

Ondrusek says, "Anyone else?"

Eve says softly: "Doctor Mojica."

Ondrusek says, "*Crap.*"

A light goes on. Eve's half-blinded again but sees Ondrusek's face illuminated briefly. She puts her hand up to shield her eyes and tells Ondrusek: "I'm out of ammo."

Ondrusek takes Eve's gun, reloads it, and hands it back to her.

She says, "Did either of you hit any?"

Eve says: "Yes."

Dentino says, "Yes."

Ondrusek says, "Me, too. I must have hit five. Chest shots, head shots. They didn't go down."

Dentino says, "I know. I know. I watched them take Tillett."

Ondrusek says, "I saw them get Verbasco." Her voice quavers. "They drank his blood."

Dentino says urgently, "They're vampires. Let's get the goddamn seeds and get out of here!"

Ondrusek and Dentino are both out of breath and wheezing by the time they reach the landing between Level 128/9—just one level above the seed bank on Level 130. They're soaked with sweat and shivering. They've both lost their respirators and are so out of breath that they're stumbling.

Neither talks about resting. Neither does Eve. Not even when the two Frosties start panting hard, swaying with exhaustion, pouring sweat.

There's a whoosh behind Eve.

Something big, very big, goes by. Eve screams and fires as Dentino opens her submachine gun right into the thing's face.

Blood sprays out behind it.

It keeps moving.

It grabs Dentino.

The gun lands, pouring smoke. Its forestock light goes dark.

Eve sees the horror in Dentino's eyes as she's snatched from the platform. She goes to scream, but the thing has her over the railing before Eve can fire another round; then it's all just a swirl of black *wing* and red *blood* and pink frostbitten *face* and white bony, *grasping* hands as the thing tears into Dentino, ravening wetly in midair. Her scream vanishes into the wet sounds.

Eve fires wildly, as fast as her finger will pull the trigger.

Eve misses the black things and hits Dentino instead. Dentino screams. After that, Eve hits the black things—one, then another, then a third, fourth and fifth. They keep flying, ripping into the violently-thrashing, screaming Dentino in midair, and—

—then Eve's blind again. Ondrusek's sweeps her shotgun with its tactical light.

Eve feels the hot shotgun wind above her—three blasts in quick succession.

Then she feels the cold wind passing over.

And hears the shotgun hit the platform.

Blind and desperate, following the sound of its metal scraping towards the edge, Eve grabs for it.

Her hand comes up empty. Light spins through the stairway. The shotgun hits with a clatter far below; the light goes dead and she is in blackness.

Eve covers the tactical light on her pistol with her hand and clicks the button. The light flares once, pink across the empty platform, hot against her hand.

Eve sees shapes in the dark past the railing.

Then the light pops and goes dead.

Eve shakes it. Nothing.

Panicking, she falls backwards, and then stares up into the black. Even the best night vision won't let her see in total blackness.

She rests and waits for them to take her.

Minutes pass.

Eve lies very still. *Everything* becomes still.

Then, something moves on the platform and she feels the platform jiggle slightly.

She hears spent cartridges swept away from its path. Are the feet bare? Booted? Clawed? Hooved? Eve can't speculate. She doesn't do that.

Something hovers above her. Eve hears flapping wings, feels their cool wind. Something settles on the carbon fiber railing—Hands? Feet? *Claws?*

Eve does not move. She stares and waits.

She hears more fluttering sounds in the big empty; more scraping of hands gripping carbon fiber.

The thing high above her gets closer.

Something touches her cheek.

A hand? A claw? She can't tell. There's no heat. She can't speculate.

Eve stares up into black and says to the darkness: "Who are you?"

No answer.

The only thing she can think to do is be more direct.

She says: "I'm afraid."

A chorus of soft sibilant voices respond—much closer than she expected.

As one, they say: "We know."

How long does it take?
A minute, an hour?
Time telescopes in the darkness.

When Eve finally stands and pads barefoot down the last flight of stairs, she feels as if she's passed through a millennium or a thousand or a million of them, and arrived at the end of time.

She also has little concept of space; even a genetically-engineered dark-adapted eye can't see in the void. The big dark empty blinds all but the vampires.

But the spiral leads her. Her slim hand, held lightly on the railing, guides her down to the spiral's terminus. She nears the seed vault. She thinks: "This is their price. Is it too much?" But she knows the answer. The creatures' price is survival: Their seed for hers. Their crossbred variation on the human fugue will live in Agartha, in the shadows, as did the mythic vampires of old. She's tasted their kisses and their blood; she knows nothing else matters. They must live. Whether the City Managers will see it that way, Eve can't begin to speculate. So she won't tell them. Monsters live better in the shadows.

The seed bank is a simple affair: Eve enters a thousand-year-old code and puts her thumb in the tube; it pricks her and records her DNA.

The vault hisses open.

The full-spectrum lights inside the vault are dim enough not to hurt her eyes, but they're still poison to the vampires. Eve is alone when she enters the vault.

It takes her an hour to select the seeds and check them. They're viable.

She seals the metal backpack. Refrigerated, it steams slightly and hurts her if she holds it too closely.

Eve finds the control panel for the transmitter. The large, clunky keyboard carries the feeling of obsolescence. Designed to send minimal information at minimal energy expenditure, it can only send a single line of text at a time on the green display.

Eve types:
STAIRS DESTROYED AT LEVEL 88.
They respond immediately:
WE KNOW. SEEDS OBTAINED?
Eve types:
RESCUE AT LEVEL 88 IN 2 HOURS.

Response:
SEEDS OBTAINED?
Eve frowns and touches her belly. She types:
SEEDS OBTAINED.
Response:
RESCUE EN ROUTE.

Thomas S. Roche's debut novel under his own name is *The Panama Laugh*, a hardboiled near-term science fiction zombie apocalypse due out from Night Shade Books in 2011. He has edited three volumes of the *Noirotica* crime-noir anthology series, two anthologies edited with Nancy Kilpatrick *(In the Shadow of the Gargoyle* and *Graven Images)*, and two vampire anthologies edited with Michael Rowe *(Sons of Darkness* and *Brothers of the Night)*, and published two short story collections, *Dark Matter and Parts of Heaven.*

Beyond the Sun
By Tanith Lee

*Imagine a night that lasts for one whole year—or longer. Think
what you could achieve in a year-long night—*
That was what the recruiting flyer said, and their promise
wasn't a lie. While of course, when the sun finally constantly
rises, you're far away already. Even, if you play the roster carefully, straight into your next long nighttime.

Heth once said, in one of his more lucid moments, "It's like
a chessboard, isn't it, where the white squares don't come on
until you've won."

But I guess I've already won, me, and my kind. Present perfect,
and the future beautifully dark. It's only the past that can't be
improved. Because, I suppose, the more symmetrically fault-
less our lives become, the more dangerously unwieldy grow
the things that already happened, and the memories that *can't*
be made to fit.

We look at Anka in the mirror, Heth and I. He seems happy,
satiated. I, Anka, look—what word? *Satisfied?* Heth's one of my
two Blood-Donors aboard this ship. He loves to give of himself
and blissfully comes, over and over, (a pleasant possibility bred
into him) as I draw my meal from his smooth veins. His blood
tastes good, as ever. And he's a good-looking guy. The best wine,
in a charming champagne flute.

"That was great," he murmurs, sleepy now. He will need a
full nine hours slumber, but that's only sensible.

"Thank you, darling," say I. "What would I do without you?"

"Starve?" he dreamily asks. Oh, a snippy moment then.

One can never tell with Heth. Amber skin and ice-blond hair,
blue, blue eyes, the color of the sort of morning sky I haven't
seen, except on DV-dex, for almost 200 years.

Corvyra, my other Bee-Dee, isn't at all like him. Sex doesn't come into the equation. We use a slender crystal tube fixed in her alabaster arm. Her hair is a much darker blue than Heth's eyes—more just post-dusk—my sort of time. She has a cat's green eyes. *She* tastes of fresh oranges; breakfast in a wonderful hotel. We talk about clothes and books and politics as I leisurely drink her. She only requires an hour's rest after sessions. But it all works out okay, or so it appears, for all of us. We've been together on 7 trips now, eight and a half years, we three. And the ship, too, of course, the *Mirandusa*. What a lot of numbers. One more: Simlon 12. The new sun.

It's not even born yet. And I, the sun-hater, the one whose tribe carry the pure *gene* of sun-hatred, I'm the creator who will wake this sun, as I always do.

Once, only God woke suns—with a word or a breath or a sigh.

I, and my kind, do it with a building program and a finger on a button. The last, while we watch (and cower) in protected darkness.

And Anka said, *Let there be light.*

Or, the button says it.

After topping up from Heth, I go out to do my space-walking, and then to check Planet 3, down below. Unlike the still unborn sun, the individual worlds of this system-in-waiting don't have names yet. Though Corvyra has nicknamed them Champion (1), Cuddles (2—the planet that may not take) and Fatgirl (3). Fatgirl, fairly obviously, is the largest, and reads as the most earth-type and lush specimen. There are other little chunks and balls and slivers circling about. Not to mention the pair of handsome moons already mecho-chemically lit. They have a duration of 300-400 earth years, after which, if wanted, they and the others can be set up, and/or rekindled. But Simlon, like every sun that gets started, will last for millennia. The general consensus has it that these solarities will all exceed the span of the original earth sun, which by now, as we know, is fading fast.

Outside the airlock I drift free, pause and gaze about me. Beautiful. Can you ever tire of such a sight? The limitless heaven of space, deepest black, or luminously translucent with galactic swarms or holo-gas clouds, the inflammatory litter of distant stars—other *suns*, natural or man-and-machine created.

After a while I drift on, around the bulk of *Mirandusa*. She's in good shape, just a minor repair finishing up on her left-frontal hull. I assess the outer work-machines. One is corroding slightly, so I send it back in and tap Main Comp for a replacement.

Far off something glitters as it dives through airlessness like a flung knife. Some meteor. You often see them. A little eye blinks in the ship's side, registering that the passer-by is harmless.

Before I joined the Space Corps I worked in various nocturnal jobs—night-gardens, aviation—I had, back then, another motive to govern my life. Afterwards…space opened its glamorous arms to me instead. And here I am.

Time to go down now to Planet 3.

It's much easier, as they found out all those centuries ago, for my kind to do this. We don't need jet-boosters, or separate navigation, or suits of any sort, beyond the minimum of sensible protection. We don't need oxygen. We can levitate—or 'fly', as the earliest of our detractors described it. And since we can negate gravity for ourselves, we can also personally institute it. To lift away, select and use the correct direction, and once there anchor without fuss, is that very same thing they caught us doing back on earth in the Dark Ages, when we took off like bats across the sky, or walked upside-down from castle towers to the ground. As for the oxygen, when they were wont to find us in our graves and coffins, we didn't breathe then—we 'lay like the dead'. Our sort *only* breathe to take nourishment from oxygenated air, just as we *drink* oxygen from the clarity of human blood. But we can shut off respiration without difficulty, or ill-effect. Especially when supplied by a rich diet. We do need the power of a ship, however. No one wants to walk or fly that kind of distance. Anyhow, *we* can't travel faster than light. Despite the stories.

But you know all this.

Or not, I suppose. There's still a lot of ignorance about us. More no doubt since so many of us became employed by the Space Corps, and left earth behind forever, to make our lives in endlessly long and lovely sleepless Night.

The basement apartment on Czechoslovus Street was half a mile down, remnant of an old bomb-shelter from the '20's. In summer, it grew boiling hot. The stone walls ran with pale green water, like exquisite sweat.

He looked up, when the young woman entered.

And she stopped, and stared back at him with enlarged dark eyes. She was scared, scared to *death*. She knew what he was, this—*man?* Did you call a male Vampire a *man?* Perhaps once. And since the R.U.S.A. Alliance of '35, such a variety of mixed ethnic types... They said he was part Rus, part German, part Canad-François.

He was called Taras. No second name was to be used.

There was one window, a fake with softly grey-lighted glass. In this austere if silvery glow she took in his black hair and lens-dark eyes. He had wonderful musician's hands, and a slightly crooked nose.

"It was kind of you to visit," he said. "Anka—do I have your name correctly?"

"Yes." Her voice sounded thin to her own ears.

"Please sit down, the red chair's quite comfortable. Or do you prefer the green chair? Some of my guests..." he hesitated.

She said, brazen with nerves, "They don't like the red chair because it's the color of blood."

"It isn't, nevertheless," he flatly answered. "Have you ever seen blood? I mean *looked* at it? There's no color on earth quite like it, Anka. But please, I don't mean to make you uncomfortable. Would you like a drink?"

"Water," she said.

"Water." He lowered his eyes and smiled slightly. "You all want water." He added with a strange and unsuitable urbanity, "As if you can wash your insides clean of what I'll do. As if it will stain. It won't, Anka. I swear it."

Anka sat in the red chair. She crossed her legs so the short skirt—short was the fashion that summer—rode up. He glanced, no more. "I'll have a geneva then, thank you."

Then he laughed. This was a fantastic laugh, like that of a very young man. But he was, she had been told, about 190 years of age. He looked barely forty. Lean and strong, elegant. Yet... old too, in there behind the polarized dark of his eyes.

It was part of her Citizen Service, to be here. Others took up assistant teaching or nursing, or police work, or training-and-enactment in the Military Corps. But those options all entailed one full year stint. While to do *this*, help maintain the Vampire population—who were turning out to be so useful—was only a matter of three months with, if properly performed, a guaranteed financial increment.

Anka had not been afraid. She had believed this work was straightforward. By then no Vampire would harm you, for if such a thing occurred, they were subject to the force of a computerized and infallible law, equally paramount and non-negotiable. Any trespass would result in what was known as Expungement.

Why then this terror that assailed her the moment she was shown the image of Taras on a screen? And why too had she not backed out? There were always three choices of client. Why was she *here*? She was just nineteen.

He brought her the geneva and she drank it in a gulp. He sat down again, facing her.

"Well," she said briskly. "Let's get on."

He cleared his throat. "Anka, I don't want you if you're frightened."

"Oh, aren't any of your—*visitors* ever nervous?"

"Yes, but there's a difference between uncertainty and terror."

"I'm not terrified."

"Thank you," he said, rising, "for calling. Don't worry, I'll be tactful with the agency. Nothing to concern you."

She too flung up from her chair. "No! I'm not going anywhere." Her heart raced, she felt her face scald with passion—was it anger or panic? She heard herself cry in a wild pleading voice, "Don't send me away—"

And then he laughed once more, a laugh quite unlike the first, soft and dark and very low. "My God," said Taras, "you're in love with me. I didn't know I could still do that."

"What?" But her mind was caught up on his use of the term 'God', now generally obsolete. Her mind could not get past the odd 'God' word. And so she began to feel what the rest of her was really saying. Anka wilted, now white as the electra-light inside the silver window.

And Taras came to her and took her in his arms and held her gently, inescapably, pressed the length of his body, and through the blackness of his shirt she felt the slow steady immortal thunder of his own almighty heart.

"My love," he said into her hair, against her lips as he kissed them, "I don't deserve such a beautiful gift, after so many years. My love," he said. "My Anka."

While he drank directly from her neck, she started only vaguely at the initial deflowering sting. She was already falling down and down through the illimitable haven of *him*, of Taras. As if through the star-streamed heaven of space. Never so lost, never so found. Safe in abandon. Like death. Better even than sex, (even the glorious sex they two would also partner in) this psychic orgasm of consensual surrender.

There's a painting you can see in the Venezi-Gifford Gallery, New Kroy, or else reproduced here and there in various art books or dealers' on-screen catalogues. It's called *Planting Out the Sheaves*, and is a cute enough take on old Earth-west farming techniques, as applied to the 'seeding' of about-to-be-solar-system planets. (I hope that's helpful, and not patronizing, to suggest it might assist you to get some idea of how I work out here, how it *looks*, vertically levitate-flying across the wide open plains and soaring mountain-sides, attended by my flock of clever machines. Some of the little robots and autohands are well-reproduced in this painting, particularly the tiny drivers that prepare the ground ahead and below. The male figure on the canvas, the painted Vampire overseer-farmer, of course, is romanticized to an ultimate degree. He looks like a cross between some gorgeous Earth Pre-Raphaelite saint—and one of their 21st Century superheroes, and his golden hair flows behind him as he strides the midnight airlessness, mysteriously lit by chemo-mech moons.)

I travel usually about three meters above the surface. Sometimes I go up a bit higher, or dip down, more closely to inspect what the machines are doing. Occasionally I call them off one area, or send them to another they've missed. Robotics isn't perfect, even now. Perhaps a good thing or would any of us have a job out here at all? Probably. There's still enough human life in most of our genes to assess terrain and feasibility with—as they now call it—psycho-voyance. (Human intuition, I believe that means.)

Planet 3 is vast. The cliffs and mountains are colossal, evidence of thinned atmosphere even in the era of the first sun. Waterless seabeds, and the gigantic arteries of dead rivers, fissure its surface. The moons softly shine on all this; when they vanish to the planet's far side, the stars render light. But I can see in total darkness.

Planet 2 (Corvyra's *Cuddles*) is far less featured than 3 (*Fatgirl*). And Planet 1 (*Champion*) is mostly a defunct ocean. But oh, we'll change all that. I've already seen to it there are myriad atoms and organisms peri-dormantly at work on Planet 1. Even Cuddles has a chance.

Inevitably, since building, I've checked the sun, too, during the months we've been here. An unlit solar-disc is no problem for my kind. And when that alters, *Mirandusa*, and all of us, Vampire, Bee-Dees, robot crew, Main Comp, will be standing way off. Down in her jet-black chamber, like a nice cozy tomb, Anka will only watch her viewer. And what will I see? A vacant

lot, where suddenly a gargantuan explosion happens: it is im-
pressively spectacular, aqua, emerald, scarlet. And then, behind
the display, a tiny fiery yellow dot is burning through, the eye
of Things To Come...

And that's the new sun alight.

One question is often asked, despite the images freely available.
Until ignition, what does a solarity—a constructed sun—look like?

Picture a huge spider's web spun from black sapphire, with
sapphire rods, lobes and weird antennae poking out of it. It hangs
there, this exquisite mechanized chemecular skeleton, immobile,
to all intents and purposes quiescent, purposeless. Till I press
that magic button.

Maybe you see a psychological analogy... The seemingly mori-
bund solar disc, the solarity Simlon 12. Inert—then galvanized
awake, on fire, radiating and incinerous, *alive*. But no. That isn't
like Vampiric life.

Do you *know* what it's like? Like memories that don't fit anymore, that won't lie still. Like old love that is dead and mummified
to corundum, but which never *can* die because, after however
many million centuries of forgetting, a moment's recollected
whisper or touch will raise it from the grave, and bring it back
to searing, quenchless flame.

We have a communal evening on the ship later. I say evening,
since the time-pieces aboard mark solar planet time in the 'human' crew areas. Corvyra and Heth eat steaks and green apples
from the store, and drink white champagne. I eat and drink my
synth version of those items, all of which carry my essential
nutrient, even in the alcohol.

After, we watch an old movie, I forget what it was. C and H
pay little attention either, necking like a couple of kids. (I don't
mind this, why should I? I can have sex with Heth whenever I
think I'll enjoy it.) When they go off together to combine, machines
neatly tidy the room.

Back in my cabin I update my work-journal and send it off
to the receptors at New Kroy.

I sit looking out the port, watching the three planets infini-
tesimally turn, and the moons setting over their shoulders. My
kind can see that sort of motion, just as we do the circling hands
on an old clock.

And if there's no sunrise to hide from, we never need sleep.
Sleep is only our massive all-over shut-down in the face of an

untenable foe—sunlight. So out here in Endless Night, we have a lot of extra time. Just what humans constantly say they crave.

But *that* much time needs to get filled.

That much time.

You think you'll never have enough. But then, you do.

She had been his only constant 'partner' for a year, when they decided that he would 'turn' her. Anka had known for several months that this was what she wanted most.

Taras then spoke very seriously to her, with an intense and almost paternal manner he sometimes assumed—which, by then, made her insanely and amusedly happy. She knew she could change him back into a thirty-five-year-old boy in seconds, into a sort of pantherine demiurge even. But she listened very carefully.

"No," Anka said. "I don't want to become what *you* are, for any of those reasons—longevity, strength—the power of levitating—God knows—" (by then too she had caught his habit of profaning 'God') "—I'd probably get vertigo—*no,* don't interrupt me, Taras. I heard you out. But I *know* these things, and *you* know I don't give a *fuck*—" (also obsolete obscenity, but it had made him smile) "— I want to be what *you* are because of what I feel about you, *for* you— I want to live as you do. I want to—to—"

"To *be* me?" he asked her quietly. "The absolute in possession?"

"No, no. *Surely* you must understand?"

She was only twenty, and her eyes had filled with tears. Of course, it had been she who had instigated the conversation. He said to her, a decade afterward, that *he* could not have presumed. At the time he said, now, gravely, "You realize that I shall need other partners for blood? As indeed, sweetheart, will you."

"Yes, naturally I know that too."

"Will it offend you? Hurt you?"

"No," she said firmly. "So long as we stay lovers. More importantly, so long as we still have *this.*"

At which he lowered his eyes, that nearly feminine response he sometimes gave her. "My kind, *our* kind if you join us, live a great while. Maybe not forever, but for centuries. And we do age a little, too. You're twenty, Anka. Perhaps in 150 years you'll appear to be thirty, thirty-five. But inside, my love, you'll have the experience and the *passions* of a woman far older. Will you still want me? Don't forget, I'll grow older too, and in both those same ways."

But at this she laughed. "Does that mean you agree, then? Yes?"

The City Corps was pleased as well. They generally let such liaisons as hers with Taras continue well over term, in the hopes of a human deciding to 'turn'. Vampires, now collated as they had been for some twenty-seven years into the mortal Life-Way, were proving virtually hourly of more value, their practical scope and physical talents far exceeding those of the best of mankind. So, there was no difficulty, and indeed a legal civil ceremony took place, reminding Anka of an old-fashioned marriage, and followed by a party.

Nor was she afraid of what had come to be called D & R, (Death and Resurrection). She fell asleep inside the fortress circle of his arms, and woke into the dawn of dark without a solitary regret.

Tonight, that is *ship's*-night, I alone look at Anka in the mirror.

I know her pretty well after all this time, that dark-eyed, young-ish woman of 212. So why look? Because, it sometimes seems to me, on these long nights amid the Endless Night, that I have an actual *look of him*. Of Taras. I dyed my hair black once, to enhance this illusion. That was about seventeen years after we parted. But strangely—or logically perhaps—to me I seemed *less* like him, then. They say too, don't they, people (even un-people?) who stay connected, come to resemble each other. Even people who don't live together, as he and I never did. Yet are close, in *some* way together, a great while.

Down the corridors of the *Mirandusa* the other lovers are mak-ing their love. Different, we know, from the mere ecstatic delights of really good sex, the sort I get with Heth, and he with me. I'm fond of them, my Bee-Dees, it's more than sustenance. We three have grown together too, I suppose, over the eight and a half years we've shared this peripatetic life. I remember once, one of the hull shields malfunctioned during a meteor storm. We worked with the machines, Corvyra, Heth and I, and got the thing patched up and saved our skins. And when it was all over the three of us ran together, thoughtless as water-drops on a pane, there in the control room, under the Main Comp's big blue benign maternal eye, and held each other close. Only for a moment. But it marks out that hour for Corvyra and Heth, for me, too. We are our own type of family. I never had one before I knew them. And with Taras, evidently, with him—'God' knows what unnamable entity we two formed. But those uncountable hours were marked indel-ibly. And it lasted. It lasted all of seventy-one years.

This cabin, mine, is the only room that ever sees me cry now. I'll cry tonight.

Chasing the moons over the saucer-rim of a world, Planet 1, the Champion. The exhilaration of it—to fly—yes, fly, I'm flying—skimming the wide lake of black space with its shimmers and shallow skerries of rippling particles, gaseous flumes—down to the sunless seabed, with canyons deep as any philosopher's abyss, and all of it now a fallow field that, with the coming of great Light, may—will—must blossom, bloom and grow. In a quadrennium, less, a fast-built home for humans, as they range forever outward through the stars.

But from here the stars aren't suns. They're friendly sprigs of neon hung in the night sky. And over there the big moon at full, and the smaller crescent that the planet's shadow makes, even though the lunar fire is inside.

Where I've set down I stand, though my personally-engendered gravity already means I could run over the surface. I'll be careful anyway, not to disturb the plantings.

Because I don't breathe, there's no waver to the vistas of space or landmass.

Despite the lack of breath, or air, a faint esoteric scent comes to me. The odor of an ancient past. The planet's. My own.

I walk the world.

And through my mind my life spills, like a phantom of the planet's ocean. My days, my years. And so I come again to Taras, and begin with and am *with* Taras, and at last, as it has to, the tide reaches its height, and brings to me that ultimate month we were together, when he told me we should part.

It wasn't, he said, so tenderly and kindly, that he had ceased to love me, nor, he said, did he think I had yet grown tired of him. There was no other he wanted, or thought that *I* did. But this had been enough, he said. What, *what* did that mean—I cried to him. Enough? *Enough?* But he only repeated, in his wonderful dark voice, the same litany. We must leave each other and go our separate ways. We must do it before our union, our love—if I preferred that name—was stale. What we had had, still had, must never be spoiled by becoming *less.*

I raged and begged. I mocked him. He said no more. I didn't believe he had not found another he liked better than me. Much farther on, knowing him as I had, I *did* believe, however. There had been no replacement. Which made what happened worse.

By the month's finish I reckoned he had come around. I had
arranged quite ordinarily to see him the next day, to which he
seemed to agree. But when I went to his apartment, he was gone.
It's unachievable, to trace our kind, as you may be aware, if they
legally refuse it. He did, it seems, so refuse. I never saw him, my
Vampire lover, ever again. Except, you'll guess, in my mind, the
high tide of memory, by such and similar means.

If he lives still, or is dead, I don't, I never shall, know.

And now—

Anka discovered the cave in the ravine wall almost inadvert-
ently; her thoughts had been otherwise engaged. A warped black
stalagmite pillar guarded the entrance.

Inside, lightglow arrested and astonished her.

With enormous care, she moved forward. The roof of the cave
was quite high, and then the sides of it opened out. A sheer black
chamber, bright at the centre with a chem.-burner...reddish light.

There were other things in the cave, which plainly was being used as a sort of living room. A rock—a *chair?* (how had it
been brought here?) on one side of the burner. A second chair
waited back in the shadows. Moisture gleamed on the walls but
the scent in the cave was wholesome and quite dry.

He stood behind the light. A tall silhouette.

Having no breath to catch, her ribs involuntarily convulse
as she *catches* it. Vacuum, for a split second, sucks at Anka's
lungs. She begins to double over, though already her Vampire
stamina has corrected the silly physical mistake. And then from
dark through light to dark he springs toward her, grips her—
inexorable, gentle—in a hold that paralyses with its *knownness.*

"How can you be here," she mutters into the shoulder of his
coat. "Have I gone mad?"

She can speak without breath. She has needed to.

"Oh, my love," he says, in such a tired, sad, *gladdened* voice.
"We—our kind—can go anywhere, do anything—didn't I teach
you that?"

Then she's herself again, the older wiser Anka he warned her
of and promised, in the time before he left her. She straightens
and stares up into his face. The face of Taras.

He is real, sentient. *He* is older. Now his hair is iced silver, his
face everywhere finely lined. He looks...like a beautiful, hale,
thin, indomitable man, perhaps sixty-five, sixty-seven. His teeth,
what else, are flawless. His black eyes clear as space itself inside
a lens. And he has not let her go.

He says, "We'll drink geneva. Then."

"Then," she answers. "Then."

Their entity formed, body to body, mouth to mouth, there could be, and was, no margin or necessity for any explanation or debate, no other element but this love, this truth, vaster than a world, more infinite than time. Life after death.

I cry my heart out, as I was aware I should. They leave me to myself, my Blood-Donors. My work is in-date, the program on target. They've learnt, after a few hours I'll be back to normal. This has happened before.

I loved him so much, Taras. I'll always love him like that. A dead coal in my guts that flares up like an igniting sun, just as Simlon will, in seven more months.

No one can be blamed for their dreams. Particularly not us, the *Vampire* kind. Out here, in perpetual darkness where we never need to sleep...*our* dreams take on a specialized waking form. We *hear* them approach, like footsteps, but can't hold them off. Conveyed by an *awake* consciousness, they have a potency, a *realness* as vital—more—than reality itself. *Our* dreams come *true*. While they last. And when they're done, what's left—is cobwebs. Dust.

Tonight we were lovers again, Taras and Anka. And I was alive as never otherwise I shall be, even if my body lasts forever.

This dream visits me quite often. I dread it. I welcome it. I pray to God it will come back.

But now, on and on, I shed my tears.

In Endless Night, the ghost of lost love shines so brightly it fades the stars. Such fire—is *beyond* the sun.

Tanith Lee was born in 1947, in North London, England. She didn't learn to read until nearly 8, and started writing at 9. After schooling, she worked at a variety of jobs (badly), until DAW Books of America liberated her into full time professional writing by publishing her novel, *The BirthGrave*. Since then she has written almost 100 books, and almost 300 short stories. She has also written for TV and radio, and certain of her stories are still regularly broadcast. At present she is working on a new Paradys collection. She lives on the South East Coast with her husband, writer/artist/photographer John Kaiine, and The Cats.

The Slowing of the World
By Sandra Kasturi

The earth is cooling.

I know this because Aurore has told me, yet again, that it is happening. Even the climatologists are beginning to notice now, and there has been some mild talk, but not in any seriously scientific way. And soon it will be too late to do anything about it. Most people are still going on about global warming. Which, incidentally, Aurore tells me isn't really going to be relevant any more. Not for a long time.

I'm new to the vampire game—I've been "Turned" (they use this term with amusement, having cribbed it from films), but the changes are slow ones. My blood is still mostly my own and my genitals haven't entirely retreated and changed. When I think of the hunger I used to feel for Aurore, it seems distant. Pleasant, but far away, like a rewritten childhood memory, or some mild opiate-induced haze.

I notice the deepening chill for the first time in many springs. It takes longer than usual for the ice to retreat from the lake's shore, snow stays on the foothills permanently, and the returning swallows don't make it back until July. But these are small things. Maybe the scientists are worried, but if they are, they're not telling anyone. And the vampires think in terms of millennia, epochs and eons. They've been a perpetual whisper on the crust of this planet since before the dinosaurs. Evolution, adaptation—it's rote now, so easy, it's a parlour trick.

Most of the Elders have retreated into the mountains, laid themselves ready for the Long Night. It started back in the 2060s, when things had gotten too hot, and there were too many of us. Too many of *them*, rather. Too many humans. I'm not one of them anymore, but the Change comes like a glacier, so sometimes I forget.

The humans were just making things hotter, and the birth rate was climbing even further. The Elders decided it was time to cool things down, cull the herd. They—we—need humans to live, but if there are too many—too many cars, too many hamburgers—it becomes dangerous for everyone, predators and prey. Too many shoes and Q-tips and Tupperware containers, too many vacationers in the Caribbean, too many paper clips and rock songs and lap dogs, and everything falls apart.

They've done it before, with the dinosaurs who were getting uppity, vicious and overly smart. With previous civilizations. They've done it with water, fire, with stars falling from the sky. But the ice is their favorite. Ice works best. It's quiet, slow and soothing. It takes time, and they, *we*, like things that take time. We are more patient than trees, than dust.

The Long Night will start in the mountains. As the Elders' bodies cool, the glaciers will make their slow way down, until humanity is contained in one small area. Our cities will be ironed to nothing, our pills and pornographies forgotten, our words and wisdom gone to smoke. Only then, when we—when they—are manageable again, will the ice retreat as the Elders wake.

I've asked Aurore: how long? The answer? *As long as it takes.* Which is no answer at all. But then, I am still young, filled with impatience. The fact that two sentences with Aurore take a year bothers me until I remember again that we will have nearly forever for conversation, the earth whizzing around the sun in an eyeblink.

Aurore and I will be the last. I am almost completely Turned now, my body smooth, but for a fine layer of something like down, my genitals retracted within my body cavity. To the vampires, "male" and "female" have no meaning. They—we—are both. And neither.

Aurore tells me of a time, centuries ago, as the humans reckon it, when the vampires tried to breed with humans, mix their DNA, raise hybrids that weren't dependent on blood supply. It never worked well. And so the vampire fables started—half-breeds crazed with desire or bloodlust, Vlad the Impaler, Wendigo, mutants and myths. The vampires put a stop to it and went another route.

"We cultivated humans, raised them like...not cattle. Pets? Beloved intelligent pets," says Aurore. This conversation takes nearly a decade, but I don't notice the time passing like I used to.

I've changed. My body and Aurore's have Slowed too. The blood we need is minimal. Once we've made sure the Elders and the rest of our population are suspended and safe, then we, too, will retire into the Long Night. The entrances to our cave system are well hidden by the brambles and spiny trees they encouraged everyone to grow before the world cooled; the encroaching ice is an added protection.

In the stories, I don't think the bad fairy stayed with Sleeping Beauty in the castle, but maybe that's how the story should really have gone: the two of them together, cooling bodies entwined, dreams meshing in warp and weft, and the spinning wheel turning endlessly, a metaphorical perpetual motion machine.

"If we—I mean *they*, the humans—were beloved, why didn't it work out?" I ask Aurore.

Another year goes by. "I don't know," comes the answer, finally. "You bred too fast. Your blood thinned. You were too violent. All or none of the above. It grew harder for us to feed from you, and the world was growing too warm."

"And it had happened before," I say, after another year passes, our talks taking on the steady rhythm of stars wheeling in the sky.

The world is asleep, under ice. The noise of the humans and the remaining animals, a distant chatter.

"How will we know to wake?" I ask.

Meteors fall, humans breed, it grows colder before Aurore answers me. "When the blood we have stored runs out, we will wake. It will be quieter. We can begin again."

"How many times have you done this?"

The pause is longer. A century goes by. Aurore is nearing the Long Night. "Many," is the answer. "Many times."

And then—nothing.

It's just me left. I'm on the path to the final Slowing.

To awaken in a century or seven or a thousand and seven. When the thrum of the blood supply is done. The hunger will be the kiss that wakens us, and our bodies will warm, and the ice will retreat. And the humans will scurry and breed.

Perhaps this time we'll play at being gods once more, demand blood sacrifice. Or maybe we'll go the Fairyland route, whisking humans away to Tir-na-nog, Under-the-hill, Brigadoon. Or we'll try interbreeding again. We have better data now, better knowledge.

I lie down in the sleeping pod next to Aurore. My body Slows further. The machinery whirs gently, and the blood—just enough to keep me alive, suspended—begins its slow journey through my system. I begin the final wind-down, the unspringing of the body's clock.

When we waken, the world will be cleansed of its fever; the cool palm of ice laid on the brow of the earth will give us all a new beginning, an immaculate story.

Sandra Kasturi is a writer, editor, publisher and book reviewer living in Ontario. She is co-publisher of *ChiZine Publications* and poetry editor at *ChiZine.com*. Sandra's work has appeared in various places, including *Prairie Fire, Contemporary Verse 2, TransVersions, On Spec, Taddle Creek, Shadows & Tall Trees, Other Tongues: Mixed Race Women Speak Out, Chilling Tales* and several books in the *Tesseracts* series. She managed to snag an introduction from Neil Gaiman for her first full-length poetry collection, *The Animal Bridegroom* (Tightrope Books). She won the *ARC* Poem of the Year award in 2005 and the Whittaker Prize for poetry in 2010.